St. Lunatic High School

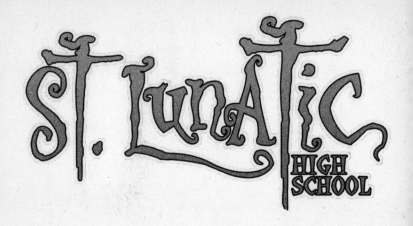

Volume Two
by Majiko!

TOKYOPOP®

HAMBURG // LONDON // LOS ANGELES // TOKYO

St. Lunatic High School Volume 2
Created by Majiko!

Translation - Alethea & Athena Nibley
English Adaptation - Barbara Randall Kesel
Retouch and Lettering - Star Print Brokers
Production Artist - Erika Terriquez
Graphic Designer - Jose Macasocol, Jr.

Editor - Katherine Schilling
Digital Imaging Manager - Chris Buford
Pre-Production Supervisor - Erika Terriquez
Production Manager - Elisabeth Brizzi
Managing Editor - Vy Nguyen
Creative Director - Anne Marie Horne
Editor-in-Chief - Rob Tokar
Publisher - Mike Kiley
President and C.O.O. - John Parker
C.E.O. and Chief Creative Officer - Stuart Levy

A  Manga

TOKYOPOP and 🌀 are trademarks or registered trademarks of TOKYOPOP Inc.

TOKYOPOP Inc.
5900 Wilshire Blvd. Suite 2000
Los Angeles, CA 90036

E-mail: info@TOKYOPOP.com
Come visit us online at www.TOKYOPOP.com

ISBN: 978-1-59816-945-4

First TOKYOPOP printing: December 2007
10 9 8 7 6 5 4 3 2 1
Printed in the USA

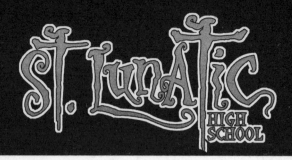

St. Lunatic HIGH SCHOOL

Majiko!   Volume 2

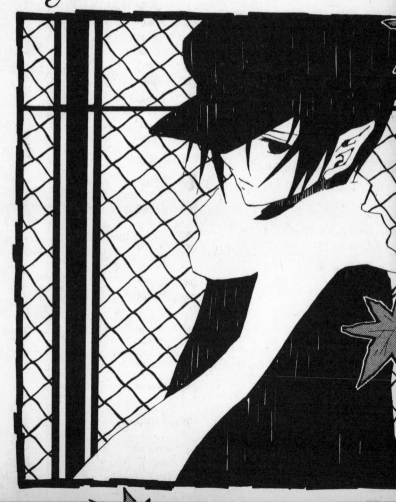

CONTENTS

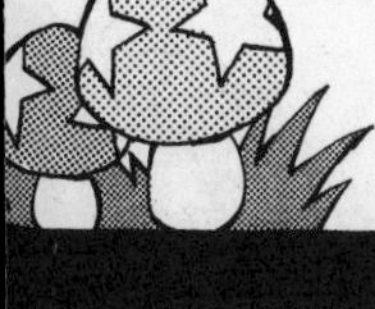

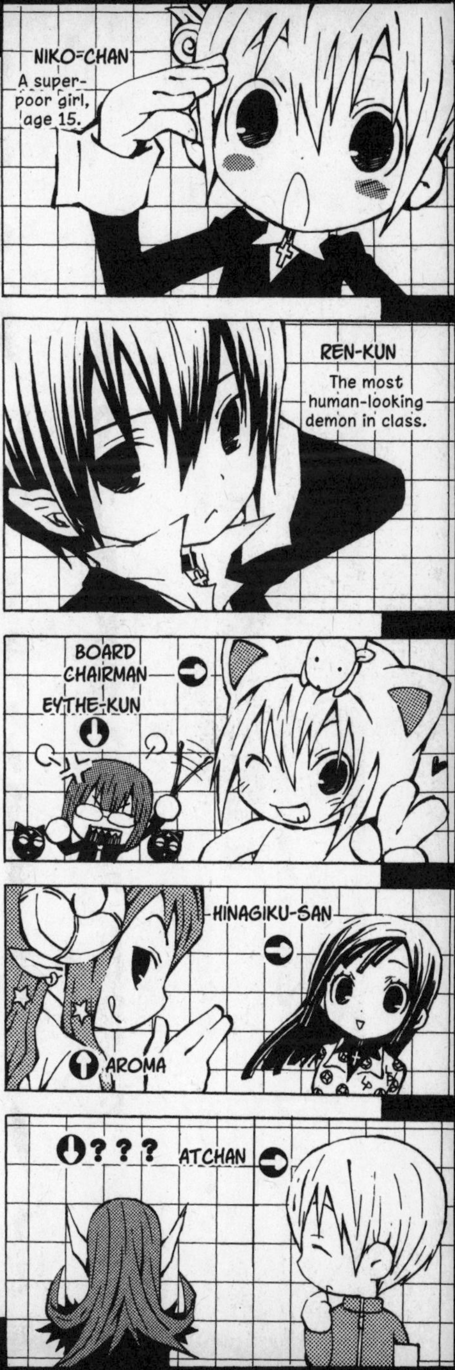
NIKO=CHAN
A super-poor girl, age 15.
REN-KUN
The most human-looking demon in class.
BOARD CHAIRMAN
EYTHE-KUN
HINAGIKU-SAN
AROMA
???
ATCHAN

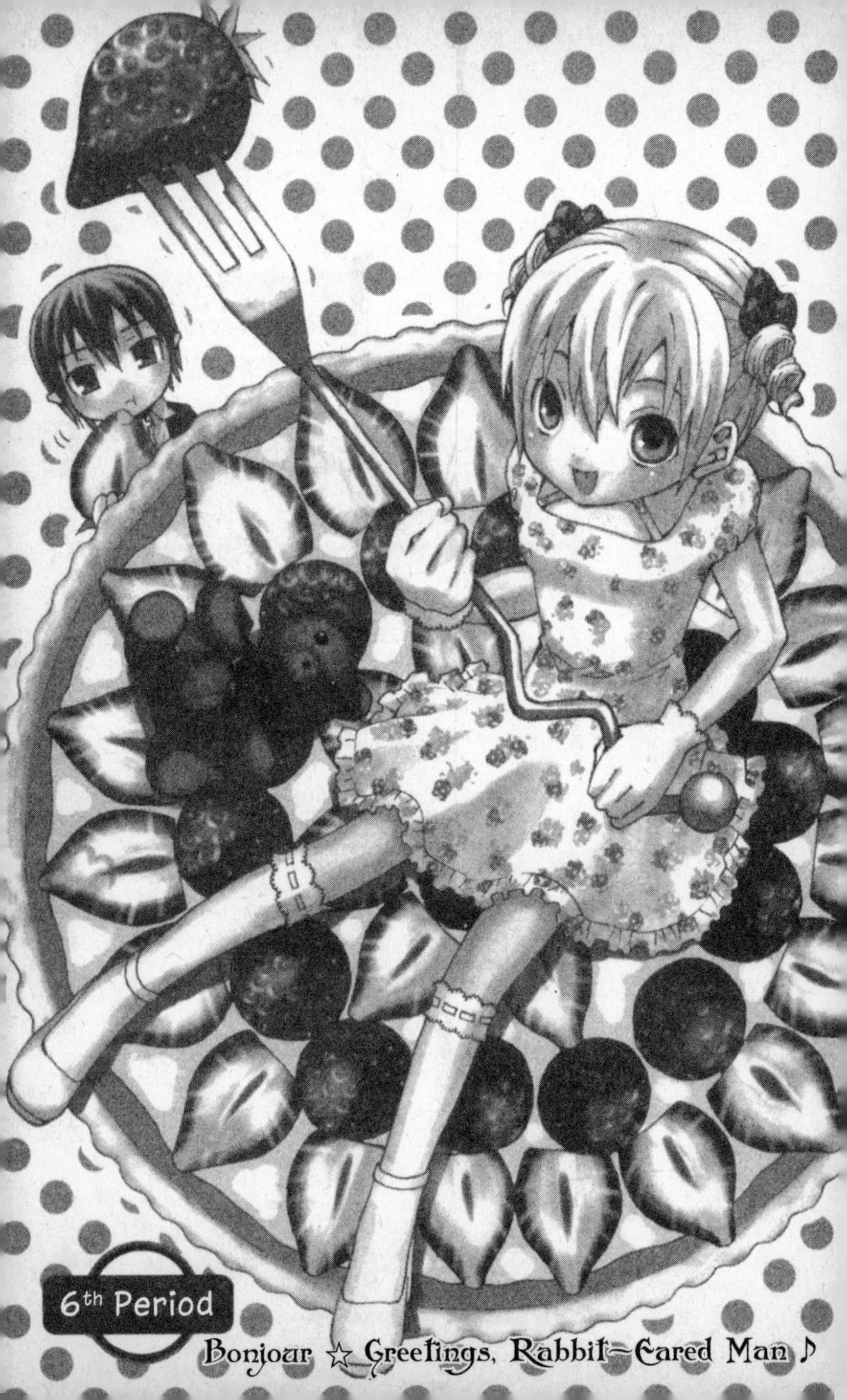
6th Period
Bonjour ☆ Greetings, Rabbit-Eared Man ♪

AT THE NIGHT CLASS TEACHER INTERVIEW.
I think it really is impossible to hire a human teacher, after all.
One look at us, and this is their reaction.
Assistants
Hmm ...
のびてる
Hm?
Every-one is so unique! ♡
Tee-hee!
You're hired !!!
And while we're at it, your sister's hired, too!!
Resume
Photo sticker
She's kind of cute. ♥
AND THAT'S HOW ATCHAN WAS HIRED.

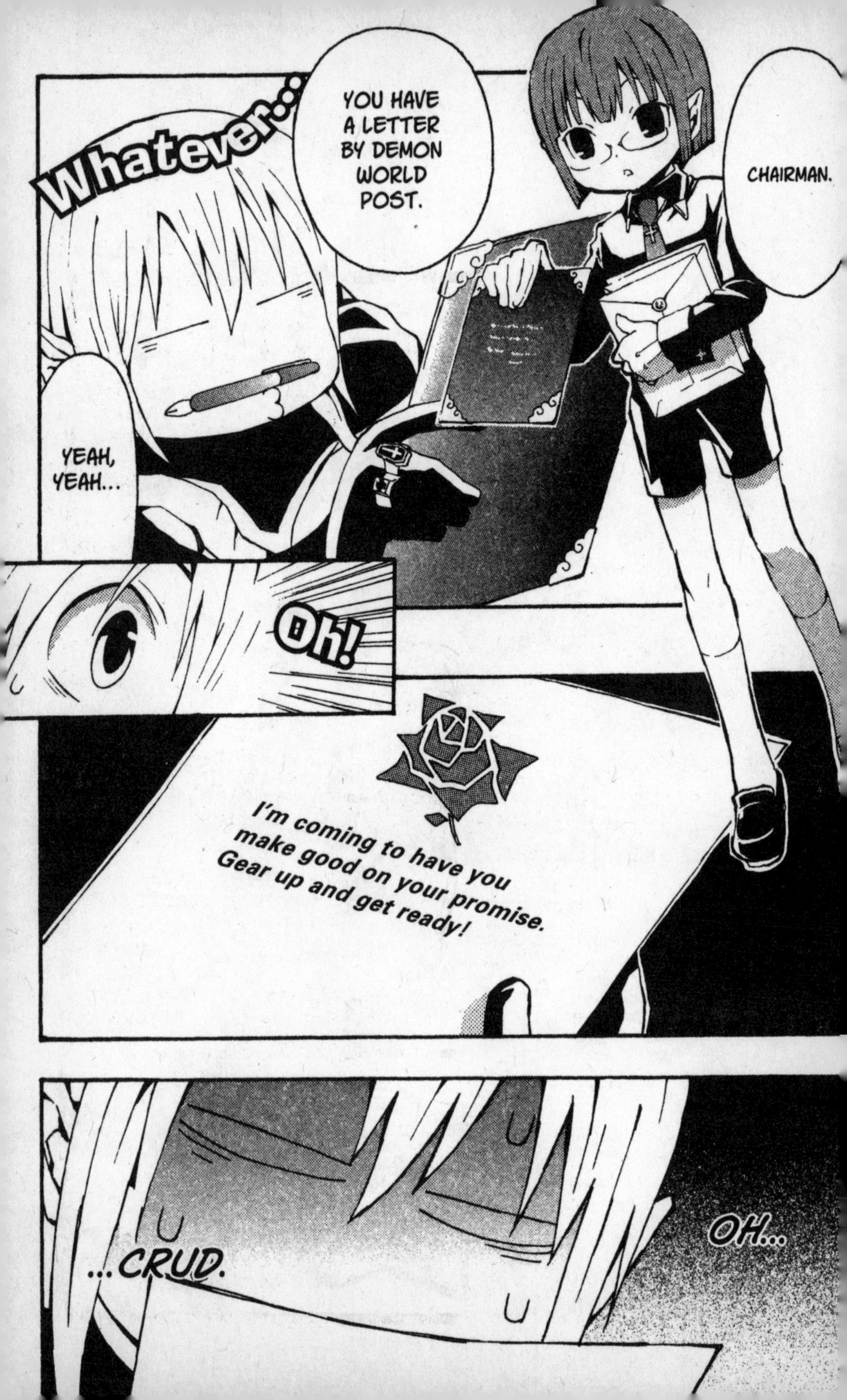
CHAIRMAN.
YOU HAVE A LETTER BY DEMON WORLD POST.
Whatever...
YEAH, YEAH...
Oh!
I'm coming to have you make good on your promise. Gear up and get ready!
OH...
...CRUD.

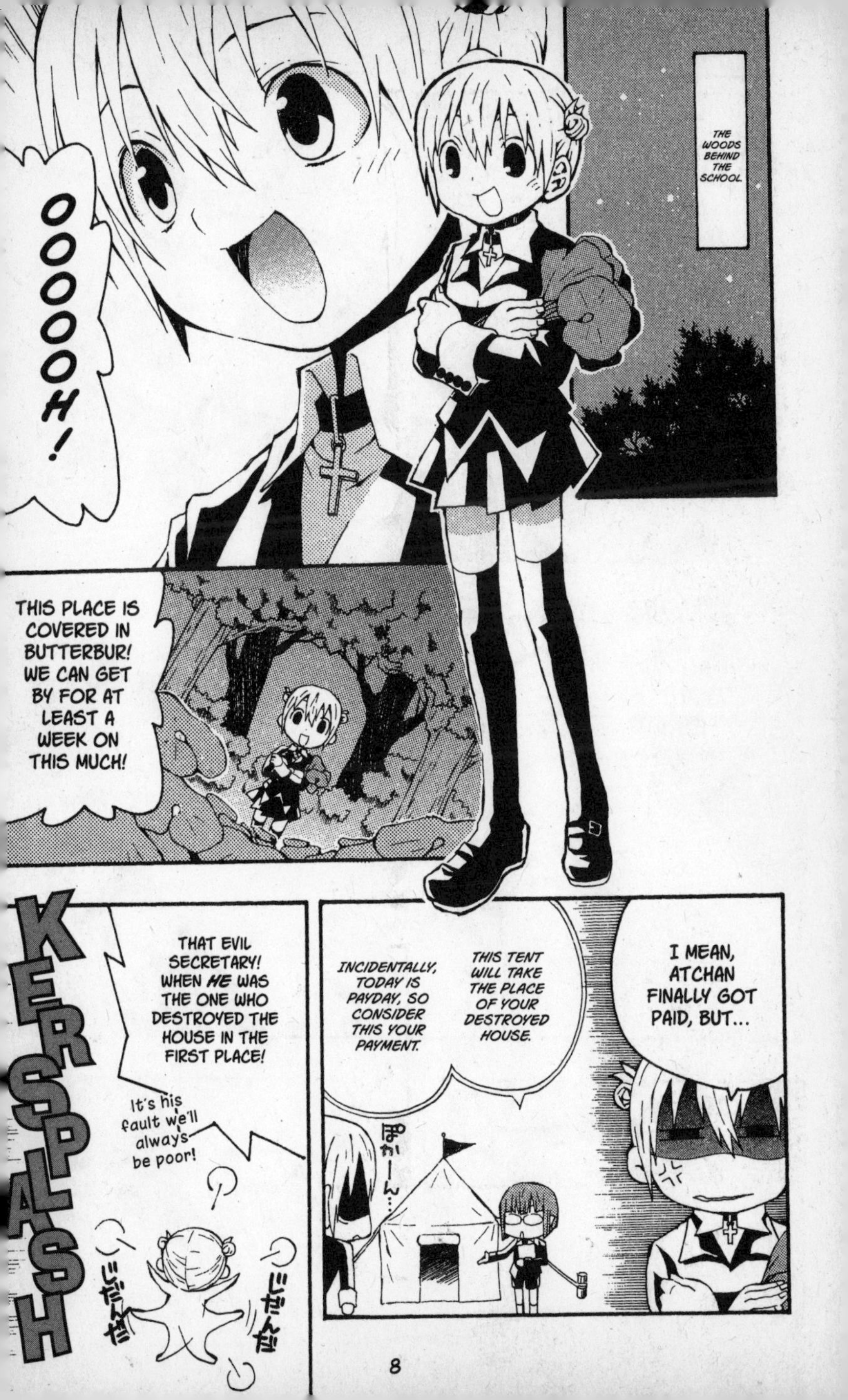
THE WOODS BEHIND THE SCHOOL.
OOOOOOH!
THIS PLACE IS COVERED IN BUTTERBUR! WE CAN GET BY FOR AT LEAST A WEEK ON THIS MUCH!
I MEAN, ATCHAN FINALLY GOT PAID, BUT...
INCIDENTALLY, TODAY IS PAYDAY, SO CONSIDER THIS YOUR PAYMENT.
THIS TENT WILL TAKE THE PLACE OF YOUR DESTROYED HOUSE.
ぽかーん…
KERSPLASH
THAT EVIL SECRETARY! WHEN *HE* WAS THE ONE WHO DESTROYED THE HOUSE IN THE FIRST PLACE!
It's his fault we'll always be poor!
じだんだ
じだんだ

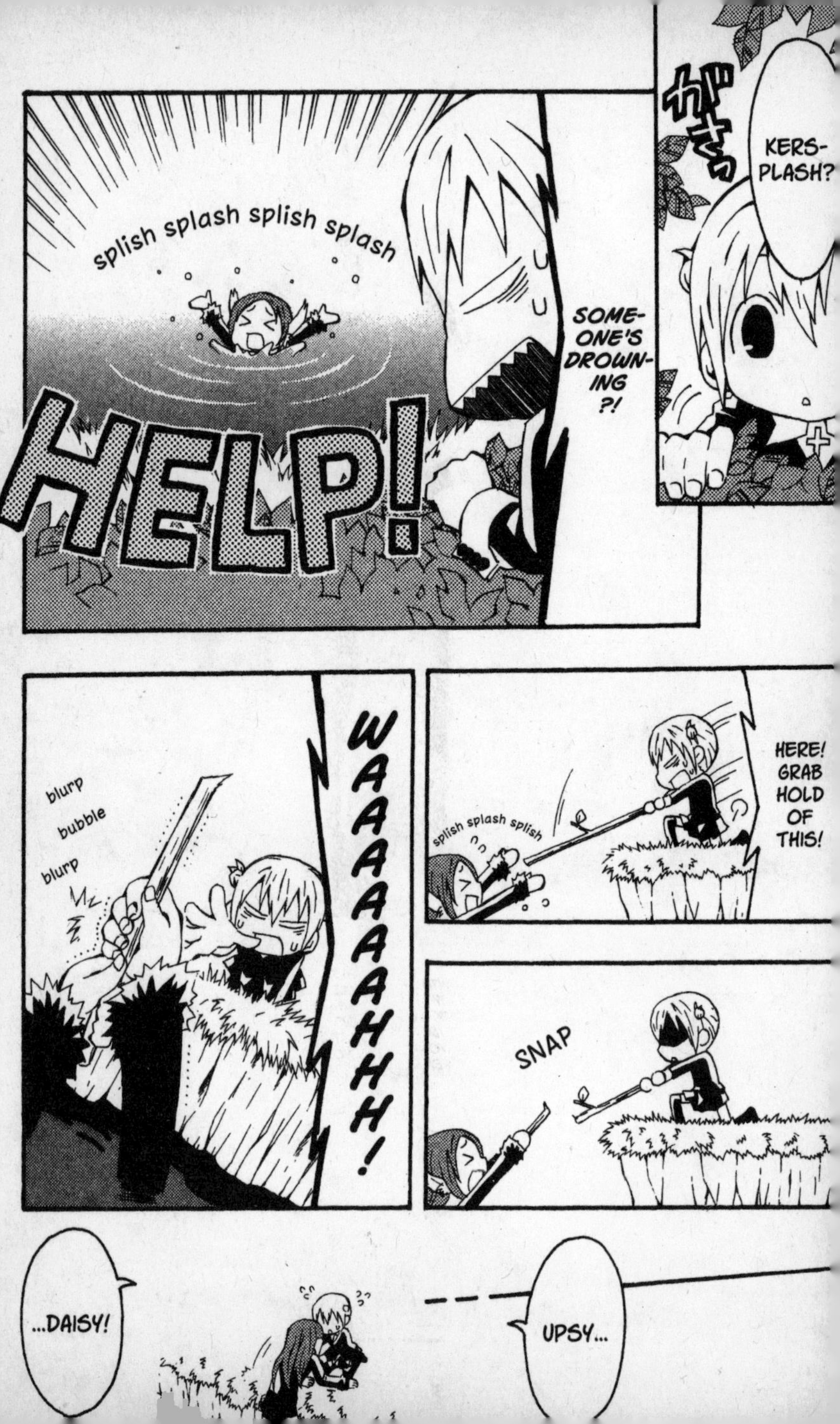
KERS-PLASH?
SOME-ONE'S DROWN-ING ?!
splish splash splish splash
HELP!
HERE! GRAB HOLD OF THIS!
splish splash splish
SNAP
WAAAAAAHHH!
blurp
bubble
blurp
UPSY...
...DAISY!

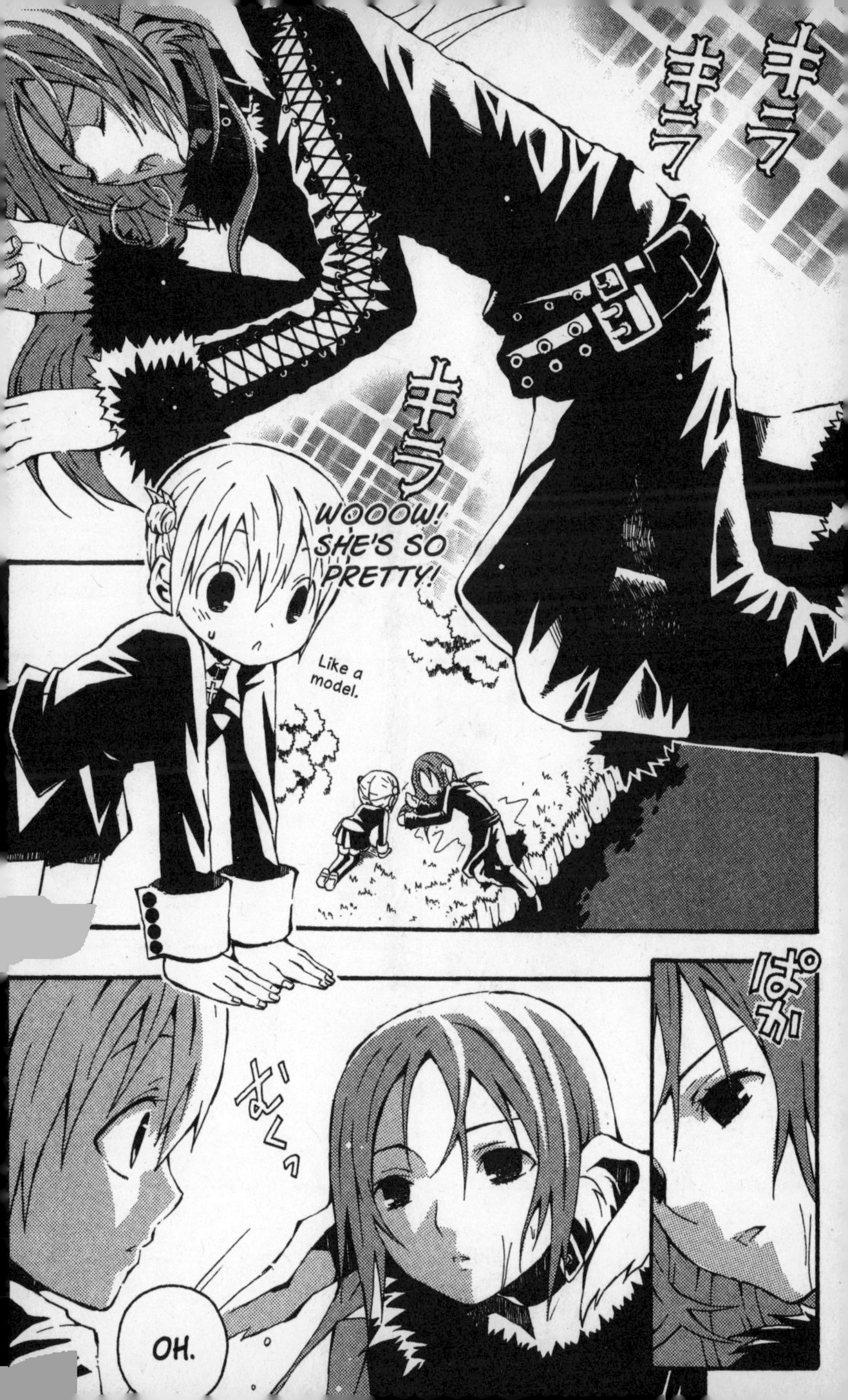
キラキラ
キラ
WOOOW! SHE'S SO PRETTY!
Like a model.
ぱか
むくっ
OH.

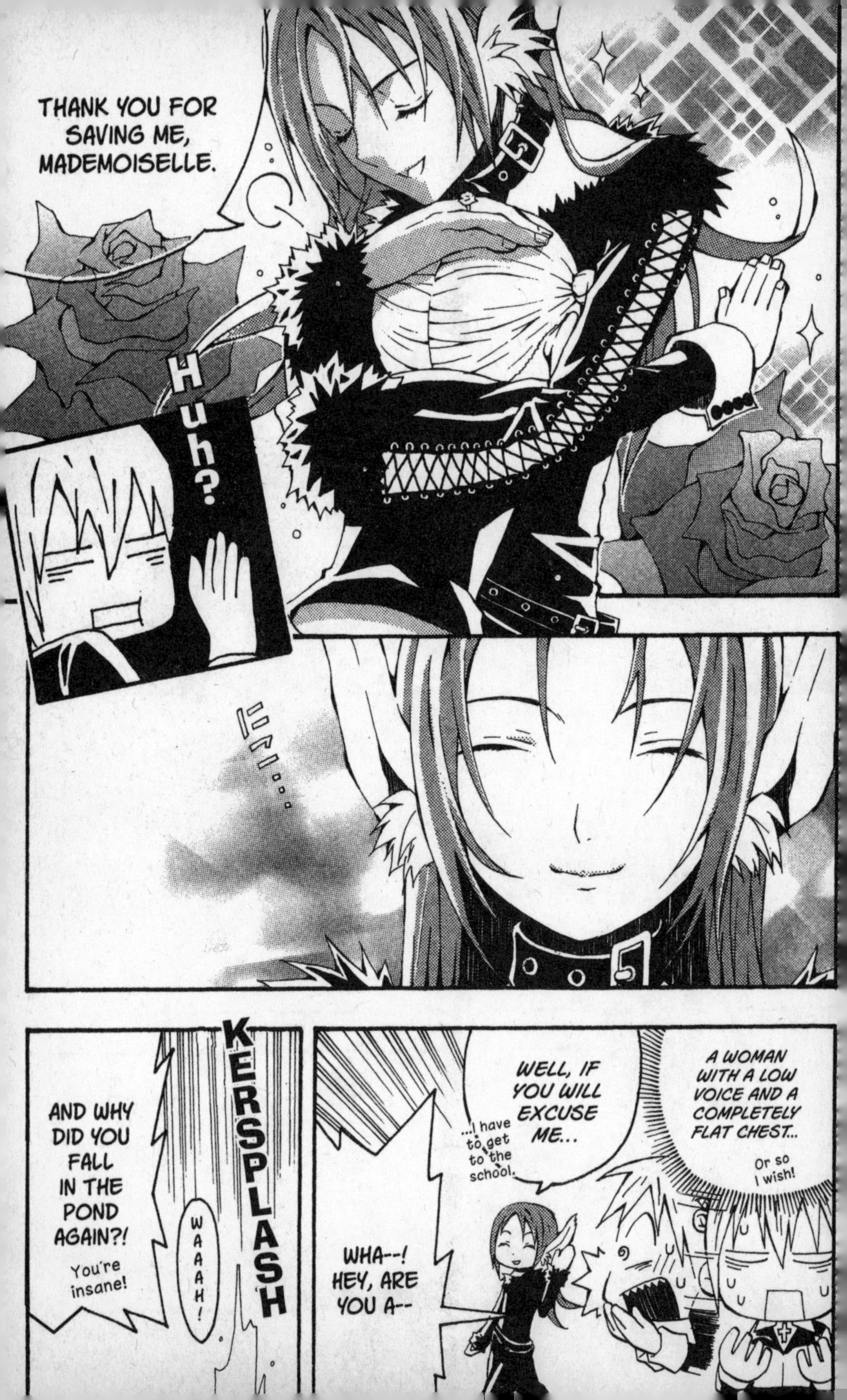
THANK YOU FOR SAVING ME, MADEMOISELLE.
Huh?
A WOMAN WITH A LOW VOICE AND A COMPLETELY FLAT CHEST...
Or so I wish!
WELL, IF YOU WILL EXCUSE ME...
...I have to get to the school.
WHA--! HEY, ARE YOU A--
KERSPLASH
WAAAAH!
AND WHY DID YOU FALL IN THE POND AGAIN?!
You're insane!

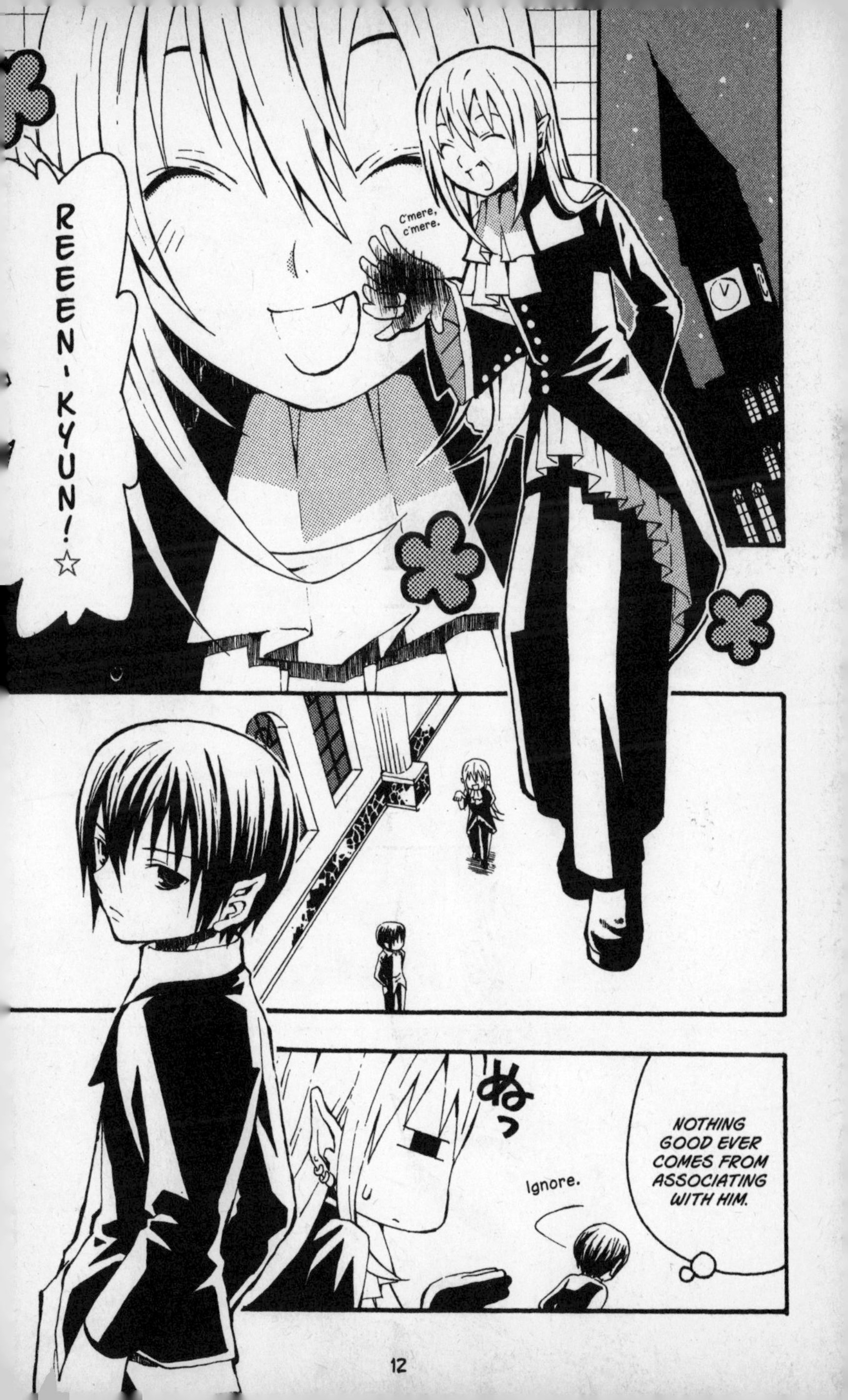
C'mere, c'mere.
REEEEN-KYUN!☆
NOTHING GOOD EVER COMES FROM ASSOCIATING WITH HIM.
Ignore.
ぬっ

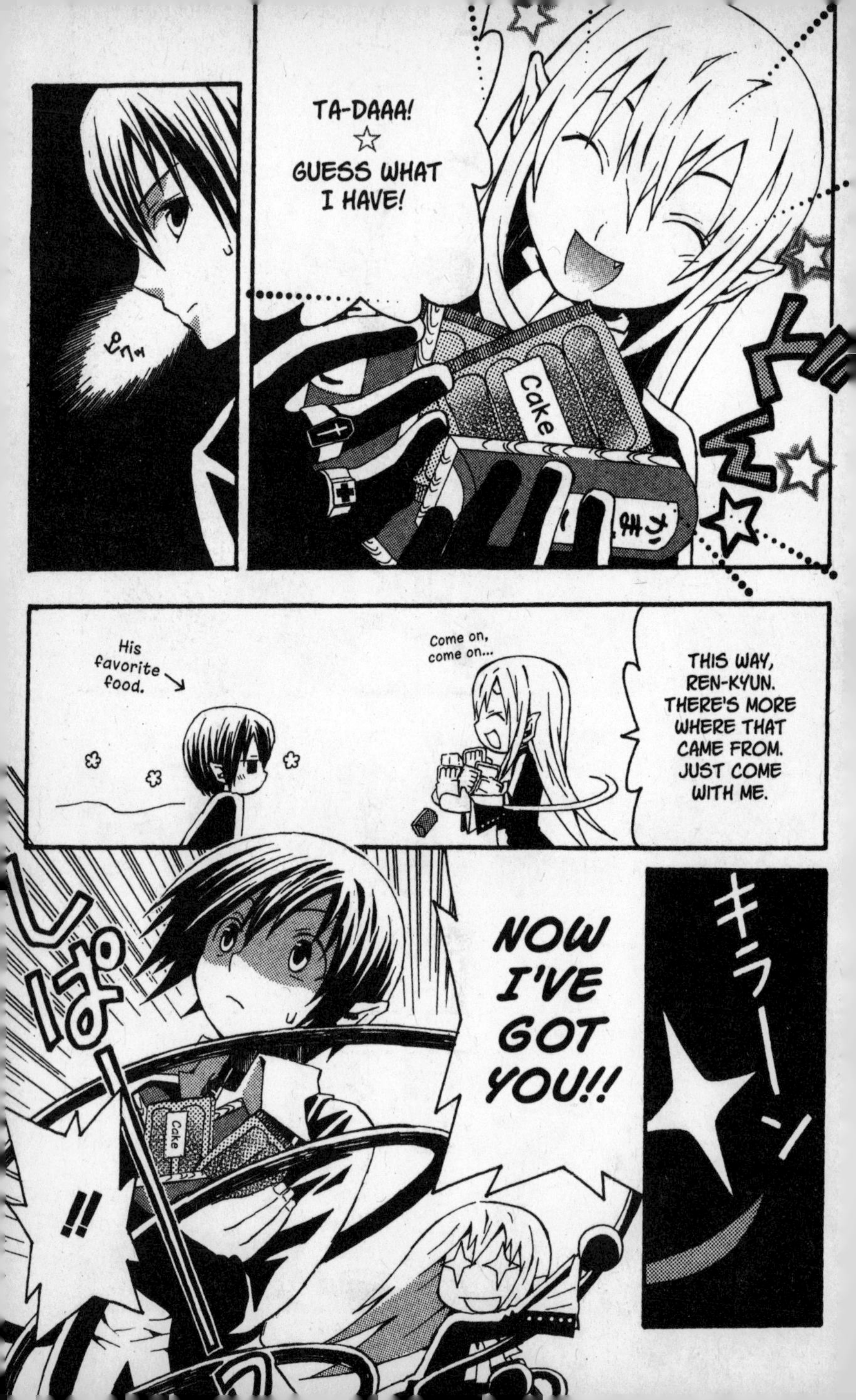
TA-DAAA! ☆ GUESS WHAT I HAVE!
Cake
THIS WAY, REN-KYUN. THERE'S MORE WHERE THAT CAME FROM. JUST COME WITH ME.
Come on, come on...
His favorite food.
NOW I'VE GOT YOU!!
!!
Cake

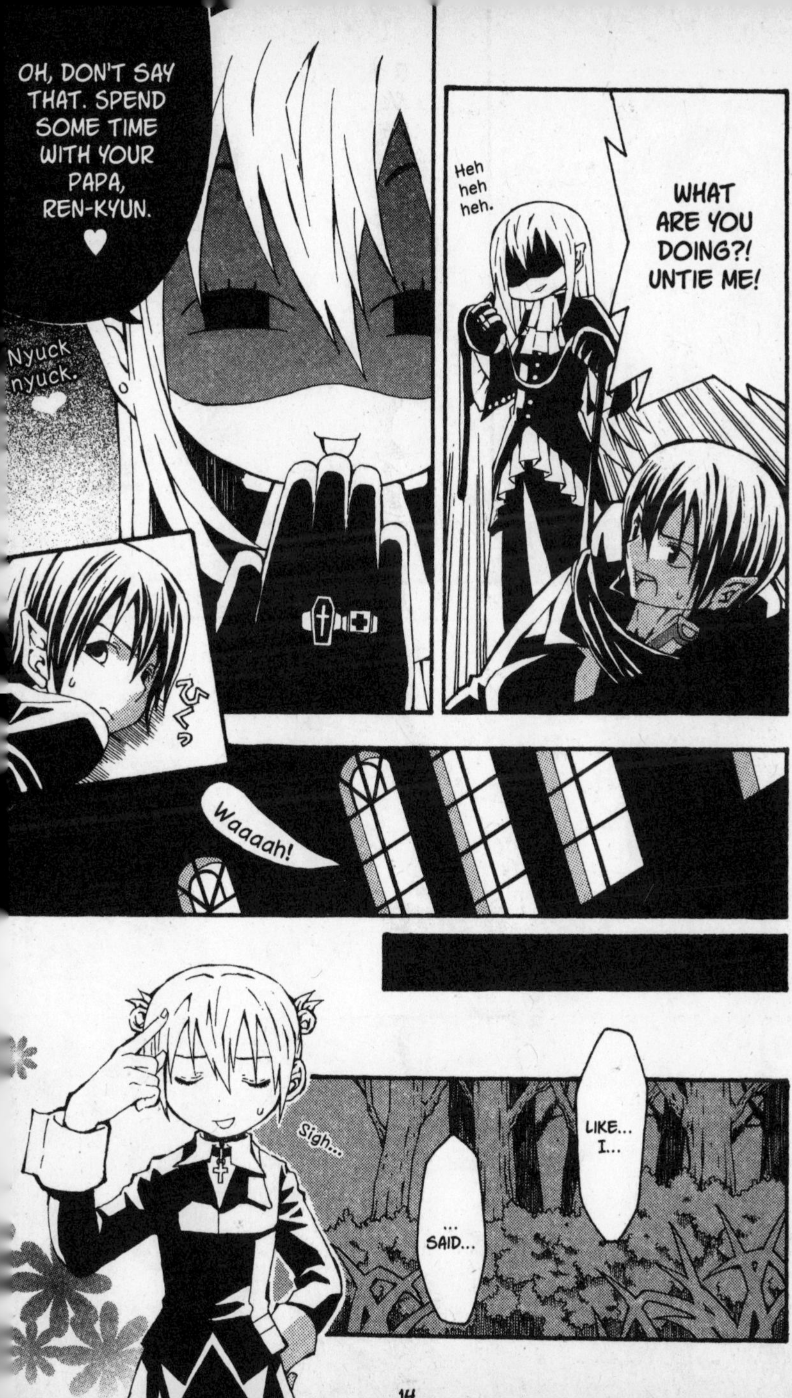
WHAT ARE YOU DOING?! UNTIE ME!
Heh heh heh.
OH, DON'T SAY THAT. SPEND SOME TIME WITH YOUR PAPA, REN-KYUN. ♥
Nyuck nyuck. ♥
Waaaah!
LIKE... I...
... SAID...
Sigh...

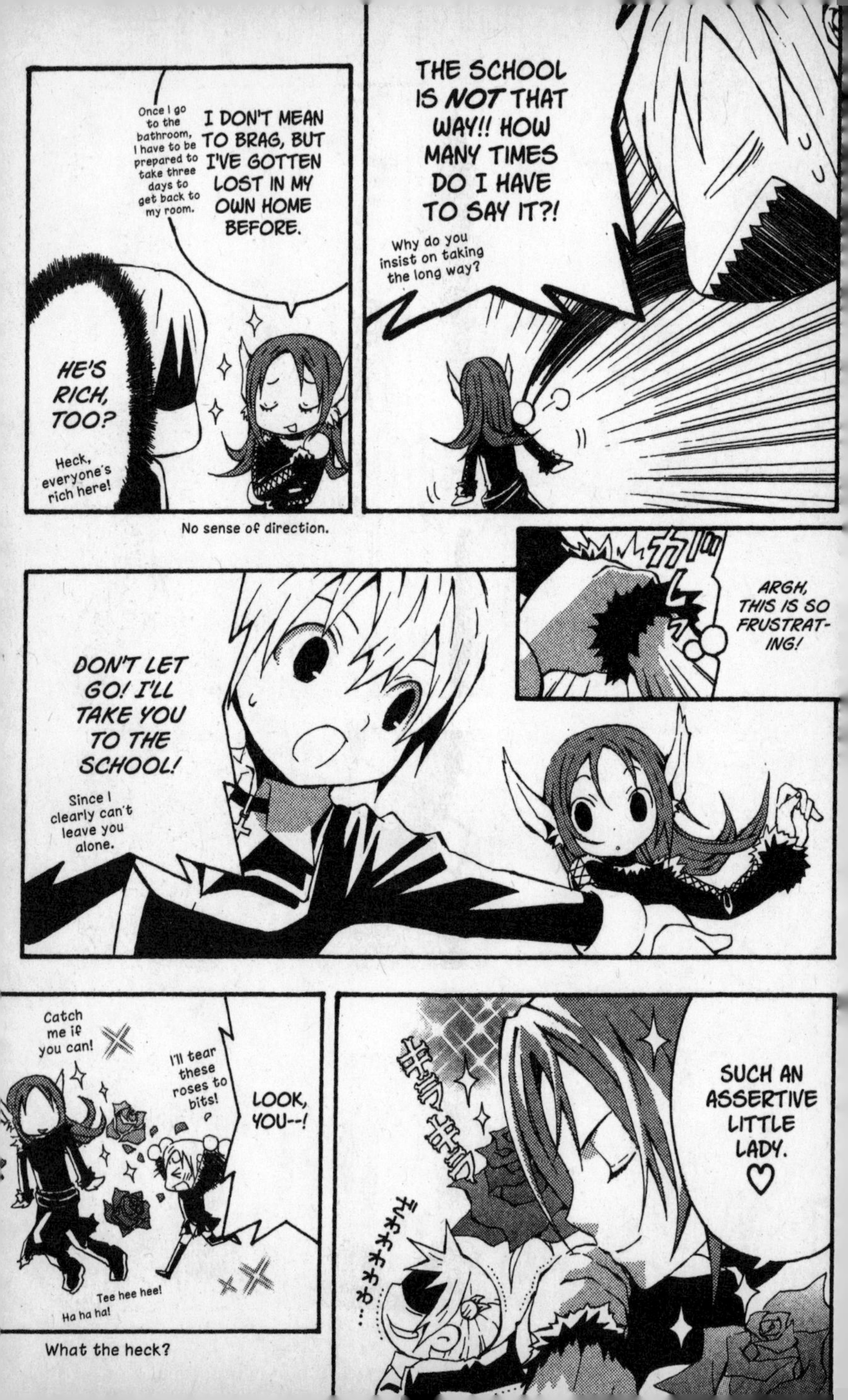
THE SCHOOL IS NOT THAT WAY!! HOW MANY TIMES DO I HAVE TO SAY IT?!
Why do you insist on taking the long way?
I DON'T MEAN TO BRAG, BUT I'VE GOTTEN LOST IN MY OWN HOME BEFORE.
Once I go to the bathroom, I have to be prepared to take three days to get back to my room.
HE'S RICH, TOO?
Heck, everyone's rich here!
No sense of direction.
ARGH, THIS IS SO FRUSTRAT-ING!
DON'T LET GO! I'LL TAKE YOU TO THE SCHOOL!
Since I clearly can't leave you alone.
SUCH AN ASSERTIVE LITTLE LADY. ♡
LOOK, YOU--!
I'll tear these roses to bits!
Catch me if you can!
Tee hee hee!
Ha ha ha!
What the heck?

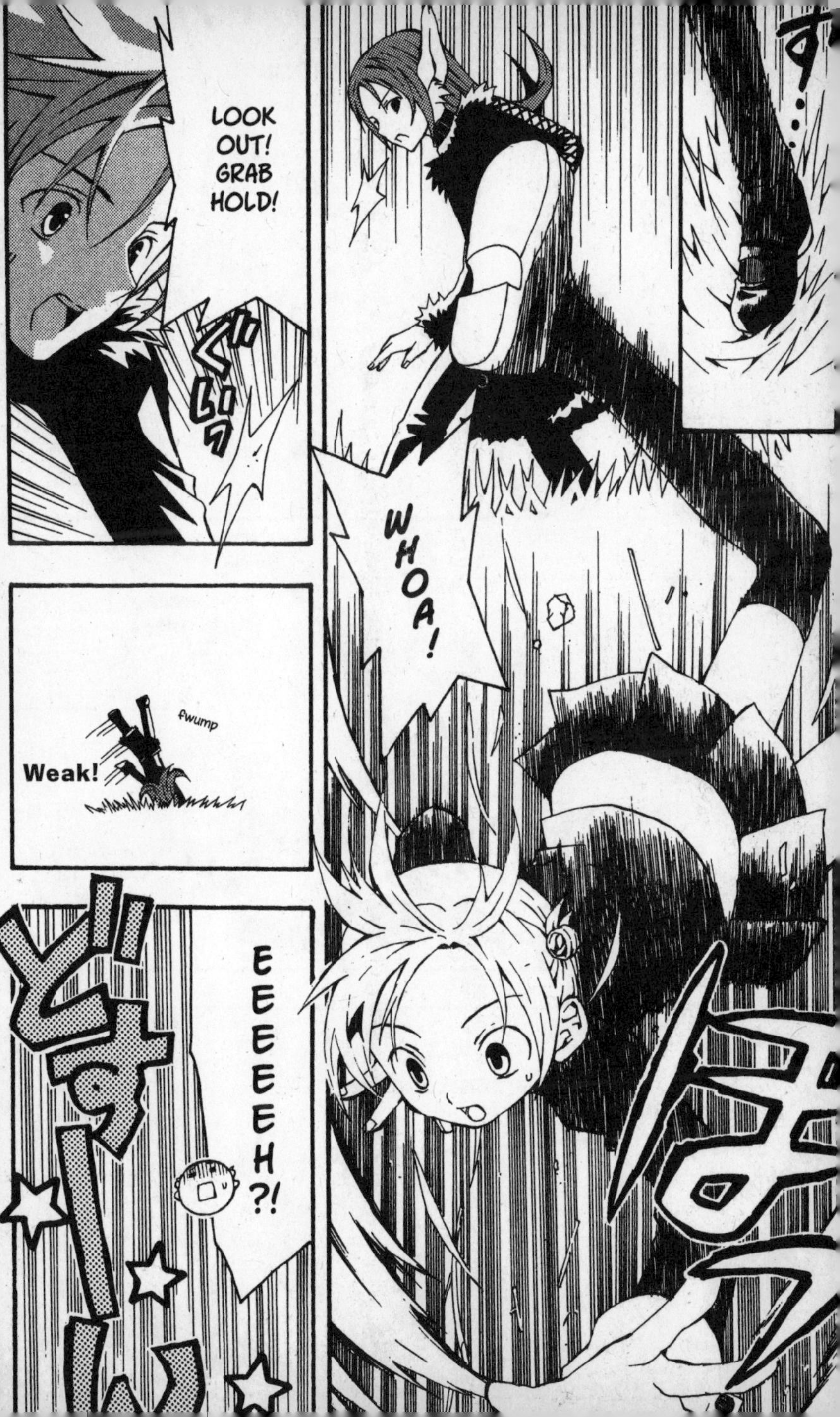
WHOA!
LOOK OUT! GRAB HOLD!
fwump
Weak!
EEEEEEH?!

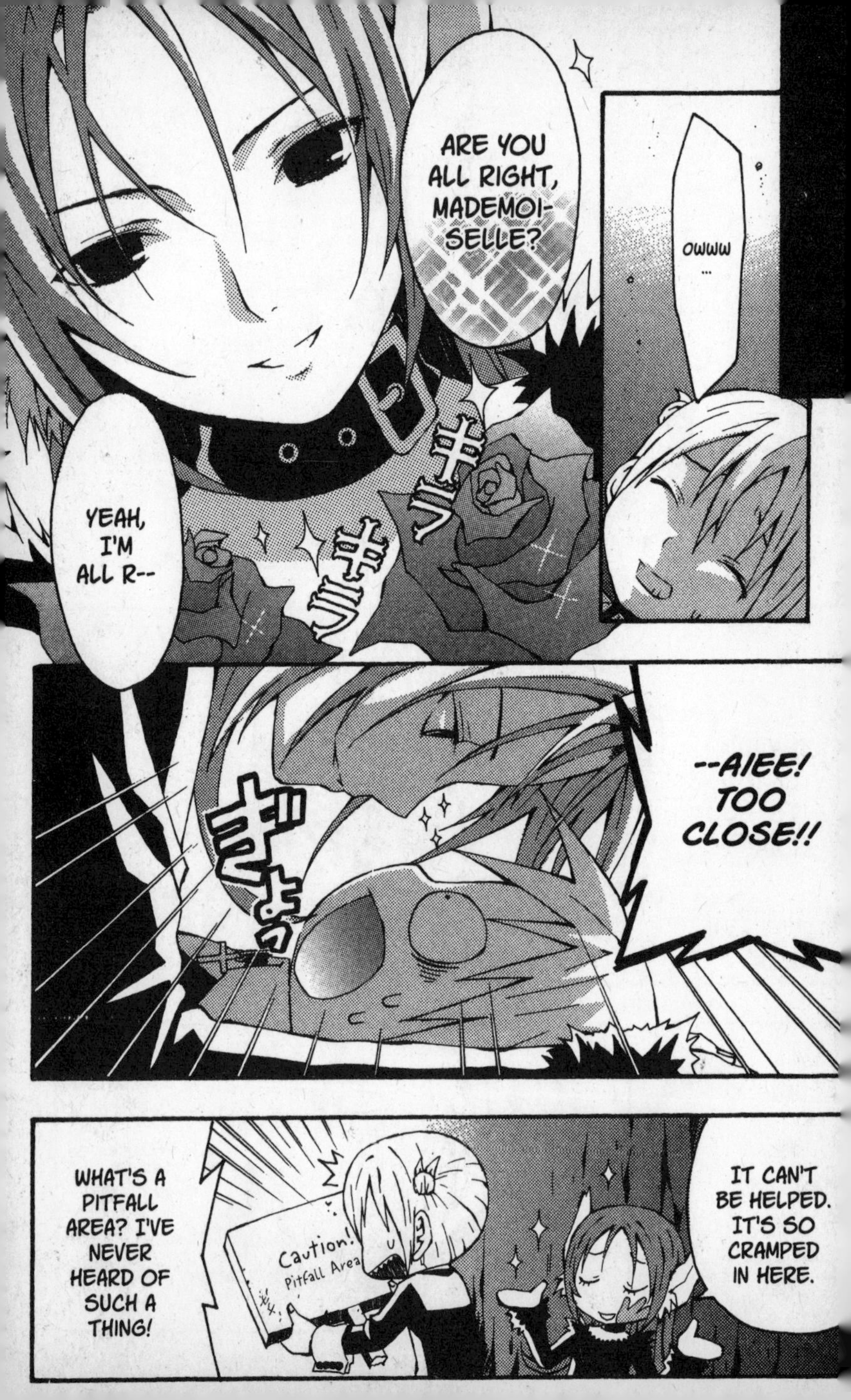
OWWW...
ARE YOU ALL RIGHT, MADEMOISELLE?
キラ
キラ
YEAH, I'M ALL R--
--AIEE! TOO CLOSE!!
ぎょっ
IT CAN'T BE HELPED. IT'S SO CRAMPED IN HERE.
Caution! Pitfall Area
WHAT'S A PITFALL AREA? I'VE NEVER HEARD OF SUCH A THING!

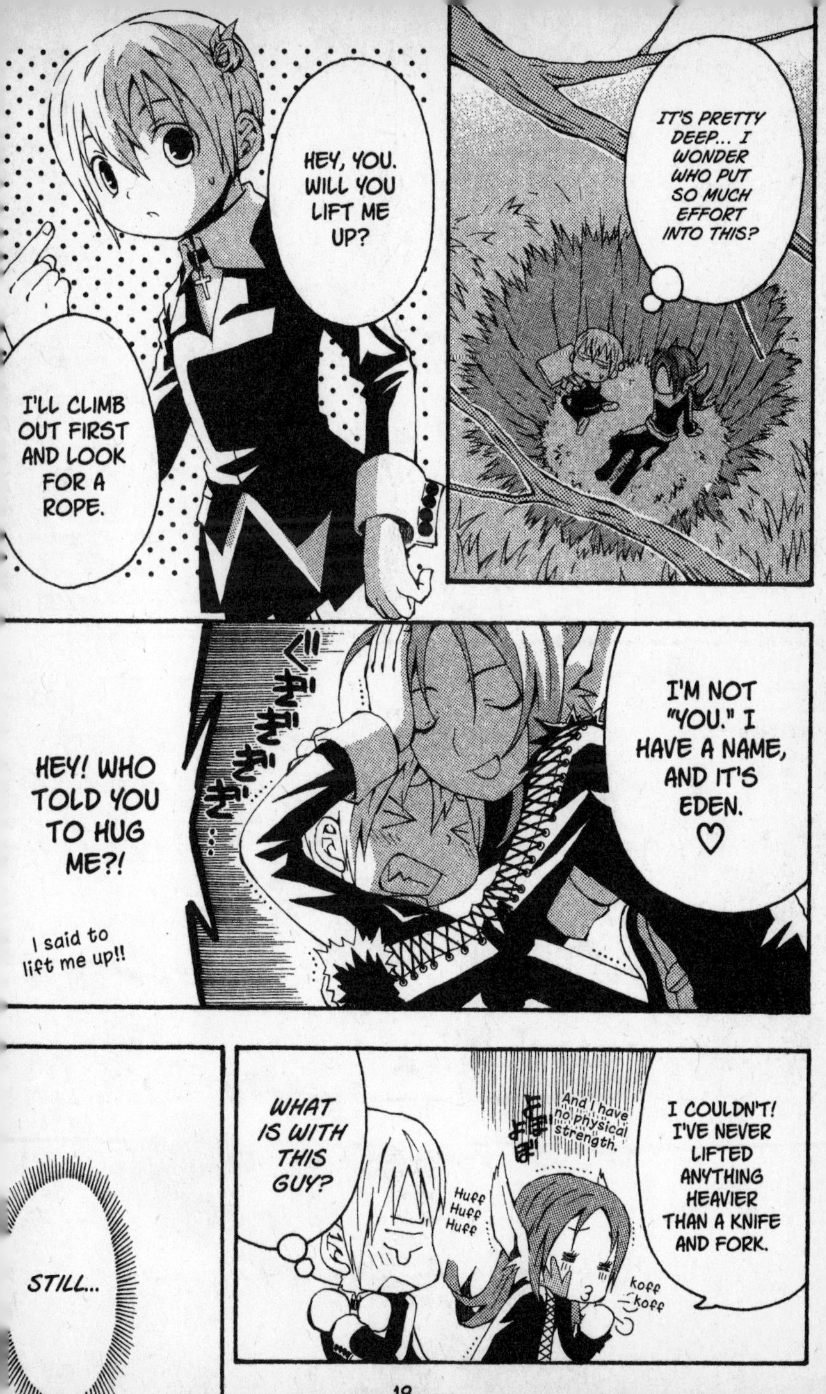
IT'S PRETTY DEEP... I WONDER WHO PUT SO MUCH EFFORT INTO THIS?
HEY, YOU. WILL YOU LIFT ME UP?
I'LL CLIMB OUT FIRST AND LOOK FOR A ROPE.
I'M NOT "YOU." I HAVE A NAME, AND IT'S EDEN. ♡
ぎぎぎぎ…
HEY! WHO TOLD YOU TO HUG ME?!
I said to lift me up!!
I COULDN'T! I'VE NEVER LIFTED ANYTHING HEAVIER THAN A KNIFE AND FORK.
koff koff
And I have no physical strength.
よぼよぼ
Huff Huff Huff
WHAT IS WITH THIS GUY?
STILL...

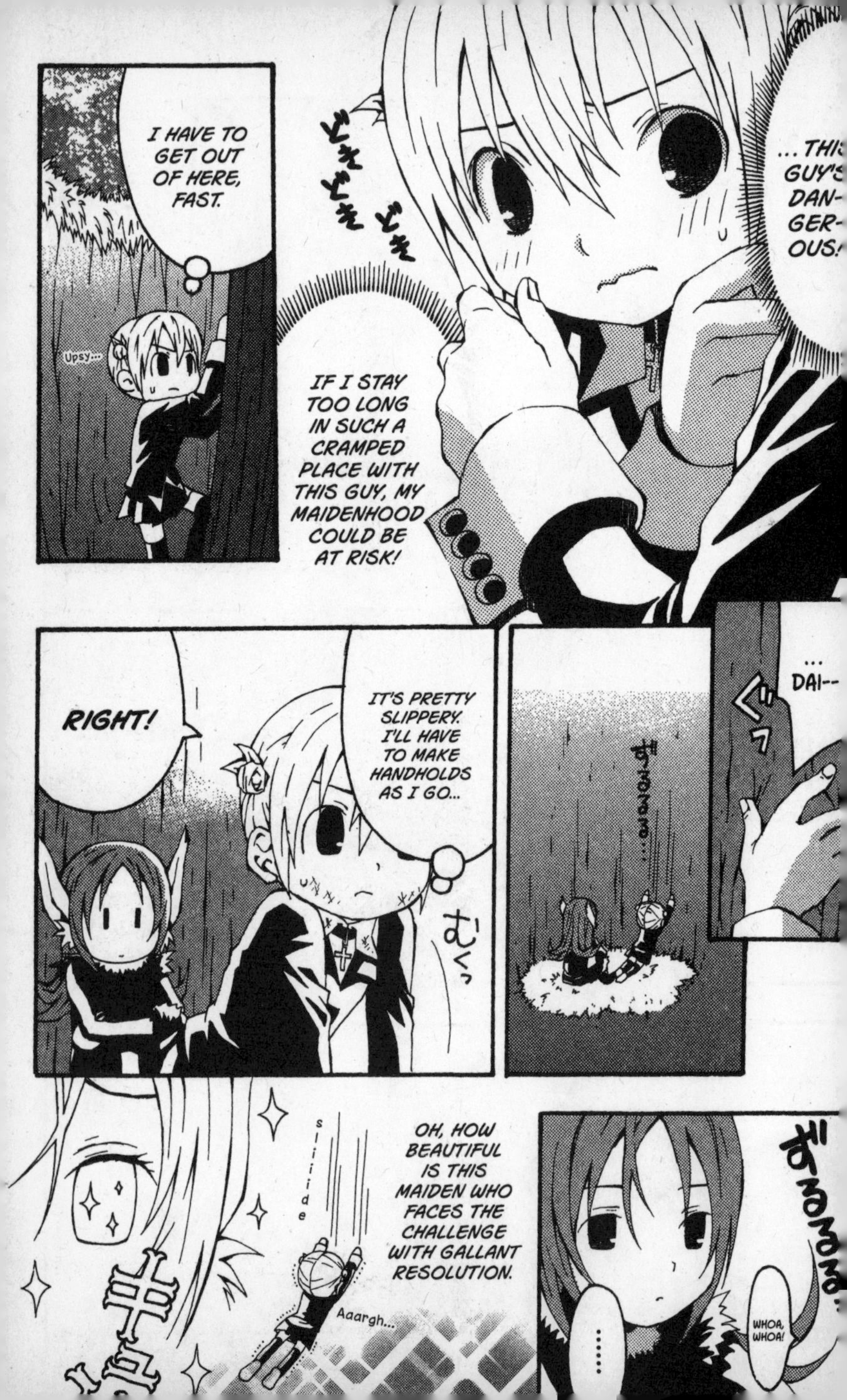
...THIS GUY'S DANGEROUS!
どきどき どき
IF I STAY TOO LONG IN SUCH A CRAMPED PLACE WITH THIS GUY, MY MAIDENHOOD COULD BE AT RISK!
I HAVE TO GET OUT OF HERE, FAST.
Upsy...
...DAI--
ぐっ
ずるるる...
IT'S PRETTY SLIPPERY. I'LL HAVE TO MAKE HANDHOLDS AS I GO...
RIGHT!
むぐっ
ずるるる...
WHOA, WHOA!
......
OH, HOW BEAUTIFUL IS THIS MAIDEN WHO FACES THE CHALLENGE WITH GALLANT RESOLUTION.
sliiide
Aaargh...

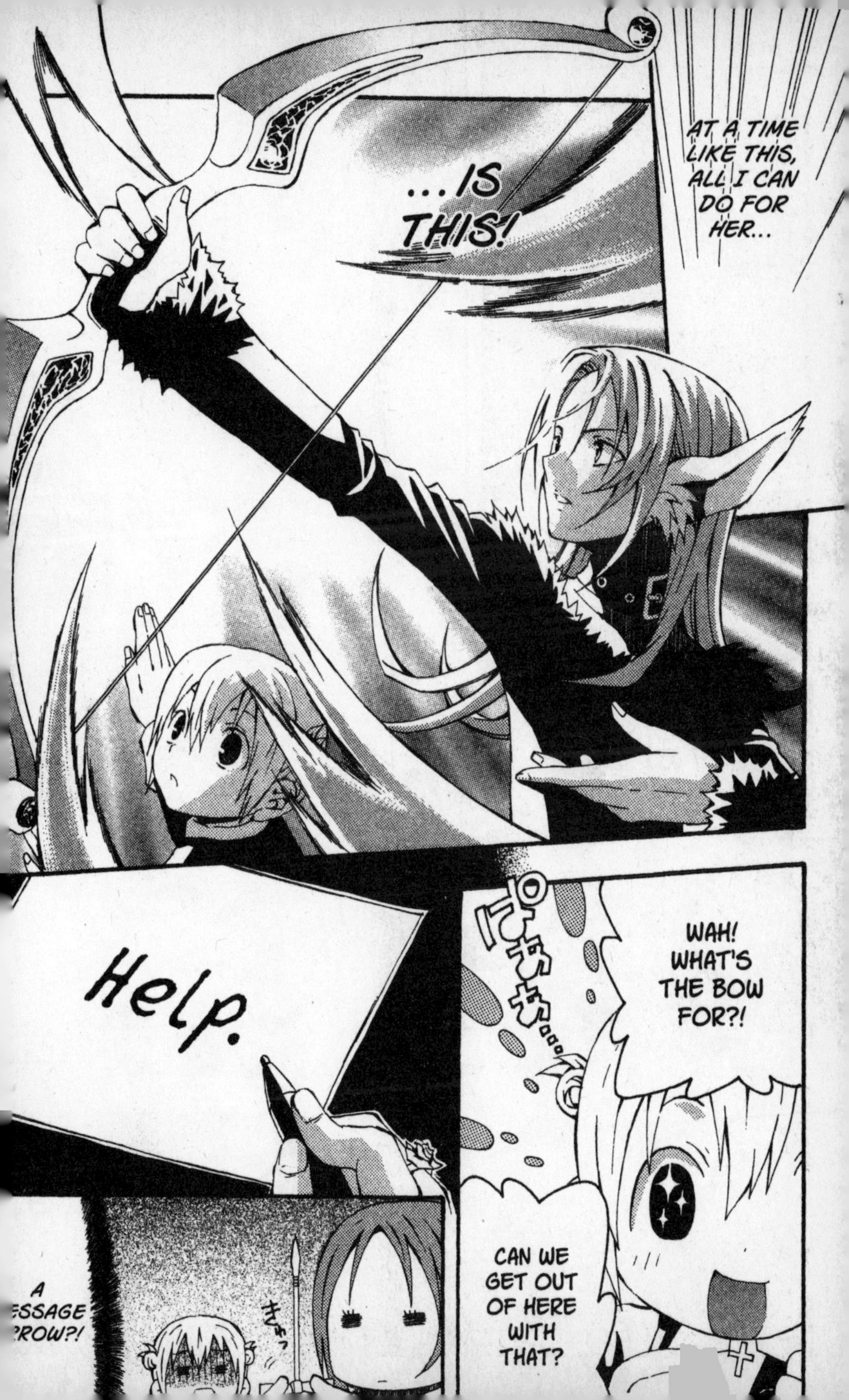
AT A TIME LIKE THIS, ALL I CAN DO FOR HER...
...IS THIS!
WAH! WHAT'S THE BOW FOR?!
CAN WE GET OUT OF HERE WITH THAT?
Help.
A ESSAGE ROW?!

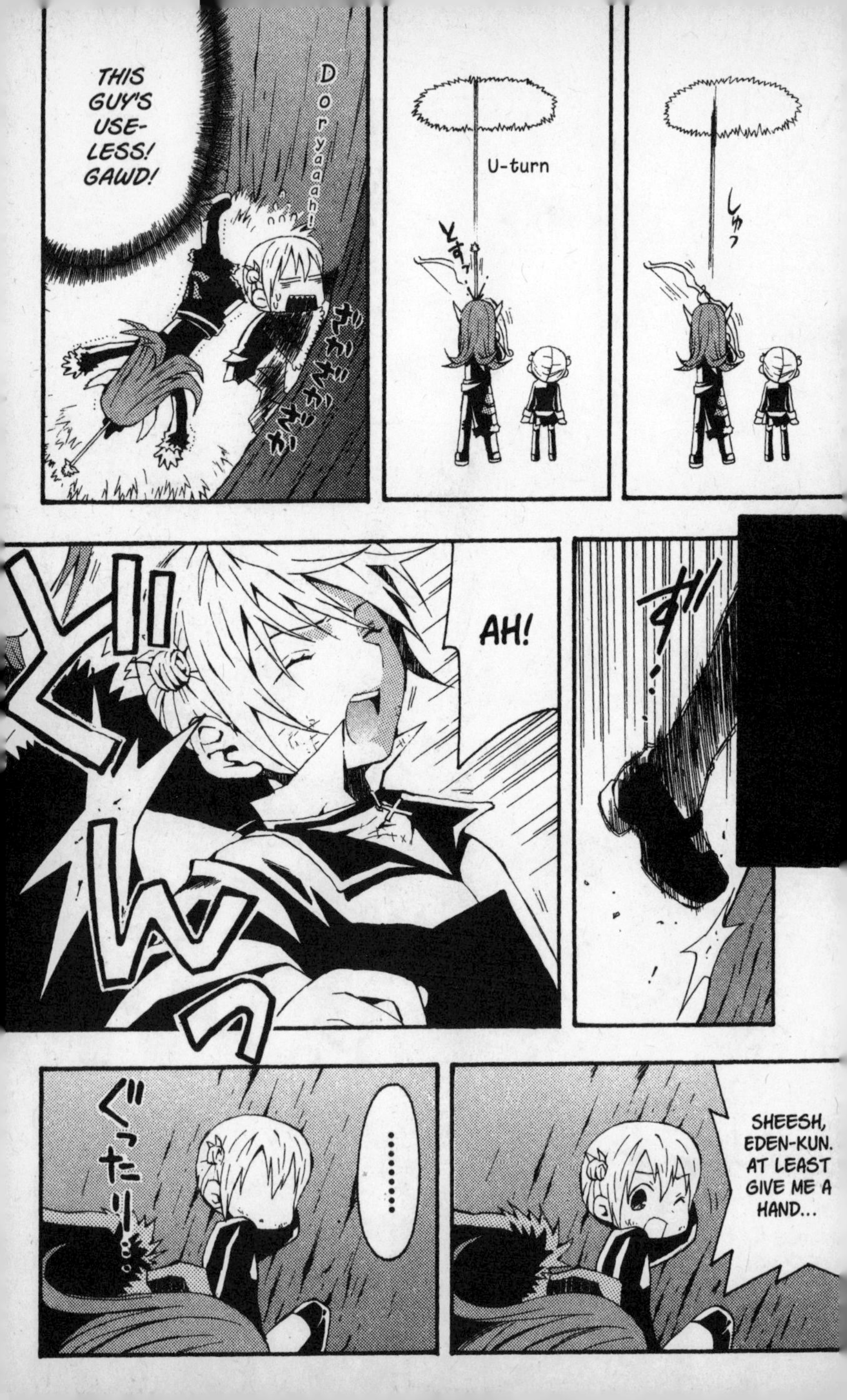
しゅっ
U-turn
とすっ
Doryaaaah!
ざかざかざか
THIS GUY'S USE-LESS! GAWD!
ずっ
AH!
SHEESH, EDEN-KUN. AT LEAST GIVE ME A HAND...
……
ぐったー…

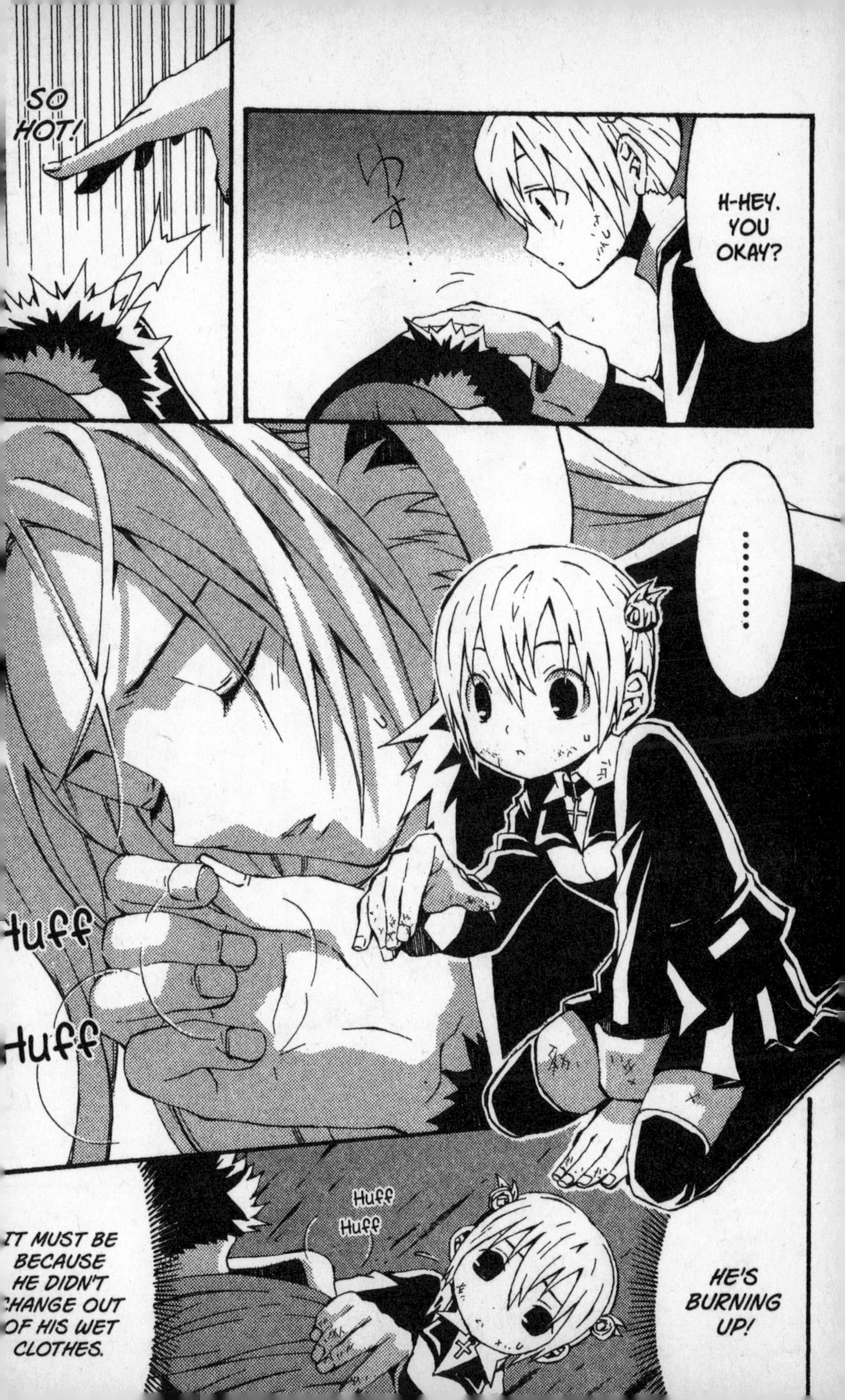
ゆす…
H-HEY. YOU OKAY?
SO HOT!
......
Huff
Huff
HE'S BURNING UP!
Huff
Huff
IT MUST BE BECAUSE HE DIDN'T CHANGE OUT OF HIS WET CLOTHES.

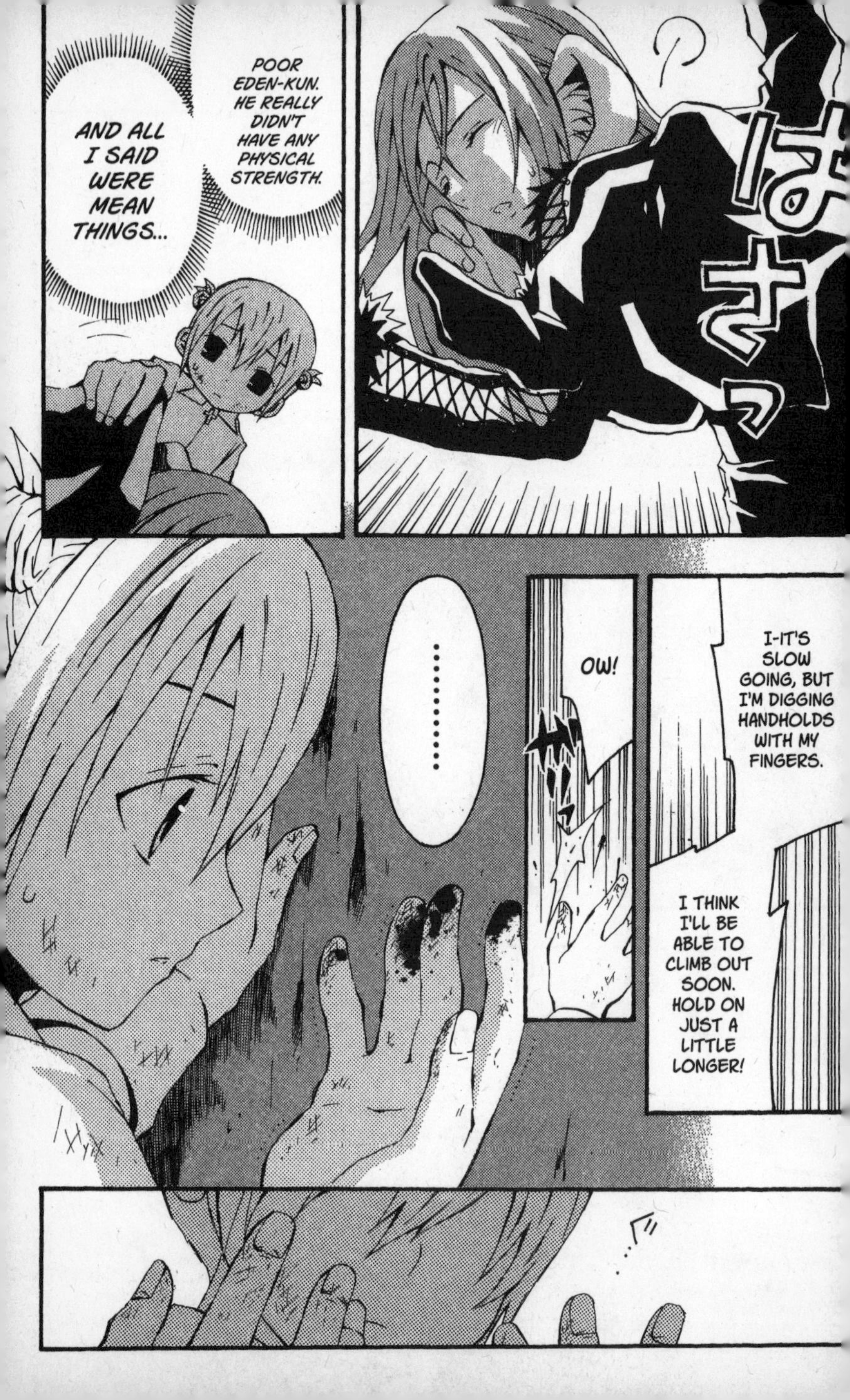
?
はさっ
POOR EDEN-KUN. HE REALLY DIDN'T HAVE ANY PHYSICAL STRENGTH.
AND ALL I SAID WERE MEAN THINGS...
I-IT'S SLOW GOING, BUT I'M DIGGING HANDHOLDS WITH MY FINGERS.
I THINK I'LL BE ABLE TO CLIMB OUT SOON. HOLD ON JUST A LITTLE LONGER!
OW!
....

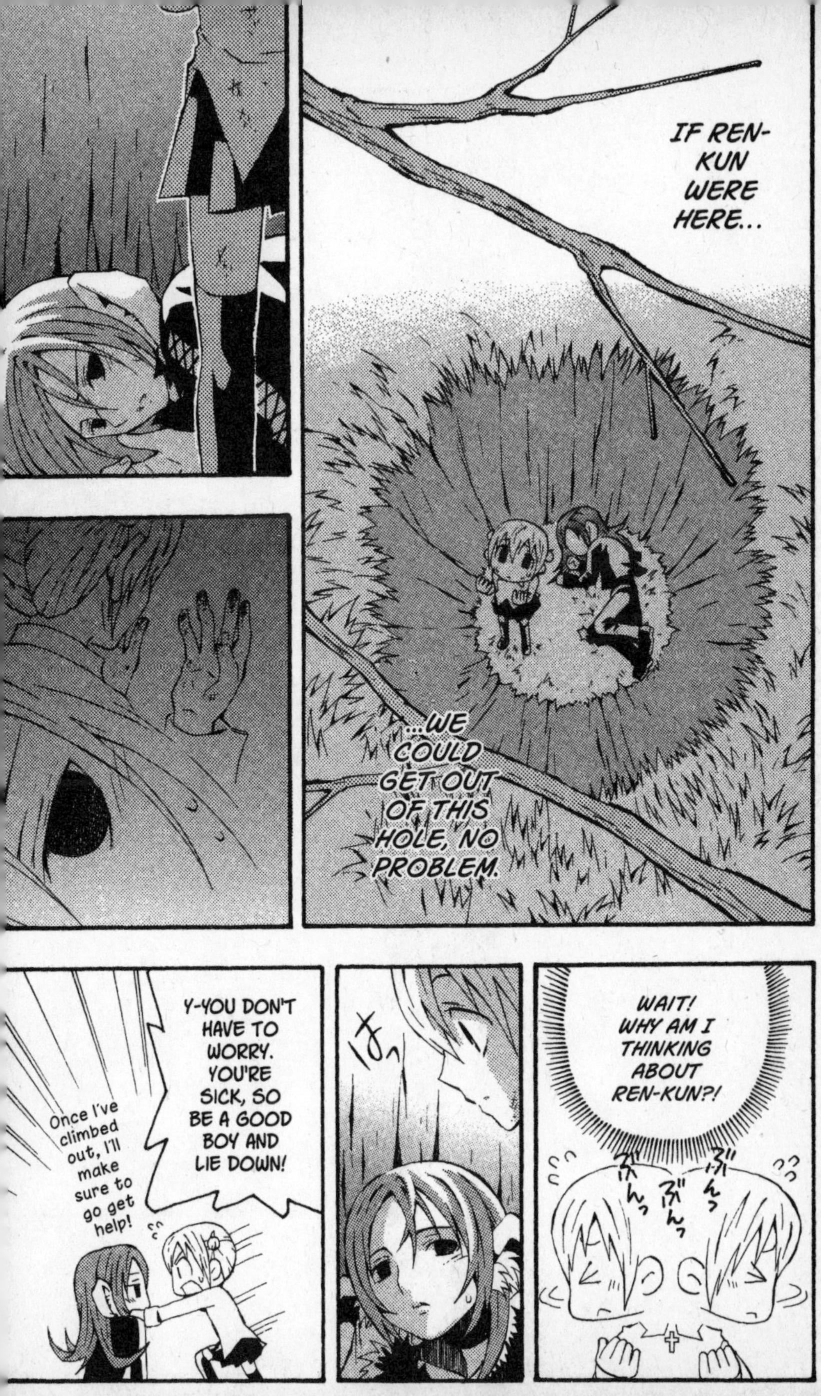
IF REN-KUN WERE HERE...
...WE COULD GET OUT OF THIS HOLE, NO PROBLEM.
WAIT! WHY AM I THINKING ABOUT REN-KUN?!
Y-YOU DON'T HAVE TO WORRY. YOU'RE SICK, SO BE A GOOD BOY AND LIE DOWN!
Once I've climbed out, I'll make sure to go get help!

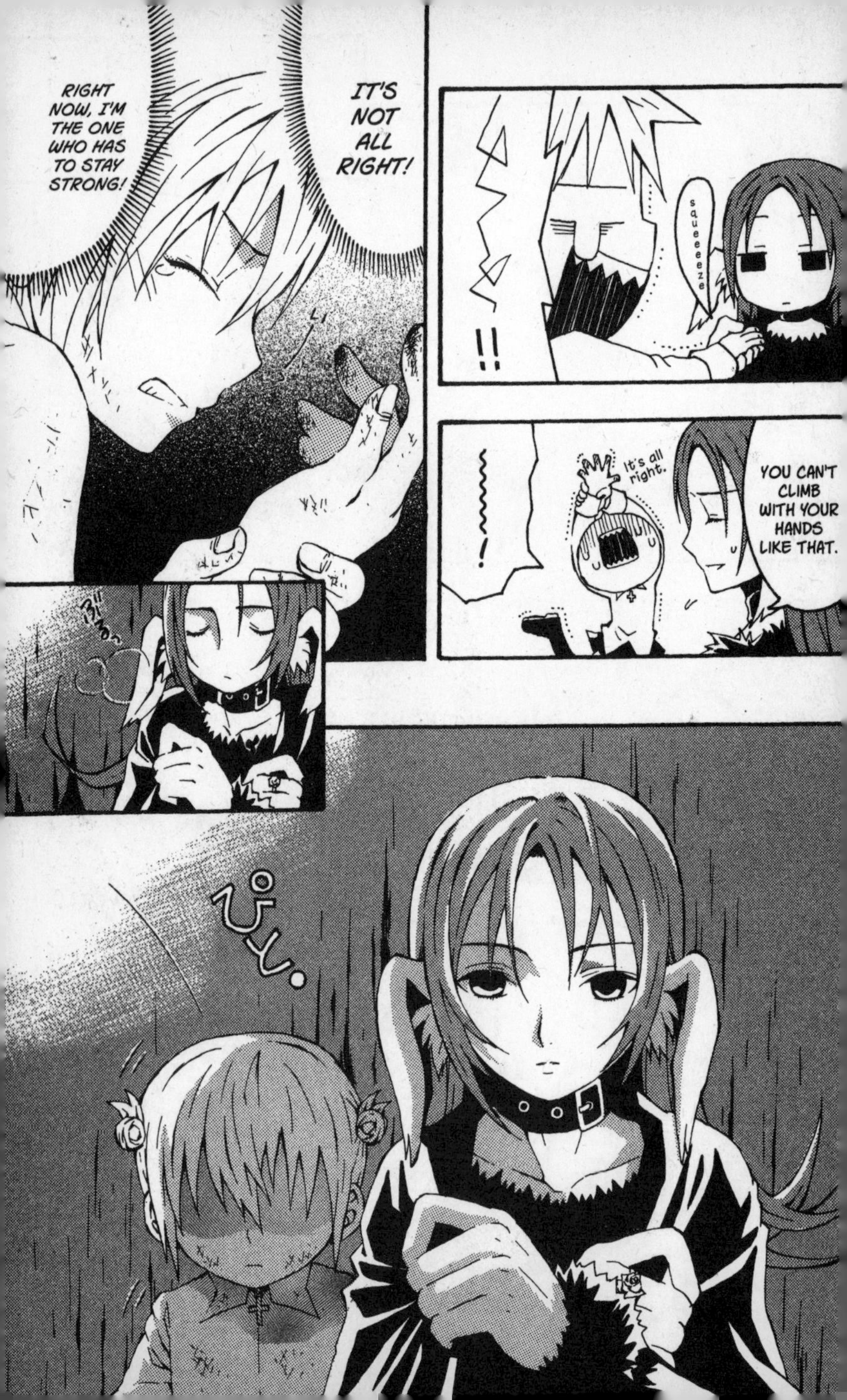
squeeeeeze
!!
YOU CAN'T CLIMB WITH YOUR HANDS LIKE THAT.
It's all right.
~~~!
IT'S NOT ALL RIGHT!
RIGHT NOW, I'M THE ONE WHO HAS TO STAY STRONG!
~~~

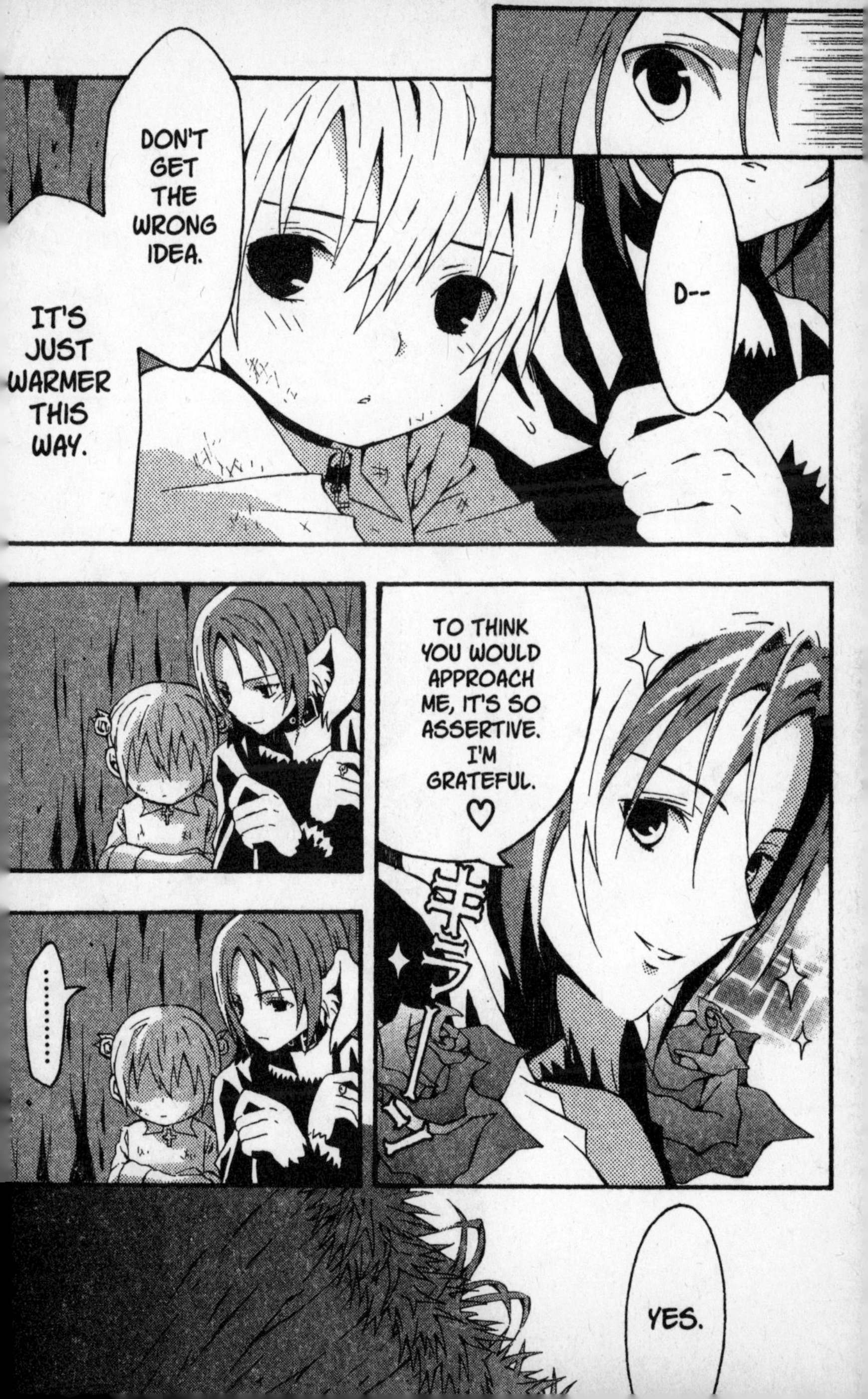
D--
DON'T GET THE WRONG IDEA.
IT'S JUST WARMER THIS WAY.
TO THINK YOU WOULD APPROACH ME, IT'S SO ASSERTIVE. I'M GRATEFUL. ♡
......
YES.

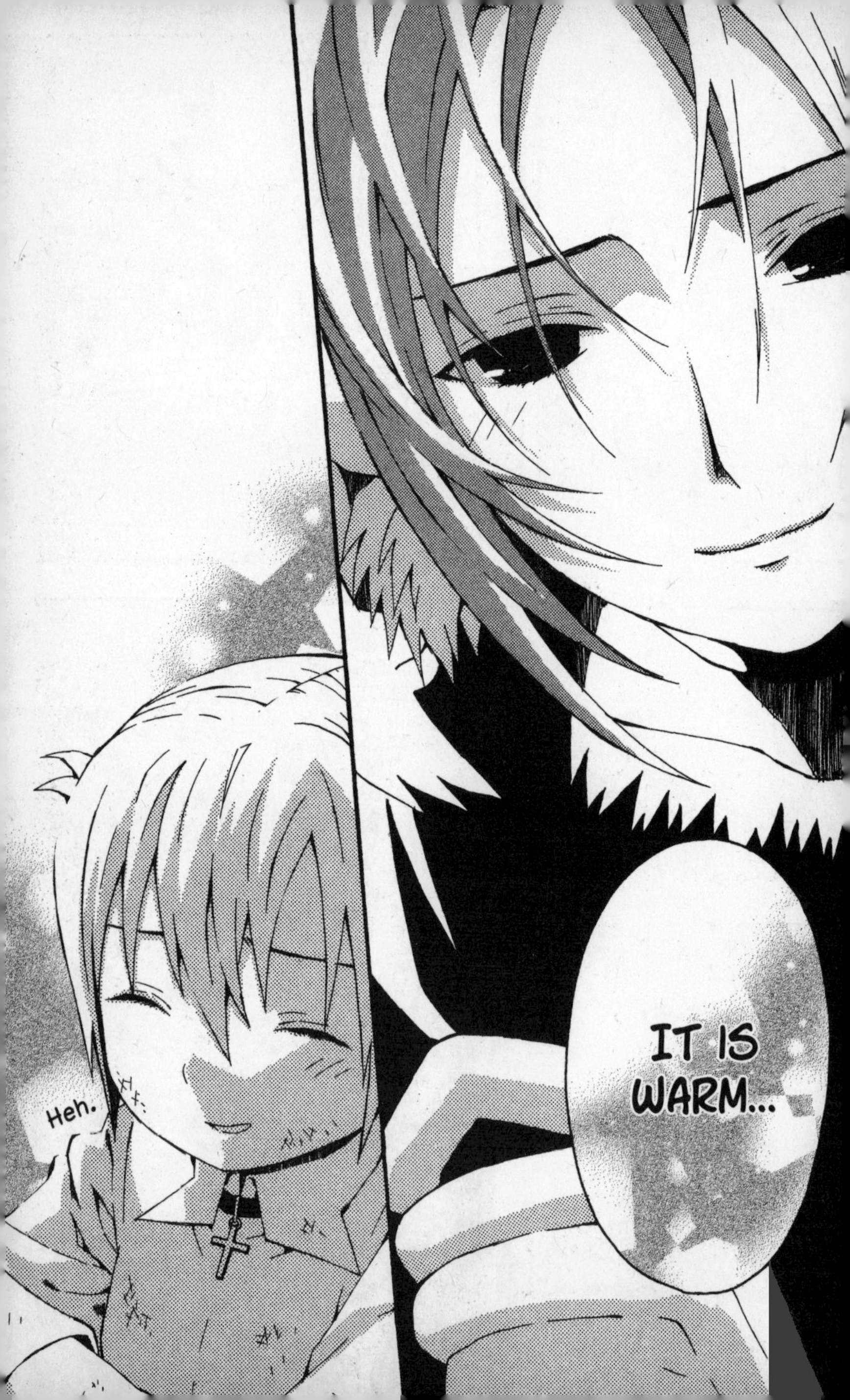
IT IS WARM...
Heh.

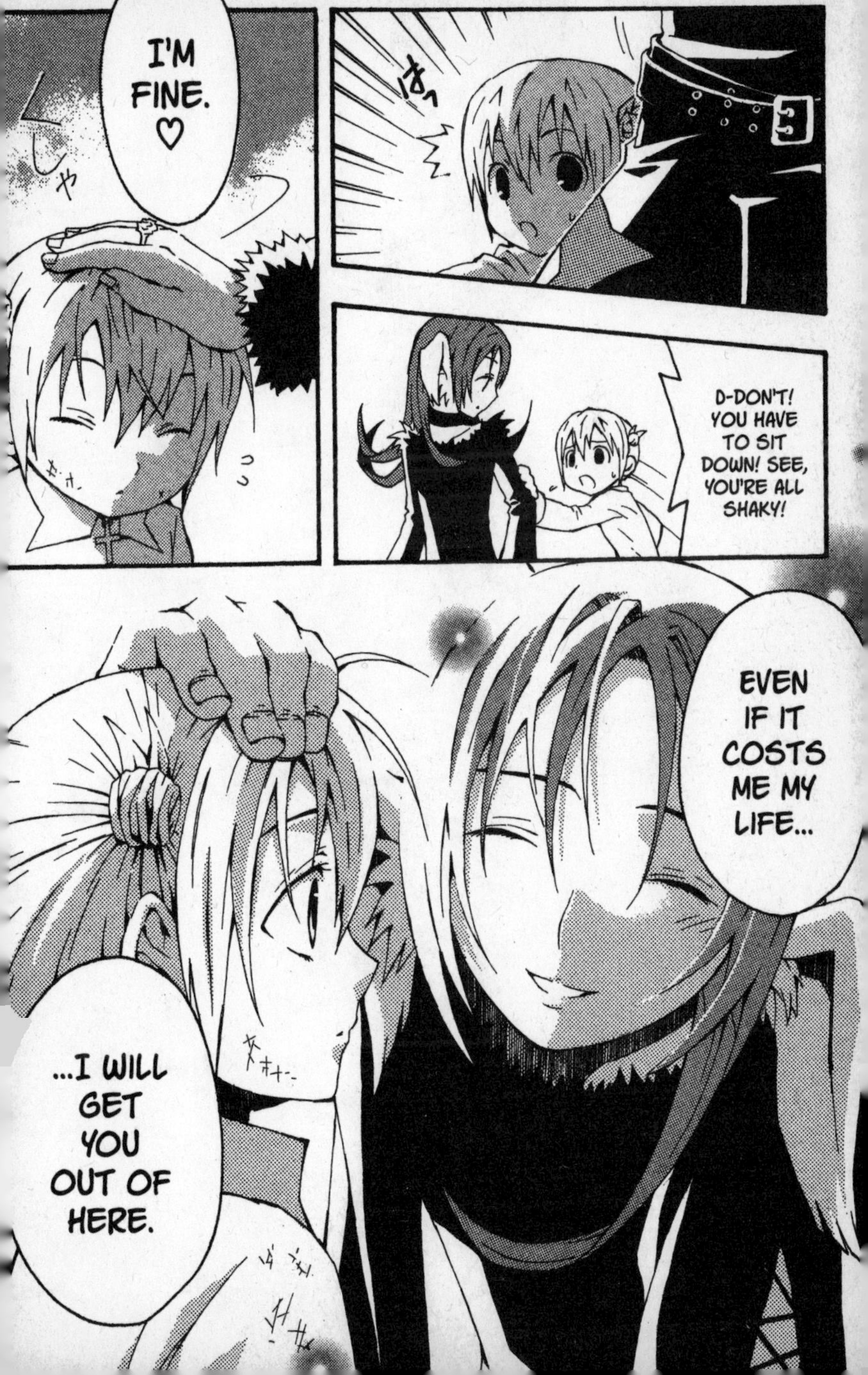
D-DON'T! YOU HAVE TO SIT DOWN! SEE, YOU'RE ALL SHAKY!
I'M FINE. ♡
EVEN IF IT COSTS ME MY LIFE...
...I WILL GET YOU OUT OF HERE.

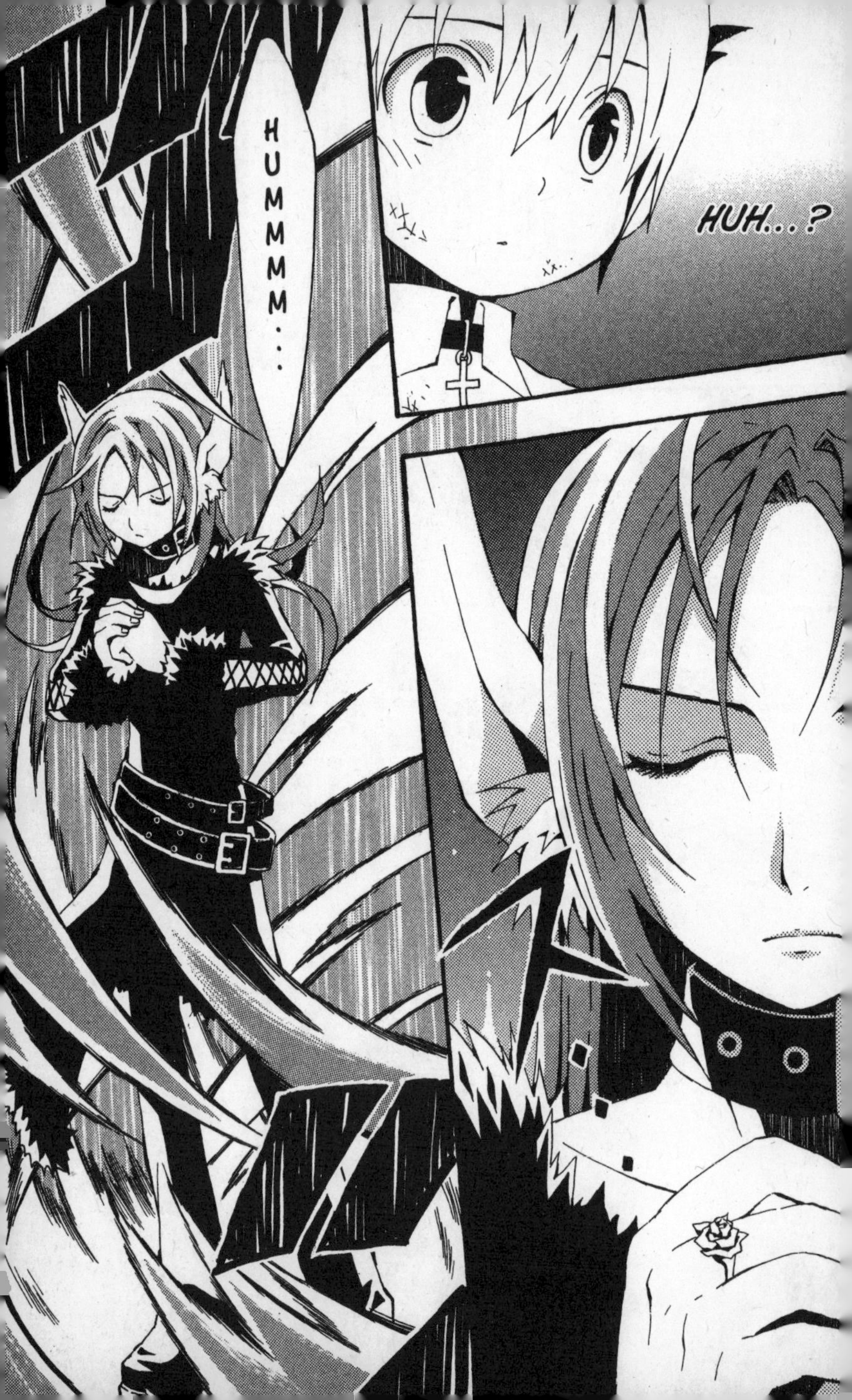
HUH...?
HUMMMM...

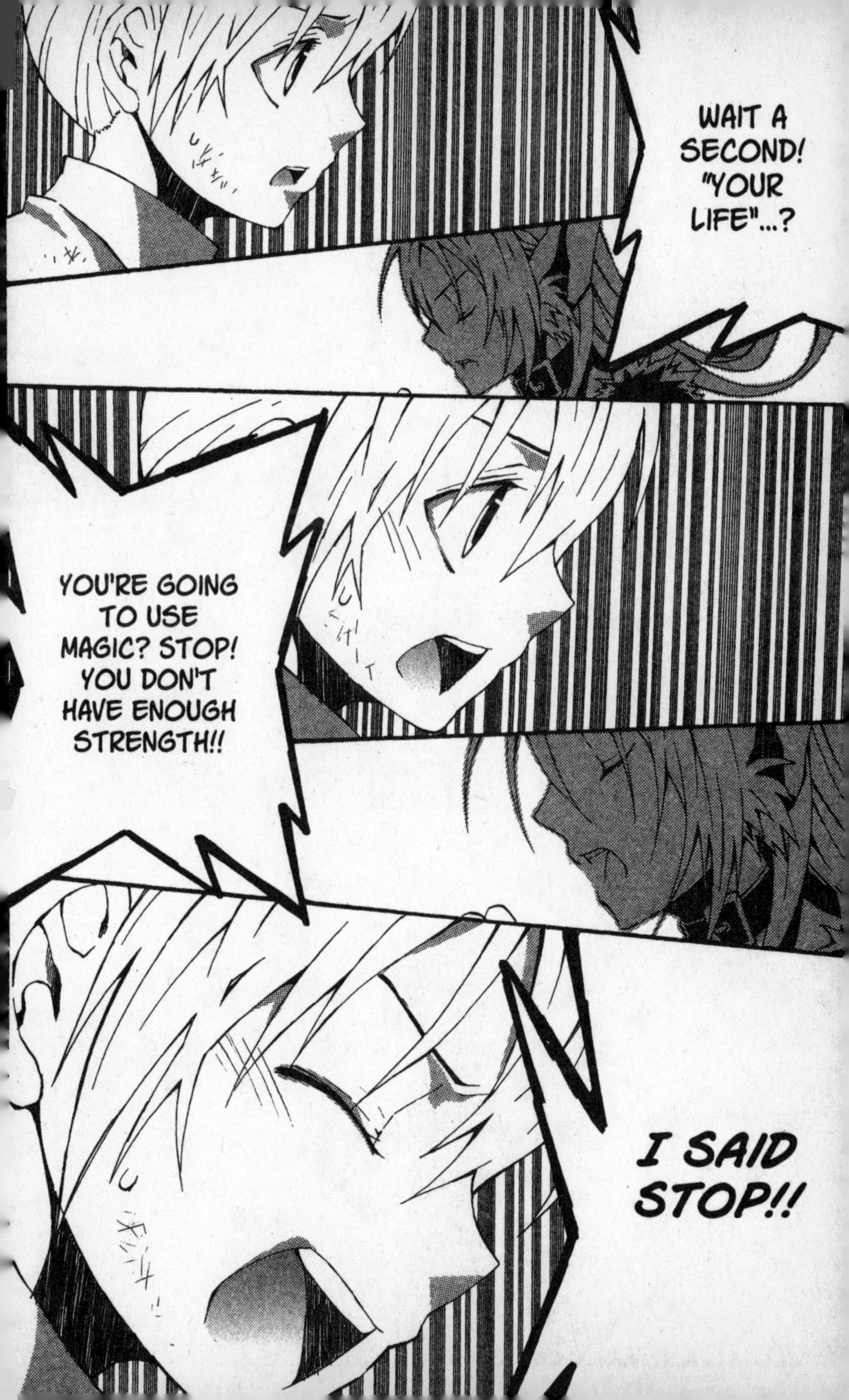
WAIT A SECOND! "YOUR LIFE"...?
YOU'RE GOING TO USE MAGIC? STOP! YOU DON'T HAVE ENOUGH STRENGTH!!
I SAID STOP!!

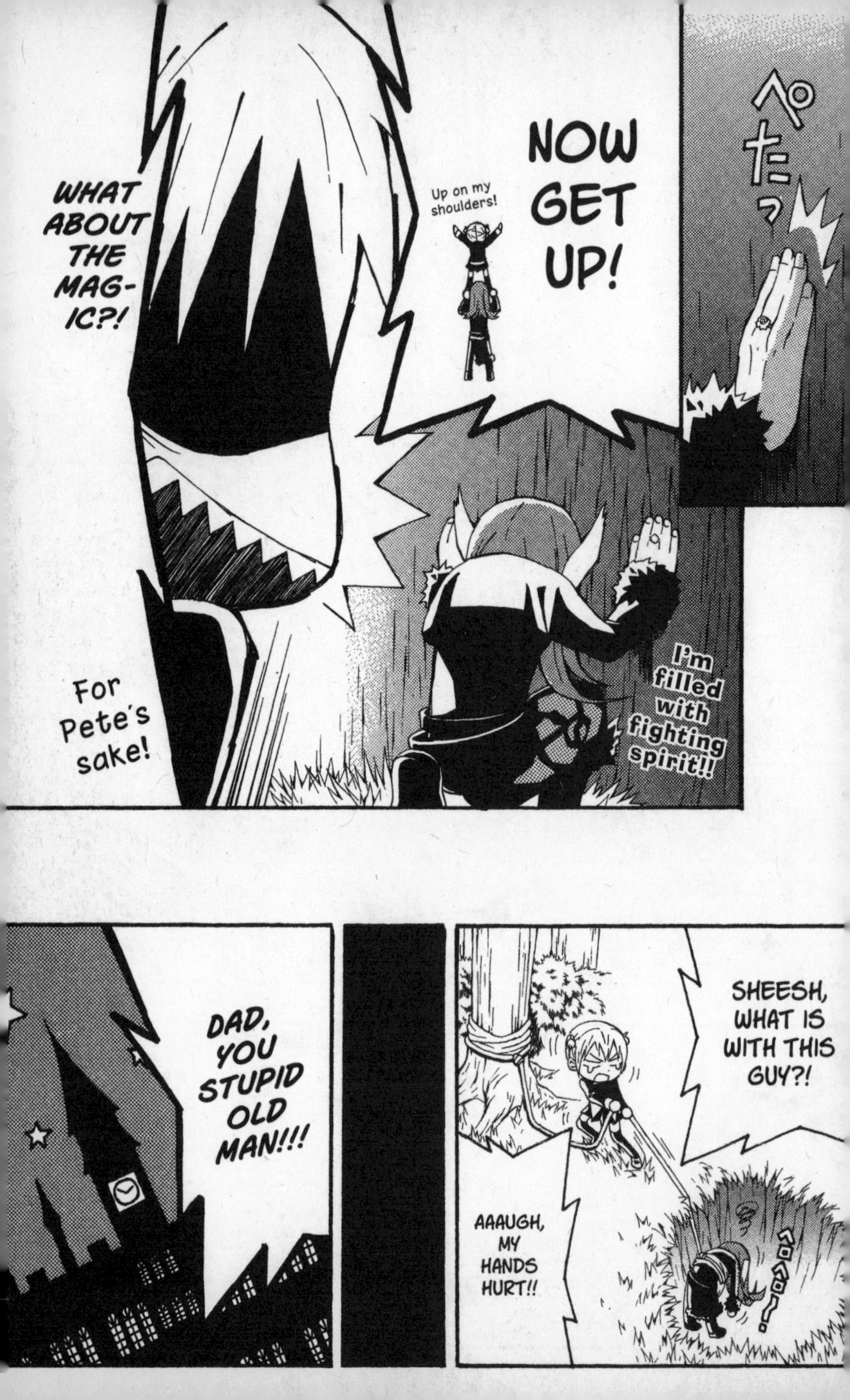
ぺたっ
NOW GET UP!
Up on my shoulders!
WHAT ABOUT THE MAG-IC?!
I'm filled with fighting spirit!!
For Pete's sake!
SHEESH, WHAT IS WITH THIS GUY?!
AAAUGH, MY HANDS HURT!!
DAD, YOU STUPID OLD MAN!!!

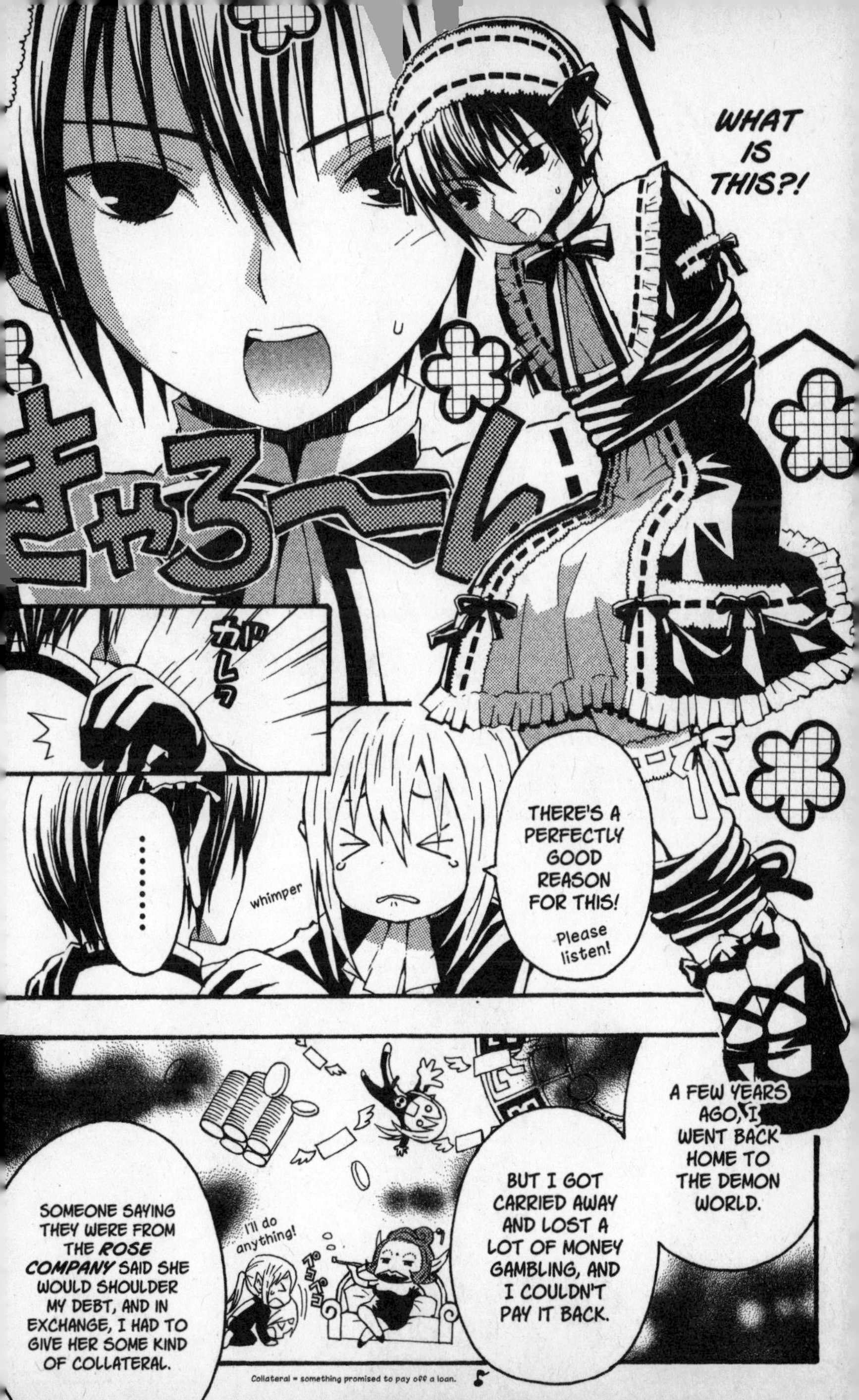
WHAT IS THIS?!
きゃろーん!!
ガしっ
THERE'S A PERFECTLY GOOD REASON FOR THIS!
Please listen!
whimper
……
A FEW YEARS AGO, I WENT BACK HOME TO THE DEMON WORLD.
BUT I GOT CARRIED AWAY AND LOST A LOT OF MONEY GAMBLING, AND I COULDN'T PAY IT BACK.
I'll do anything!
SOMEONE SAYING THEY WERE FROM THE *ROSE COMPANY* SAID SHE WOULD SHOULDER MY DEBT, AND IN EXCHANGE, I HAD TO GIVE HER SOME KIND OF COLLATERAL.

Collateral = something promised to pay off a loan.

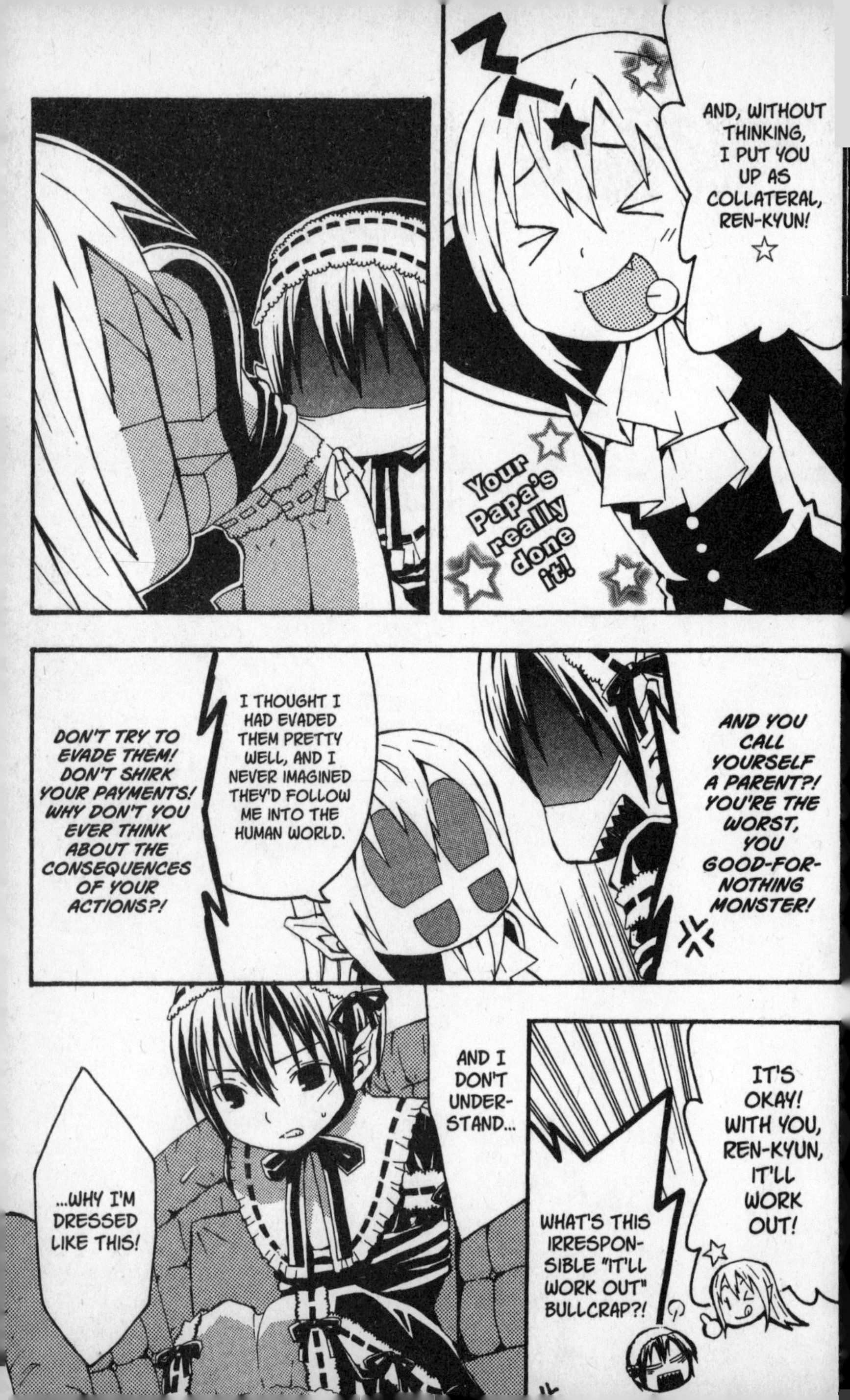
AND, WITHOUT THINKING, I PUT YOU UP AS COLLATERAL, REN-KYUN! ☆
Your Papa's really done it!
AND YOU CALL YOURSELF A PARENT?! YOU'RE THE WORST, YOU GOOD-FOR-NOTHING MONSTER!
I THOUGHT I HAD EVADED THEM PRETTY WELL, AND I NEVER IMAGINED THEY'D FOLLOW ME INTO THE HUMAN WORLD.
DON'T TRY TO EVADE THEM! DON'T SHIRK YOUR PAYMENTS! WHY DON'T YOU EVER THINK ABOUT THE CONSEQUENCES OF YOUR ACTIONS?!
IT'S OKAY! WITH YOU, REN-KYUN, IT'LL WORK OUT!
WHAT'S THIS IRRESPONSIBLE "IT'LL WORK OUT" BULLCRAP?!
AND I DON'T UNDERSTAND...
...WHY I'M DRESSED LIKE THIS!

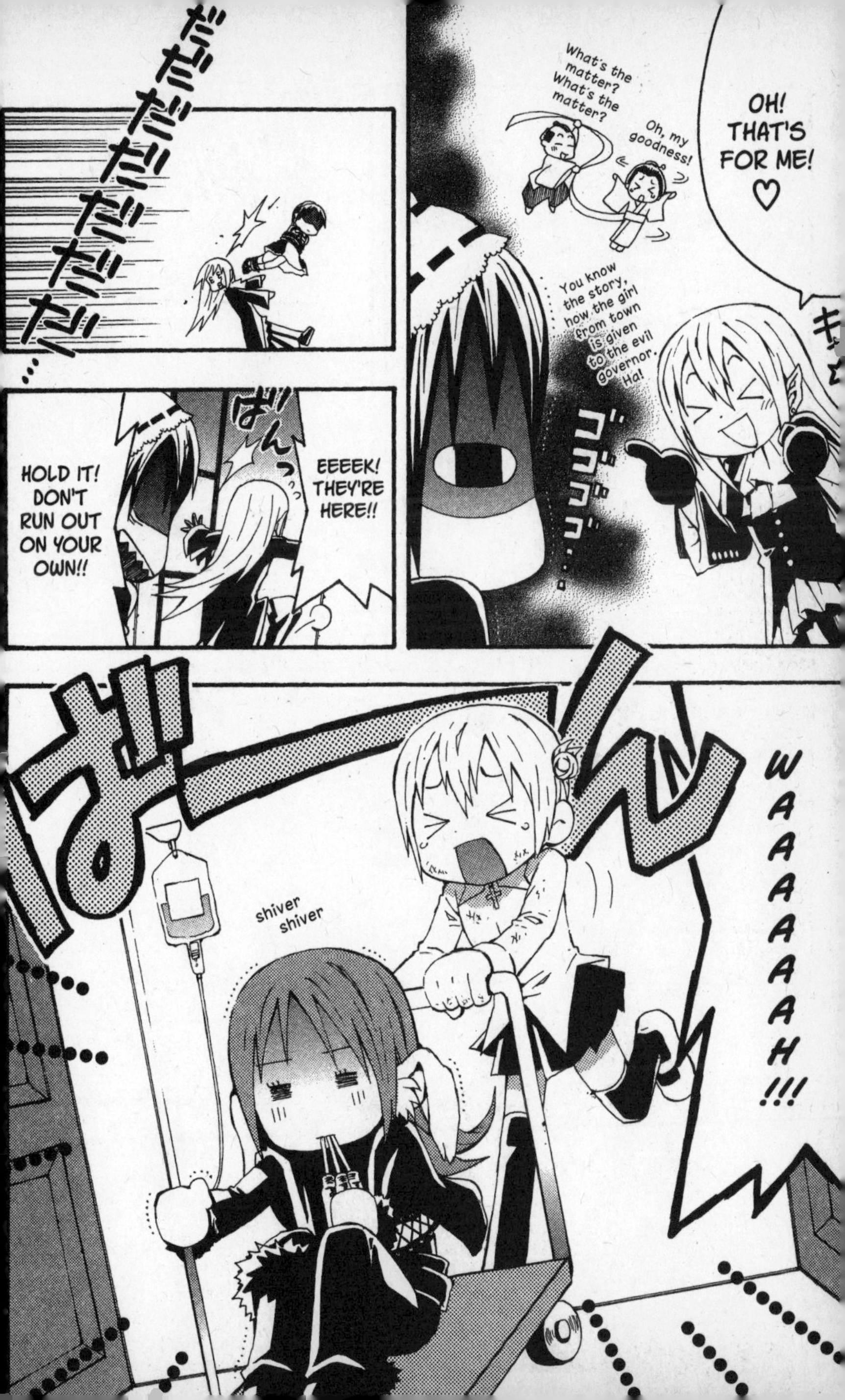
OH! THAT'S FOR ME! ♡
What's the matter? What's the matter?
Oh, my goodness!
You know the story, how the girl from town is given to the evil governor. Ha!
ゴゴゴゴ…
だだだだだだだ…
ぱんっ
EEEEK! THEY'RE HERE!!
HOLD IT! DON'T RUN OUT ON YOUR OWN!!
WAAAAAAAAH!!!
ざーん
shiver shiver

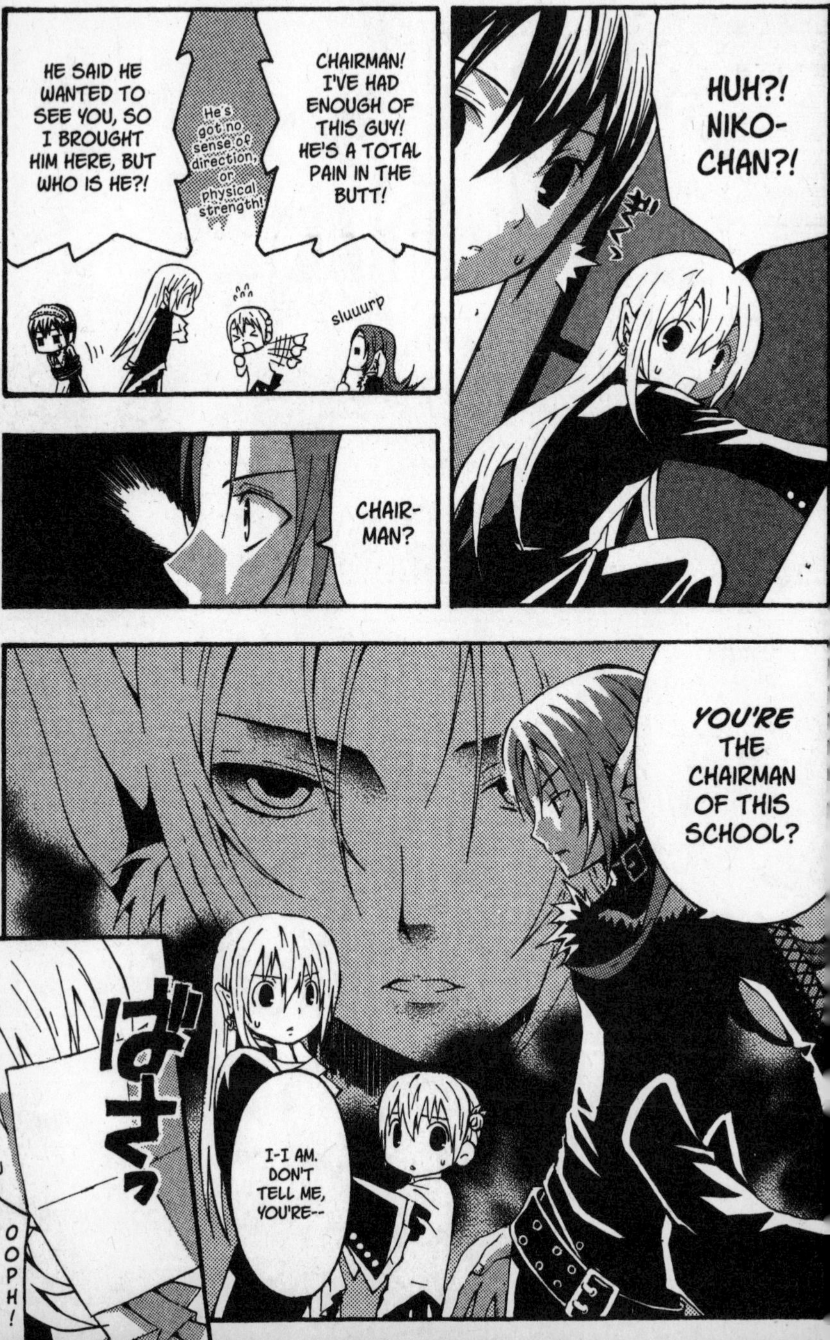
HUH?! NIKO-CHAN?!
CHAIRMAN! I'VE HAD ENOUGH OF THIS GUY! HE'S A TOTAL PAIN IN THE BUTT!
He's got no sense of direction, or physical strength!
HE SAID HE WANTED TO SEE YOU, SO I BROUGHT HIM HERE, BUT WHO IS HE?!
sluuurp
CHAIR-MAN?
YOU'RE THE CHAIRMAN OF THIS SCHOOL?
I-I AM. DON'T TELL ME, YOU'RE--
ばさっ
OOPH!

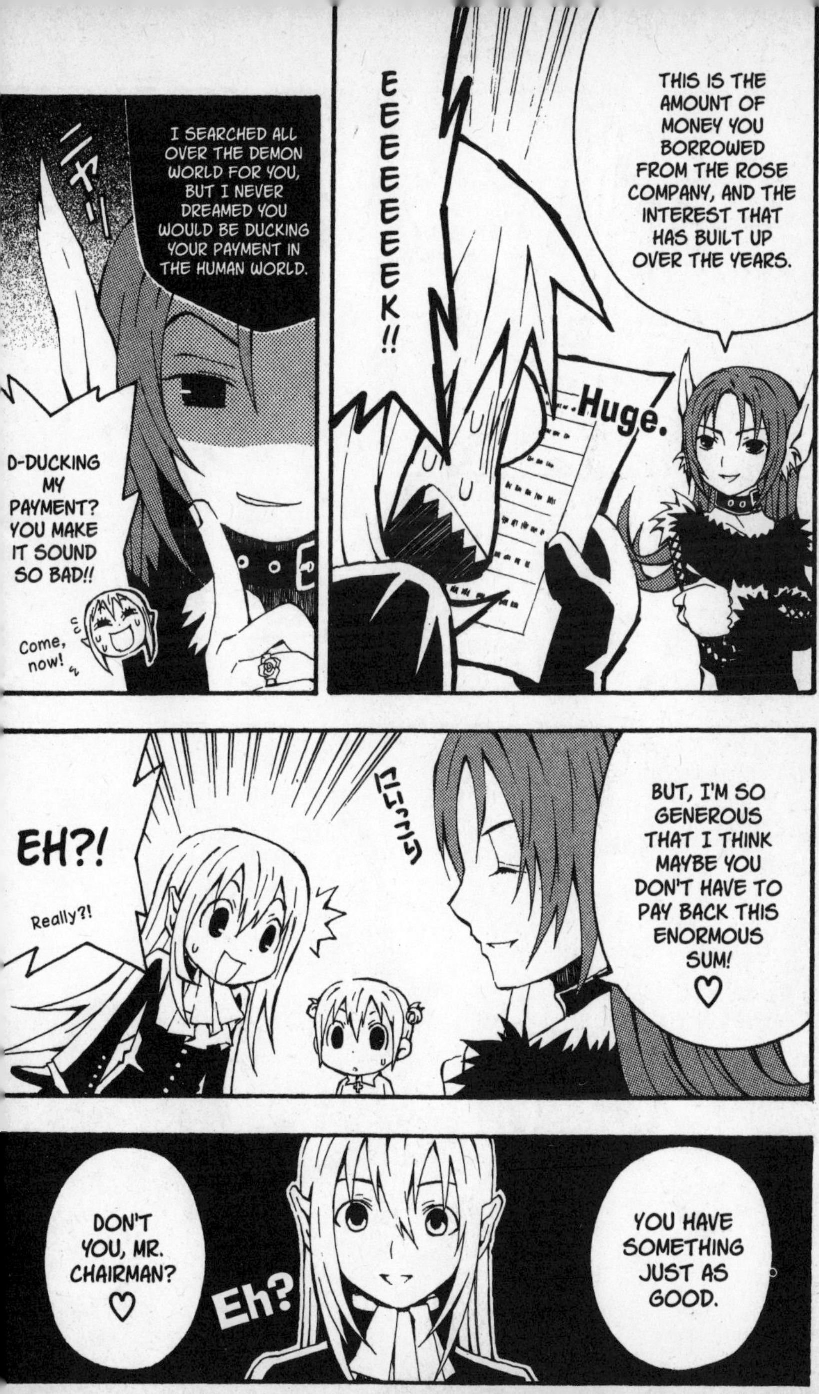
THIS IS THE AMOUNT OF MONEY YOU BORROWED FROM THE ROSE COMPANY, AND THE INTEREST THAT HAS BUILT UP OVER THE YEARS.
EEEEEEEEEK!!
Huge.
I SEARCHED ALL OVER THE DEMON WORLD FOR YOU, BUT I NEVER DREAMED YOU WOULD BE DUCKING YOUR PAYMENT IN THE HUMAN WORLD.
D-DUCKING MY PAYMENT? YOU MAKE IT SOUND SO BAD!!
Come, now!
BUT, I'M SO GENEROUS THAT I THINK MAYBE YOU DON'T HAVE TO PAY BACK THIS ENORMOUS SUM! ♡
にっこり
EH?!
Really?!
YOU HAVE SOMETHING JUST AS GOOD.
Eh?
DON'T YOU, MR. CHAIRMAN? ♡

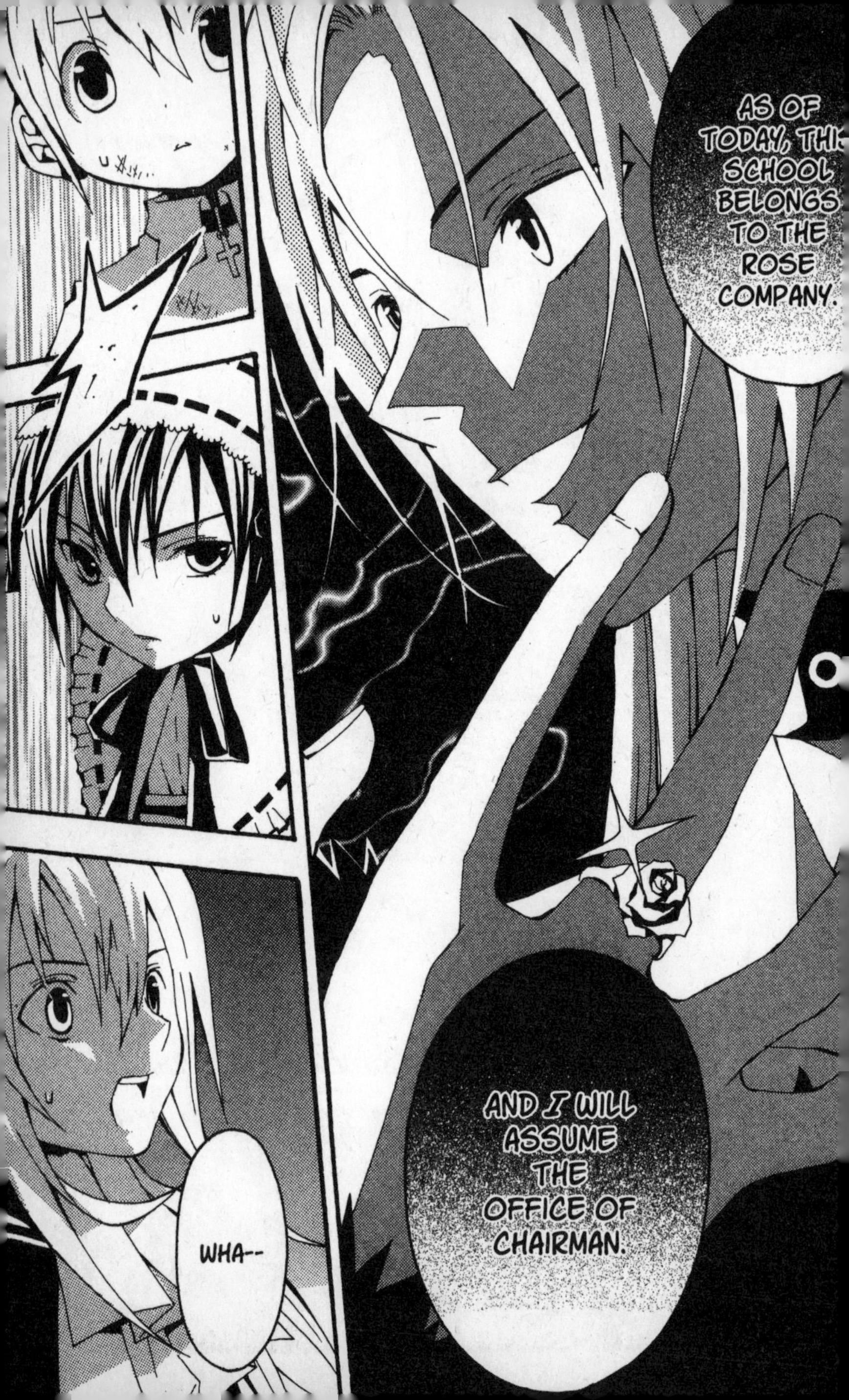
AS OF TODAY, THIS SCHOOL BELONGS TO THE ROSE COMPANY.
AND I WILL ASSUME THE OFFICE OF CHAIRMAN.
WHA--

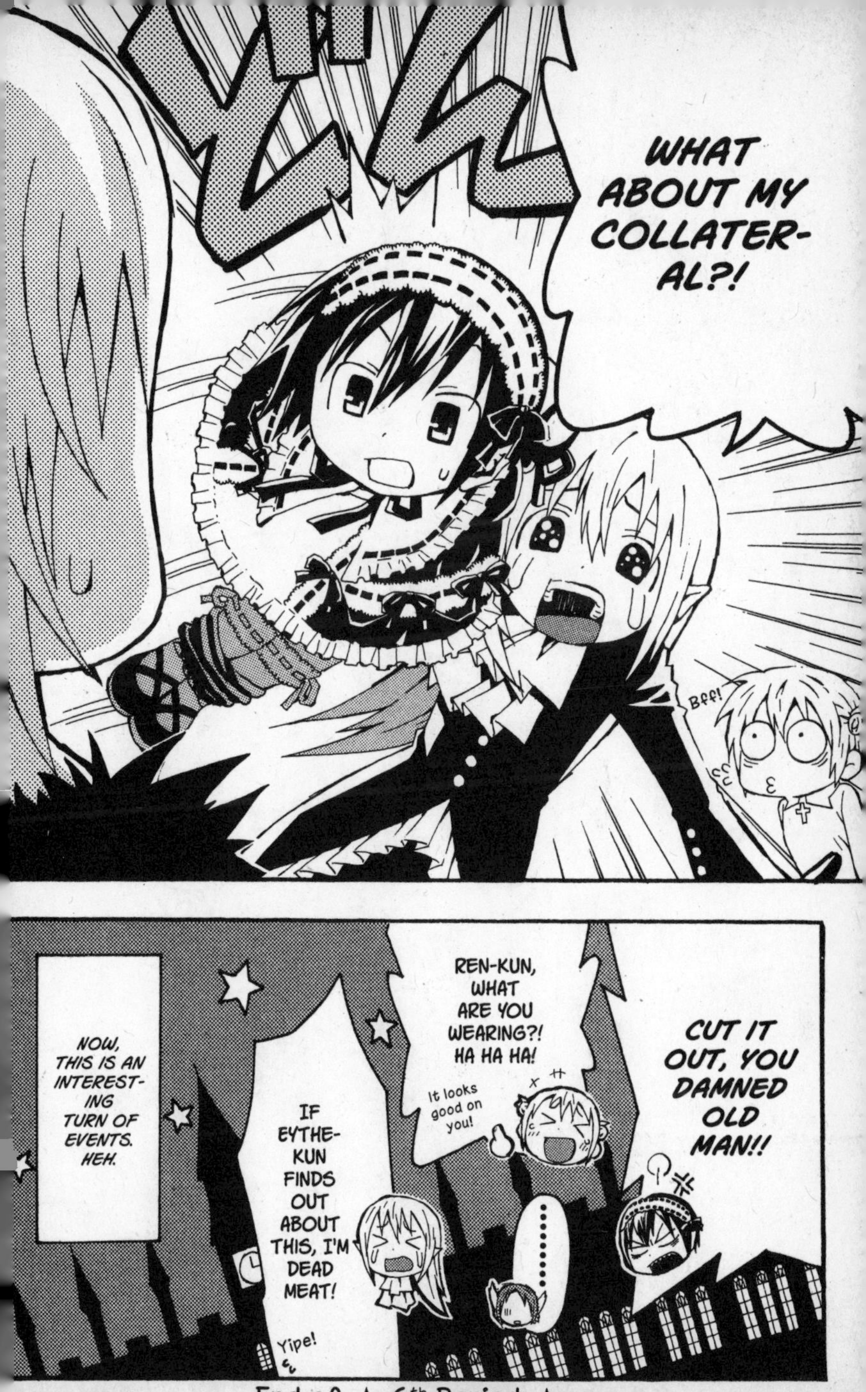
WHAT ABOUT MY COLLATER-AL?!
Bff!
CUT IT OUT, YOU DAMNED OLD MAN!!
REN-KUN, WHAT ARE YOU WEARING?! HA HA HA!
It looks good on you!
......
IF EYTHE-KUN FINDS OUT ABOUT THIS, I'M DEAD MEAT!
Yipe!
NOW, THIS IS AN INTEREST-ING TURN OF EVENTS. HEH.

End of ★ 6th Period ★

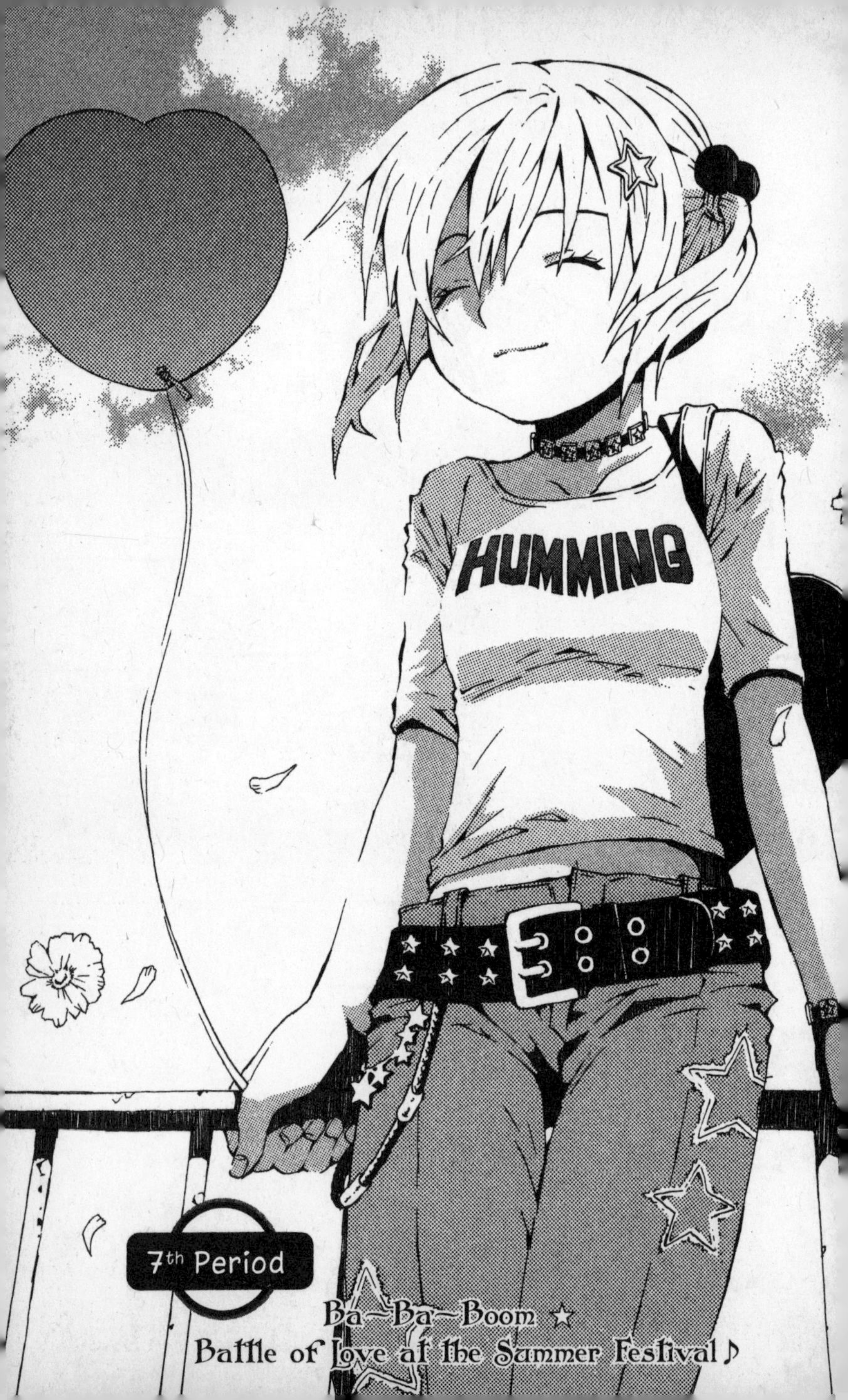
HUMMING
7th Period
Ba~Ba~Boom ☆
Battle of Love at the Summer Festival ♪

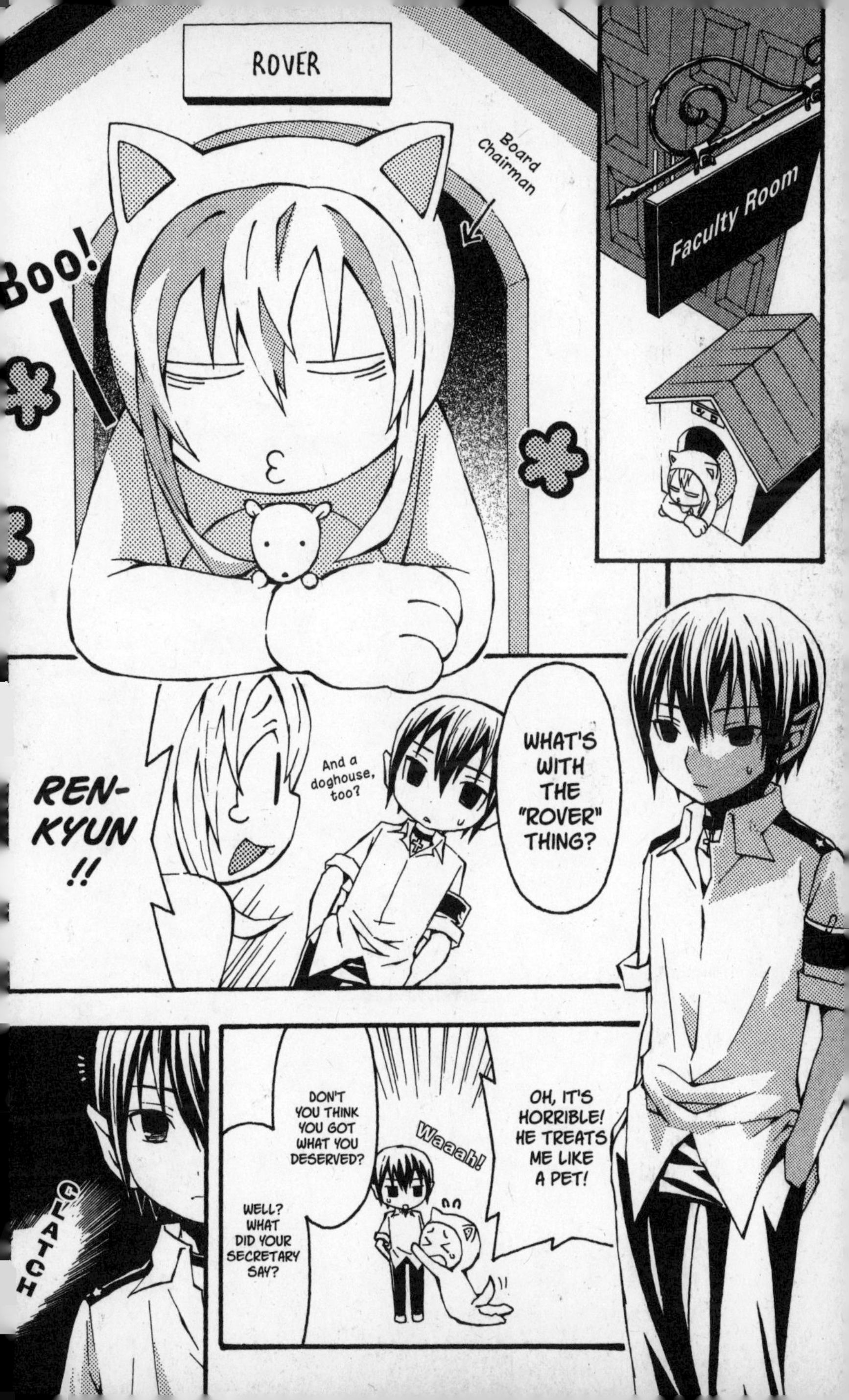
Faculty Room
ROVER
Board Chairman
Boo!
WHAT'S WITH THE "ROVER" THING?
And a doghouse, too?
REN-KYUN!!
OH, IT'S HORRIBLE! HE TREATS ME LIKE A PET!
Waaah!
DON'T YOU THINK YOU GOT WHAT YOU DESERVED?
WELL? WHAT DID YOUR SECRETARY SAY?
CLATCH

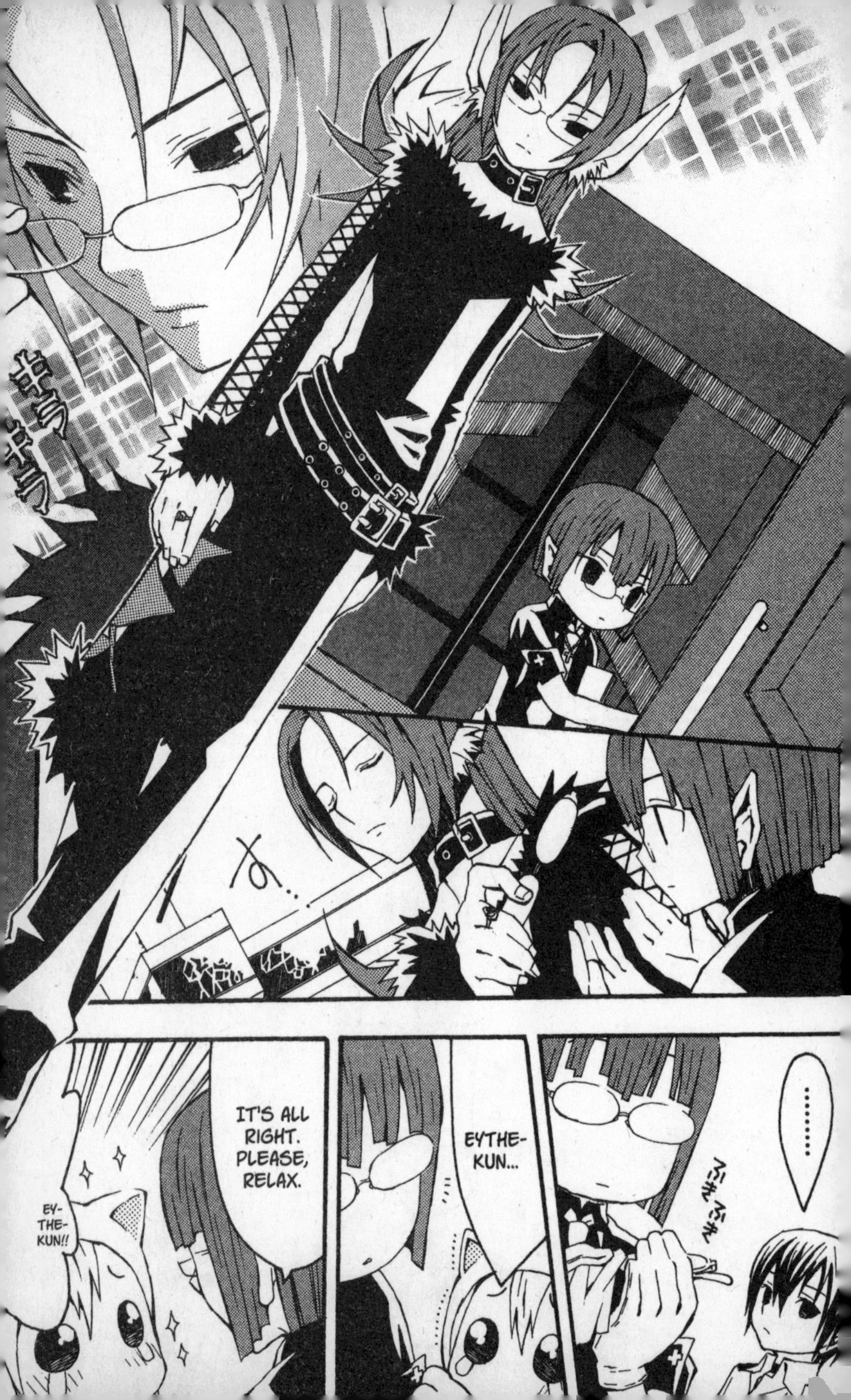
……
EYTHE-KUN...
IT'S ALL RIGHT. PLEASE, RELAX.
EY-THE-KUN!!

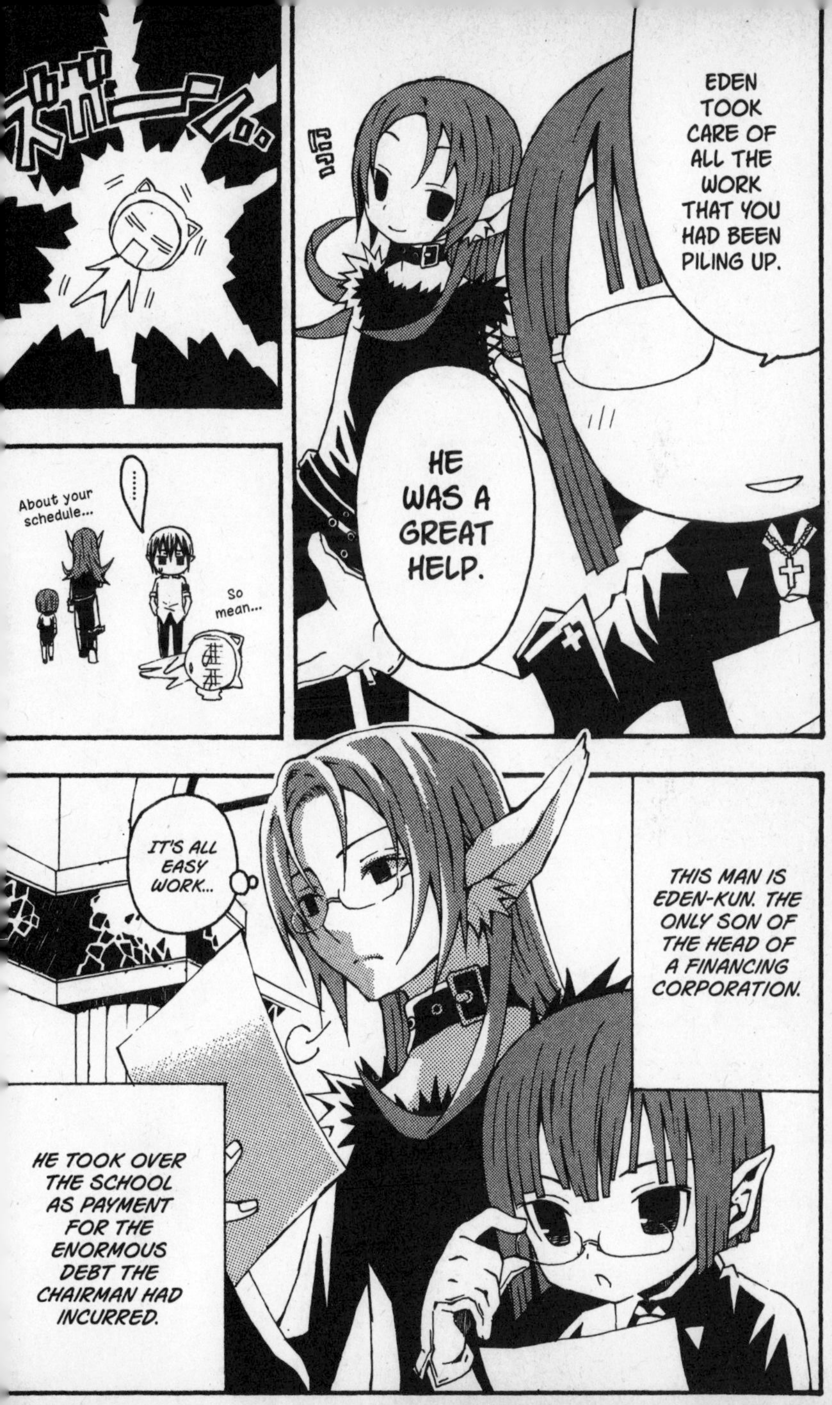
EDEN TOOK CARE OF ALL THE WORK THAT YOU HAD BEEN PILING UP.
HE WAS A GREAT HELP.
......
About your schedule...
So mean...
THIS MAN IS EDEN-KUN. THE ONLY SON OF THE HEAD OF A FINANCING CORPORATION.
IT'S ALL EASY WORK...
HE TOOK OVER THE SCHOOL AS PAYMENT FOR THE ENORMOUS DEBT THE CHAIRMAN HAD INCURRED.

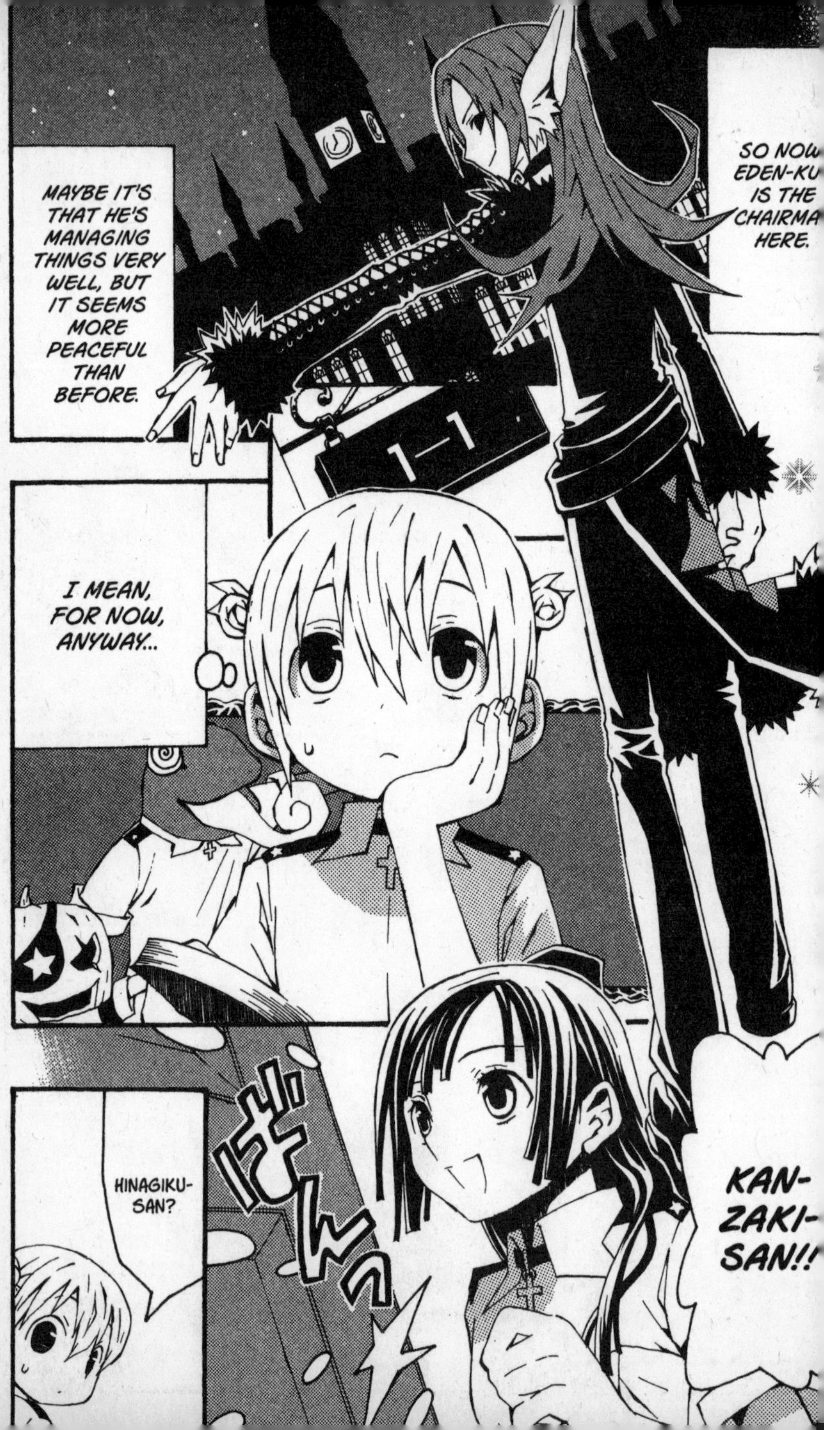
SO NOW EDEN-KU IS THE CHAIRMA HERE.
MAYBE IT'S THAT HE'S MANAGING THINGS VERY WELL, BUT IT SEEMS MORE PEACEFUL THAN BEFORE.
1-1
I MEAN, FOR NOW, ANYWAY...
KAN-ZAKI-SAN!!
HINAGIKU-SAN?

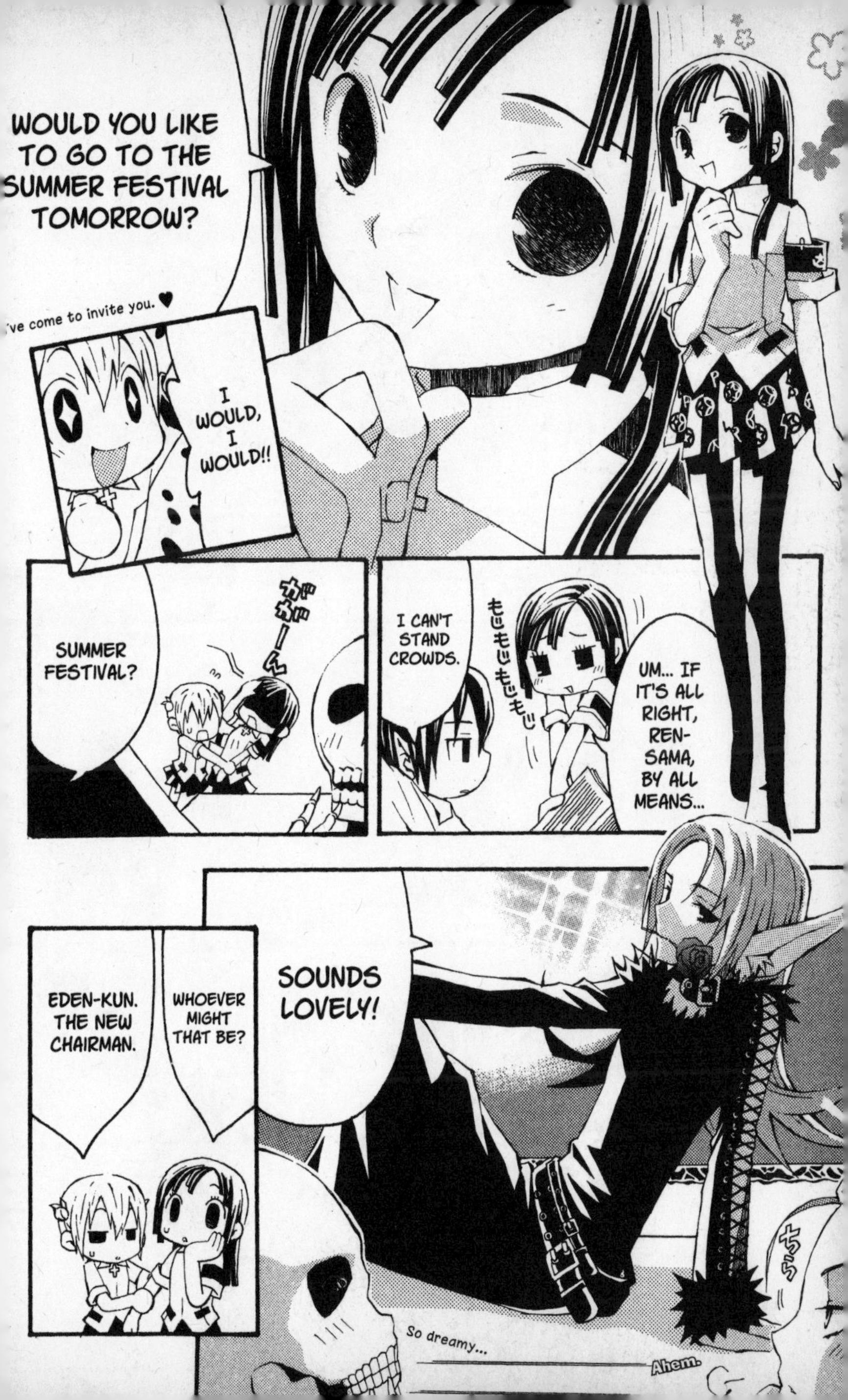

WOULD YOU LIKE TO GO TO THE SUMMER FESTIVAL TOMORROW?
I've come to invite you. ♥
I WOULD, I WOULD!!
UM... IF IT'S ALL RIGHT, REN-SAMA, BY ALL MEANS...
もじもじもじもじ
I CAN'T STAND CROWDS.
ががーん
SUMMER FESTIVAL?
SOUNDS LOVELY!
ちら
So dreamy...
Ahem.
WHOEVER MIGHT THAT BE?
EDEN-KUN. THE NEW CHAIRMAN.

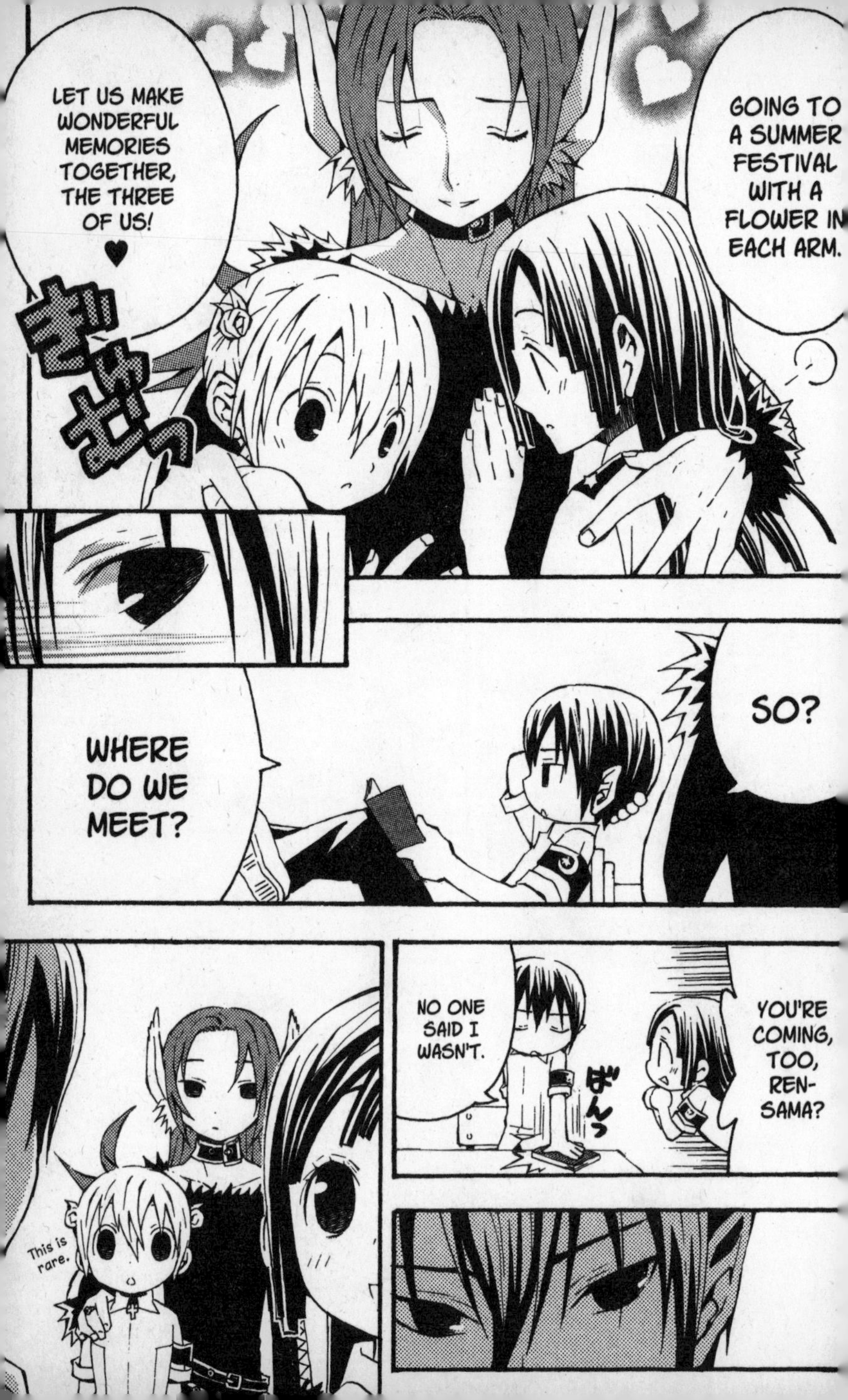
GOING TO A SUMMER FESTIVAL WITH A FLOWER IN EACH ARM.
LET US MAKE WONDERFUL MEMORIES TOGETHER, THE THREE OF US! ♥
SO?
WHERE DO WE MEET?
YOU'RE COMING, TOO, REN-SAMA?
NO ONE SAID I WASN'T.
ばんっ
This is rare.

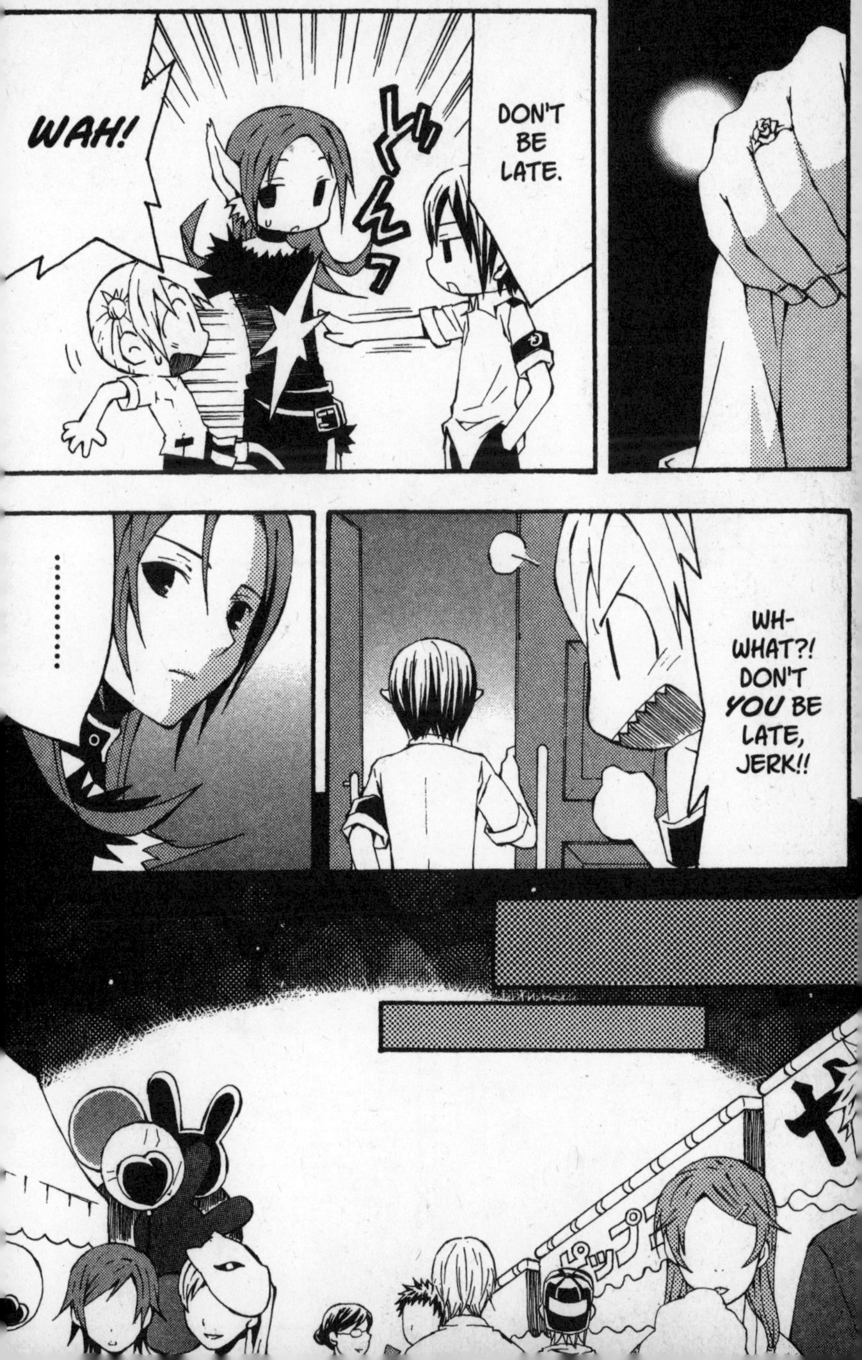
DON'T BE LATE.
WAH!
WH- WHAT?! DON'T YOU BE LATE, JERK!!
....

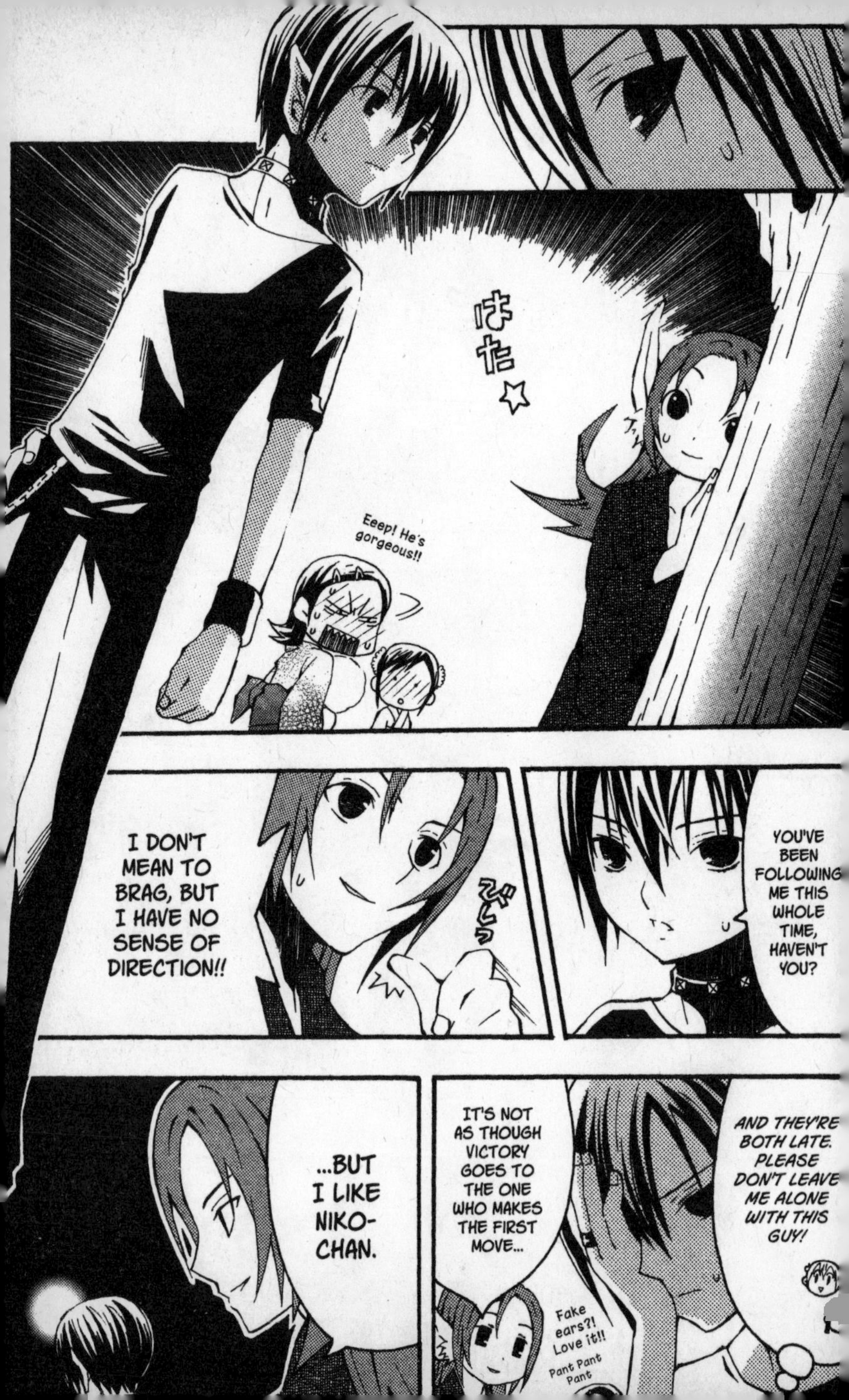
はた☆
Eeep! He's gorgeous!!
YOU'VE BEEN FOLLOWING ME THIS WHOLE TIME, HAVEN'T YOU?
びくっ
I DON'T MEAN TO BRAG, BUT I HAVE NO SENSE OF DIRECTION!!
AND THEY'RE BOTH LATE. PLEASE DON'T LEAVE ME ALONE WITH THIS GUY!
IT'S NOT AS THOUGH VICTORY GOES TO THE ONE WHO MAKES THE FIRST MOVE...
Fake ears?! Love it!!
Pant Pant Pant
...BUT I LIKE NIKO-CHAN.

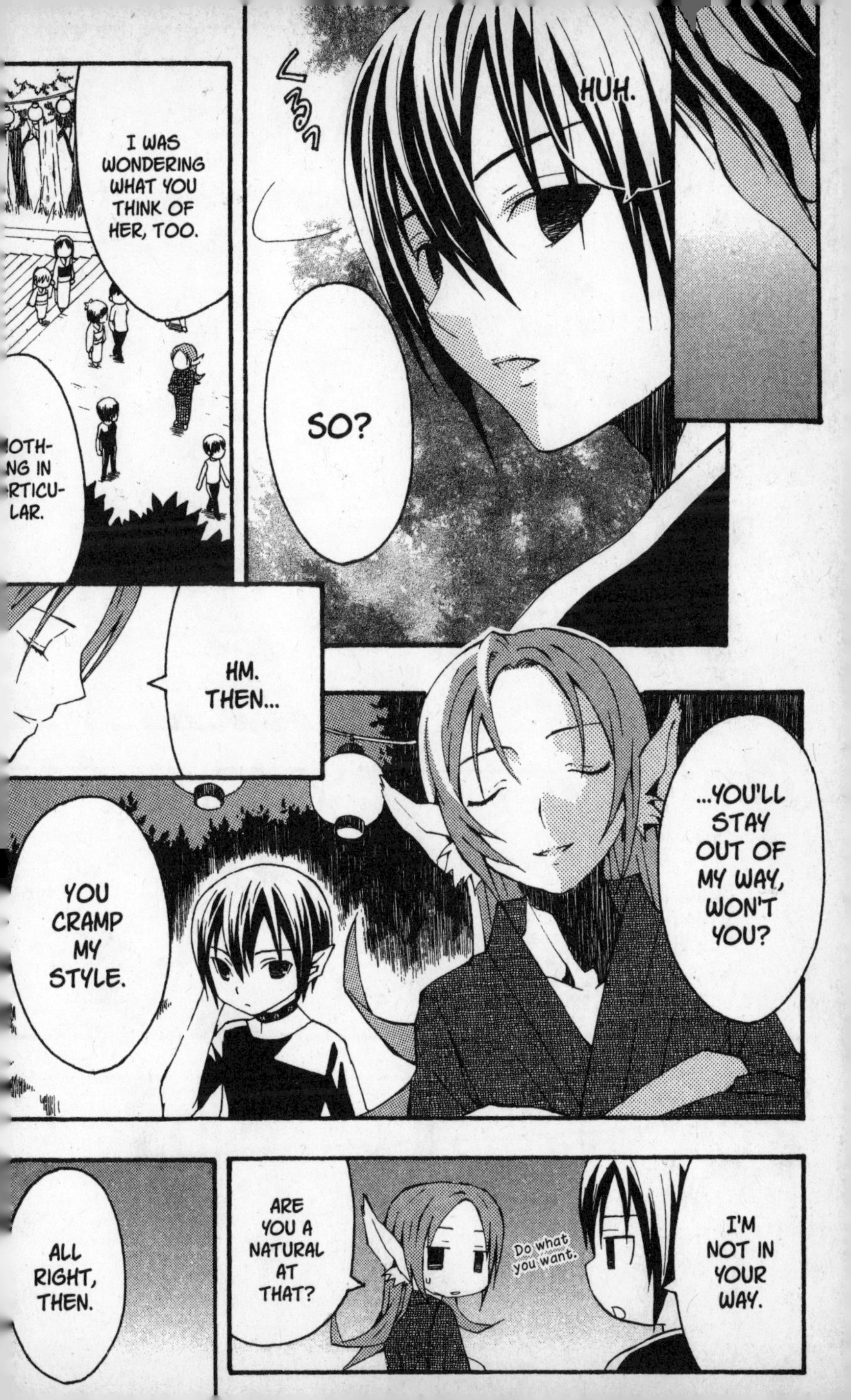
くるっ
HUH.
SO?
I WAS WONDERING WHAT YOU THINK OF HER, TOO.
OTH- NG IN RTICU- LAR.
HM. THEN...
...YOU'LL STAY OUT OF MY WAY, WON'T YOU?
YOU CRAMP MY STYLE.
I'M NOT IN YOUR WAY.
Do what you want.
ARE YOU A NATURAL AT THAT?
ALL RIGHT, THEN.

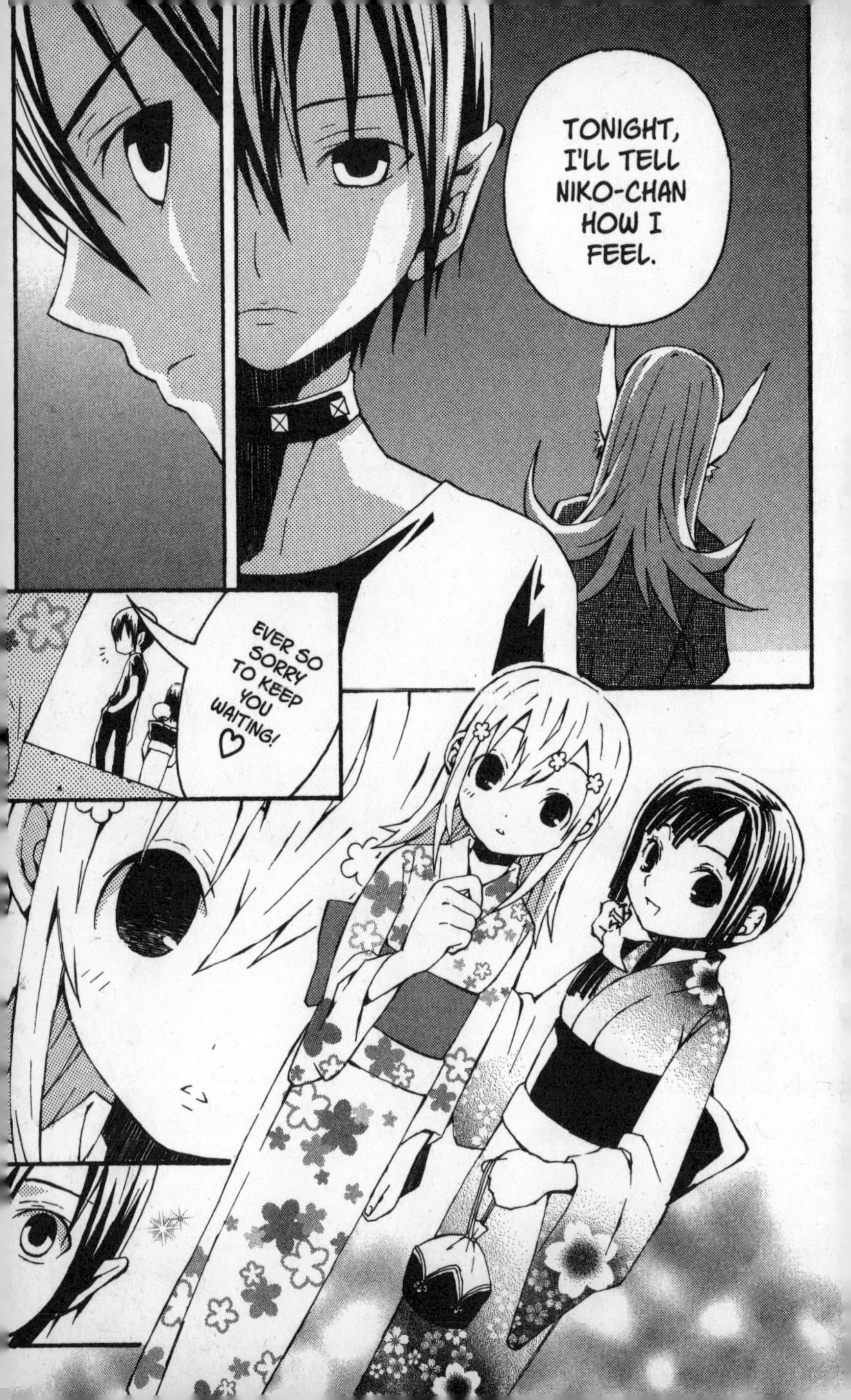
TONIGHT, I'LL TELL NIKO-CHAN HOW I FEEL.
EVER SO SORRY TO KEEP YOU WAITING! ♡

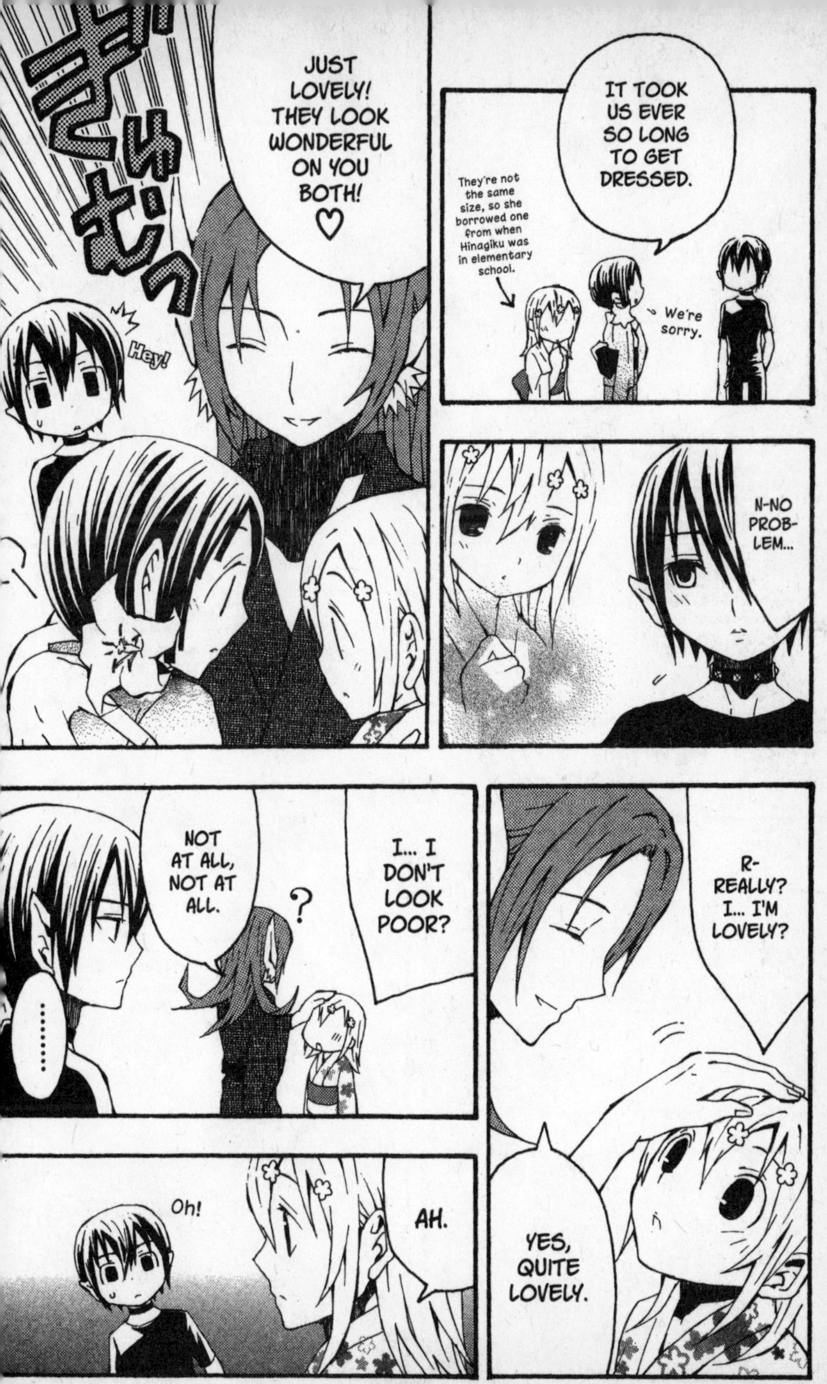
IT TOOK US EVER SO LONG TO GET DRESSED.
They're not the same size, so she borrowed one from when Hinagiku was in elementary school.
We're sorry.
N-NO PROBLEM...
ぎゅむっ
JUST LOVELY! THEY LOOK WONDERFUL ON YOU BOTH! ♡
Hey!
R-REALLY? I... I'M LOVELY?
YES, QUITE LOVELY.
I... I DON'T LOOK POOR?
NOT AT ALL, NOT AT ALL.
?
......
AH.
Oh!

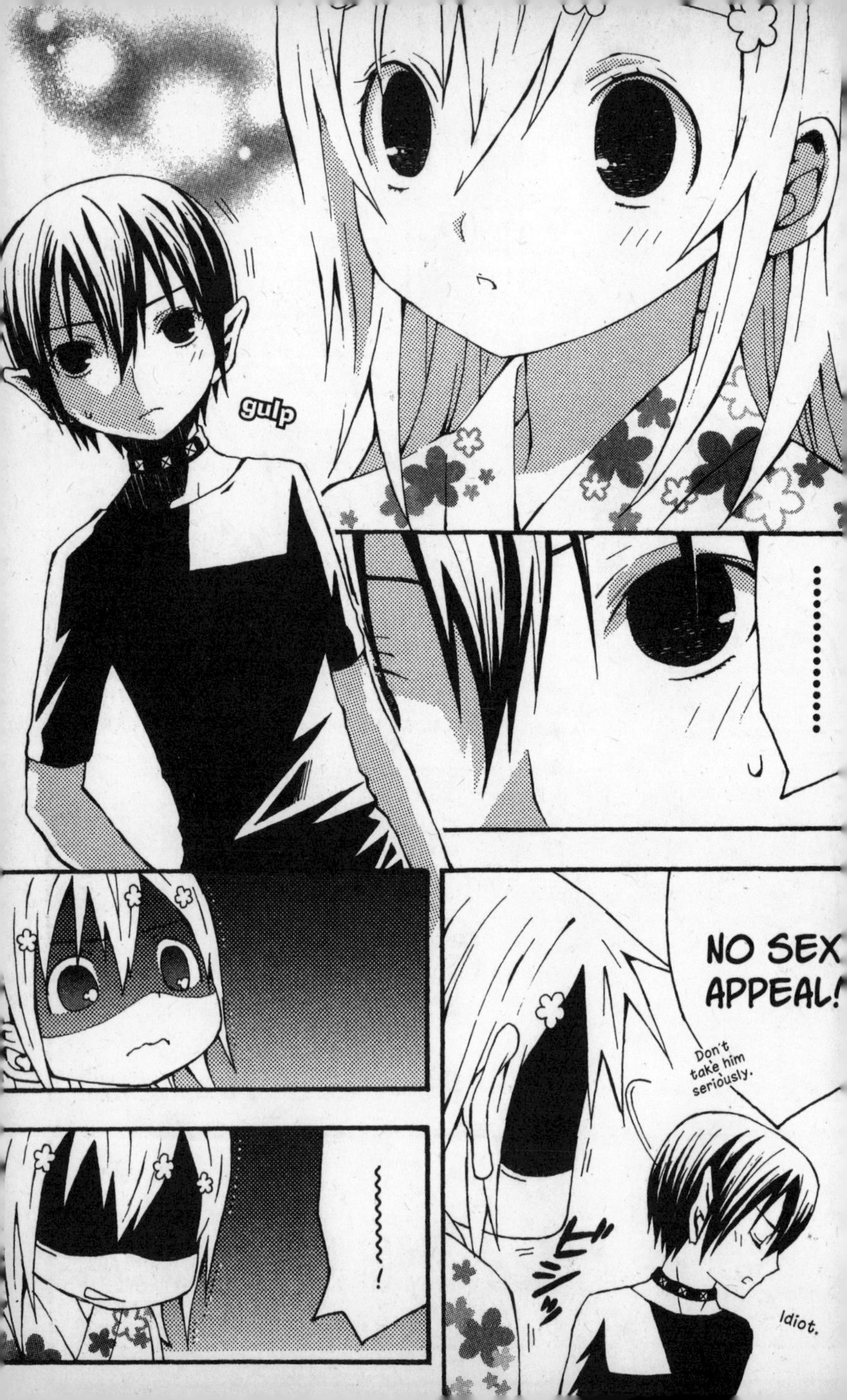
......
gulp
NO SEX APPEAL!
Don't take him seriously.
Idiot.

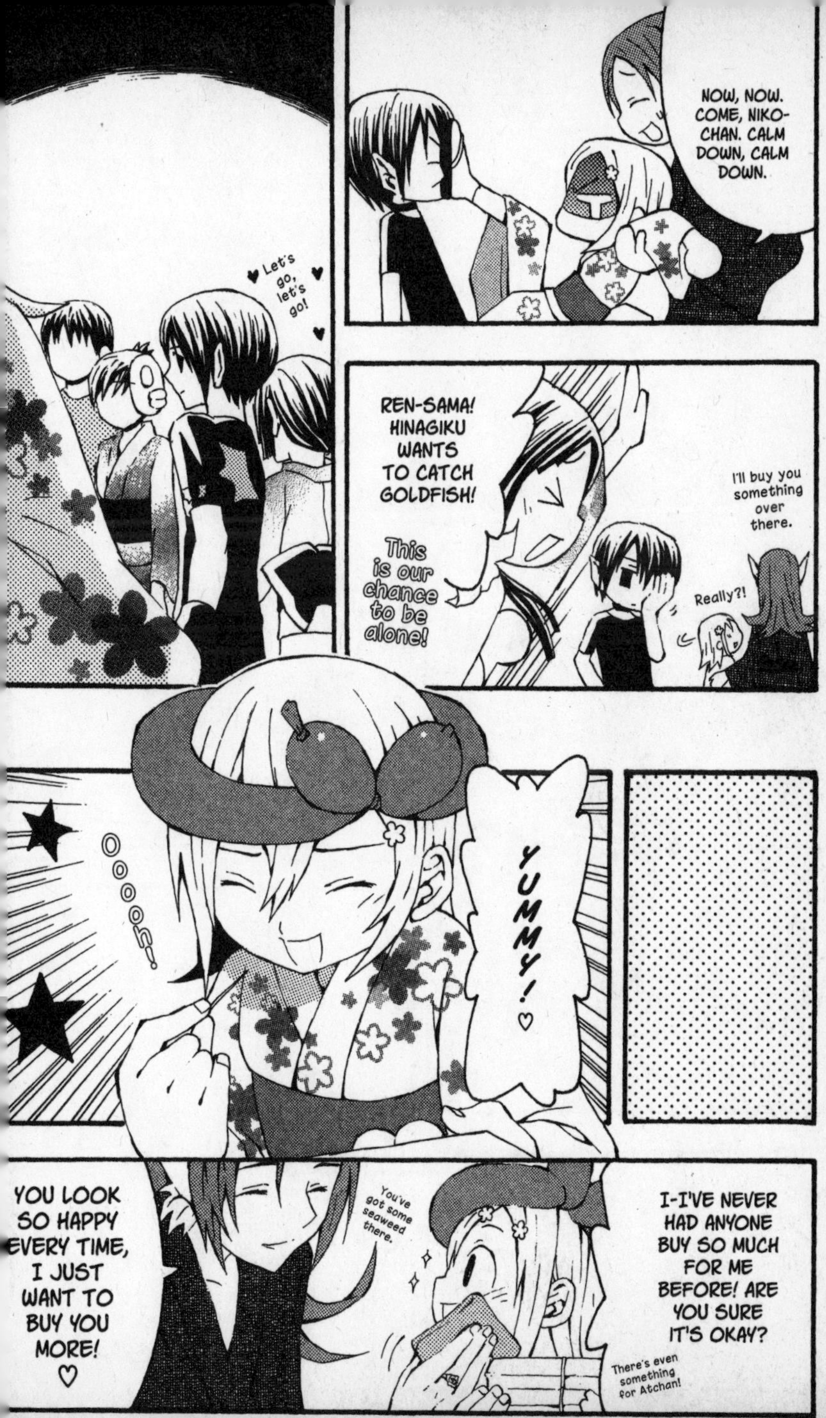

NOW, NOW. COME, NIKO-CHAN. CALM DOWN, CALM DOWN.
REN-SAMA! HINAGIKU WANTS TO CATCH GOLDFISH!
I'll buy you something over there.
Really?!
This is our chance to be alone!
♥ Let's go, let's go! ♥
YUMMY! ♡
Ooooh!
I-I'VE NEVER HAD ANYONE BUY SO MUCH FOR ME BEFORE! ARE YOU SURE IT'S OKAY?
There's even something for Atchan!
You've got some seaweed there.
YOU LOOK SO HAPPY EVERY TIME, I JUST WANT TO BUY YOU MORE! ♡

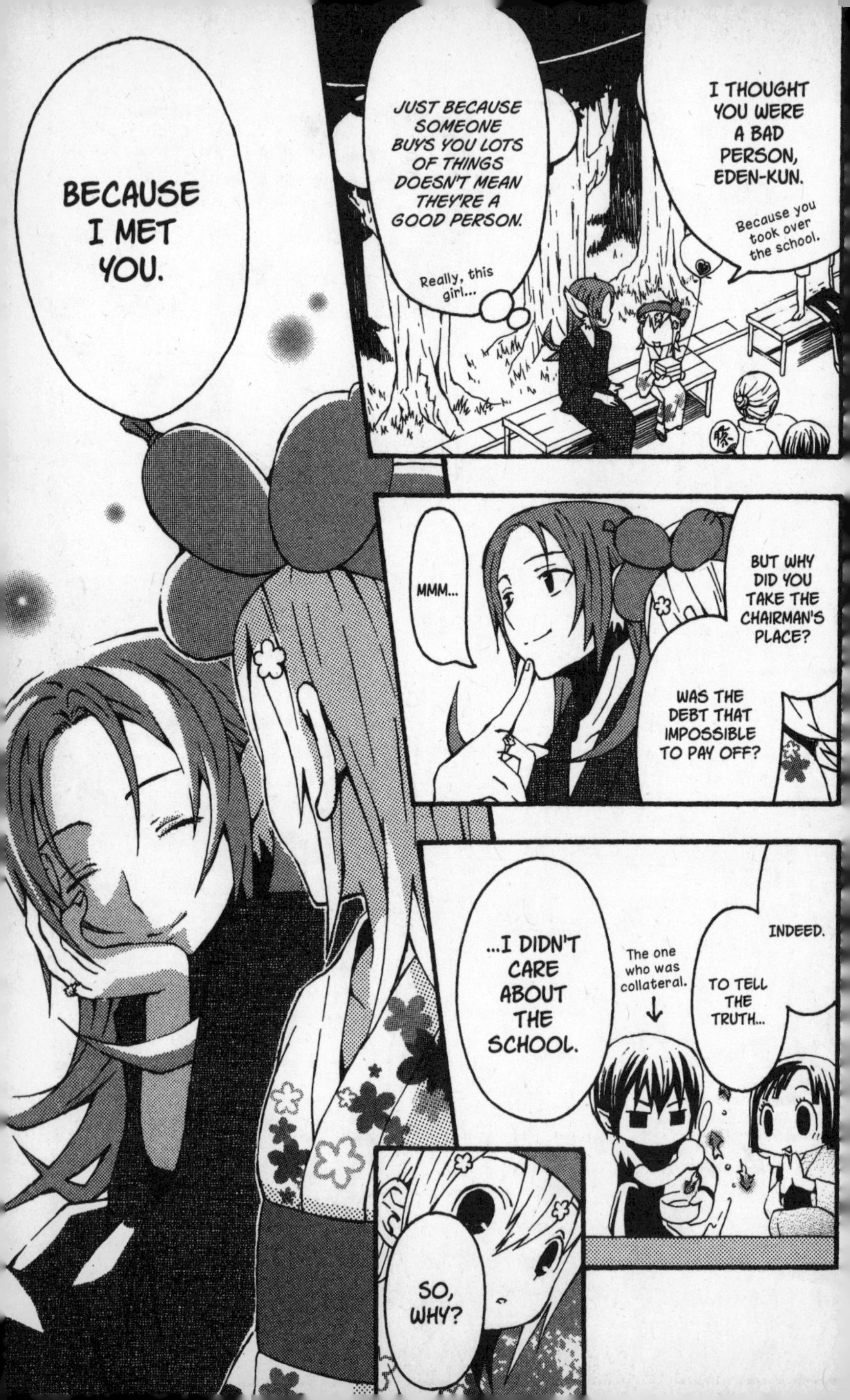
I THOUGHT YOU WERE A BAD PERSON, EDEN-KUN.
Because you took over the school.
JUST BECAUSE SOMEONE BUYS YOU LOTS OF THINGS DOESN'T MEAN THEY'RE A GOOD PERSON.
Really, this girl...
BUT WHY DID YOU TAKE THE CHAIRMAN'S PLACE?
WAS THE DEBT THAT IMPOSSIBLE TO PAY OFF?
MMM...
INDEED.
TO TELL THE TRUTH...
The one who was collateral.
...I DIDN'T CARE ABOUT THE SCHOOL.
SO, WHY?
BECAUSE I MET YOU.

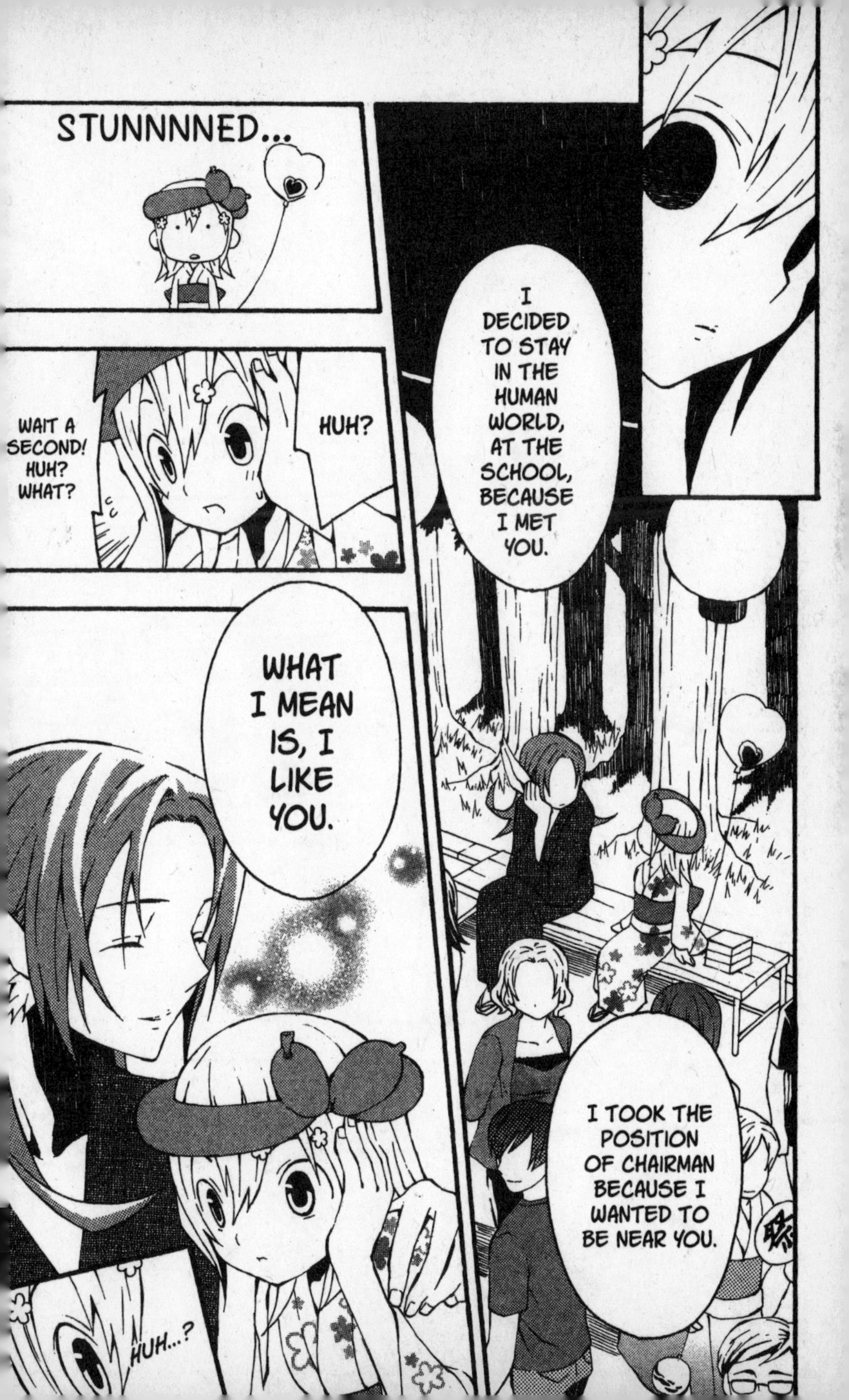
I DECIDED TO STAY IN THE HUMAN WORLD, AT THE SCHOOL, BECAUSE I MET YOU.
I TOOK THE POSITION OF CHAIRMAN BECAUSE I WANTED TO BE NEAR YOU.
STUNNNNED...
HUH?
WAIT A SECOND! HUH? WHAT?
WHAT I MEAN IS, I LIKE YOU.
HUH...?

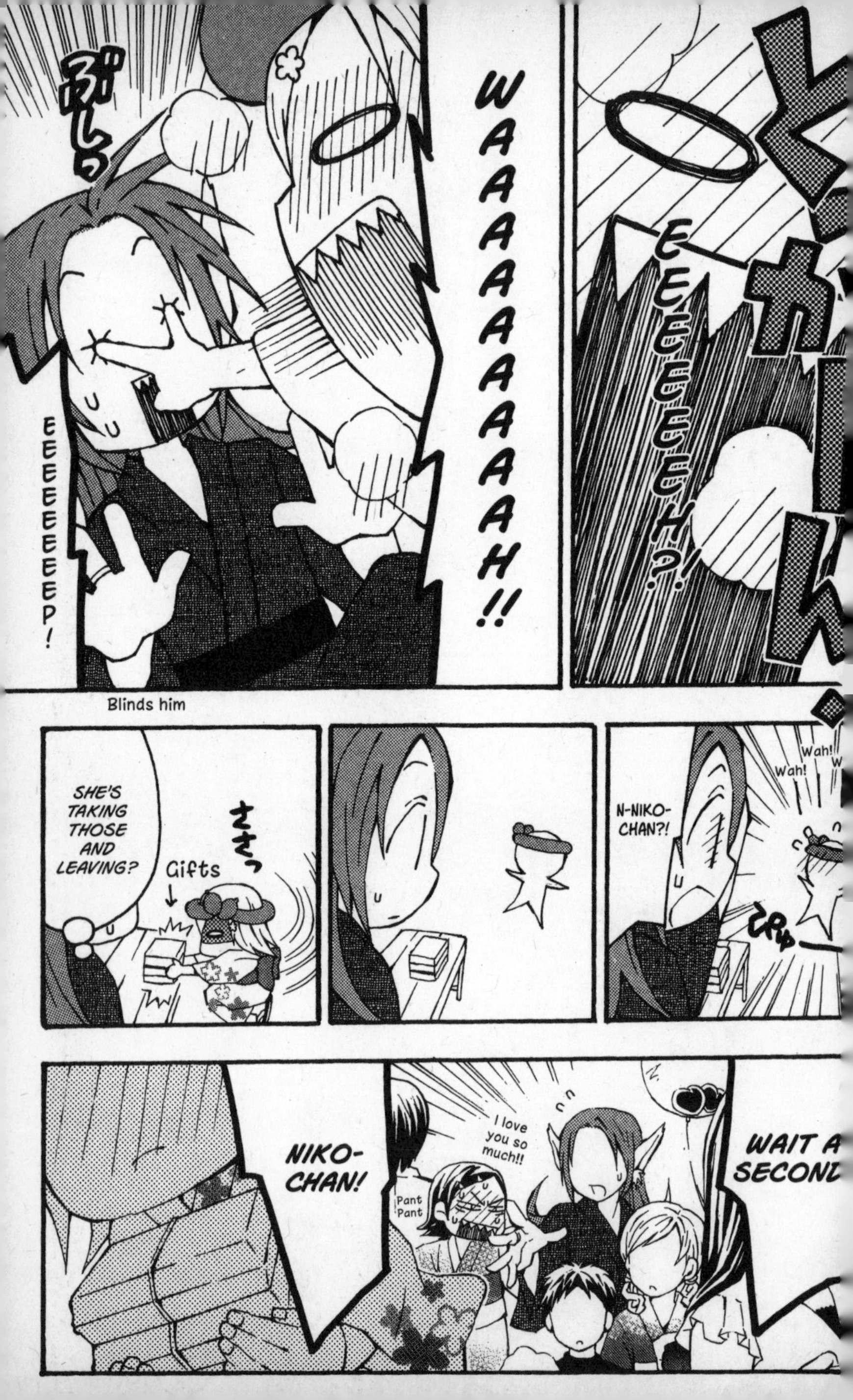
EEEEEEEEEH?!
WAAAAAAAAAH!!
ぶしっ
EEEEEEEEEEP!
Blinds him
Wah!
Wah!
N-NIKO-CHAN?!
ささっ
SHE'S TAKING THOSE AND LEAVING?
Gifts
WAIT A SECOND
I love you so much!!
Pant Pant
NIKO-CHAN!

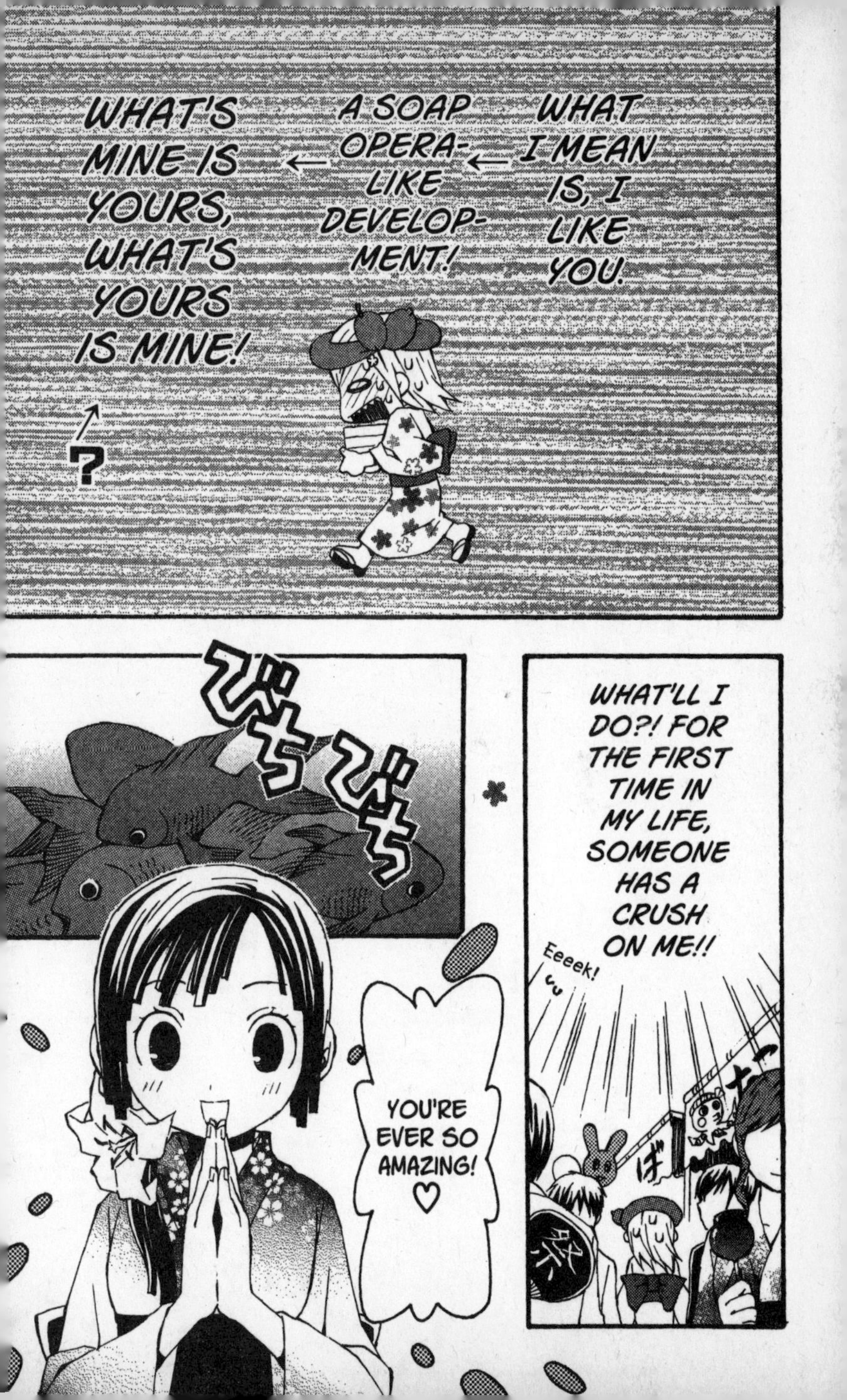
WHAT I MEAN IS, I LIKE YOU.
A SOAP OPERA-LIKE DEVELOPMENT!
WHAT'S MINE IS YOURS, WHAT'S YOURS IS MINE!
?
WHAT'LL I DO?! FOR THE FIRST TIME IN MY LIFE, SOMEONE HAS A CRUSH ON ME!!
Eeeek!
ぴちぴち
YOU'RE EVER SO AMAZING! ♡

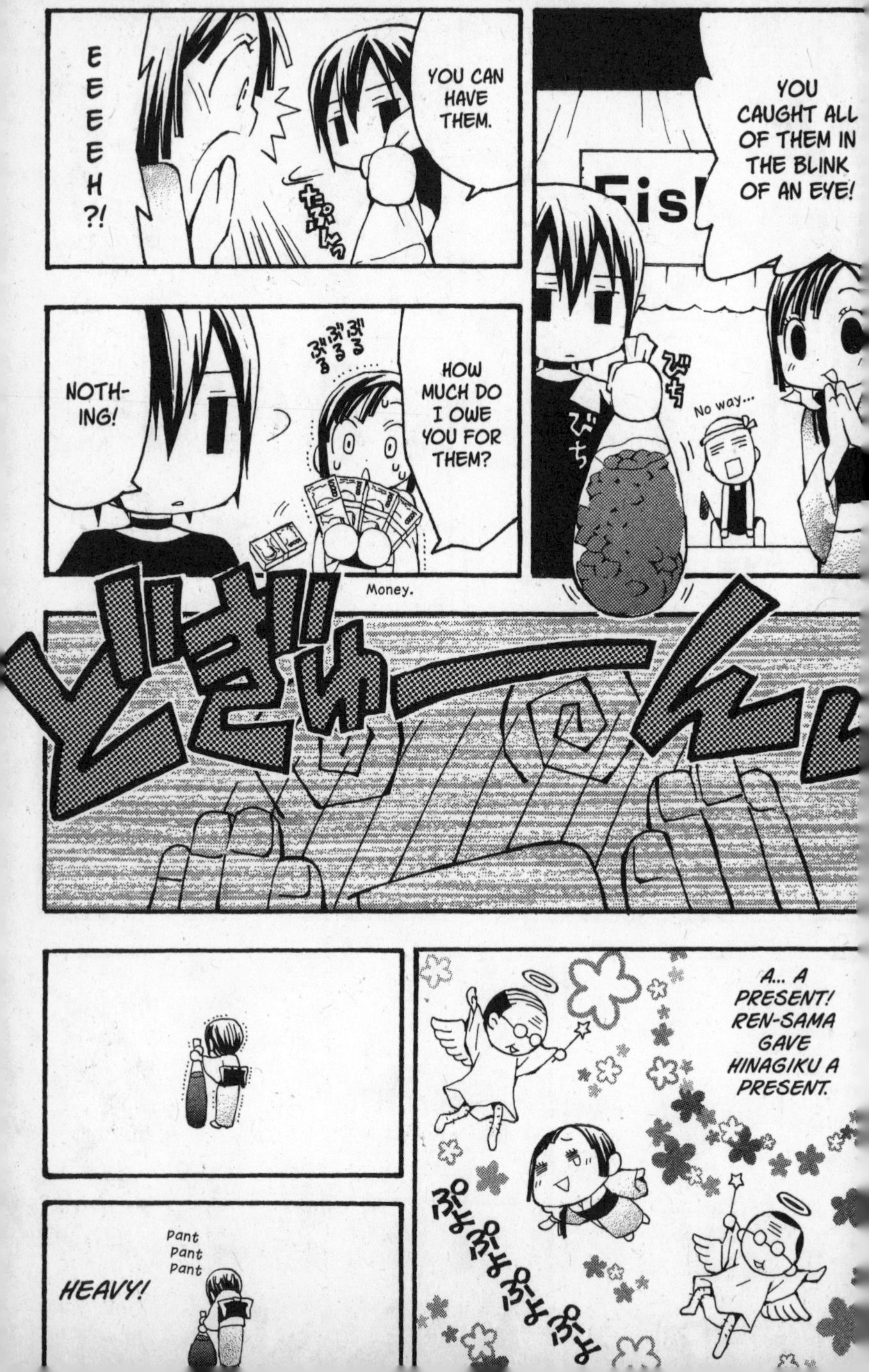

YOU CAUGHT ALL OF THEM IN THE BLINK OF AN EYE!
Fis
びち
びち
No way...
YOU CAN HAVE THEM.
EEEEEH?!
HOW MUCH DO I OWE YOU FOR THEM?
NOTHING!
Money.
A... A PRESENT! REN-SAMA GAVE HINAGIKU A PRESENT.
ぷよぷよぷよぷよ
Pant pant pant
HEAVY!

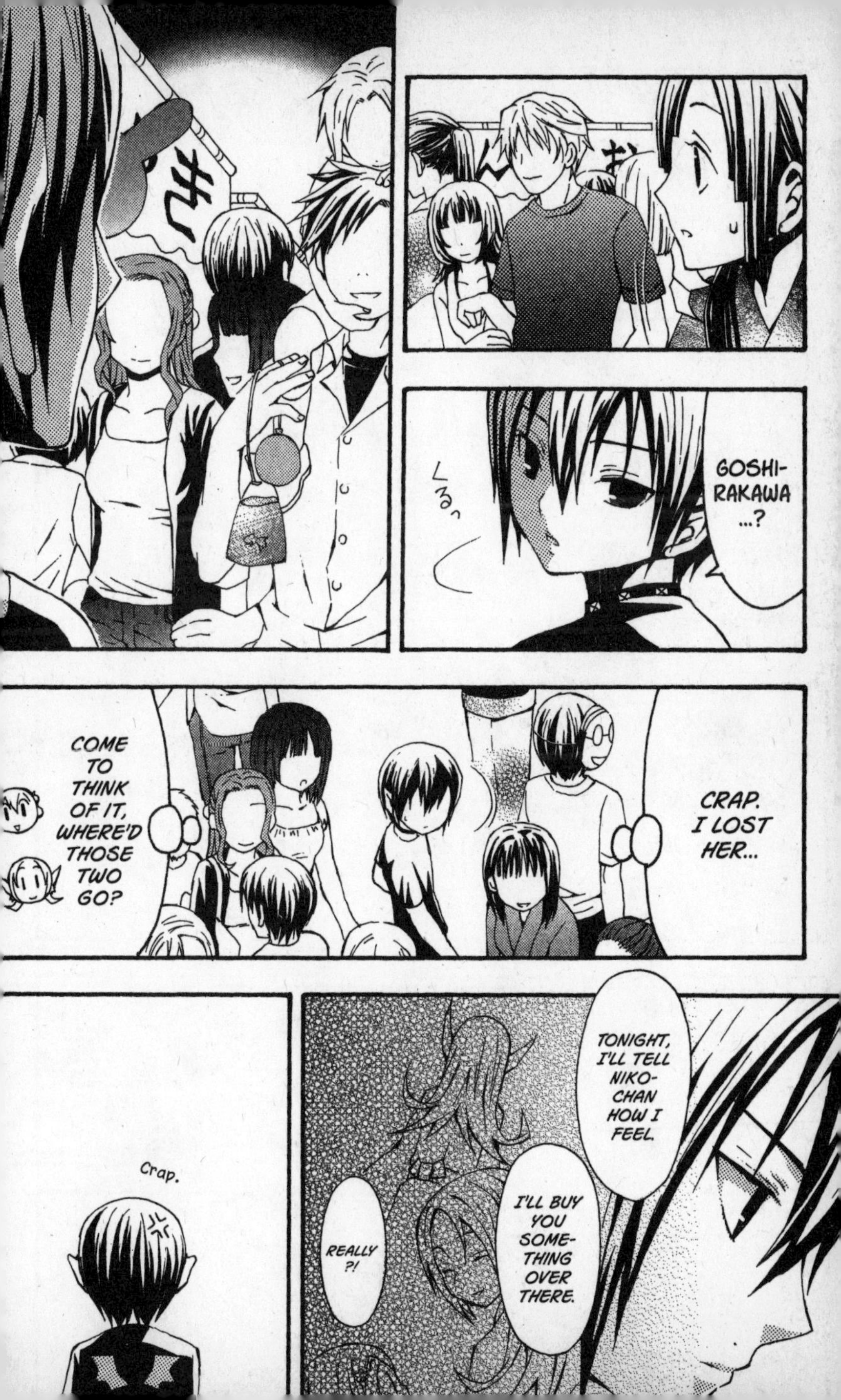
くるっ
GOSHI-RAKAWA ...?
CRAP. I LOST HER...
COME TO THINK OF IT, WHERE'D THOSE TWO GO?
TONIGHT, I'LL TELL NIKO-CHAN HOW I FEEL.
I'LL BUY YOU SOMETHING OVER THERE.
REALLY ?!
Crap.

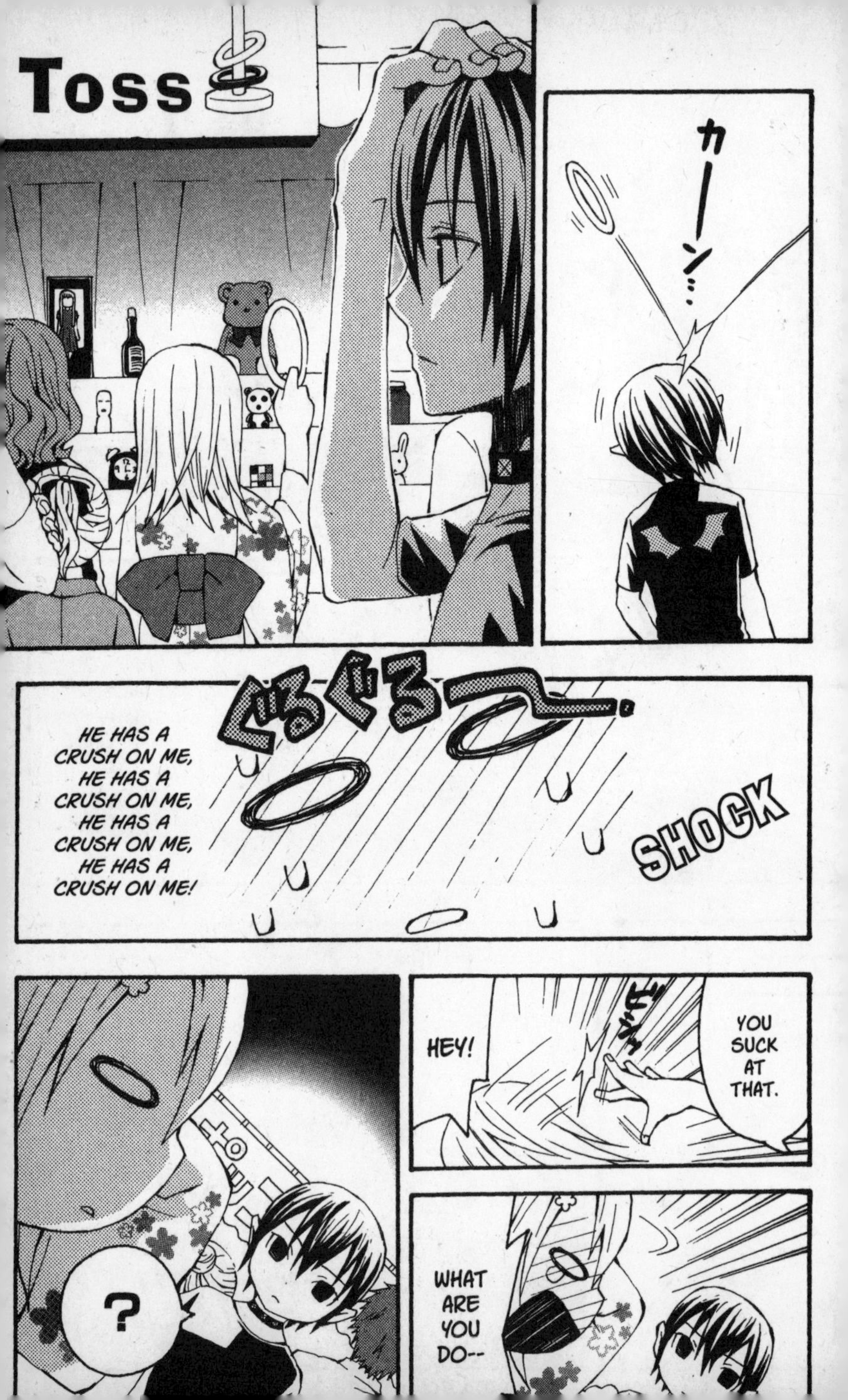
カーン…
Toss
ぐるぐる〜
HE HAS A CRUSH ON ME, HE HAS A CRUSH ON ME, HE HAS A CRUSH ON ME, HE HAS A CRUSH ON ME!
SHOCK
YOU SUCK AT THAT.
HEY!
WHAT ARE YOU DO--
?

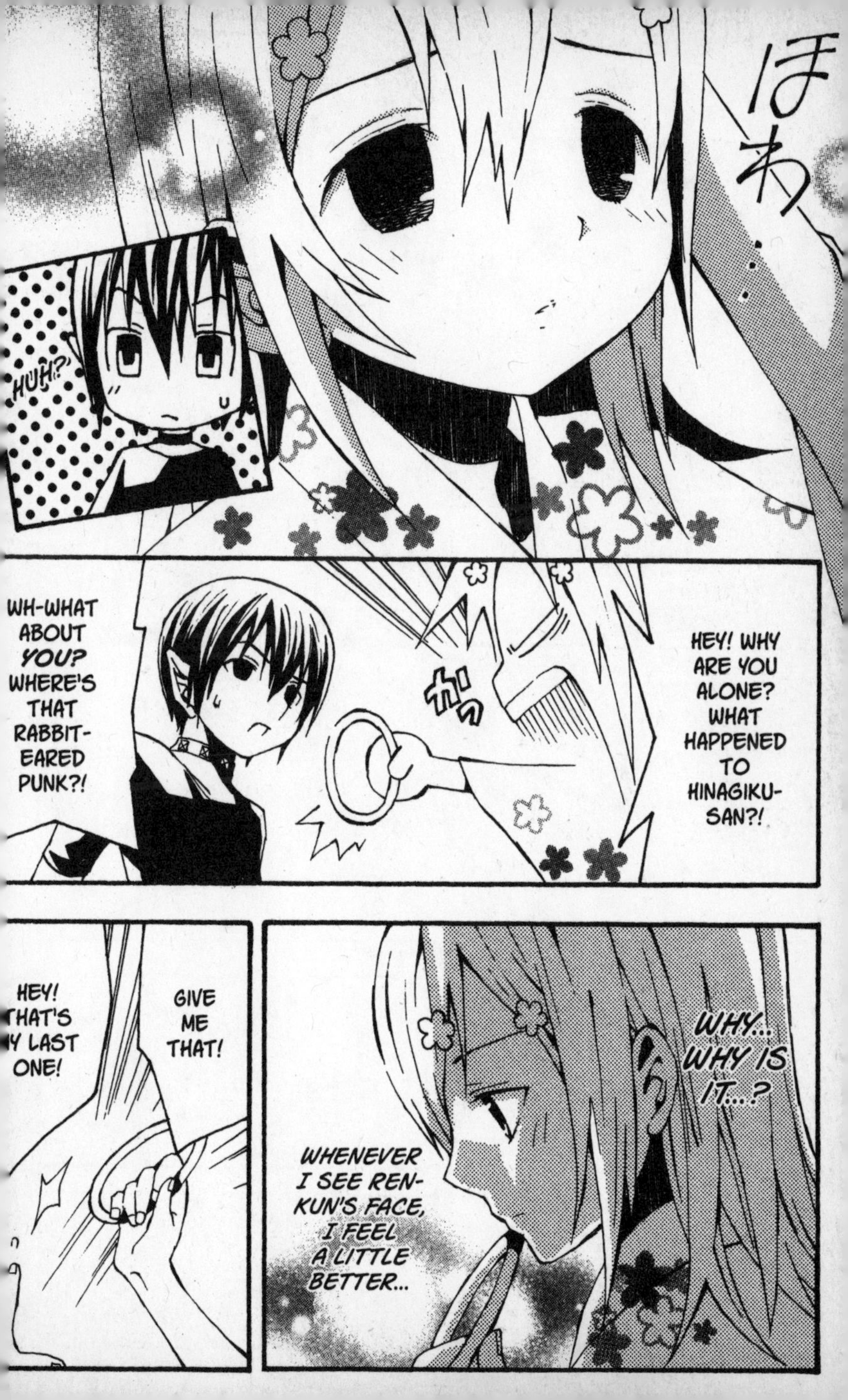
ほわっ…
HUH?!
HEY! WHY ARE YOU ALONE? WHAT HAPPENED TO HINAGIKU-SAN?!
かっ
WH-WHAT ABOUT YOU? WHERE'S THAT RABBIT-EARED PUNK?!
WHY... WHY IS IT...?
WHENEVER I SEE REN-KUN'S FACE, I FEEL A LITTLE BETTER...
GIVE ME THAT!
HEY! THAT'S Y LAST ONE!

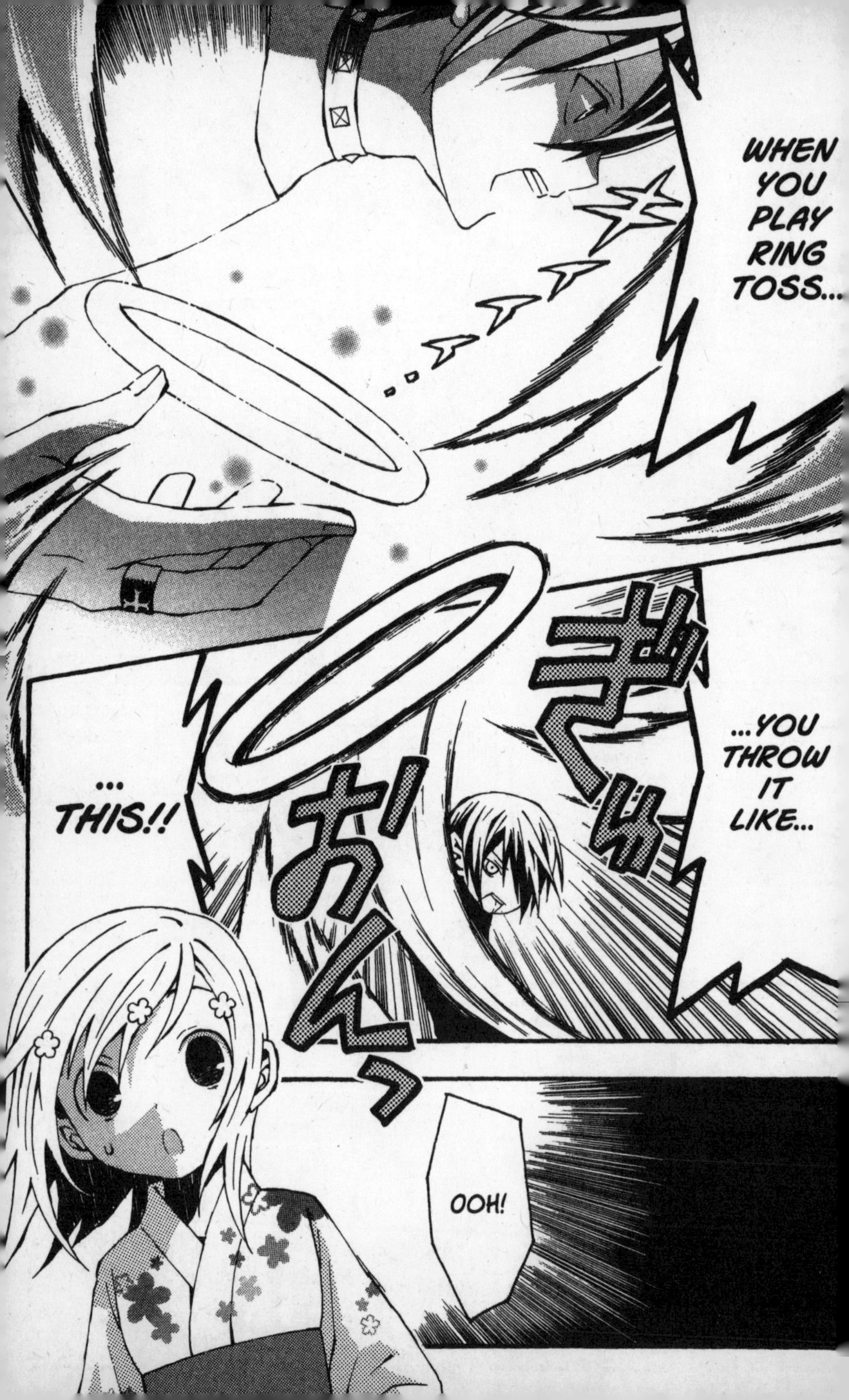
WHEN YOU PLAY RING TOSS...
...YOU THROW IT LIKE...
ぎゅおんっ
... THIS!!
OOH!

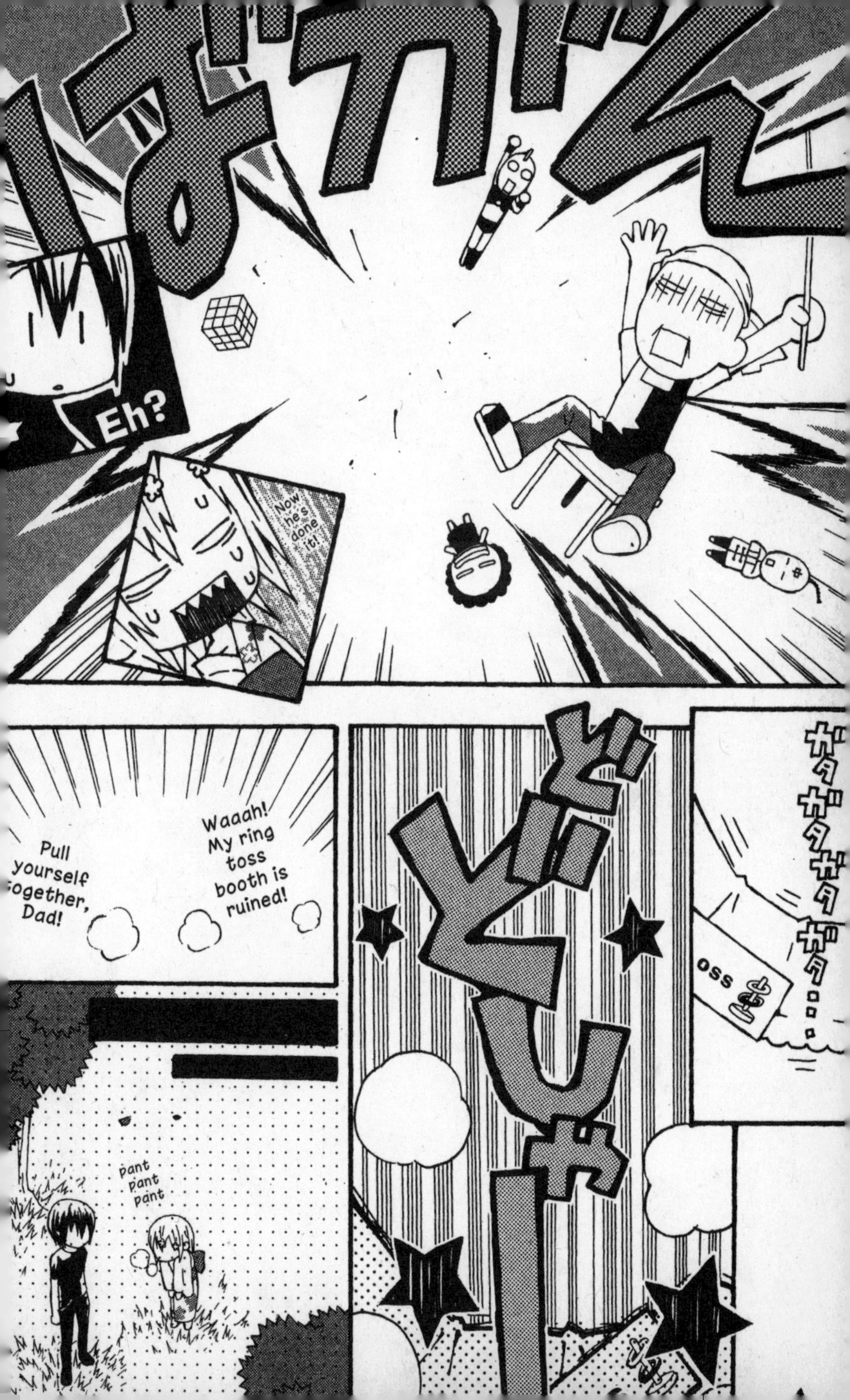
Eh?
Now he's done it!
oss
Waaah! My ring toss booth is ruined!
Pull yourself together, Dad!
pant pant pant

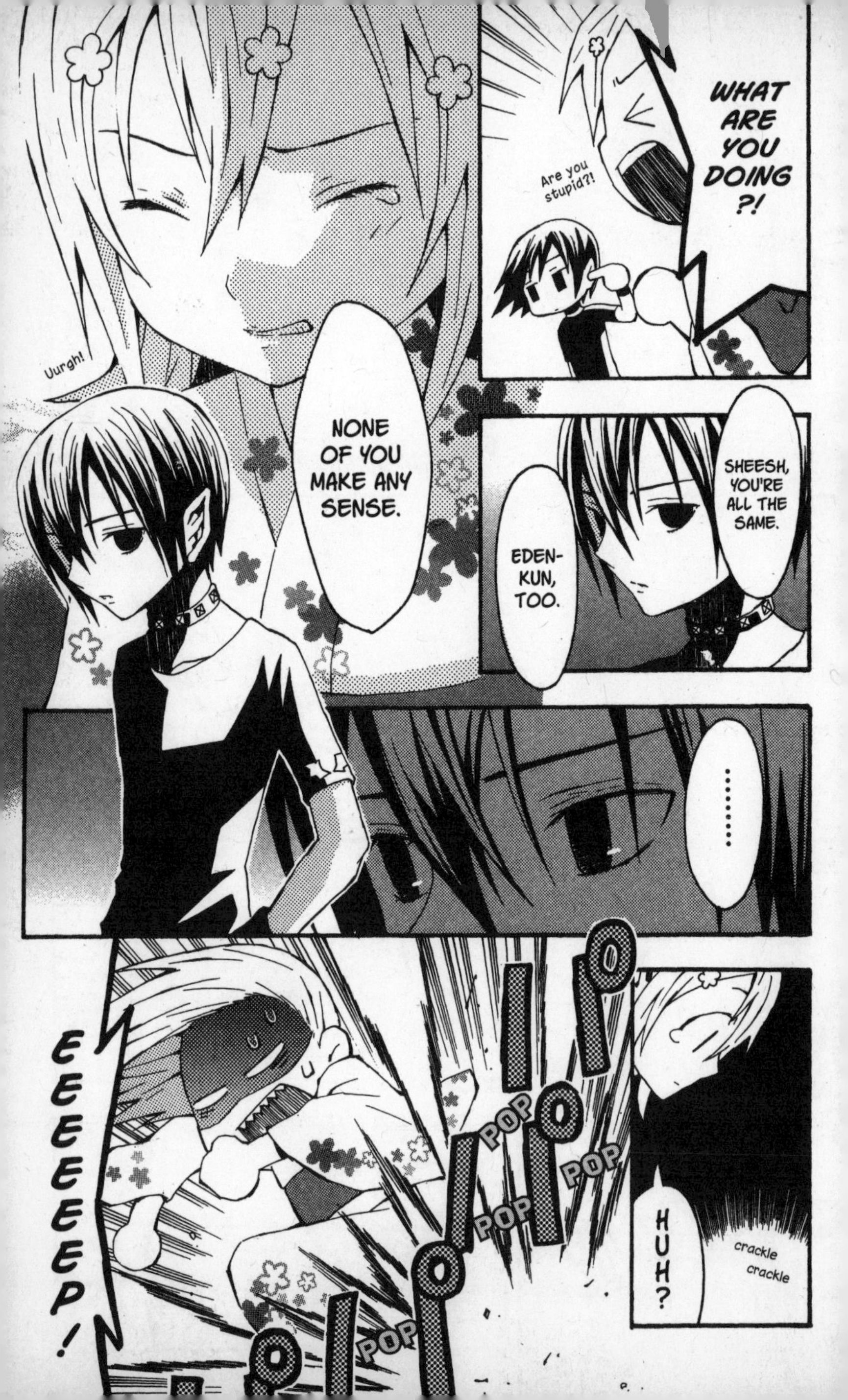
WHAT ARE YOU DOING?!
Are you stupid?!
SHEESH, YOU'RE ALL THE SAME.
EDEN-KUN, TOO.
NONE OF YOU MAKE ANY SENSE.
Uurgh!
....
HUH?
crackle crackle
POP POP POP POP POP
EEEEEEEP!

FIRE-CRACKERS.

WHAT?!
WHAT?!
WHAT?!

FIRE-CRACKERS?!
WHERE'D THEY COME FROM?!

OFFICER!

I SWIPED THEM AT THE RING TOSS.

Firecracker Set

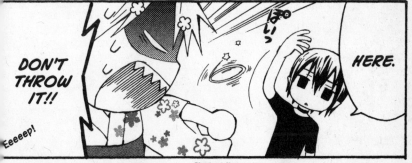

DON'T THROW IT!!

Eeeeep!

HERE.

Pinwheel firecracker

WAAAAAH!

WAAAAAH!

64

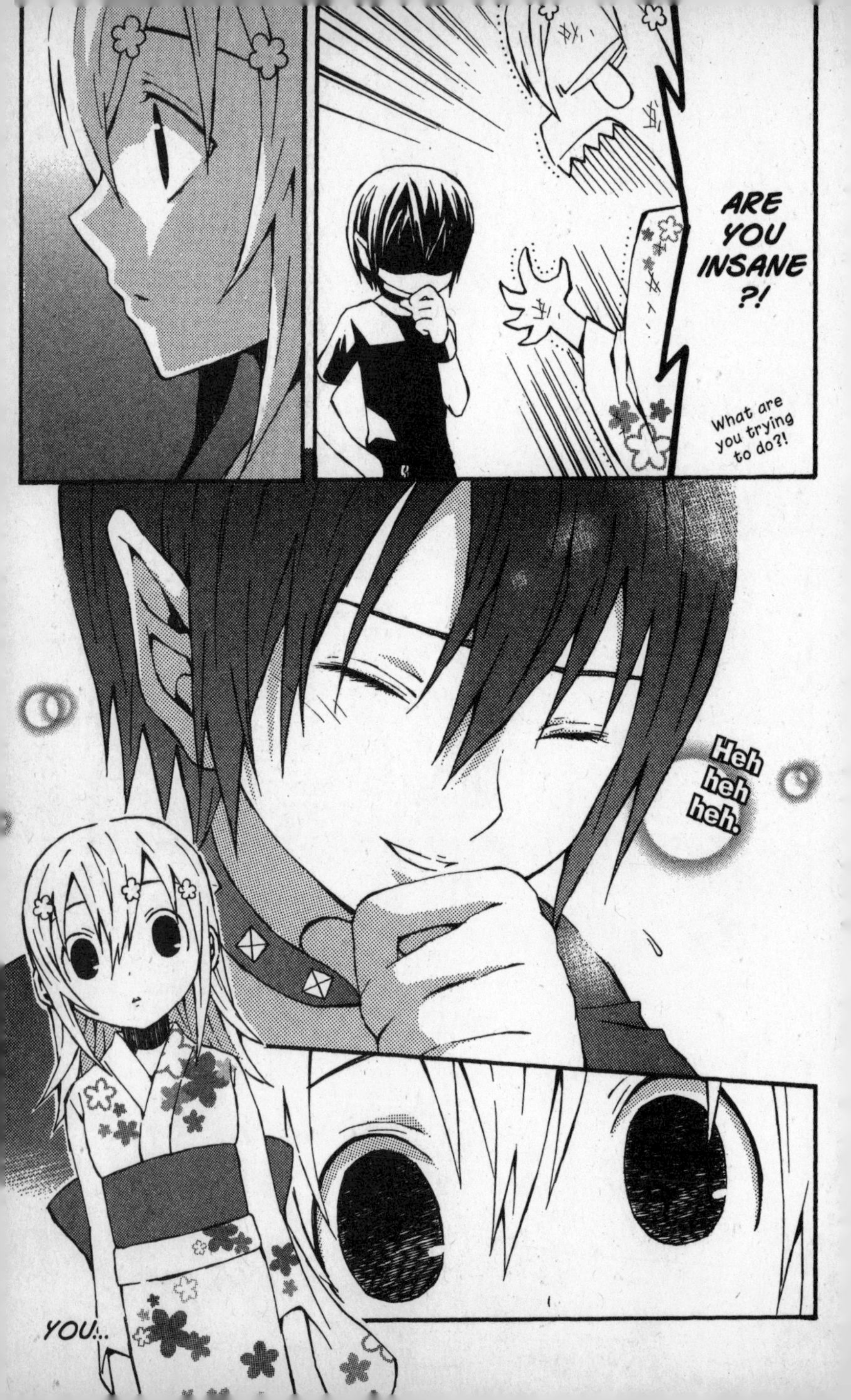
ARE YOU INSANE ?!
What are you trying to do?!
Heh heh heh.
YOU...

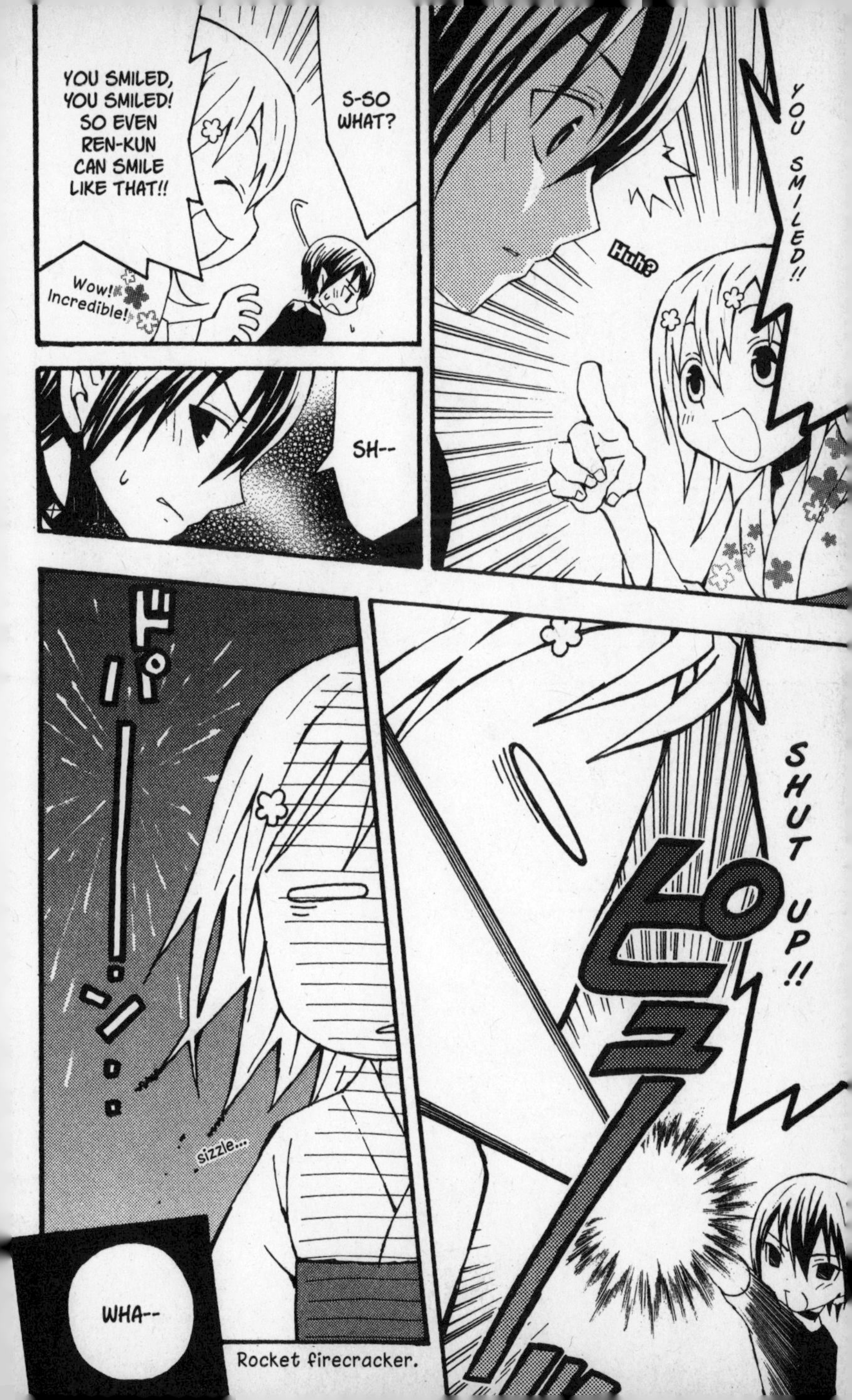
YOU SMILED!!
Huh?
YOU SMILED, YOU SMILED! SO EVEN REN-KUN CAN SMILE LIKE THAT!!
Wow! Incredible!
S-SO WHAT?
SH--
SHUT UP!!
ピュー
ドパーン!!
sizzle...
WHA--
Rocket firecracker.

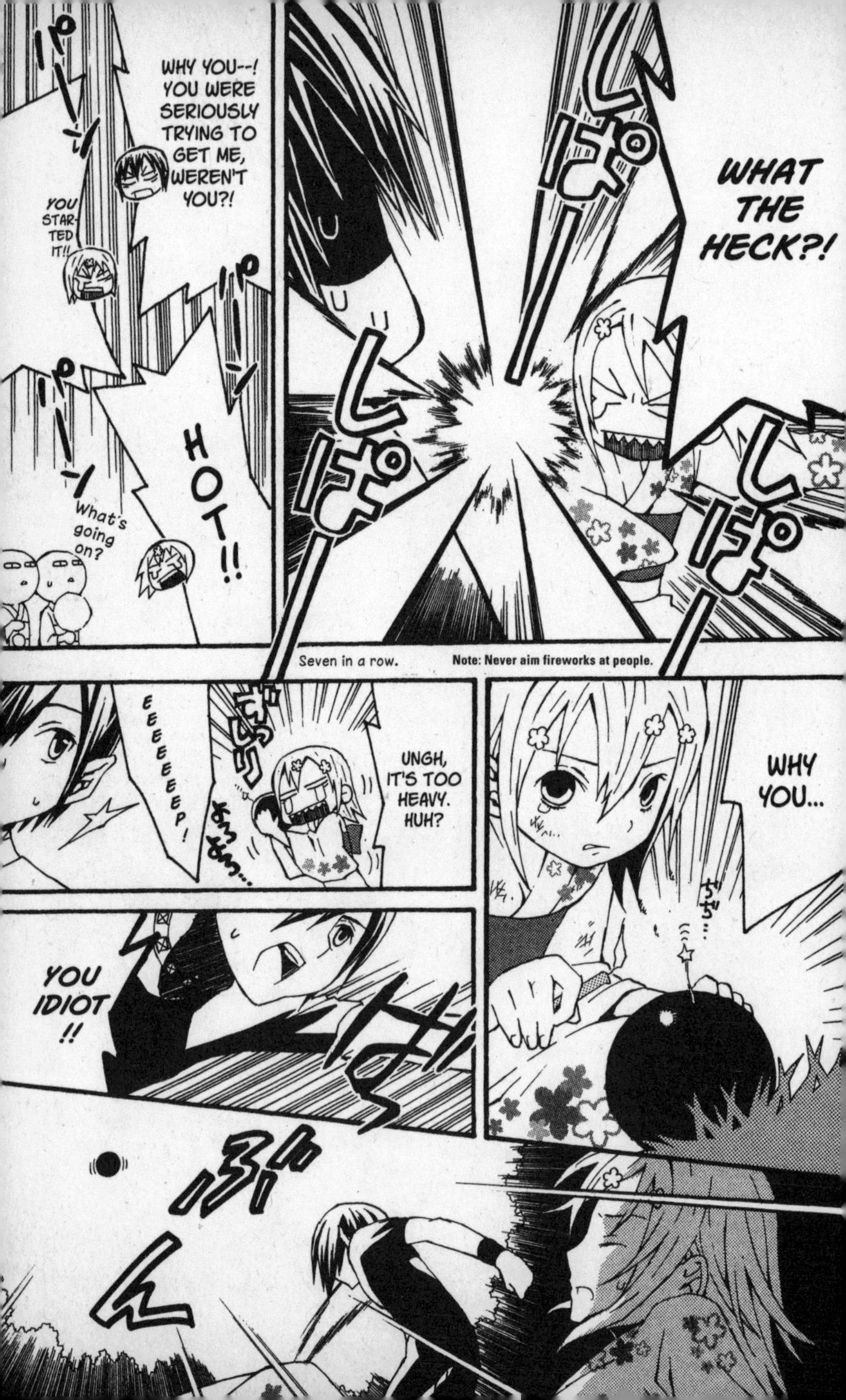
WHAT THE HECK?!
WHY YOU--! YOU WERE SERIOUSLY TRYING TO GET ME, WEREN'T YOU?!
YOU STARTED IT!!
HOT!!
What's going on?
Seven in a row.
Note: Never aim fireworks at people.
WHY YOU...
UNGH, IT'S TOO HEAVY. HUH?
EEEEEEEEEP!
YOU IDIOT!!

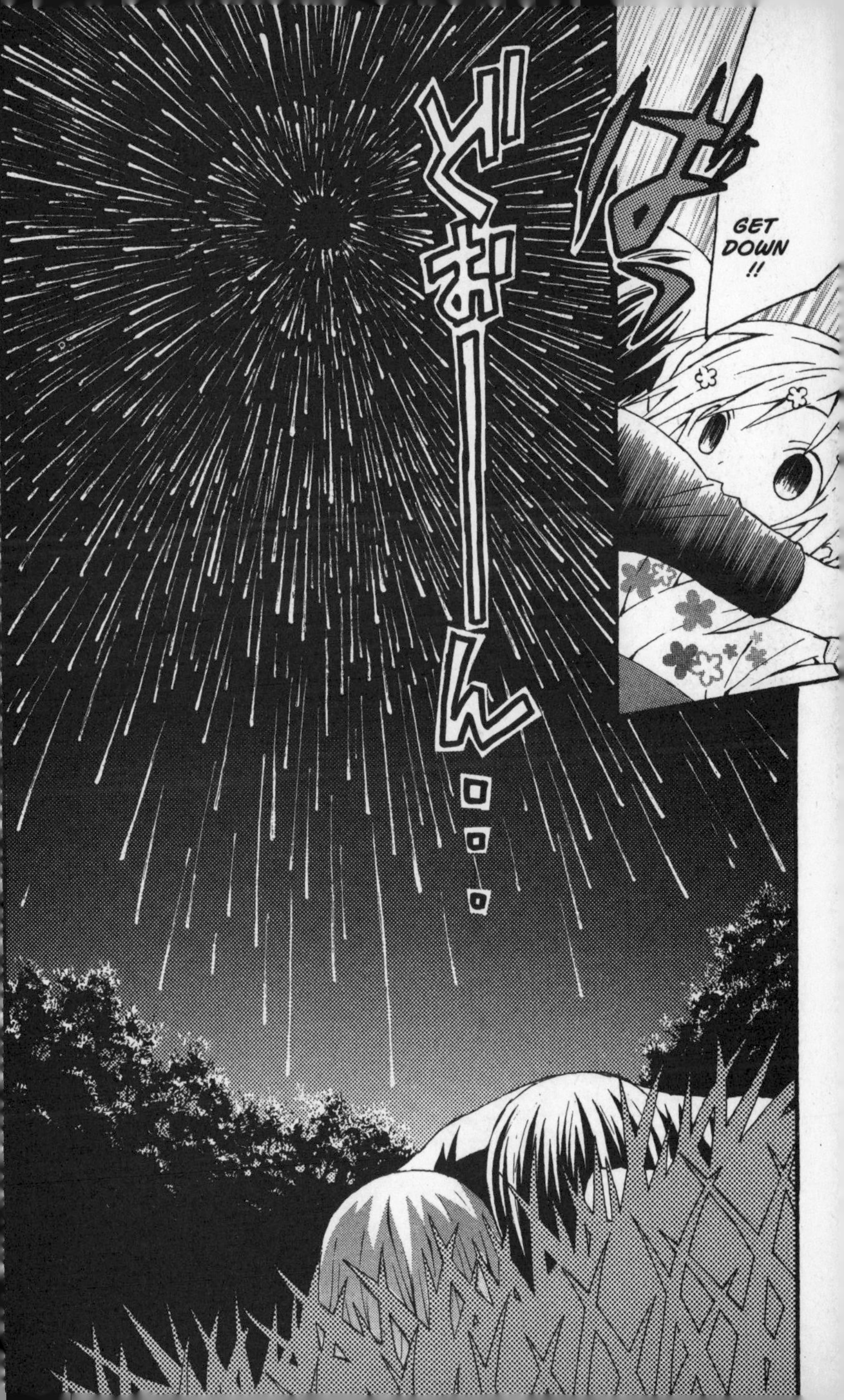
GET DOWN !!

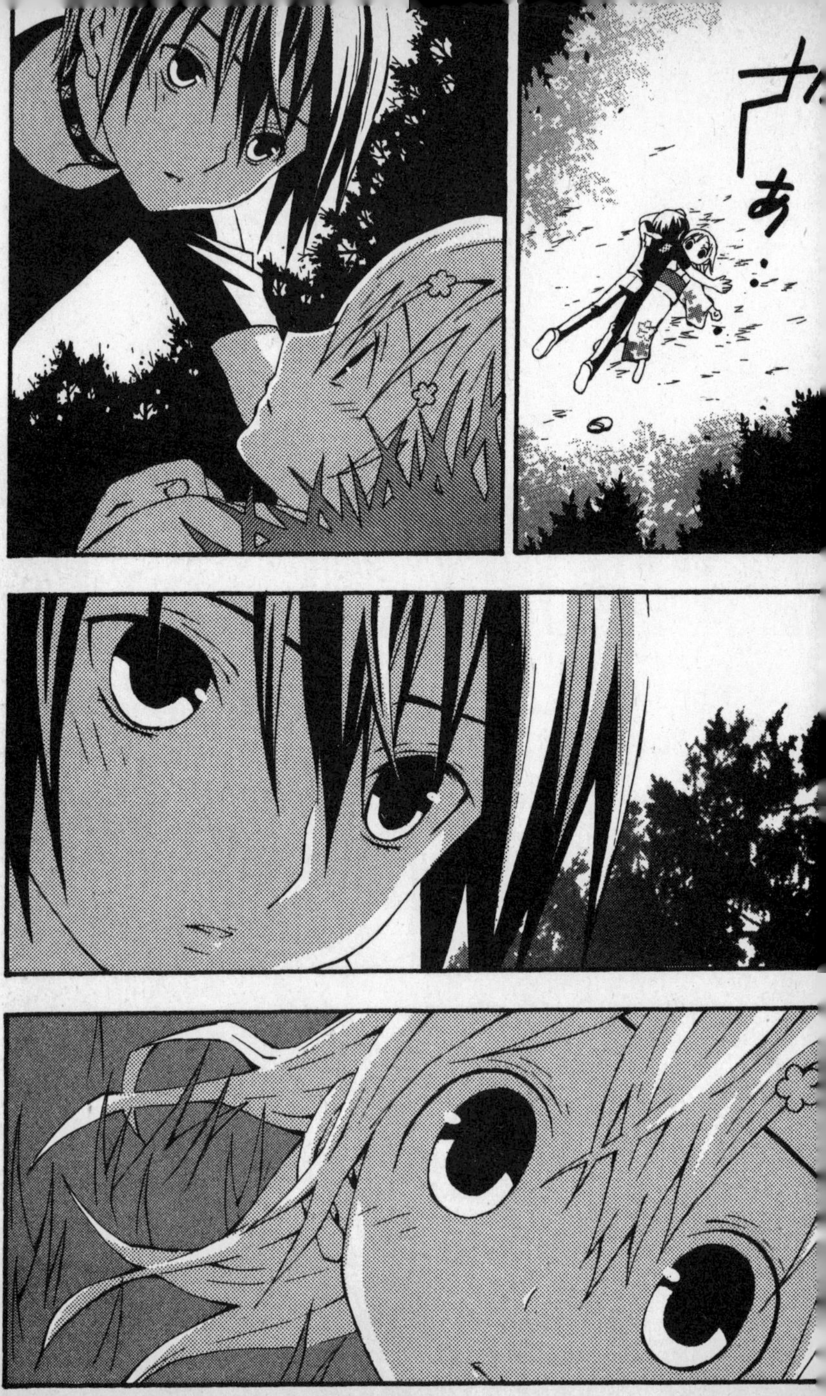
ざあ…

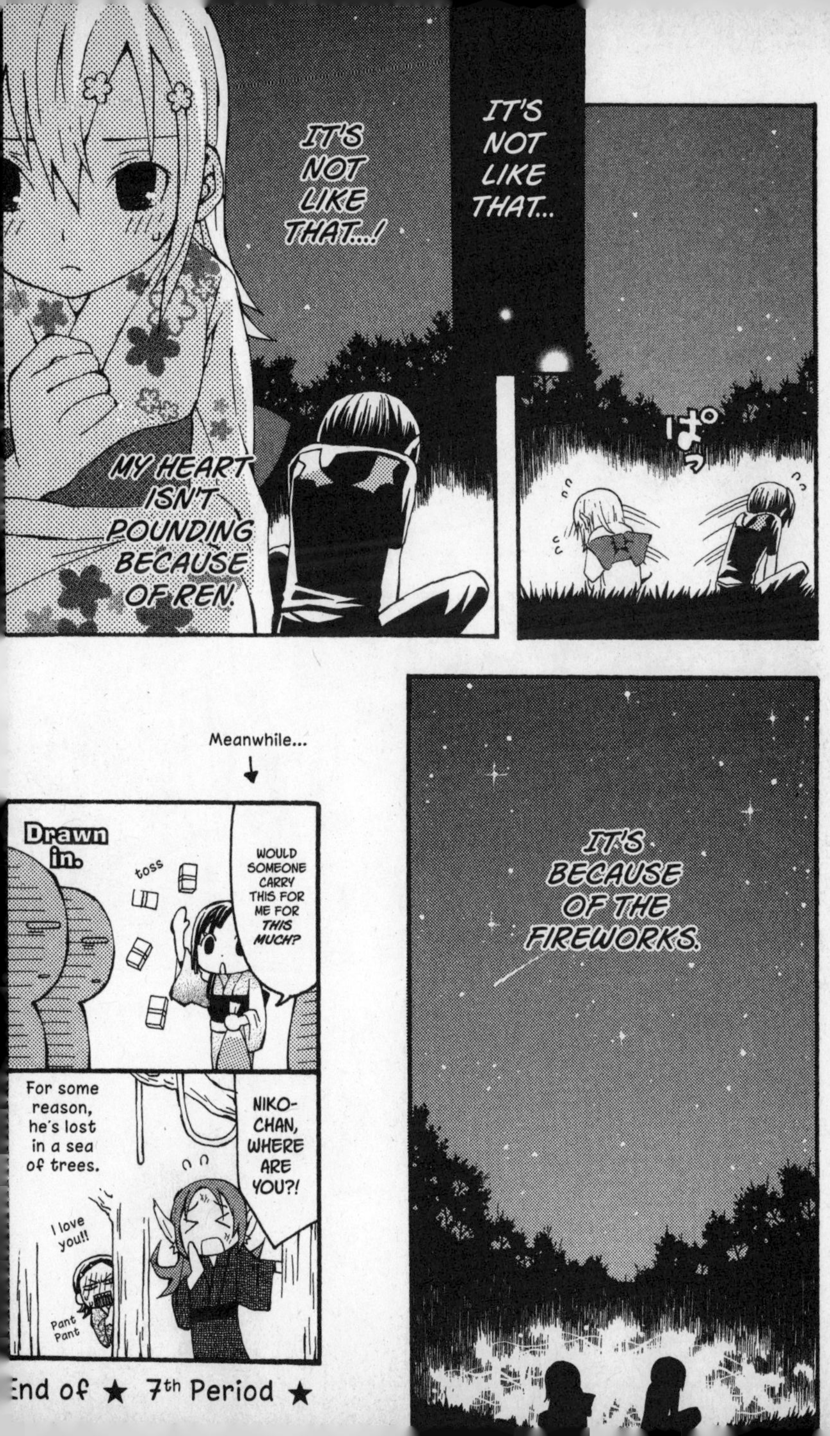
IT'S NOT LIKE THAT...
ぱっ
IT'S NOT LIKE THAT...!
MY HEART ISN'T POUNDING BECAUSE OF REN.
IT'S BECAUSE OF THE FIREWORKS.
Meanwhile...
Drawn in.
WOULD SOMEONE CARRY THIS FOR ME FOR THIS MUCH?
toss
NIKO-CHAN, WHERE ARE YOU?!
For some reason, he's lost in a sea of trees.
I love you!!
Pant Pant
End of ★ 7th Period ★

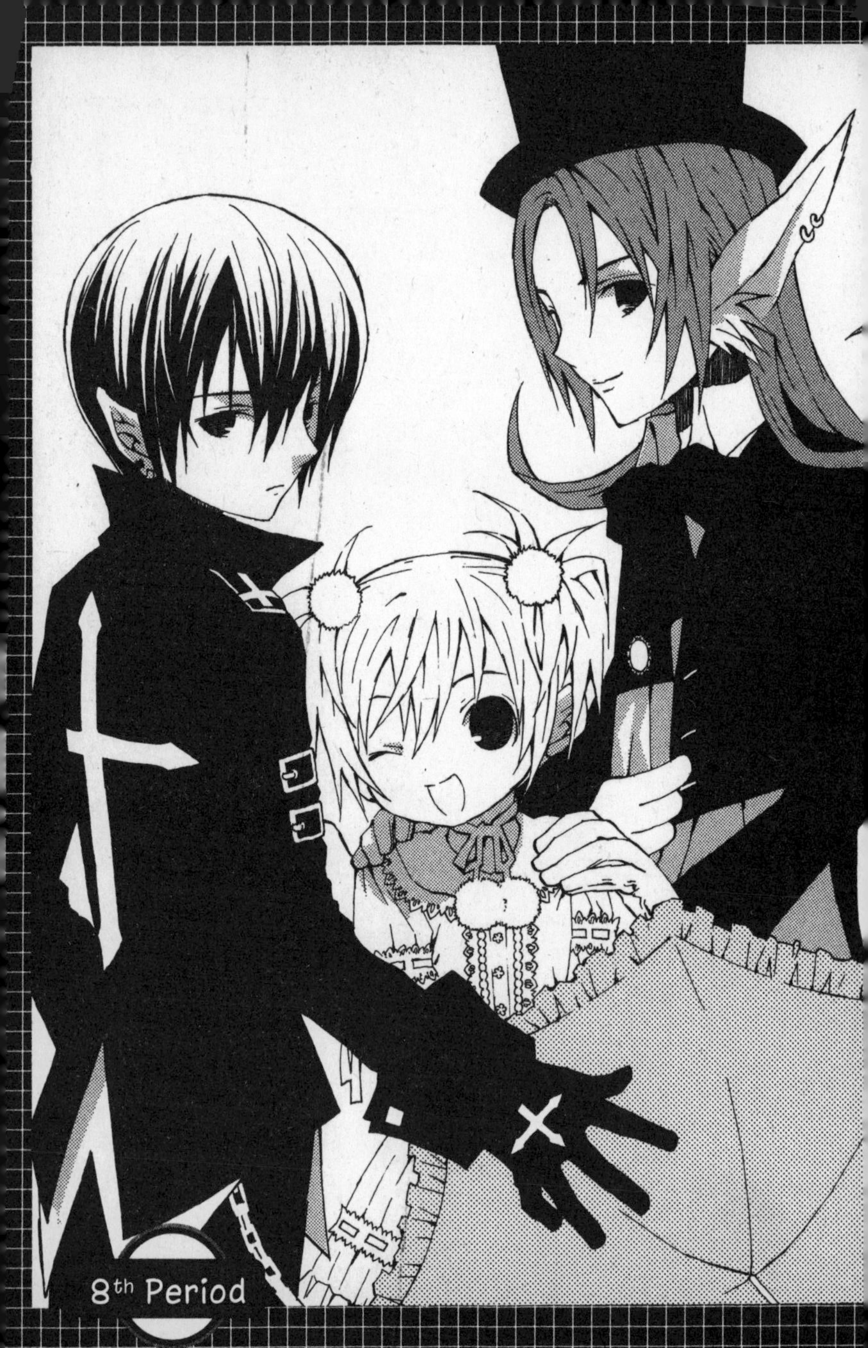

8th Period

Kersplash ★ Trouble on a Hike♪

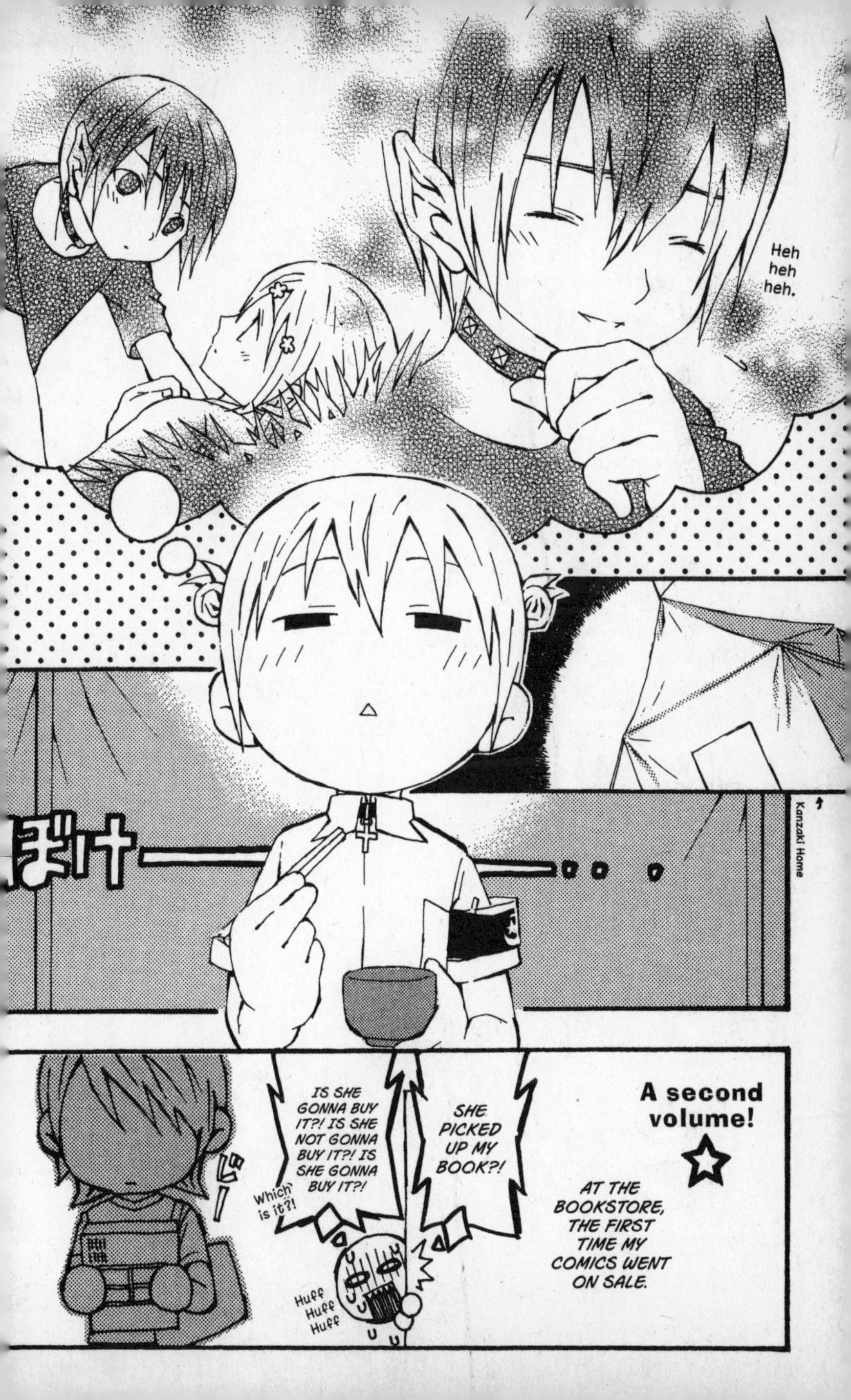
Heh heh heh.
Kanzaki Home
ぼけー
A second volume! ☆
AT THE BOOKSTORE, THE FIRST TIME MY COMICS WENT ON SALE.
SHE PICKED UP MY BOOK?!
IS SHE GONNA BUY IT?! IS SHE NOT GONNA BUY IT?! IS SHE GONNA BUY IT?!
Which is it?!
Huff Huff Huff

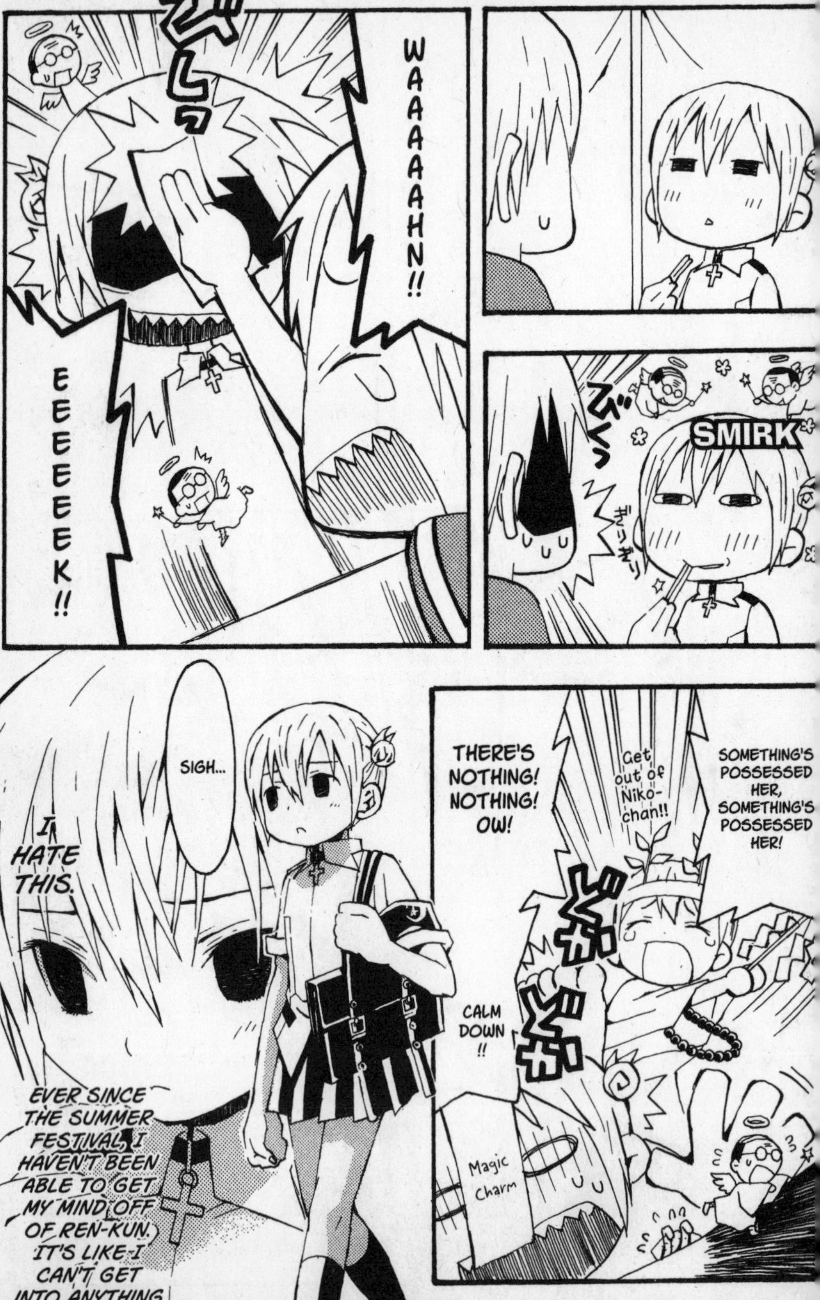
SMIRK
びくっ
ぎりぎり
びしっ
WAAAAAAHN!!
EEEEEEEK!!
SOMETHING'S POSSESSED HER, SOMETHING'S POSSESSED HER!
Get out of Niko-chan!!
THERE'S NOTHING! NOTHING! OW!
CALM DOWN!!
Magic Charm
SIGH...
I HATE THIS.
EVER SINCE THE SUMMER FESTIVAL, I HAVEN'T BEEN ABLE TO GET MY MIND OFF OF REN-KUN. IT'S LIKE I CAN'T GET INTO ANYTHING ANYMORE.

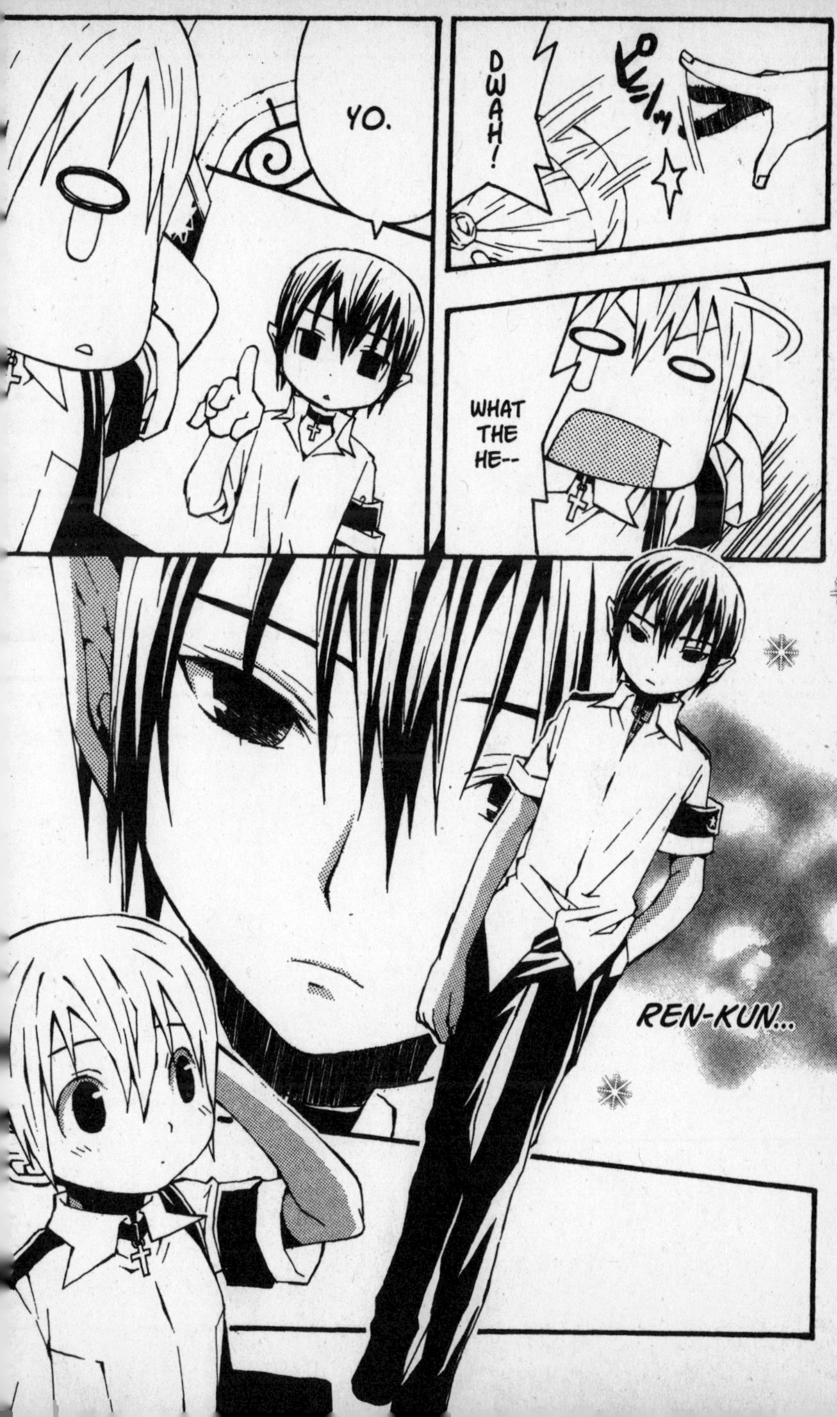
DWAH!
WHAT THE HE--
YO.
REN-KUN...

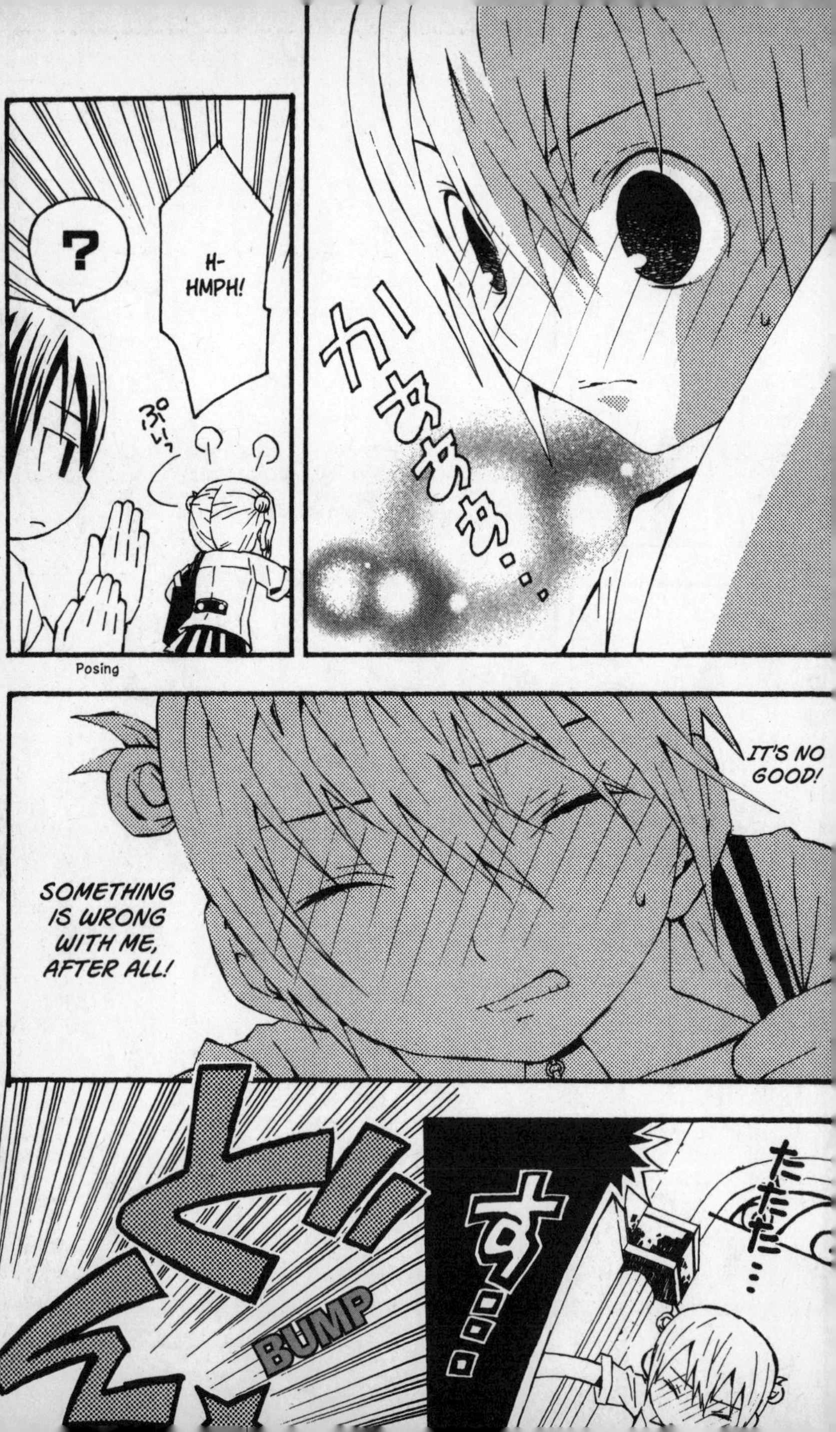
かぁぁぁぁ...
?
H-HMPH!
ぷいっ
Posing
IT'S NO GOOD!
SOMETHING IS WRONG WITH ME, AFTER ALL!
たたた…
BUMP

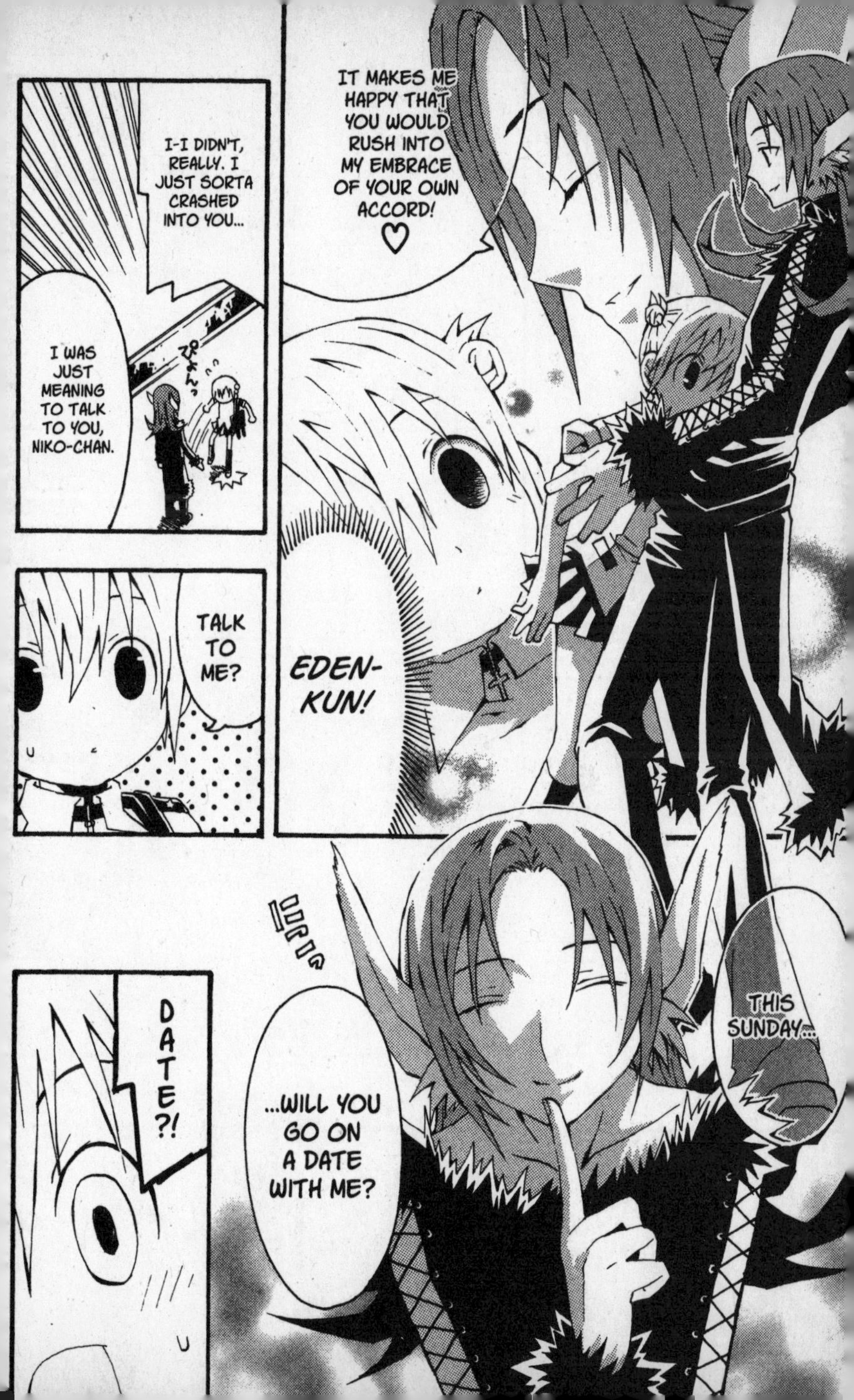
IT MAKES ME HAPPY THAT YOU WOULD RUSH INTO MY EMBRACE OF YOUR OWN ACCORD! ♡
EDEN-KUN!
I-I DIDN'T, REALLY. I JUST SORTA CRASHED INTO YOU...
I WAS JUST MEANING TO TALK TO YOU, NIKO-CHAN.
TALK TO ME?
THIS SUNDAY...
...WILL YOU GO ON A DATE WITH ME?
DATE?!

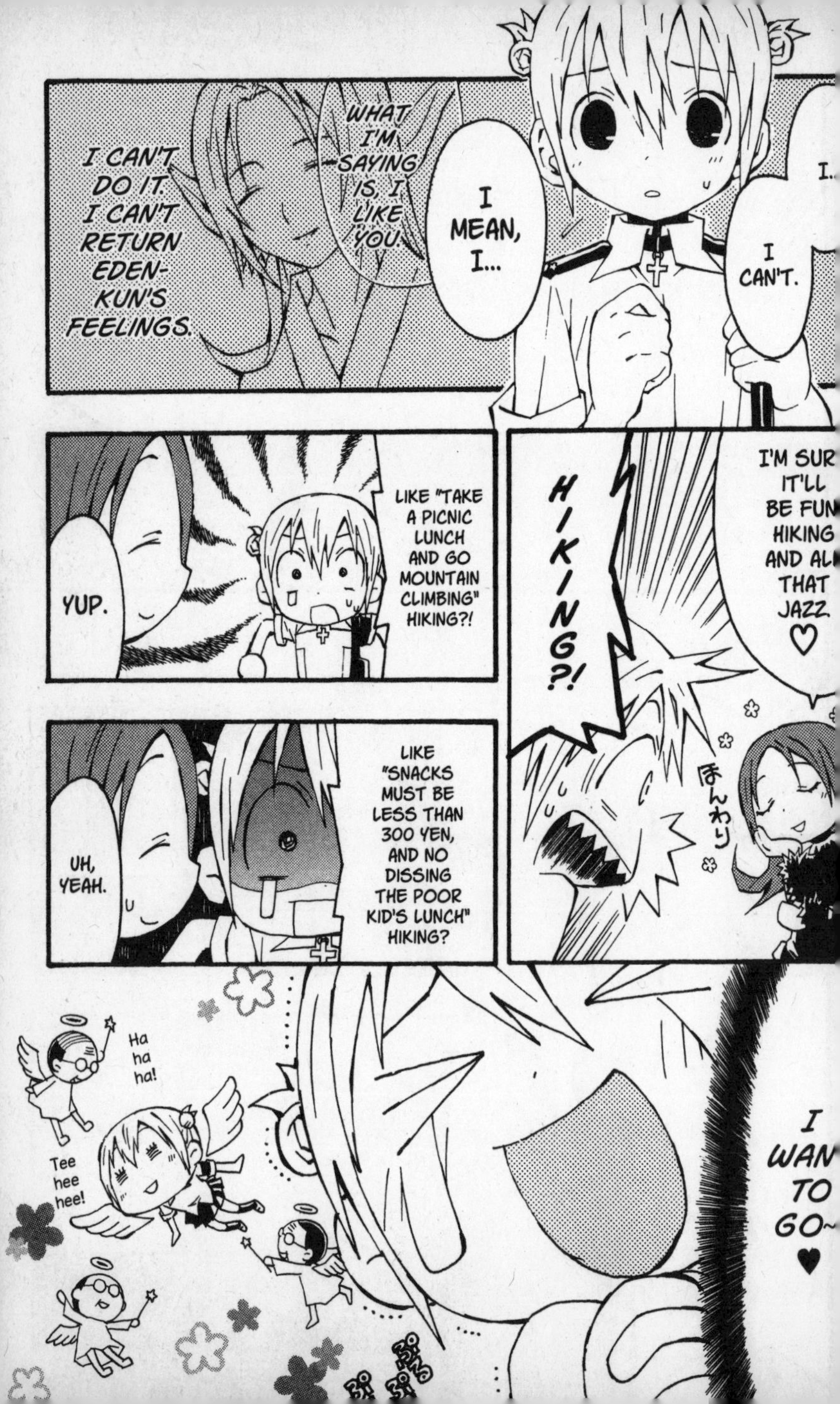
I...
I CAN'T.
I MEAN, I...
WHAT I'M SAYING IS, I LIKE YOU.
I CAN'T DO IT. I CAN'T RETURN EDEN-KUN'S FEELINGS.
I'M SUR IT'LL BE FUN HIKING AND AL THAT JAZZ. ♡
HIKING?!
ほんわり
LIKE "TAKE A PICNIC LUNCH AND GO MOUNTAIN CLIMBING" HIKING?!
YUP.
LIKE "SNACKS MUST BE LESS THAN 300 YEN, AND NO DISSING THE POOR KID'S LUNCH" HIKING?
UH, YEAH.
I WAN TO GO~ ♥
Ha ha ha!
Tee hee hee!

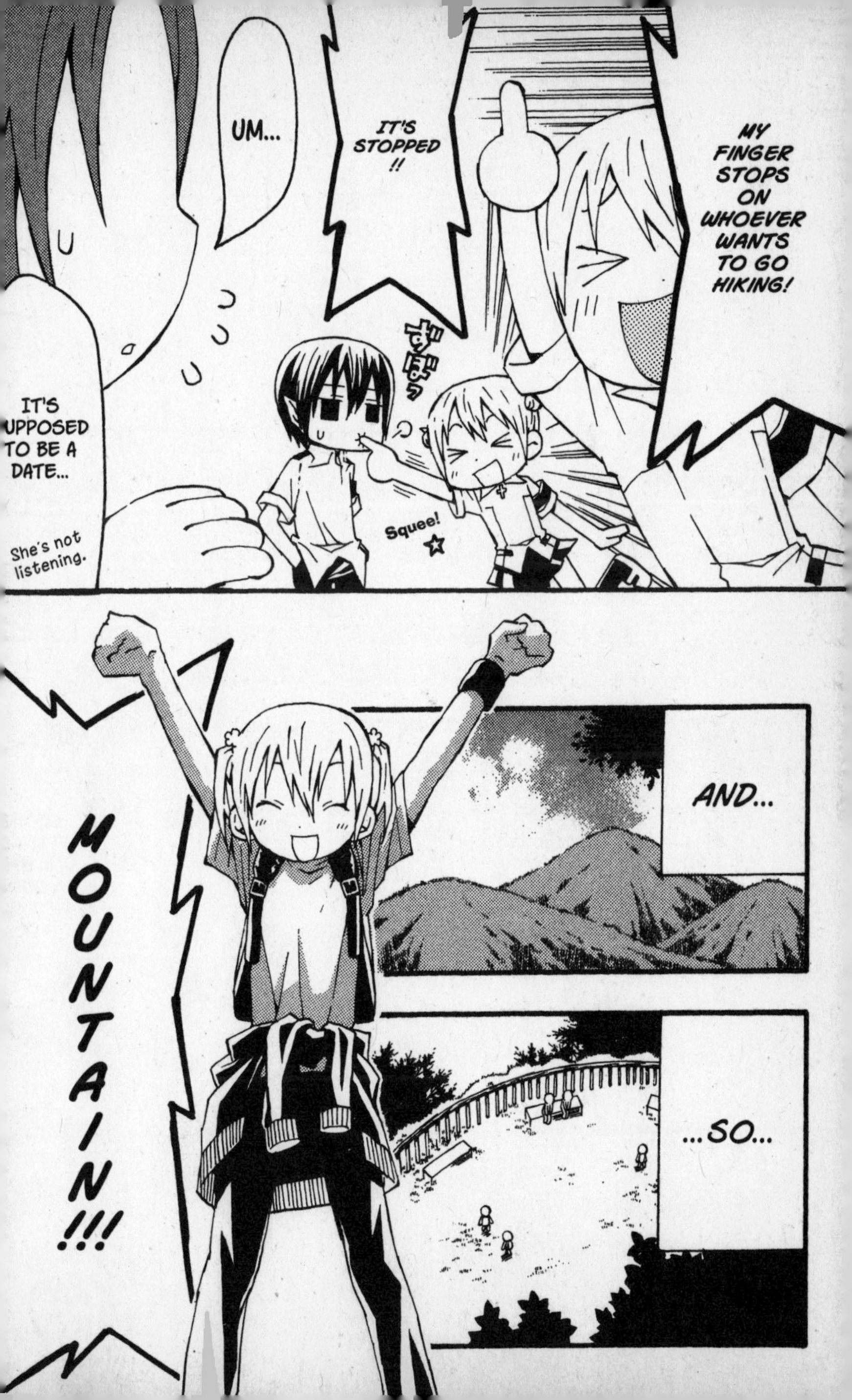
MY FINGER STOPS ON WHOEVER WANTS TO GO HIKING!
IT'S STOPPED !!
Squee!
UM...
IT'S UPPOSED TO BE A DATE...
She's not listening.
AND...
...SO...
MOUNTAIN!!!

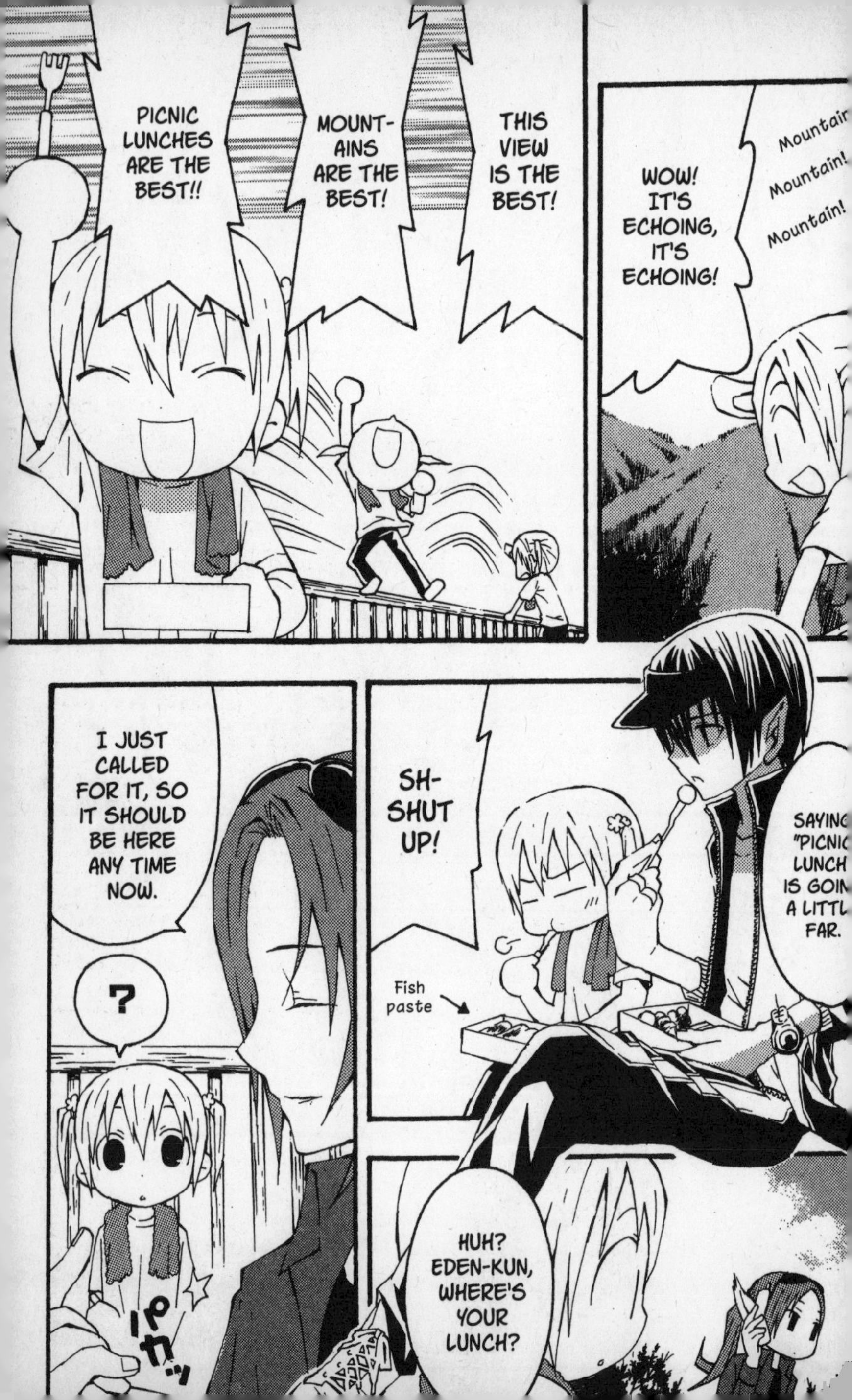
WOW! IT'S ECHOING, IT'S ECHOING!
Mountain
Mountain!
Mountain!
THIS VIEW IS THE BEST!
MOUNT-AINS ARE THE BEST!
PICNIC LUNCHES ARE THE BEST!!
SAYING "PICNIC LUNCH" IS GOIN A LITTL FAR.
SH-SHUT UP!
Fish paste
HUH? EDEN-KUN, WHERE'S YOUR LUNCH?
I JUST CALLED FOR IT, SO IT SHOULD BE HERE ANY TIME NOW.
?
パカッ

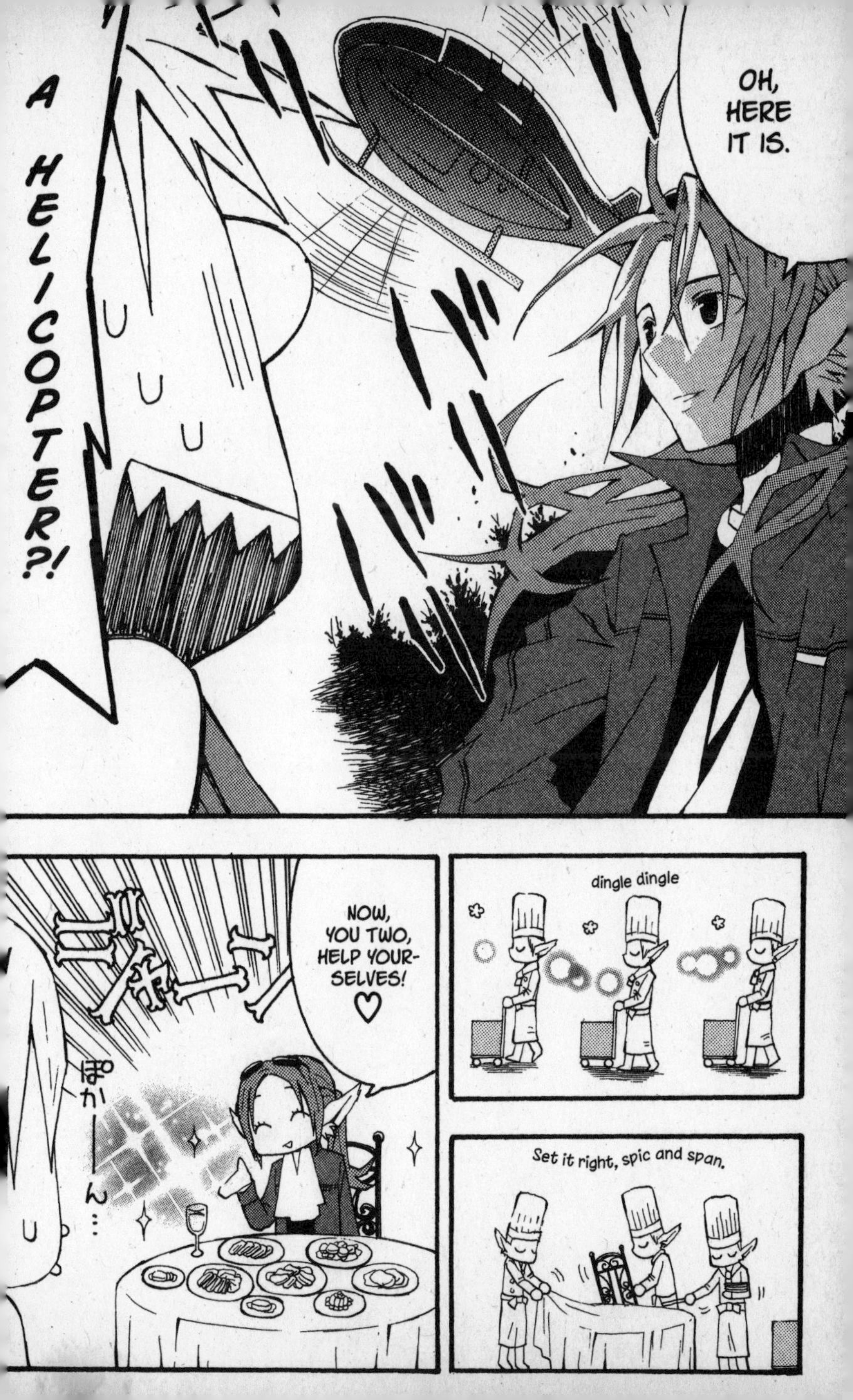
OH, HERE IT IS.
A HELICOPTER?!
dingle dingle
Set it right, spic and span.
NOW, YOU TWO, HELP YOURSELVES! ♥
ぽかーん…

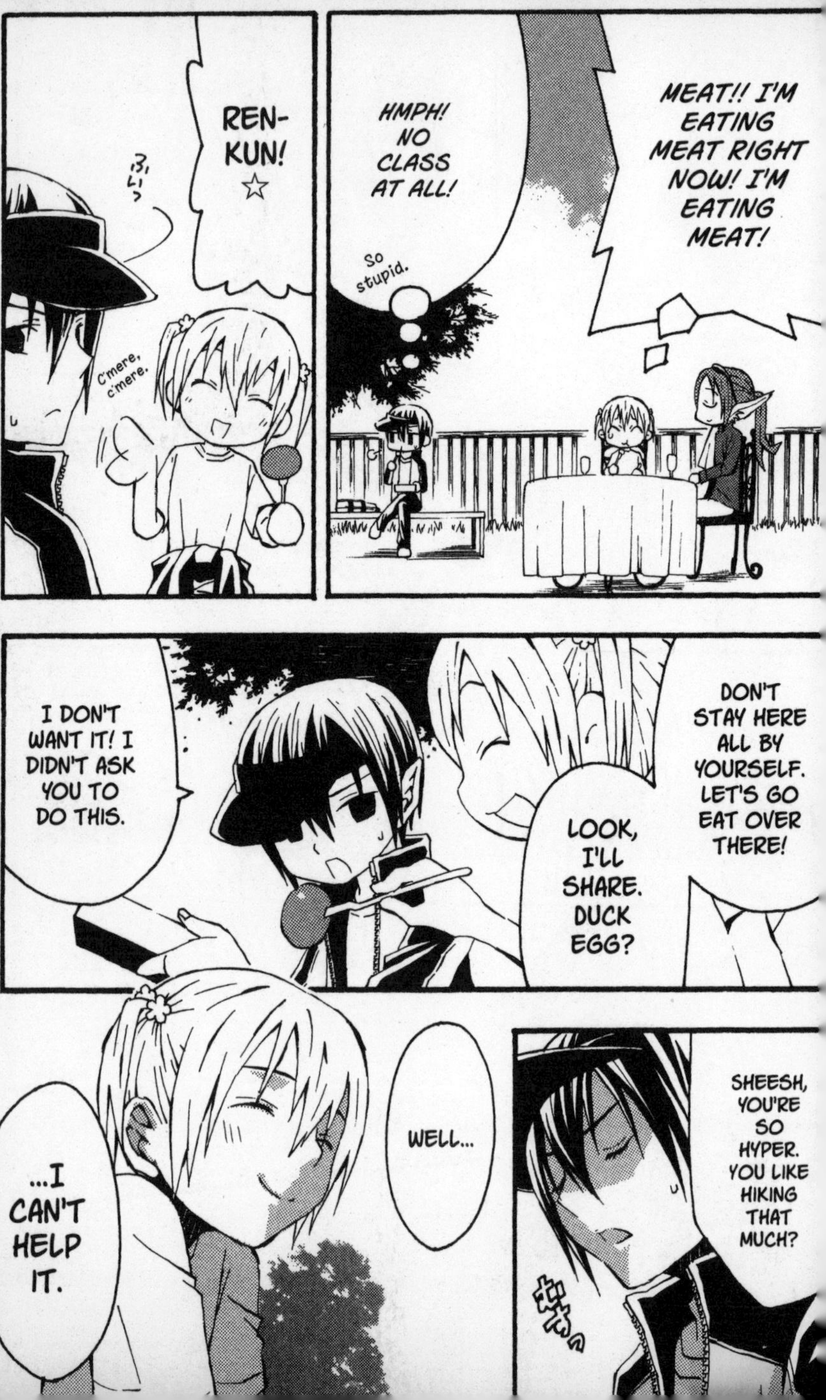
MEAT!! I'M EATING MEAT RIGHT NOW! I'M EATING MEAT!
HMPH! NO CLASS AT ALL!
So stupid.
REN-KUN! ☆
C'mere, c'mere.
DON'T STAY HERE ALL BY YOURSELF. LET'S GO EAT OVER THERE!
LOOK, I'LL SHARE. DUCK EGG?
I DON'T WANT IT! I DIDN'T ASK YOU TO DO THIS.
SHEESH, YOU'RE SO HYPER. YOU LIKE HIKING THAT MUCH?
WELL...
...I CAN'T HELP IT.

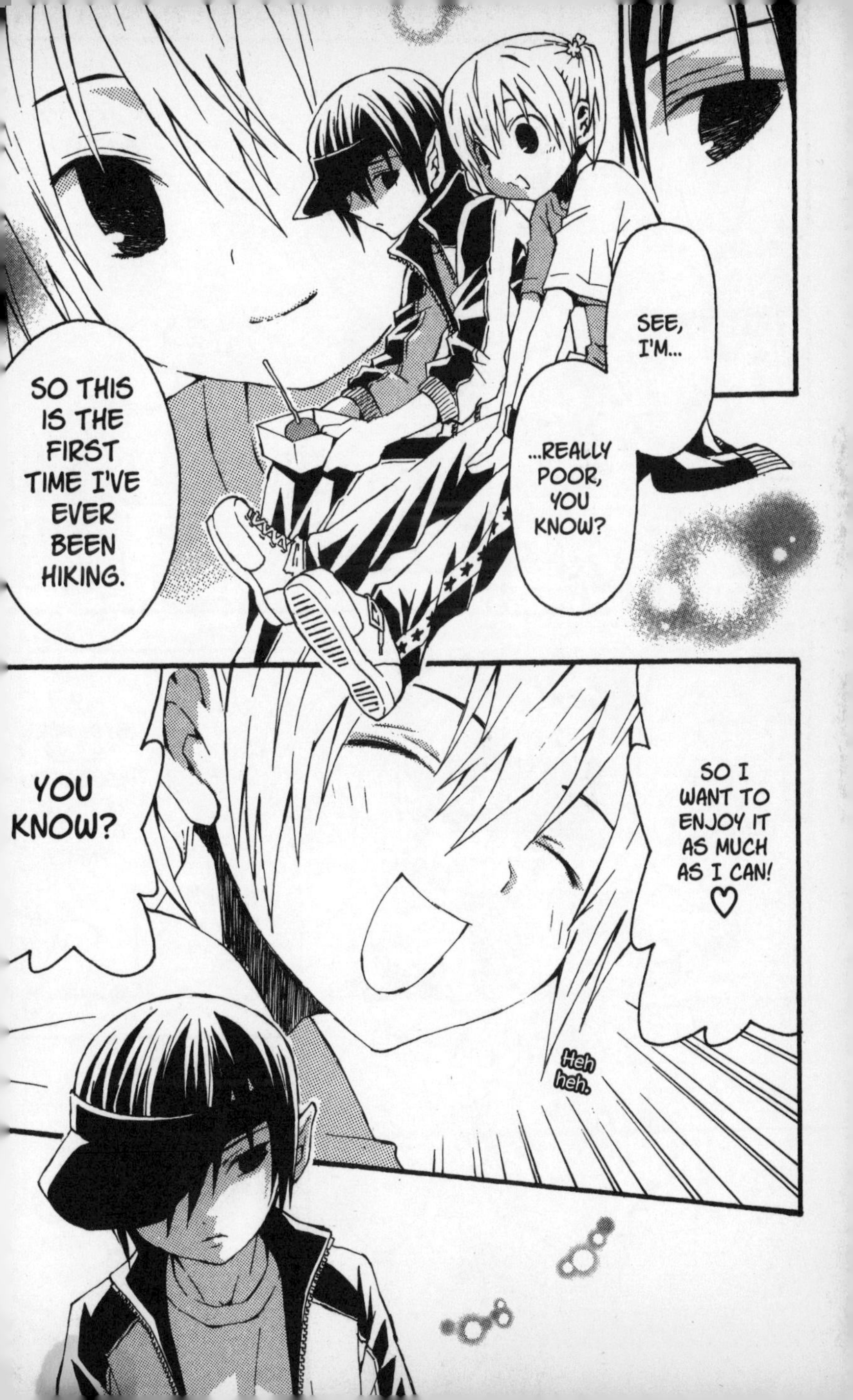
SEE, I'M...
...REALLY POOR, YOU KNOW?
SO THIS IS THE FIRST TIME I'VE EVER BEEN HIKING.
SO I WANT TO ENJOY IT AS MUCH AS I CAN! ♡
YOU KNOW?
Heh heh.

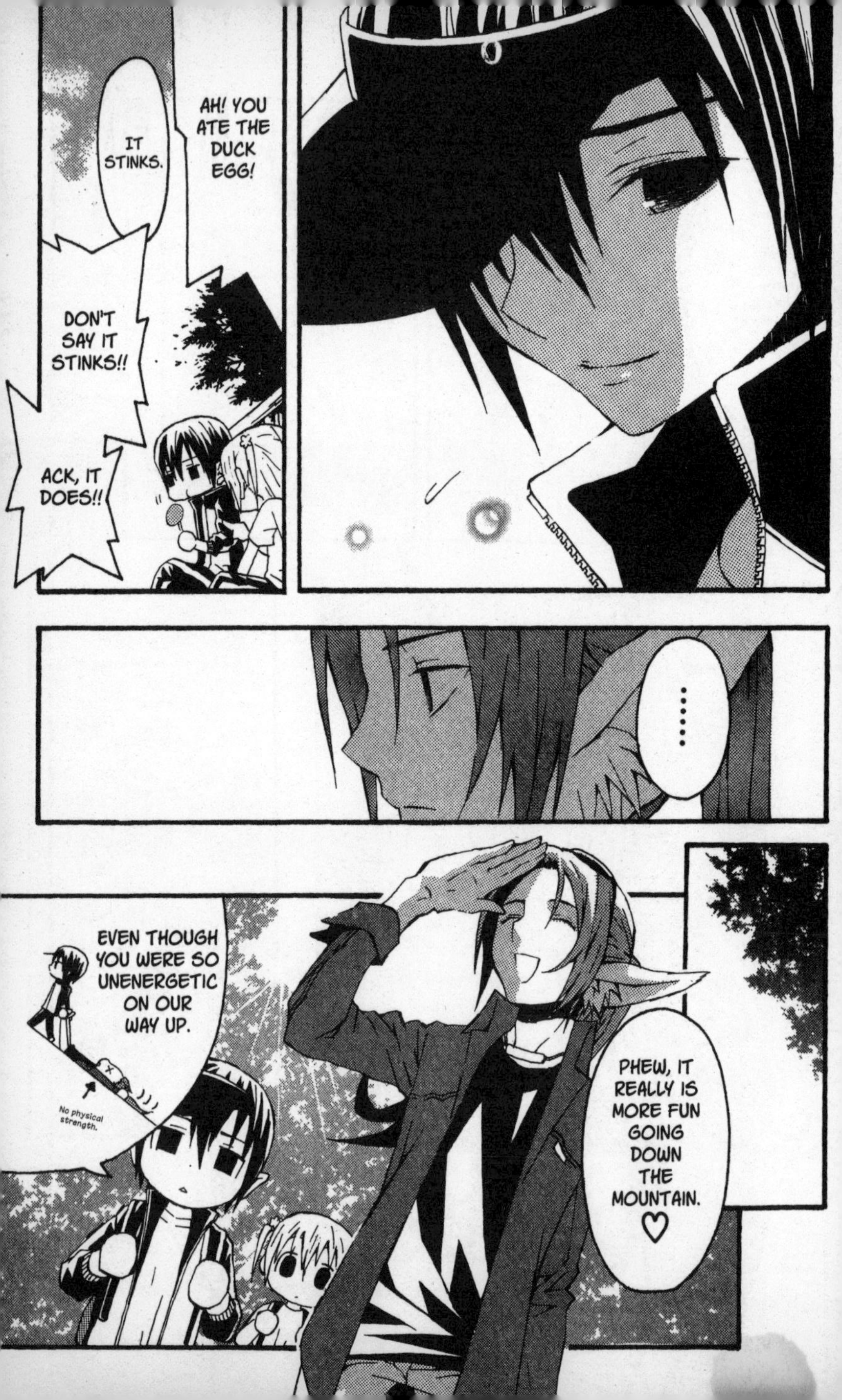
AH! YOU ATE THE DUCK EGG!
IT STINKS.
DON'T SAY IT STINKS!!
ACK, IT DOES!!
......
PHEW, IT REALLY IS MORE FUN GOING DOWN THE MOUNTAIN. ♡
EVEN THOUGH YOU WERE SO UNENERGETIC ON OUR WAY UP.
No physical strength.

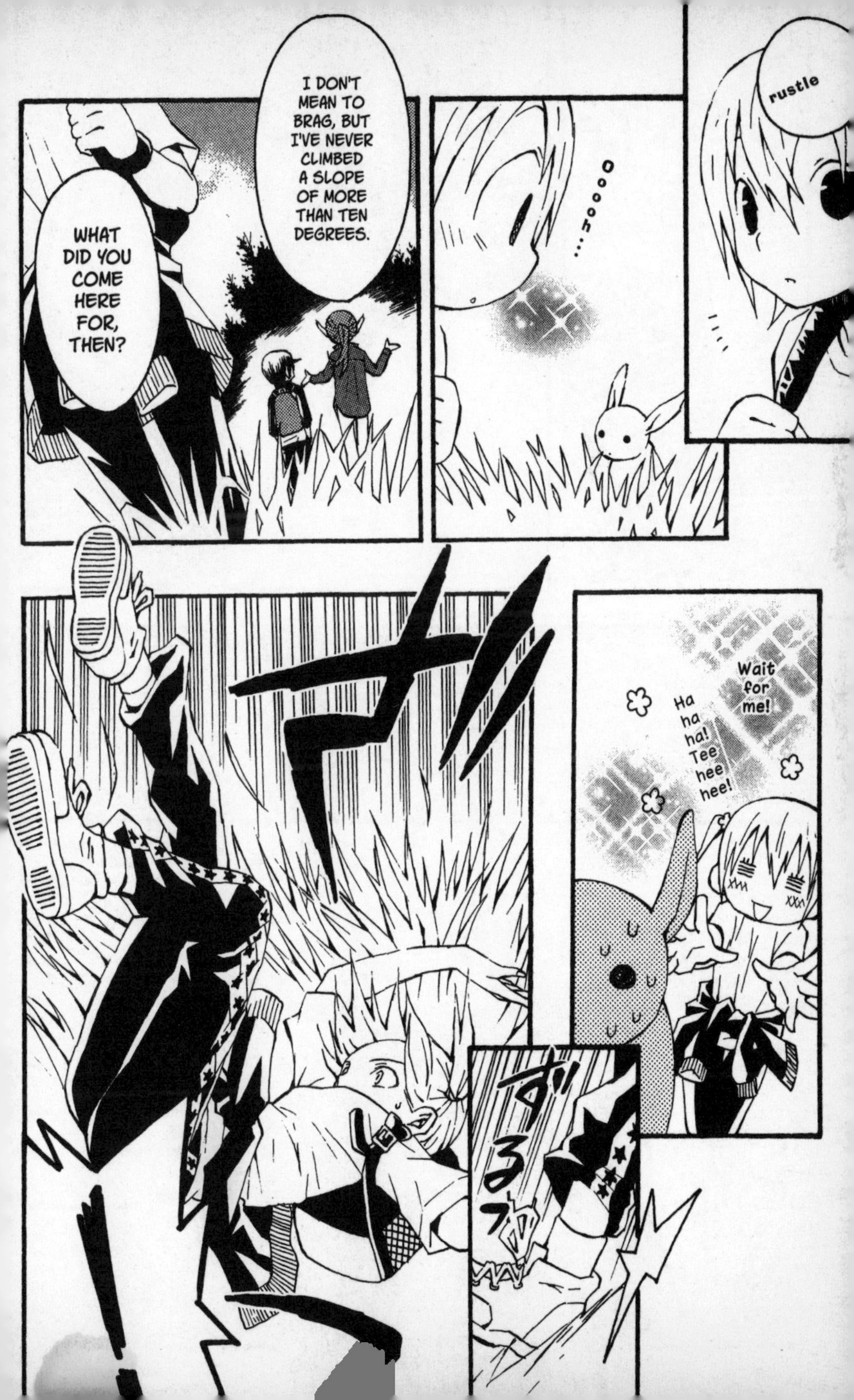
rustle
Ooooh...
I DON'T MEAN TO BRAG, BUT I'VE NEVER CLIMBED A SLOPE OF MORE THAN TEN DEGREES.
WHAT DID YOU COME HERE FOR, THEN?
Wait for me!
Ha ha ha! Tee hee hee!

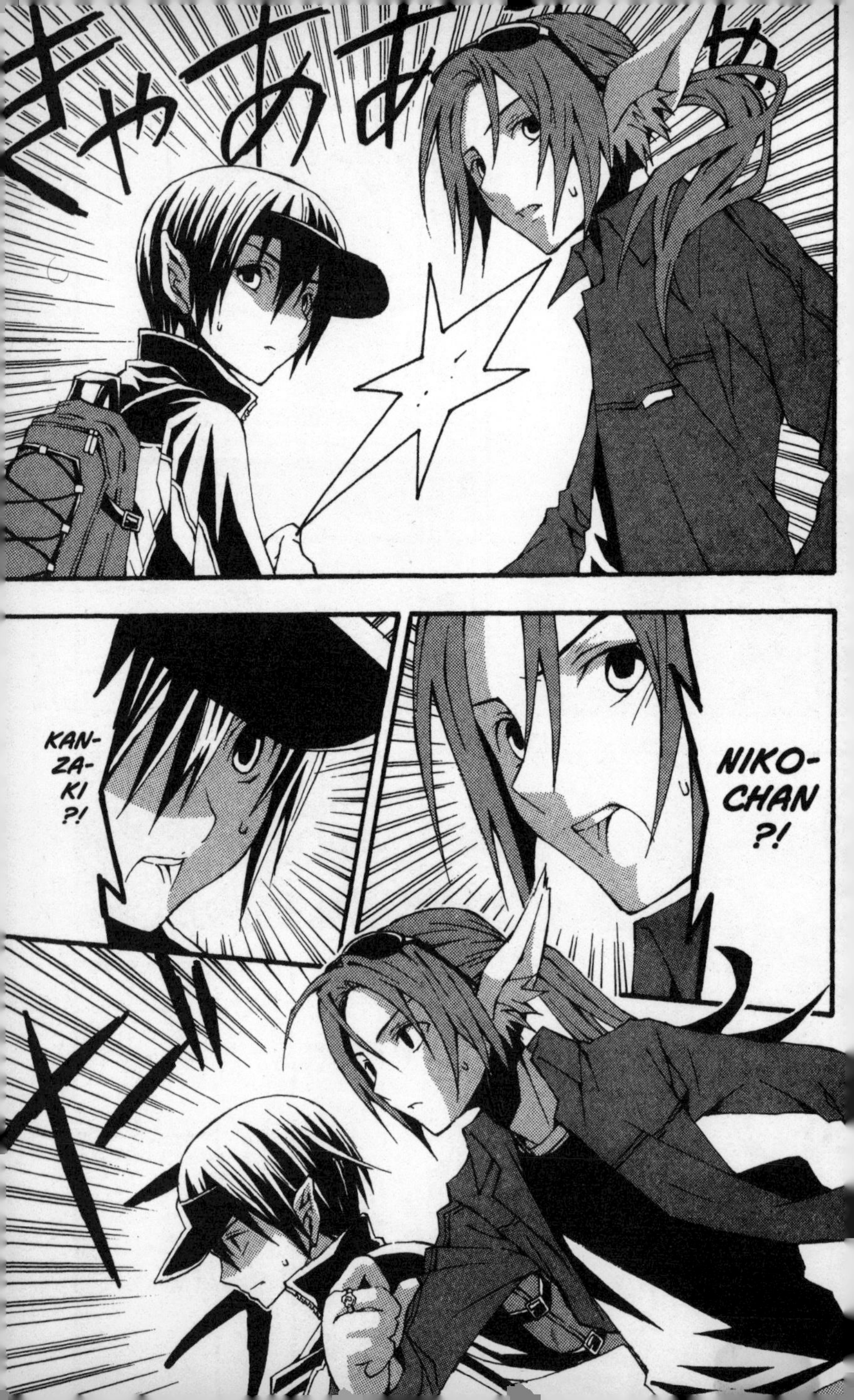

きゃあああ
NIKO-CHAN?!
KAN-ZA-KI?!

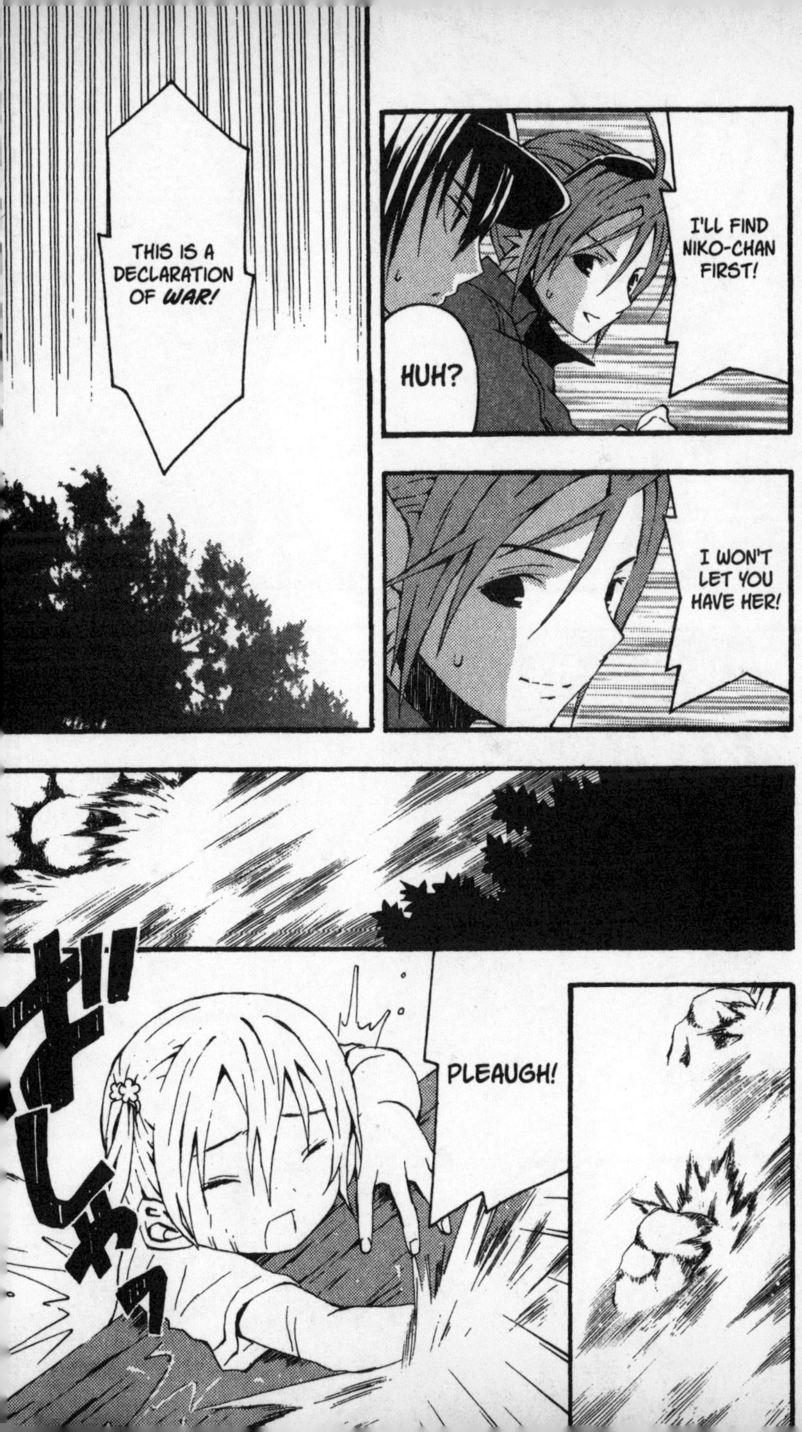
I'LL FIND NIKO-CHAN FIRST!
HUH?
I WON'T LET YOU HAVE HER!
THIS IS A DECLARATION OF *WAR!*
PLEAUGH!

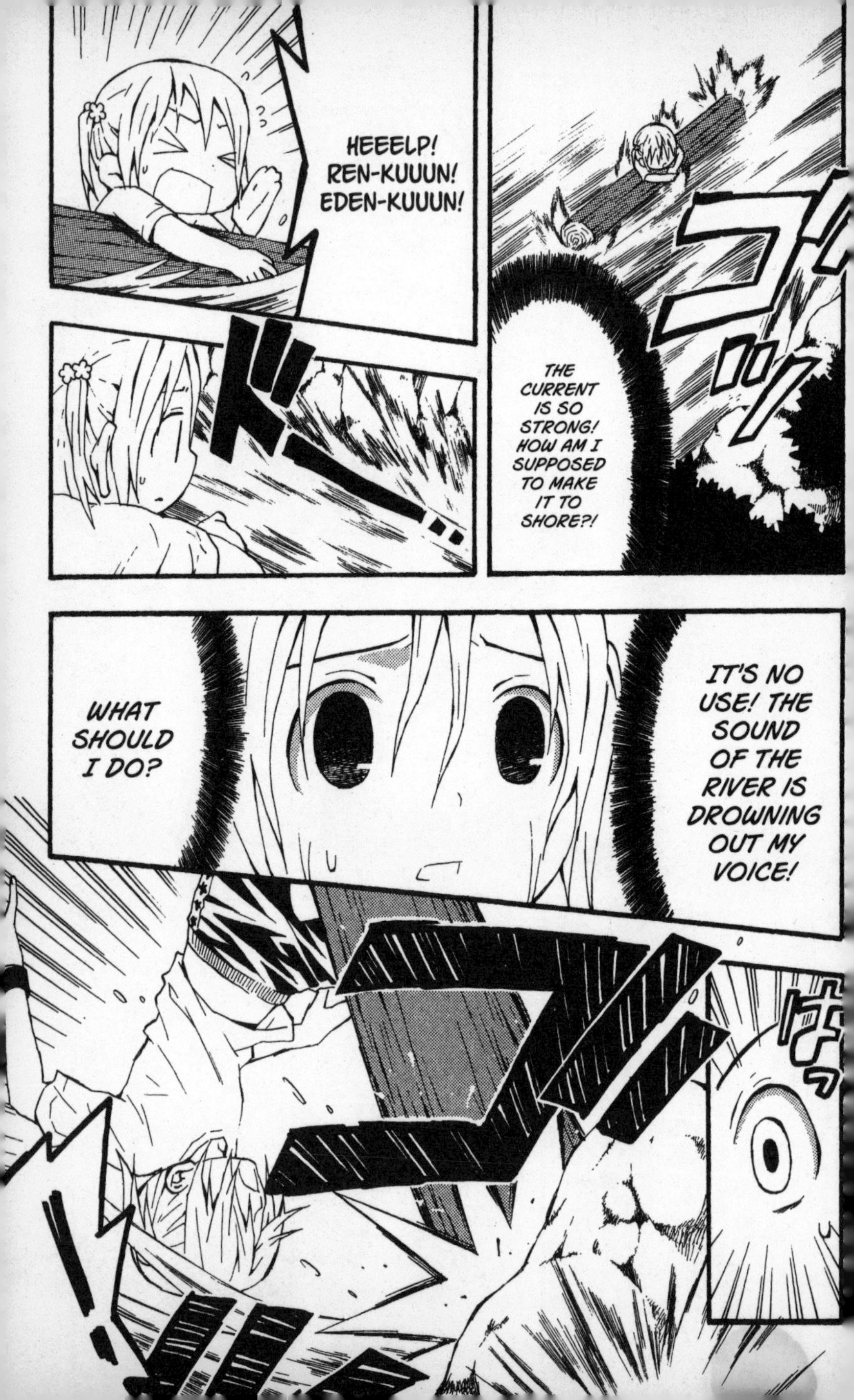
THE CURRENT IS SO STRONG! HOW AM I SUPPOSED TO MAKE IT TO SHORE?!
HEEELP! REN-KUUUN! EDEN-KUUUN!
IT'S NO USE! THE SOUND OF THE RIVER IS DROWNING OUT MY VOICE!
WHAT SHOULD I DO?

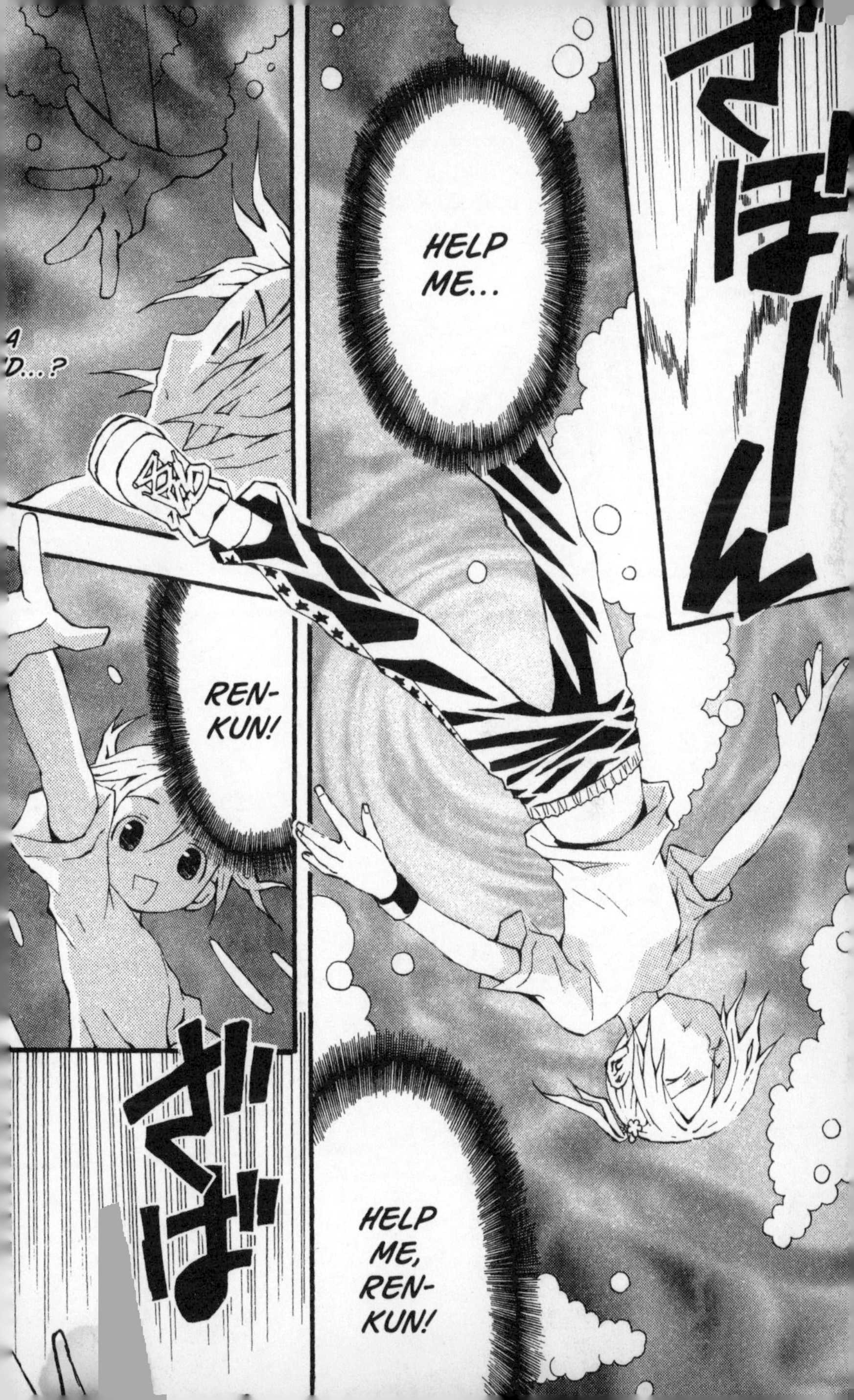
ざぼーん
HELP ME...
HELP ME, REN-KUN!
REN-KUN!
ざば

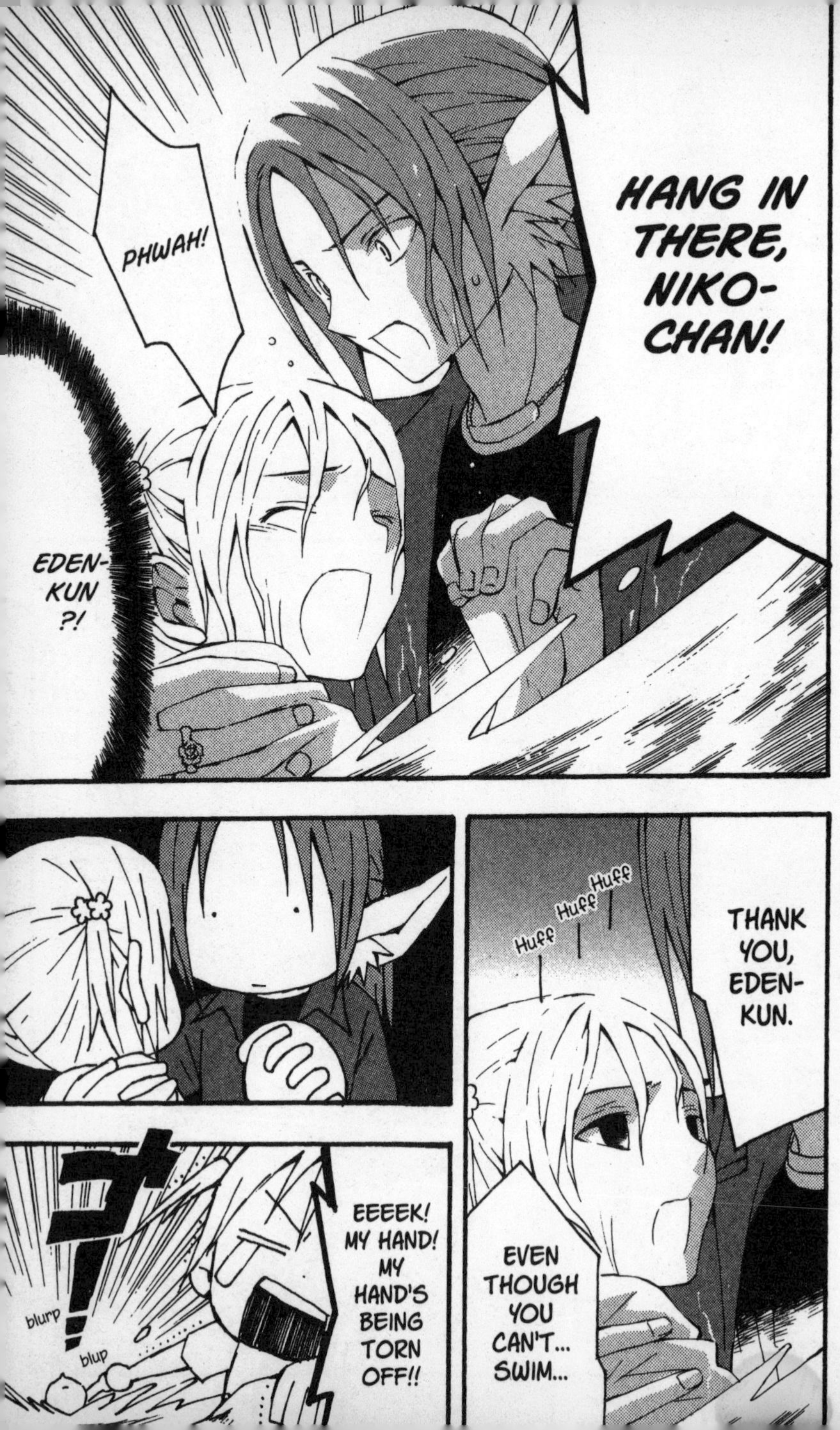
HANG IN THERE, NIKO-CHAN!
PHWAH!
EDEN-KUN ?!
Huff Huff Huff
THANK YOU, EDEN-KUN.
EVEN THOUGH YOU CAN'T... SWIM...
EEEEK! MY HAND! MY HAND'S BEING TORN OFF!!
blurp
blup

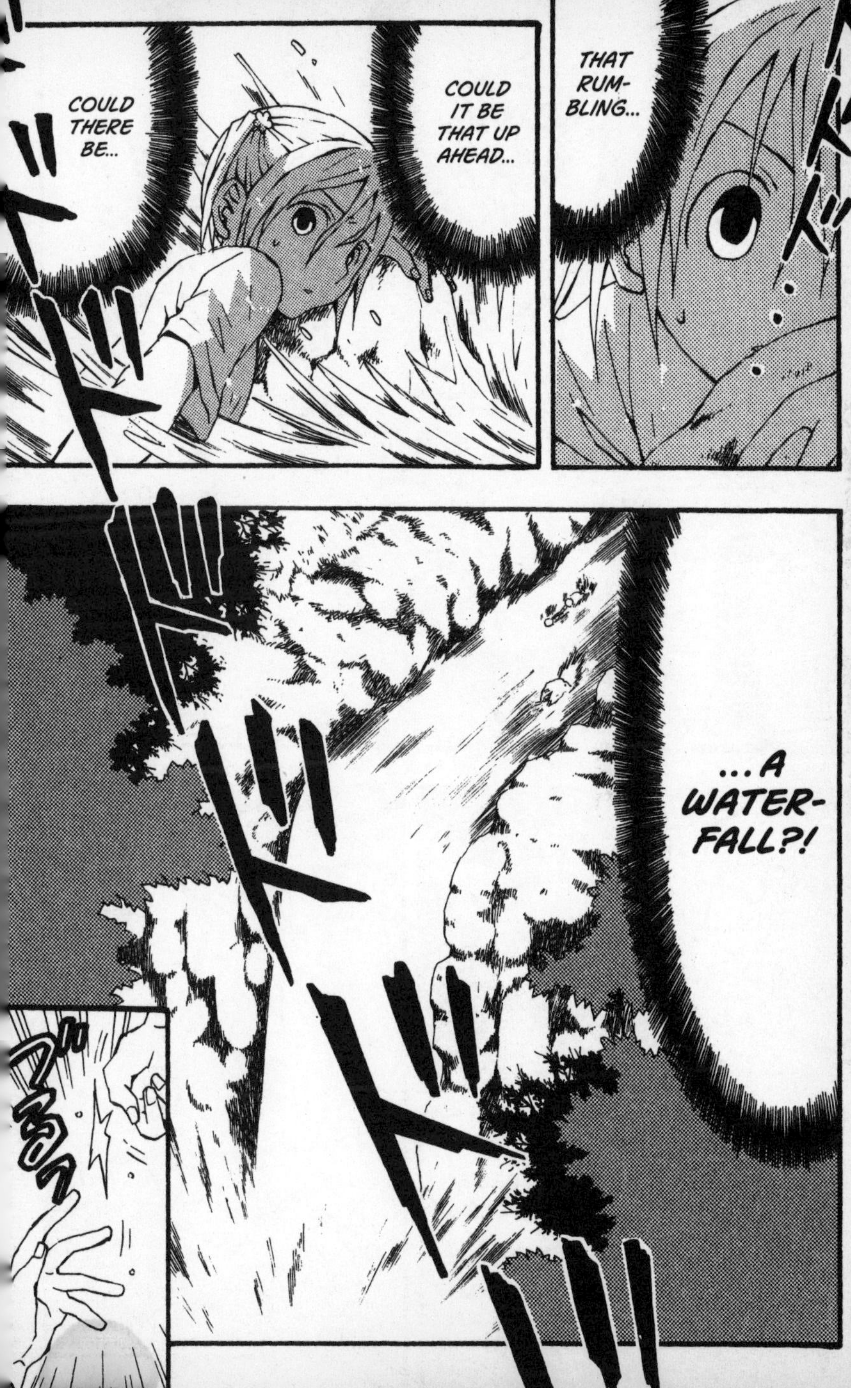
THAT RUM-BLING...
COULD IT BE THAT UP AHEAD...
COULD THERE BE...
...A WATER-FALL?!

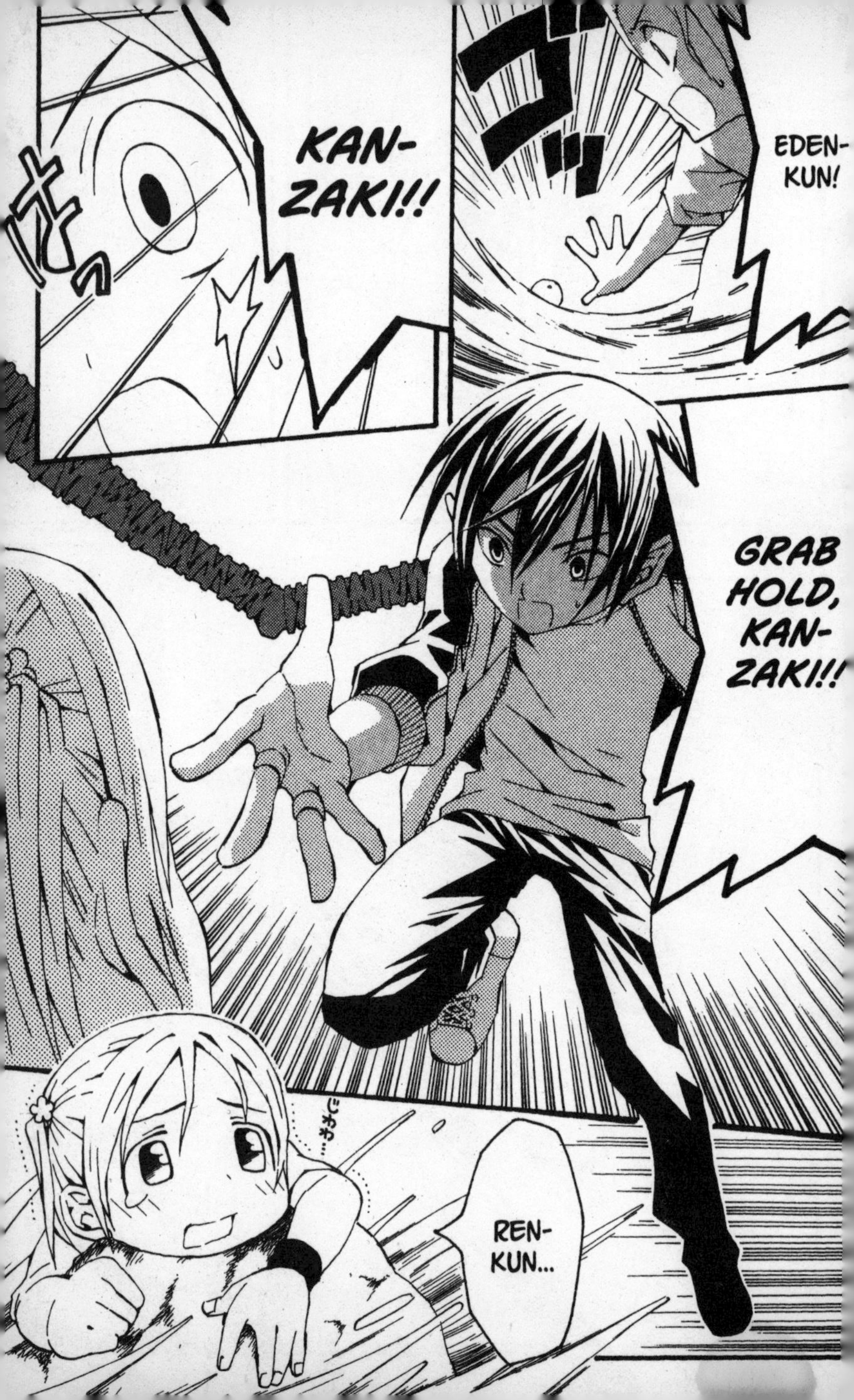
EDEN-KUN!
KAN-ZAKI!!
GRAB HOLD, KAN-ZAKI!!
REN-KUN...

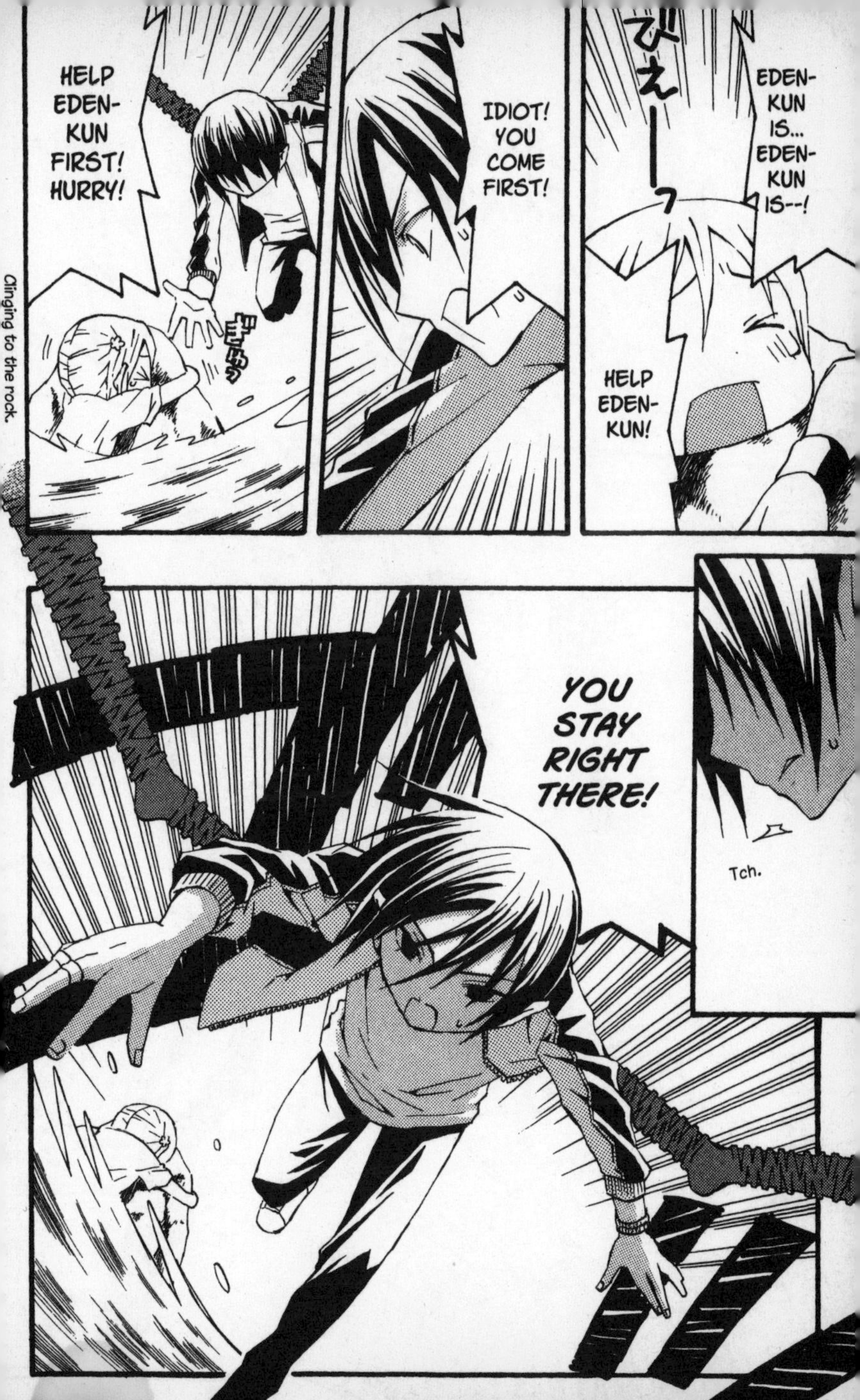
でぇーっ
EDEN-KUN IS... EDEN-KUN IS--!
HELP EDEN-KUN!
IDIOT! YOU COME FIRST!
HELP EDEN-KUN FIRST! HURRY!
Clinging to the rock.
Tch.
YOU STAY RIGHT THERE!

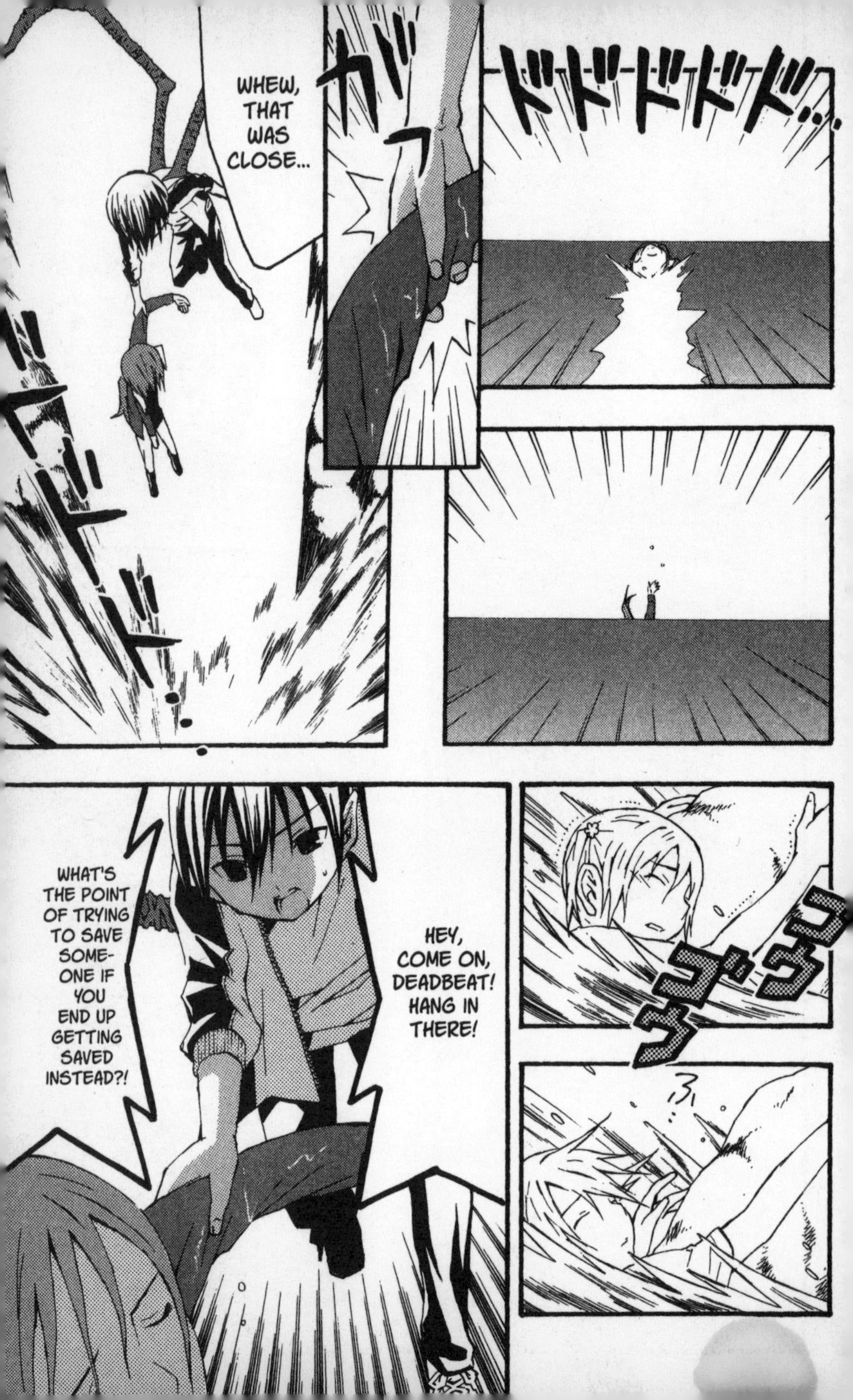
ドドドドド…
WHEW, THAT WAS CLOSE...
HEY, COME ON, DEADBEAT! HANG IN THERE!
WHAT'S THE POINT OF TRYING TO SAVE SOME-ONE IF YOU END UP GETTING SAVED INSTEAD?!

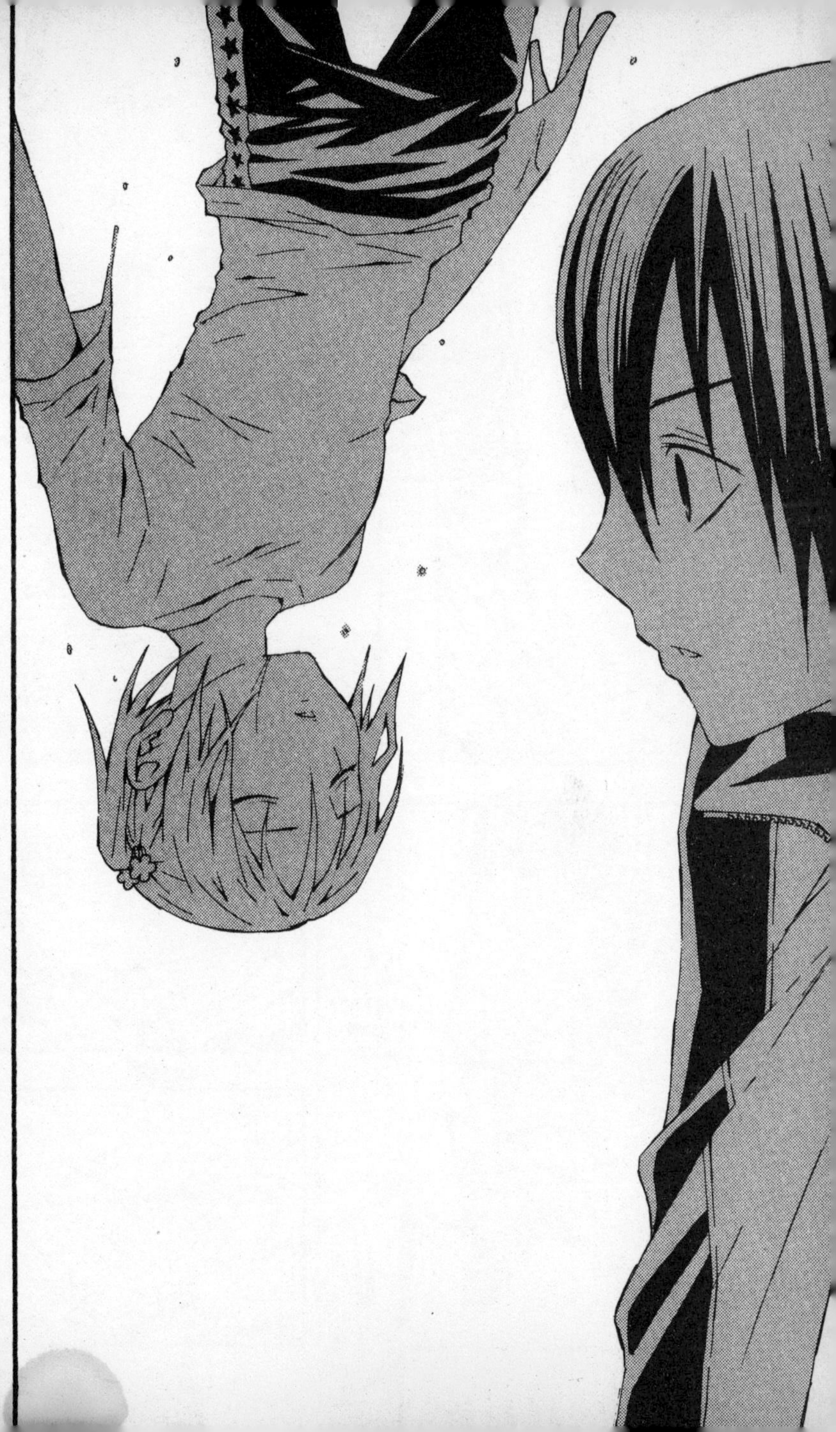

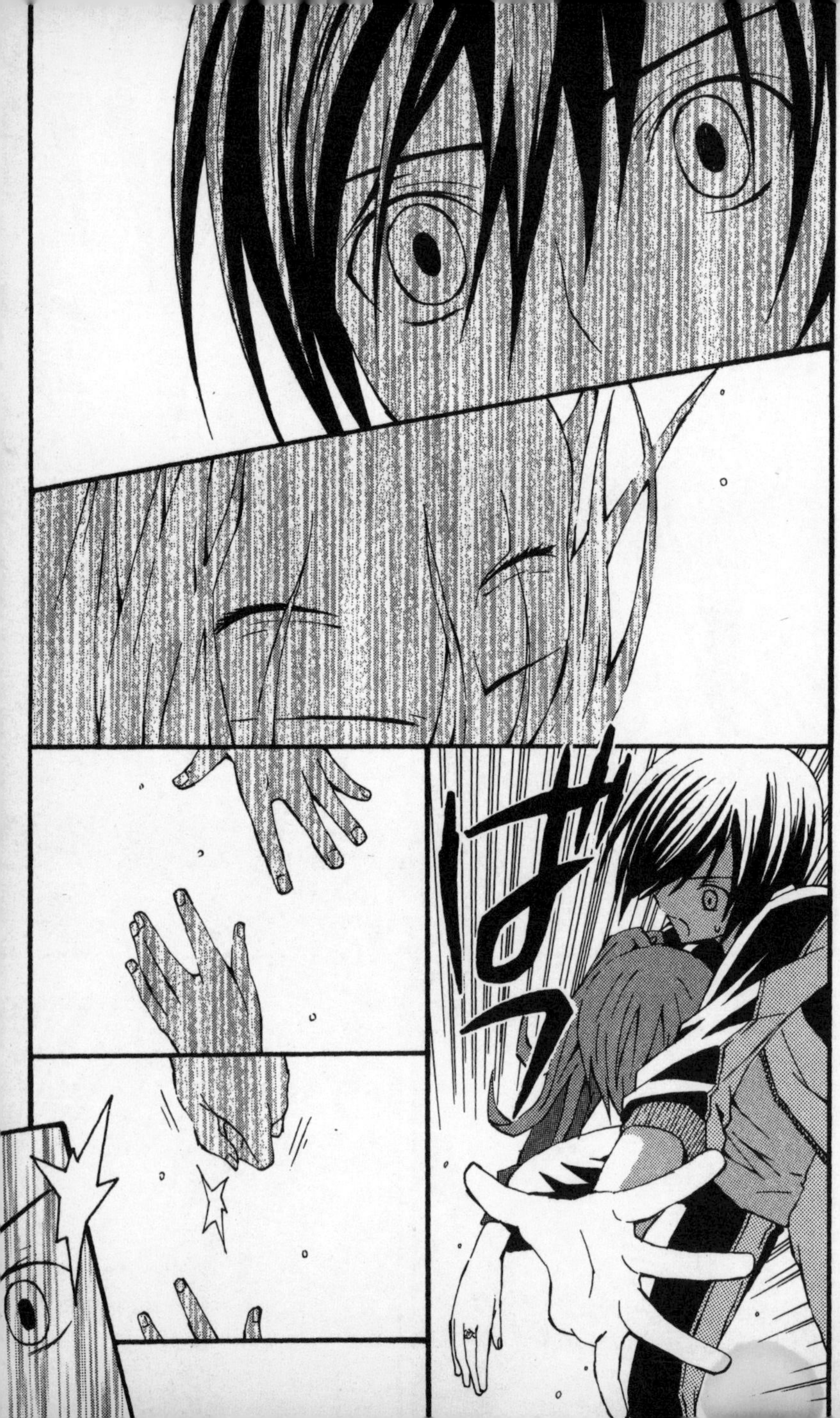
ばっ

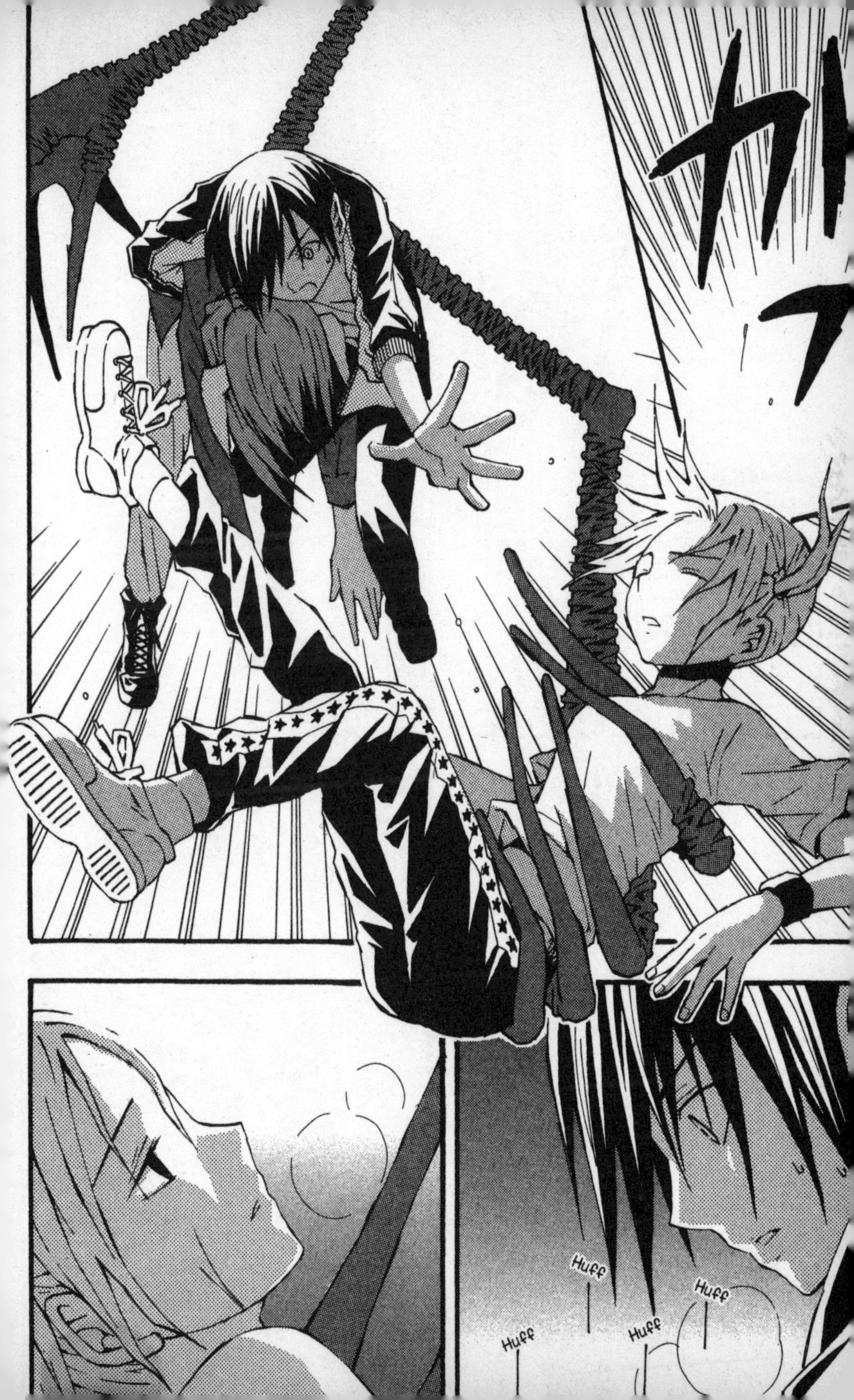
Huff
Huff
Huff
Huff

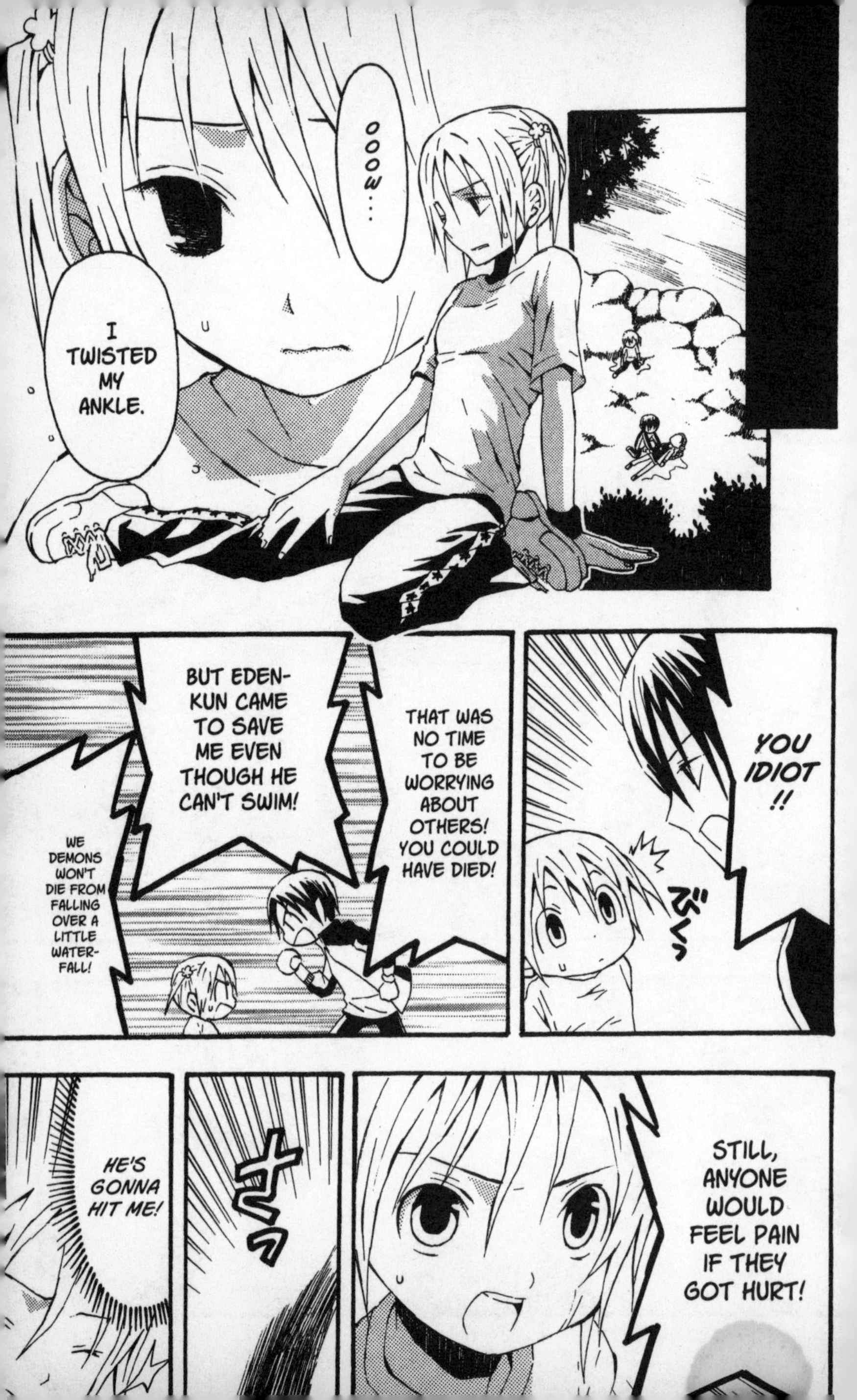
OOOW...
I TWISTED MY ANKLE.
YOU IDIOT!!
びくっ
THAT WAS NO TIME TO BE WORRYING ABOUT OTHERS! YOU COULD HAVE DIED!
BUT EDEN-KUN CAME TO SAVE ME EVEN THOUGH HE CAN'T SWIM!
WE DEMONS WON'T DIE FROM FALLING OVER A LITTLE WATER-FALL!
STILL, ANYONE WOULD FEEL PAIN IF THEY GOT HURT!
さっ
HE'S GONNA HIT ME!

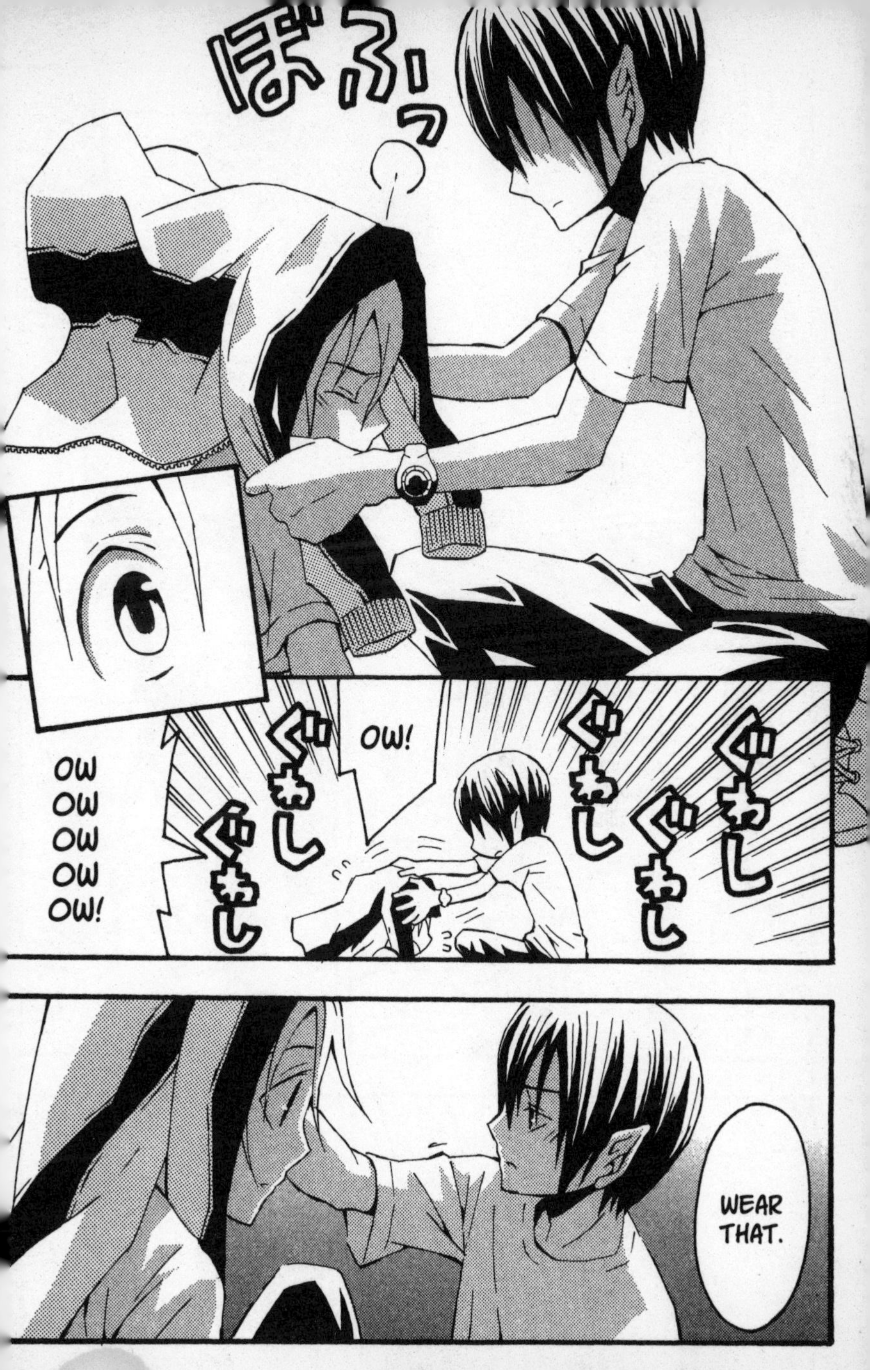
ぼふっ
ぐわし
ぐわし
ぐわし
ぐわし
ぐわし
ぐわし
OW!
OW OW OW OW OW!
WEAR THAT.

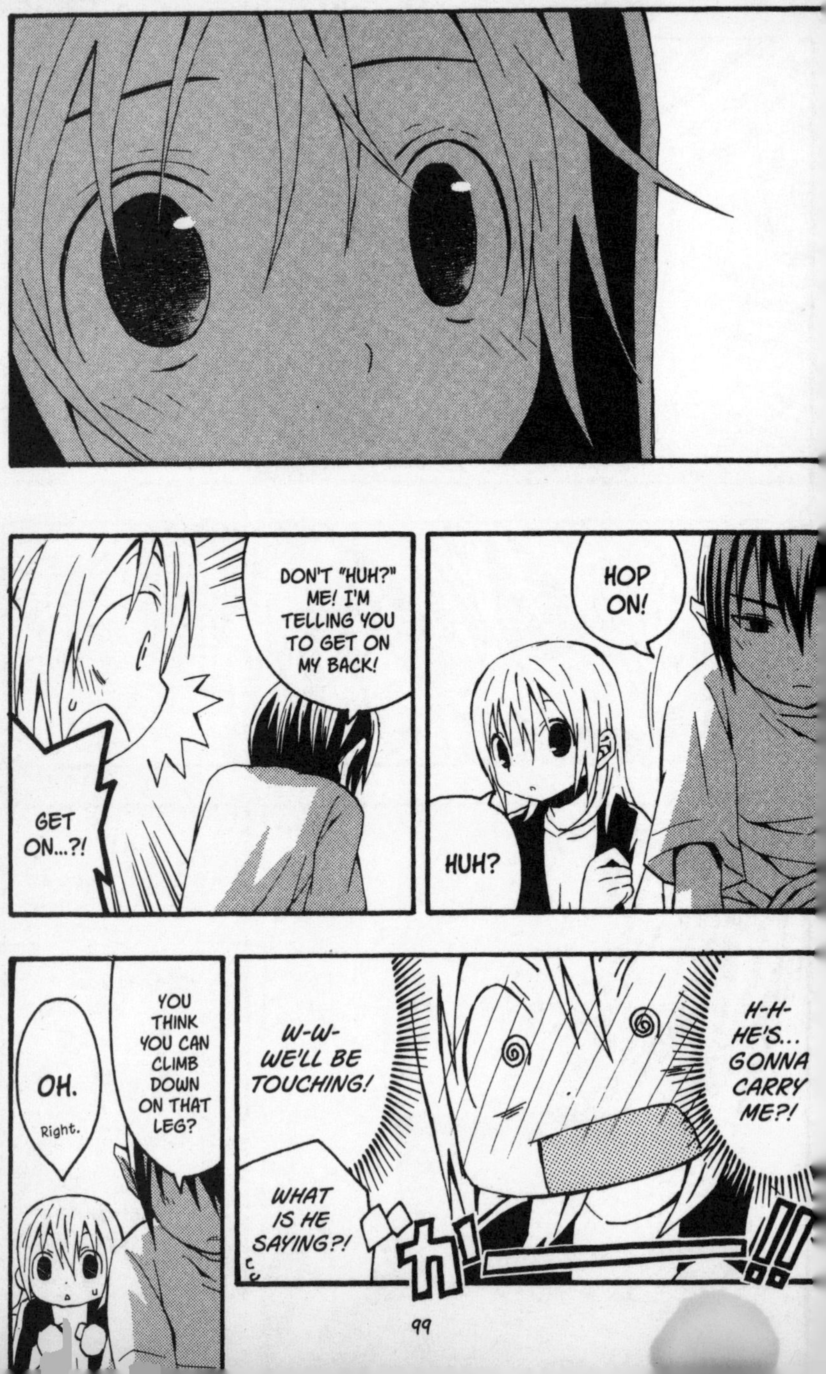
HOP ON!
HUH?
DON'T "HUH?" ME! I'M TELLING YOU TO GET ON MY BACK!
GET ON...?!
H-H-HE'S... GONNA CARRY ME?!
W-W-WE'LL BE TOUCHING!
WHAT IS HE SAYING?!
YOU THINK YOU CAN CLIMB DOWN ON THAT LEG?
OH.
Right.

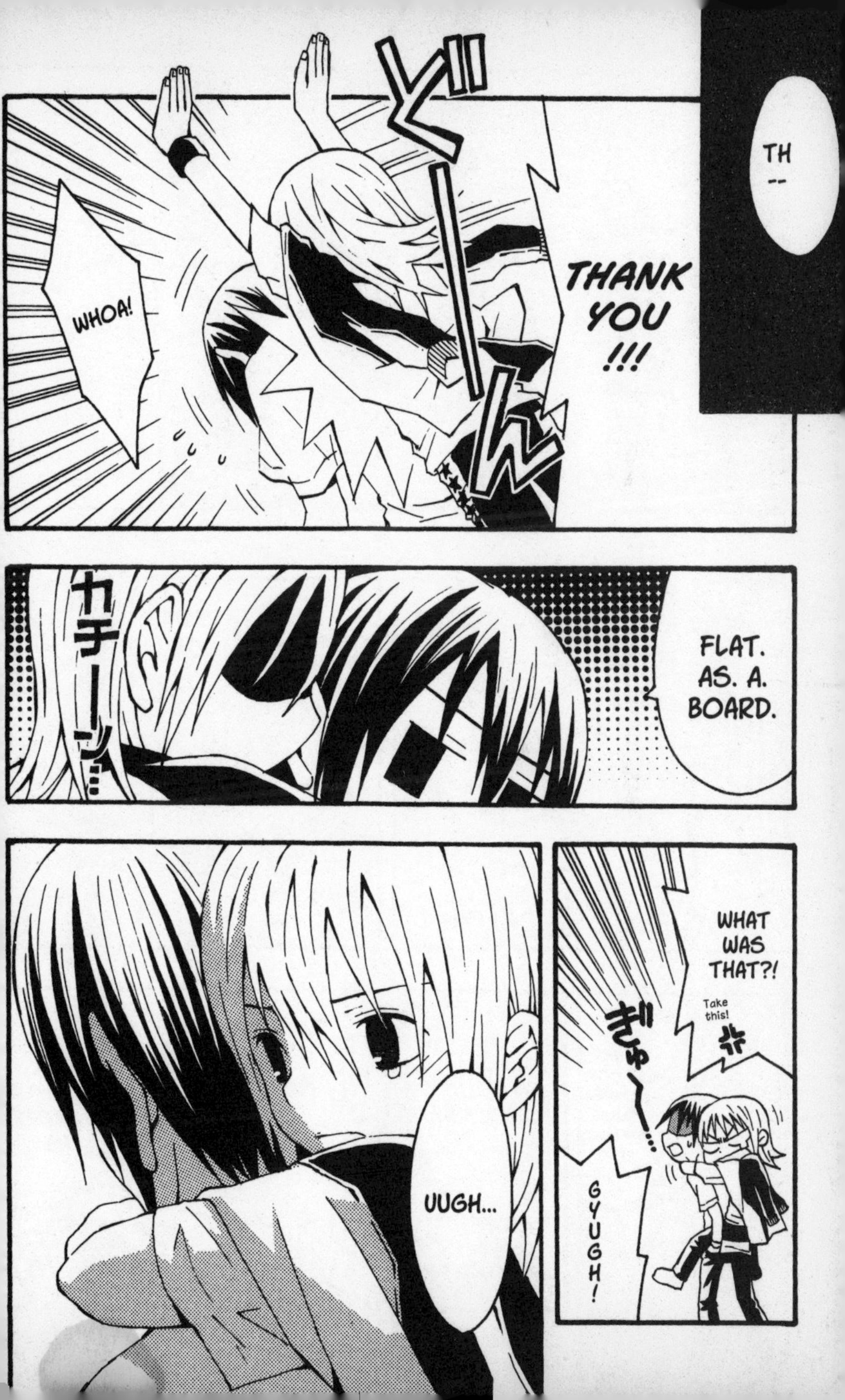
TH --
どーん
THANK YOU !!!
WHOA!
FLAT. AS. A. BOARD.
カチーン...
WHAT WAS THAT?!
Take this!
ぎゅ～...
GYUGH!
UUGH...

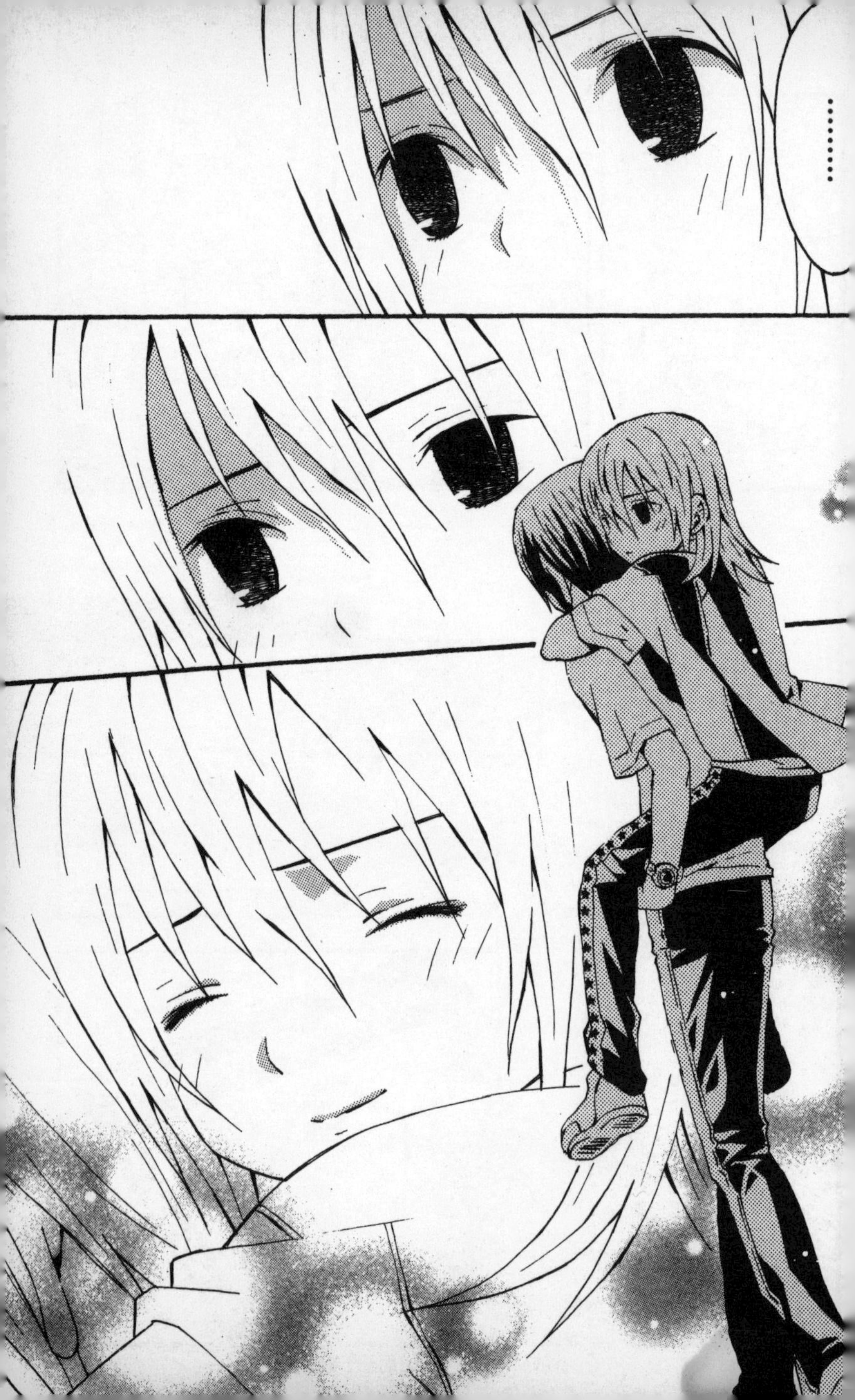
....

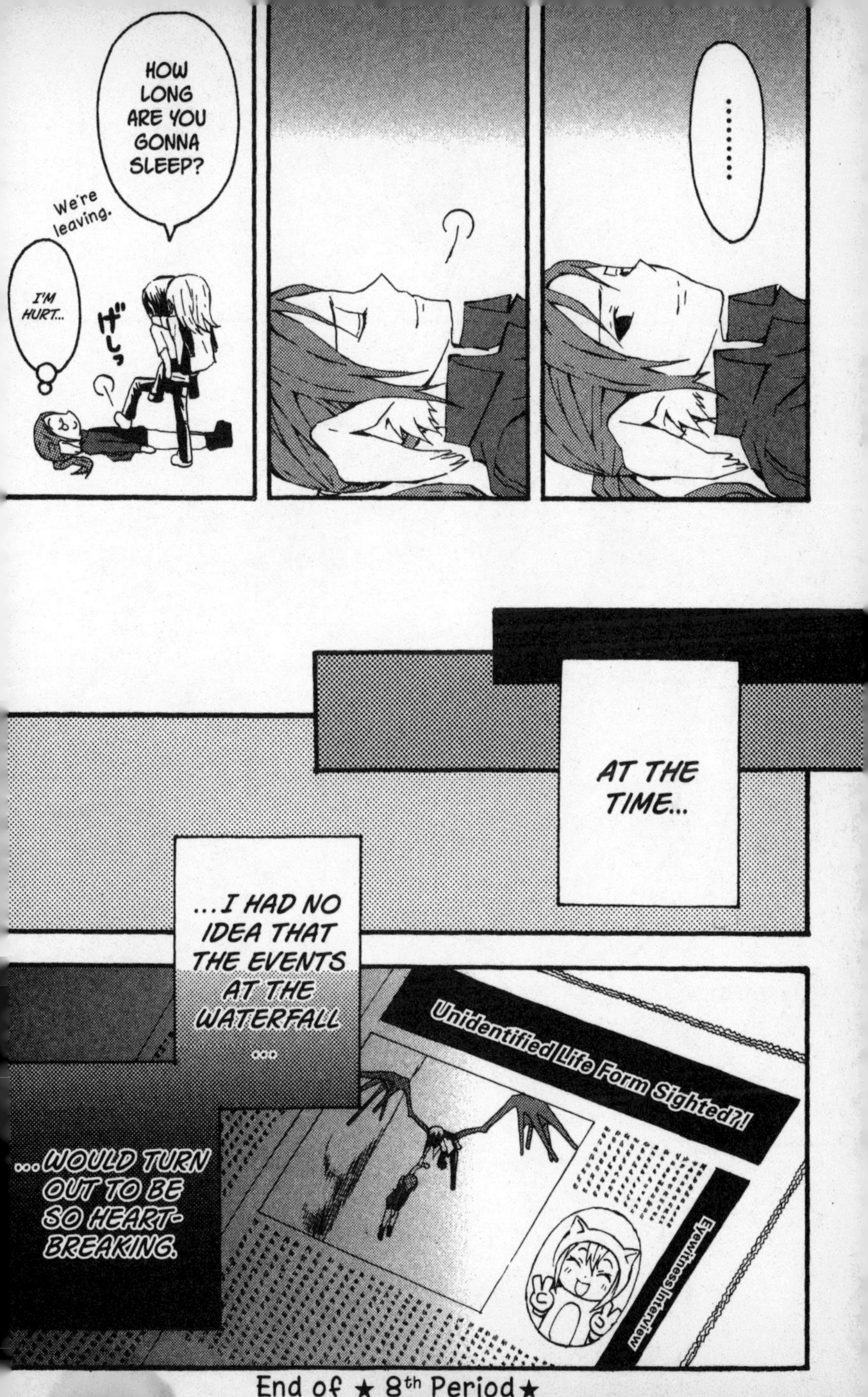
....
HOW LONG ARE YOU GONNA SLEEP?
We're leaving.
げしっ
I'M HURT...
AT THE TIME...
...I HAD NO IDEA THAT THE EVENTS AT THE WATERFALL ...
...WOULD TURN OUT TO BE SO HEART-BREAKING.
Unidentified Life Form Sighted?!
Eyewitness Interview

End of ★ 8th Period★

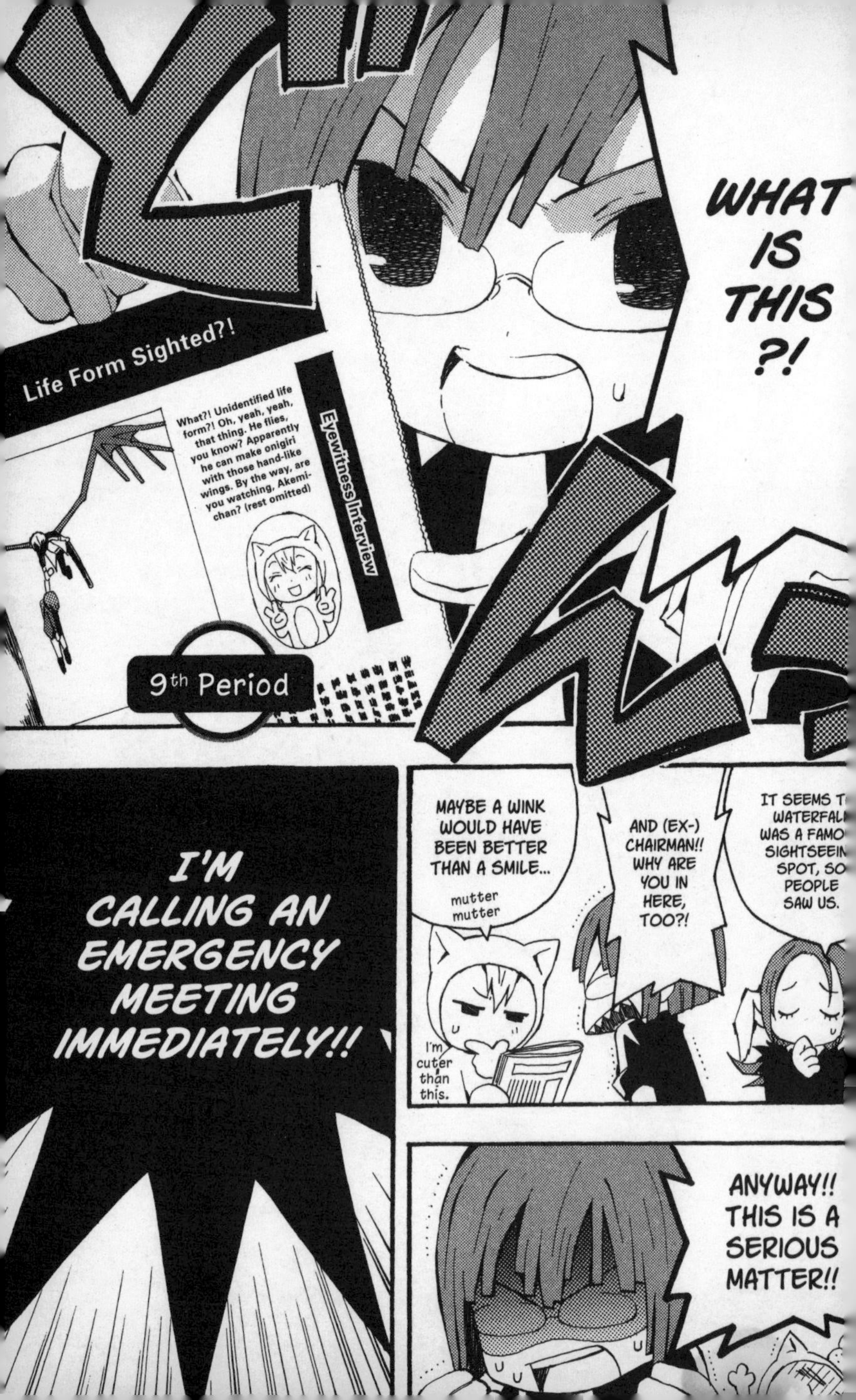
WHAT IS THIS?!
Life Form Sighted?!
Eyewitness Interview
What?! Unidentified life form?! Oh, yeah, yeah, that thing. He flies, you know? Apparently he can make onigiri with those hand-like wings. By the way, are you watching, Akemi-chan? (rest omitted)
9th Period
IT SEEMS T WATERFAL WAS A FAMO SIGHTSEEIN SPOT, SO PEOPLE SAW US.
AND (EX-) CHAIRMAN!! WHY ARE YOU IN HERE, TOO?!
MAYBE A WINK WOULD HAVE BEEN BETTER THAN A SMILE...
mutter mutter
I'm cuter than this.
ANYWAY!! THIS IS A SERIOUS MATTER!!
I'M CALLING AN EMERGENCY MEETING IMMEDIATELY!!

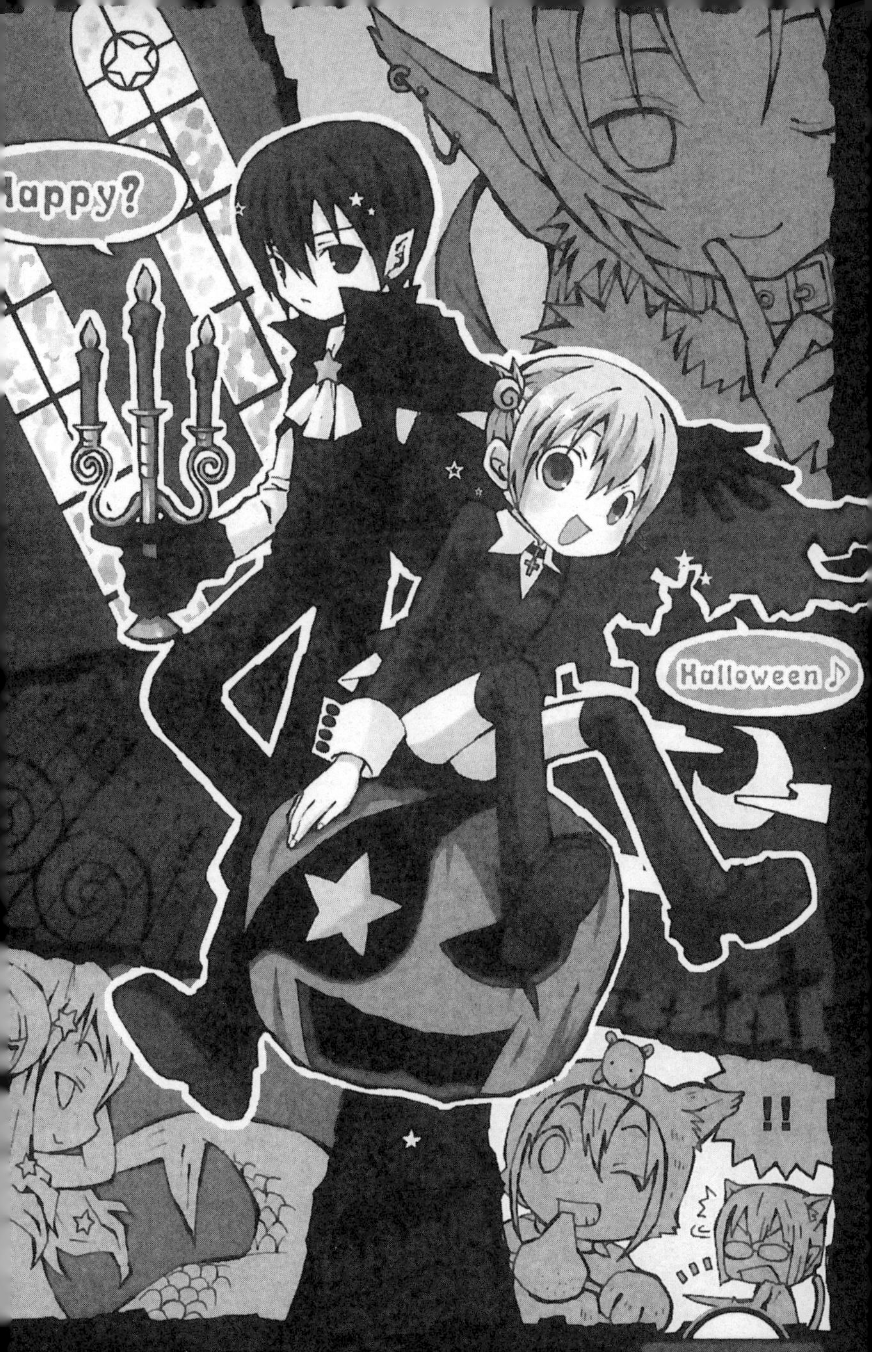
Happy?
Halloween ♪
!!

Cheers ★ A Romantic Halloween Flight ♪ 9th Period

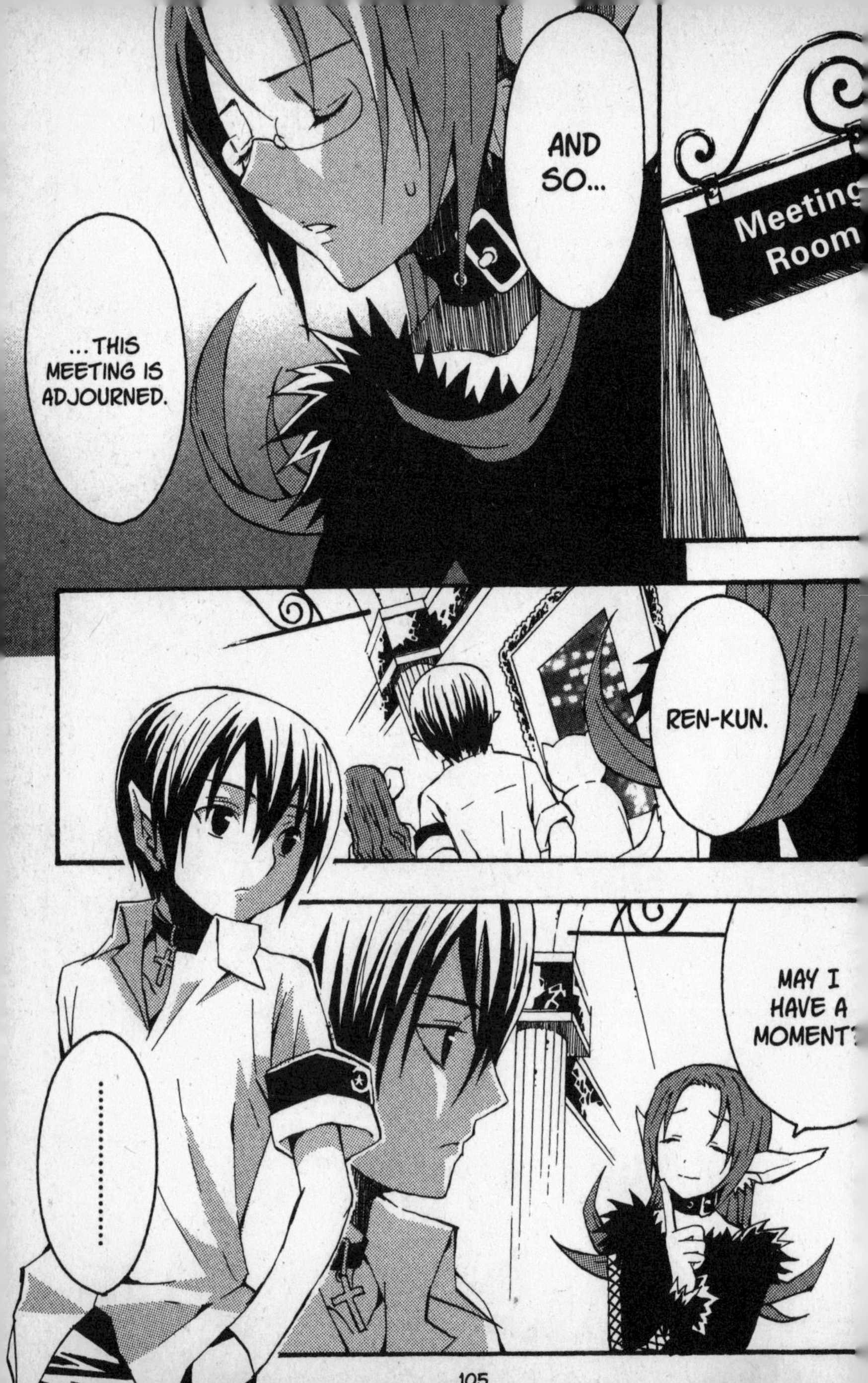
AND SO...
Meeting Room
...THIS MEETING IS ADJOURNED.
REN-KUN.
MAY I HAVE A MOMENT?
....

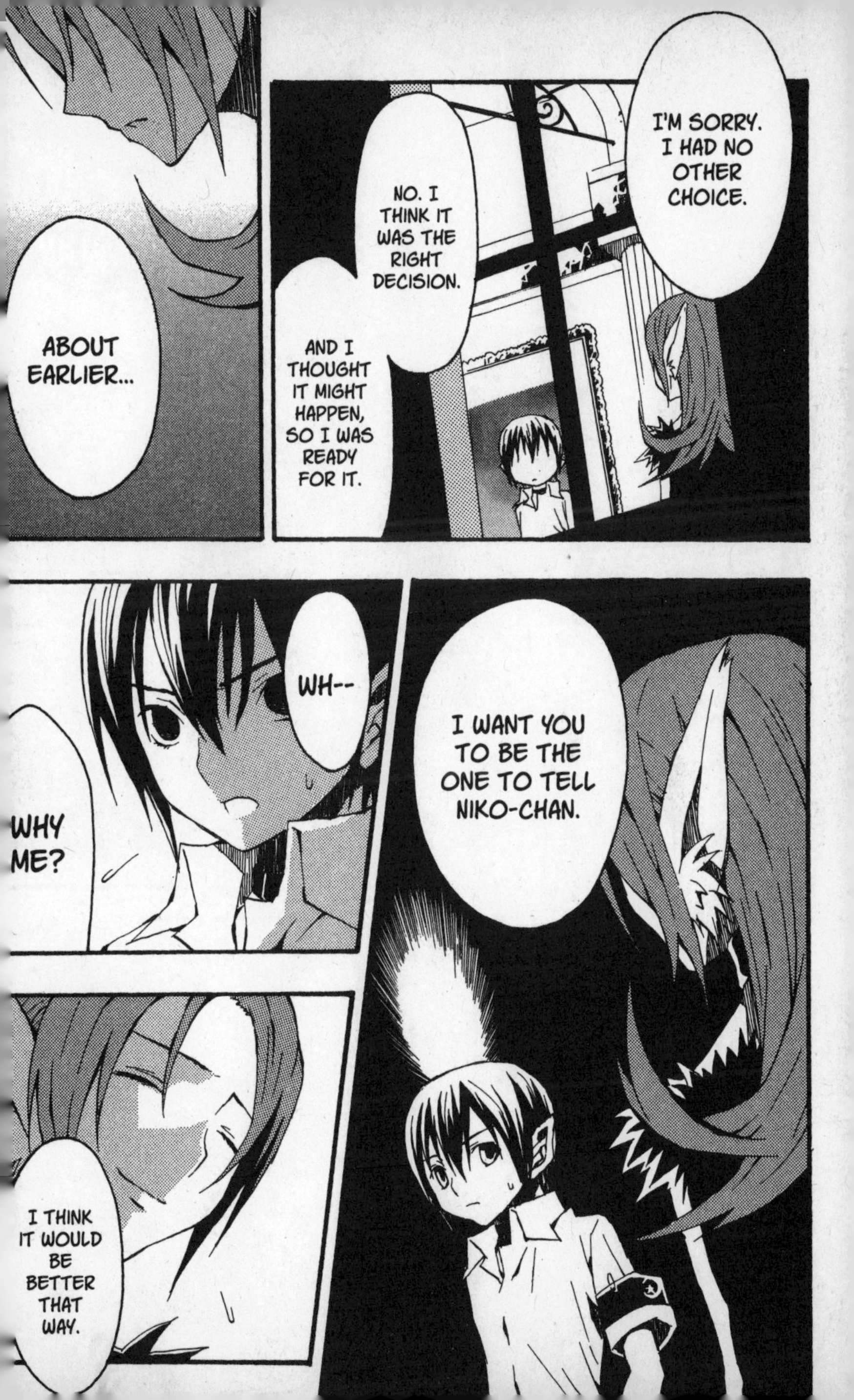
I'M SORRY. I HAD NO OTHER CHOICE.
NO. I THINK IT WAS THE RIGHT DECISION.
AND I THOUGHT IT MIGHT HAPPEN, SO I WAS READY FOR IT.
ABOUT EARLIER...
I WANT YOU TO BE THE ONE TO TELL NIKO-CHAN.
WH--
WHY ME?
I THINK IT WOULD BE BETTER THAT WAY.

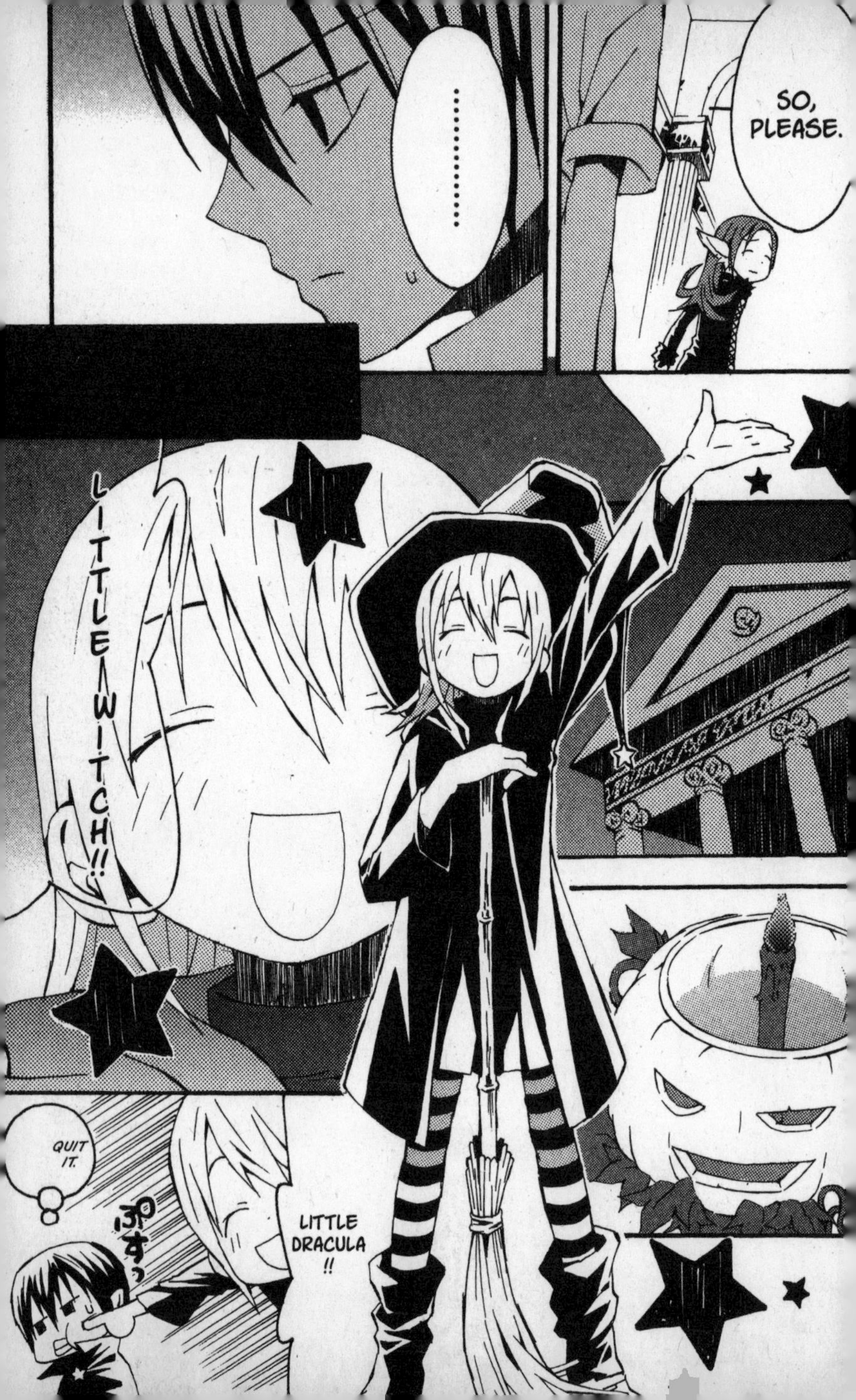
SO, PLEASE.
......
LITTLE WITCH!!
LITTLE DRACULA!!
QUIT IT.
ぷすっ

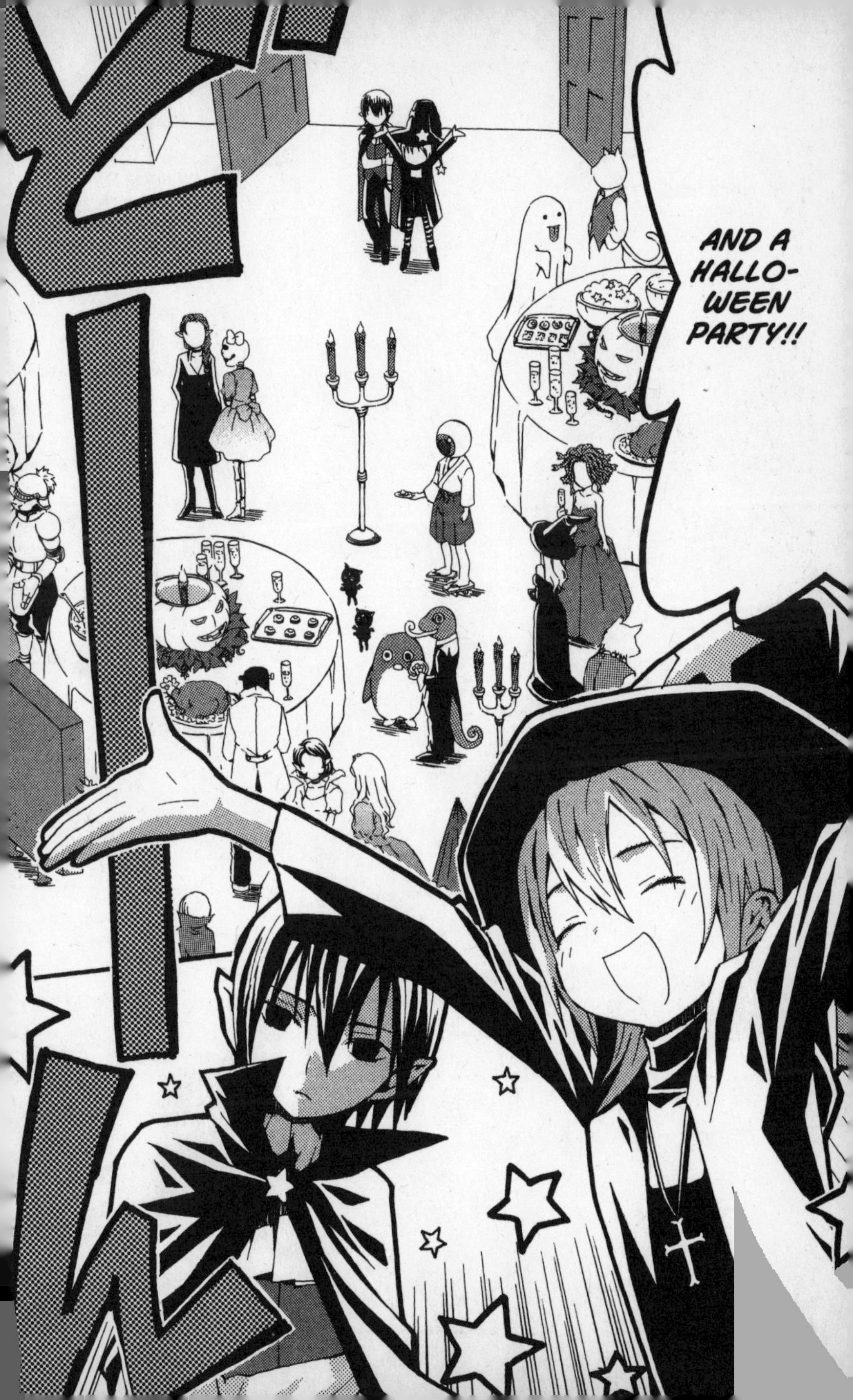
AND A HALLO-WEEN PARTY!!

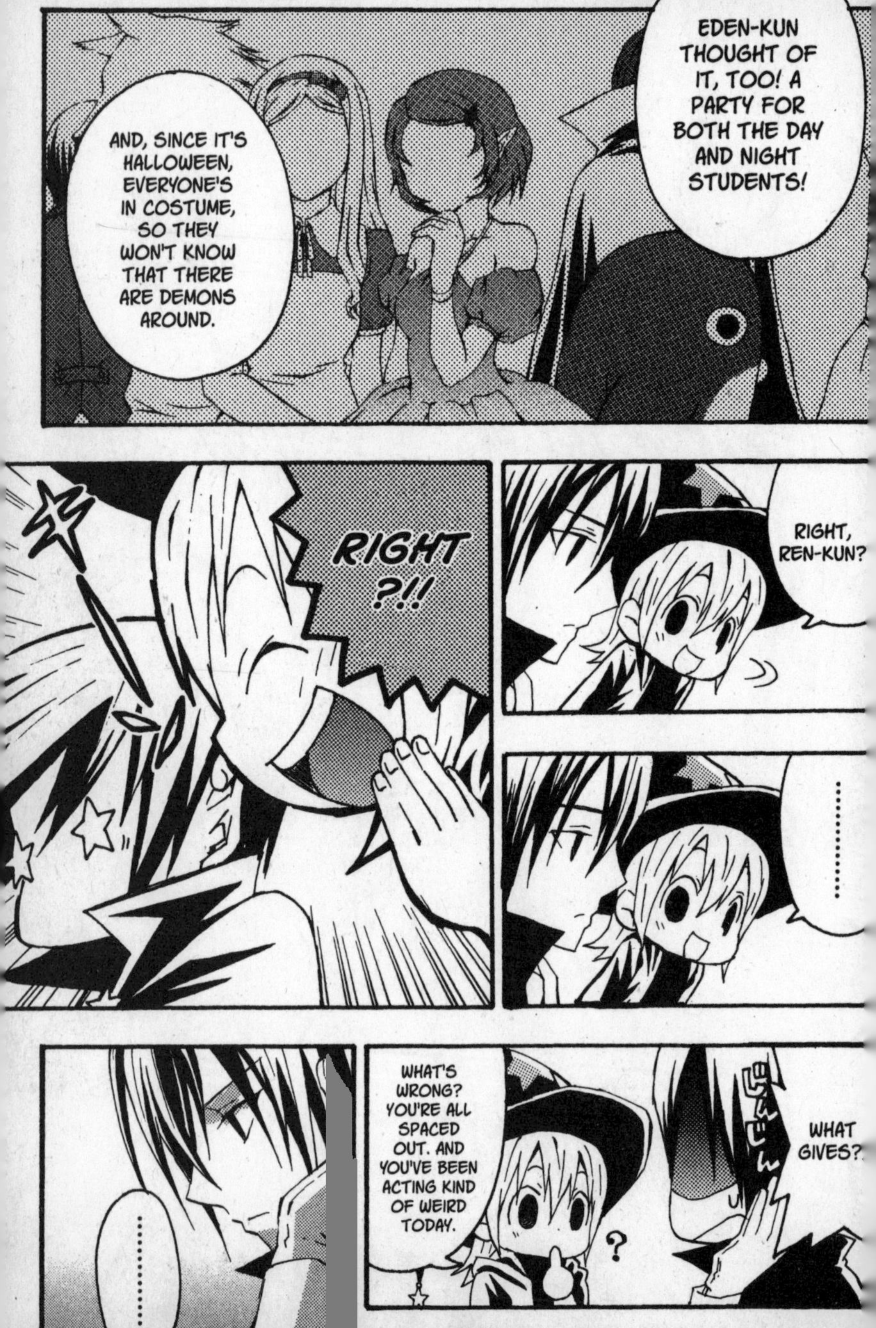
EDEN-KUN THOUGHT OF IT, TOO! A PARTY FOR BOTH THE DAY AND NIGHT STUDENTS!
AND, SINCE IT'S HALLOWEEN, EVERYONE'S IN COSTUME, SO THEY WON'T KNOW THAT THERE ARE DEMONS AROUND.
RIGHT, REN-KUN?
......
RIGHT ?!!
WHAT GIVES?
WHAT'S WRONG? YOU'RE ALL SPACED OUT. AND YOU'VE BEEN ACTING KIND OF WEIRD TODAY.
?
......

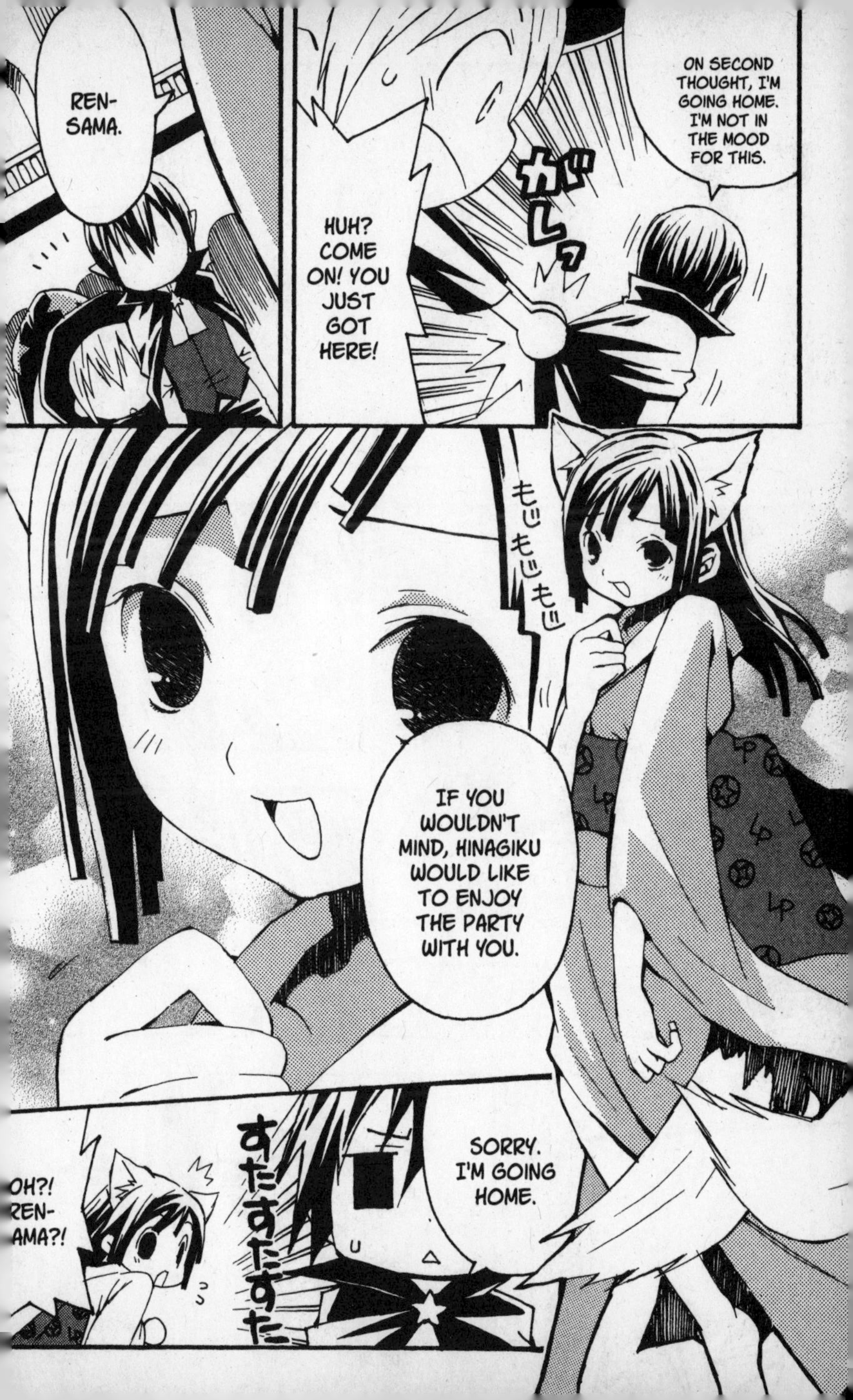
ON SECOND THOUGHT, I'M GOING HOME. I'M NOT IN THE MOOD FOR THIS.
がしっ
HUH? COME ON! YOU JUST GOT HERE!
REN-SAMA.
もじもじもじ
IF YOU WOULDN'T MIND, HINAGIKU WOULD LIKE TO ENJOY THE PARTY WITH YOU.
SORRY. I'M GOING HOME.
すたすたすた
OH?! REN-AMA?!

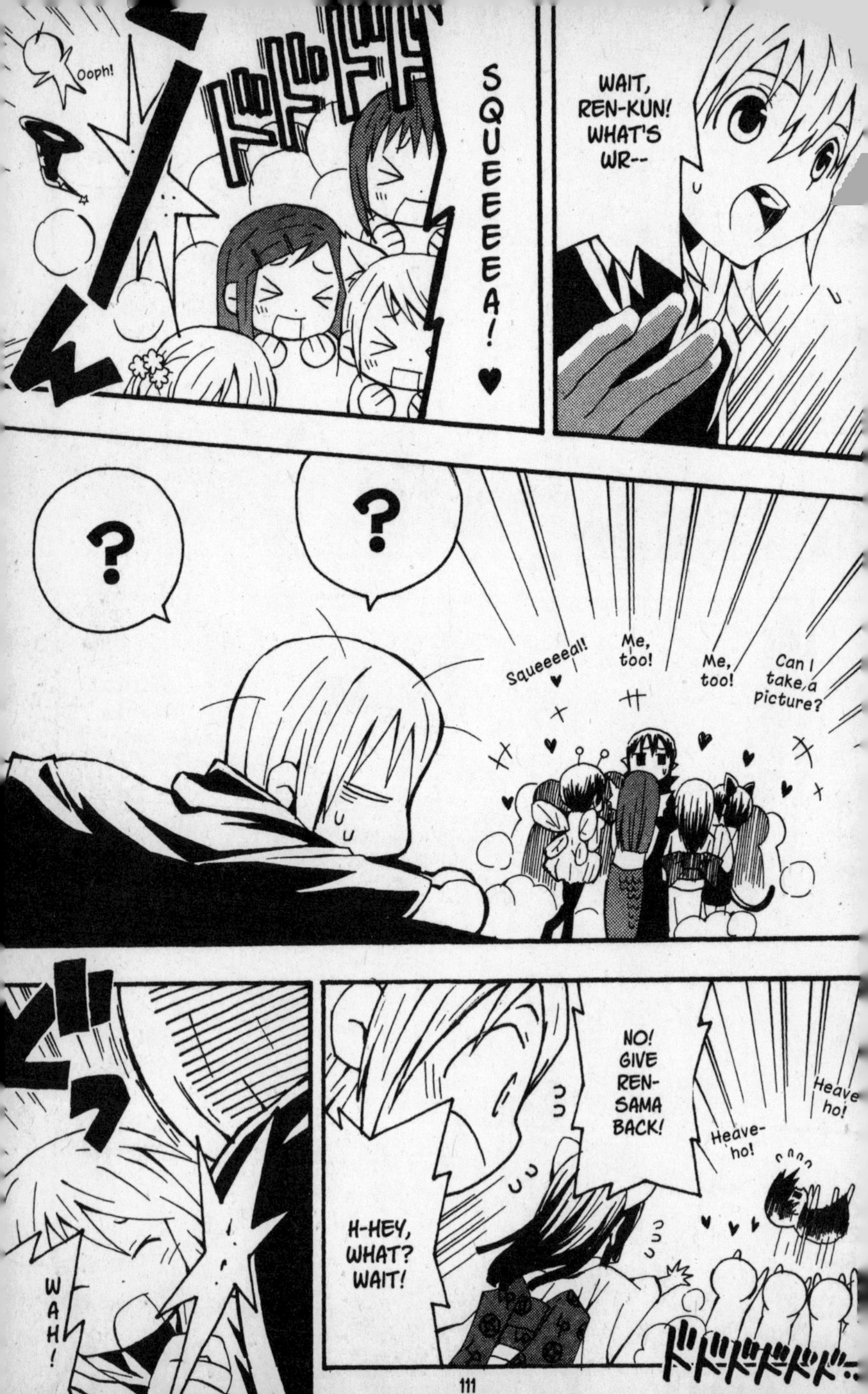
WAIT, REN-KUN! WHAT'S WR--
SQUEEEEEA! ♥
Ooph!
Can I take a picture?
Me, too!
Me, too!
Squeeeeeal! ♥
?
?
NO! GIVE REN-SAMA BACK!
Heave ho!
Heave-ho!
H-HEY, WHAT? WAIT!
WAH!

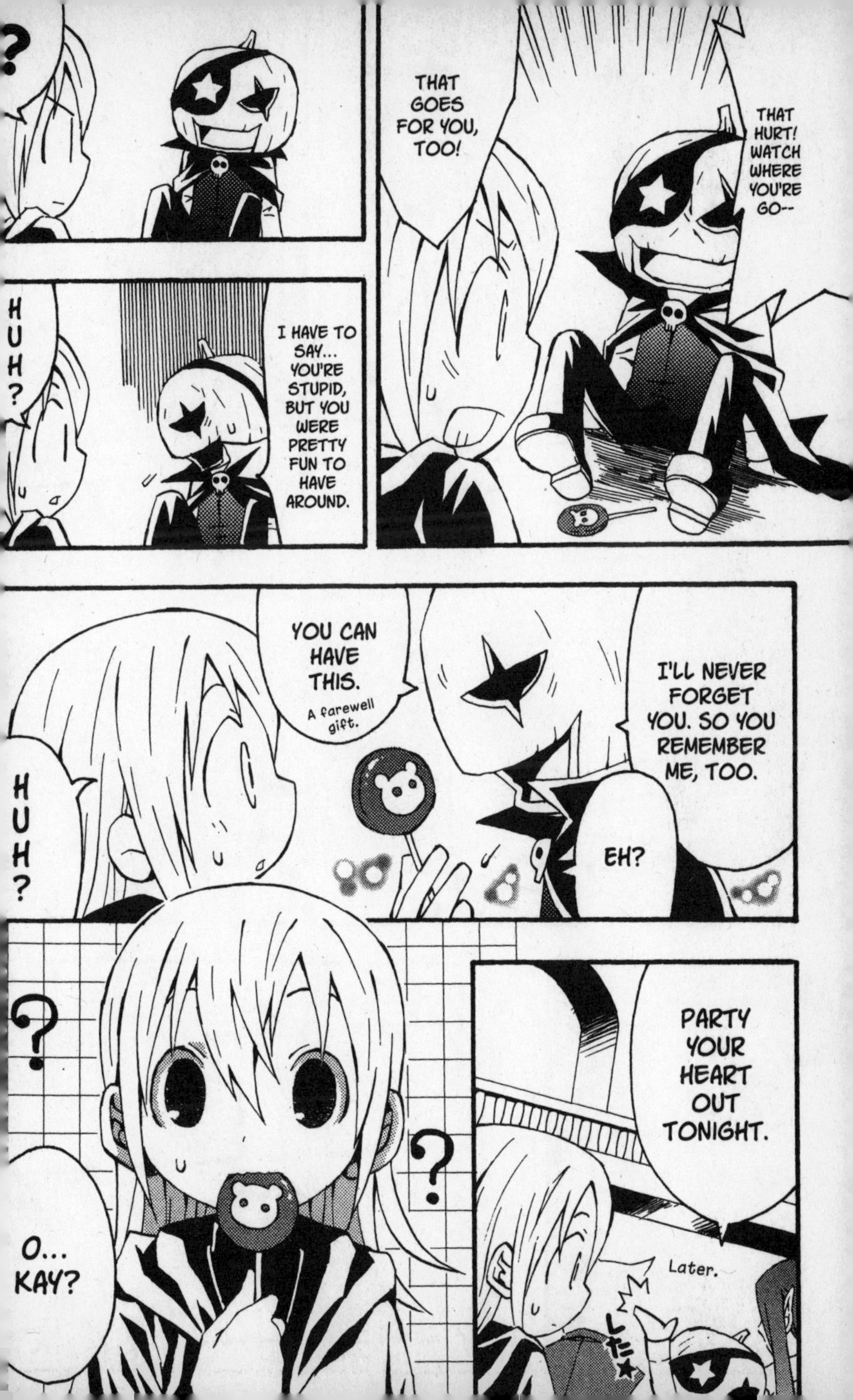
THAT HURT! WATCH WHERE YOU'RE GO--
THAT GOES FOR YOU, TOO!
?
I HAVE TO SAY... YOU'RE STUPID, BUT YOU WERE PRETTY FUN TO HAVE AROUND.
HUH?
I'LL NEVER FORGET YOU. SO YOU REMEMBER ME, TOO.
YOU CAN HAVE THIS.
A farewell gift.
EH?
HUH?
PARTY YOUR HEART OUT TONIGHT.
Later.
?
?
O... KAY?

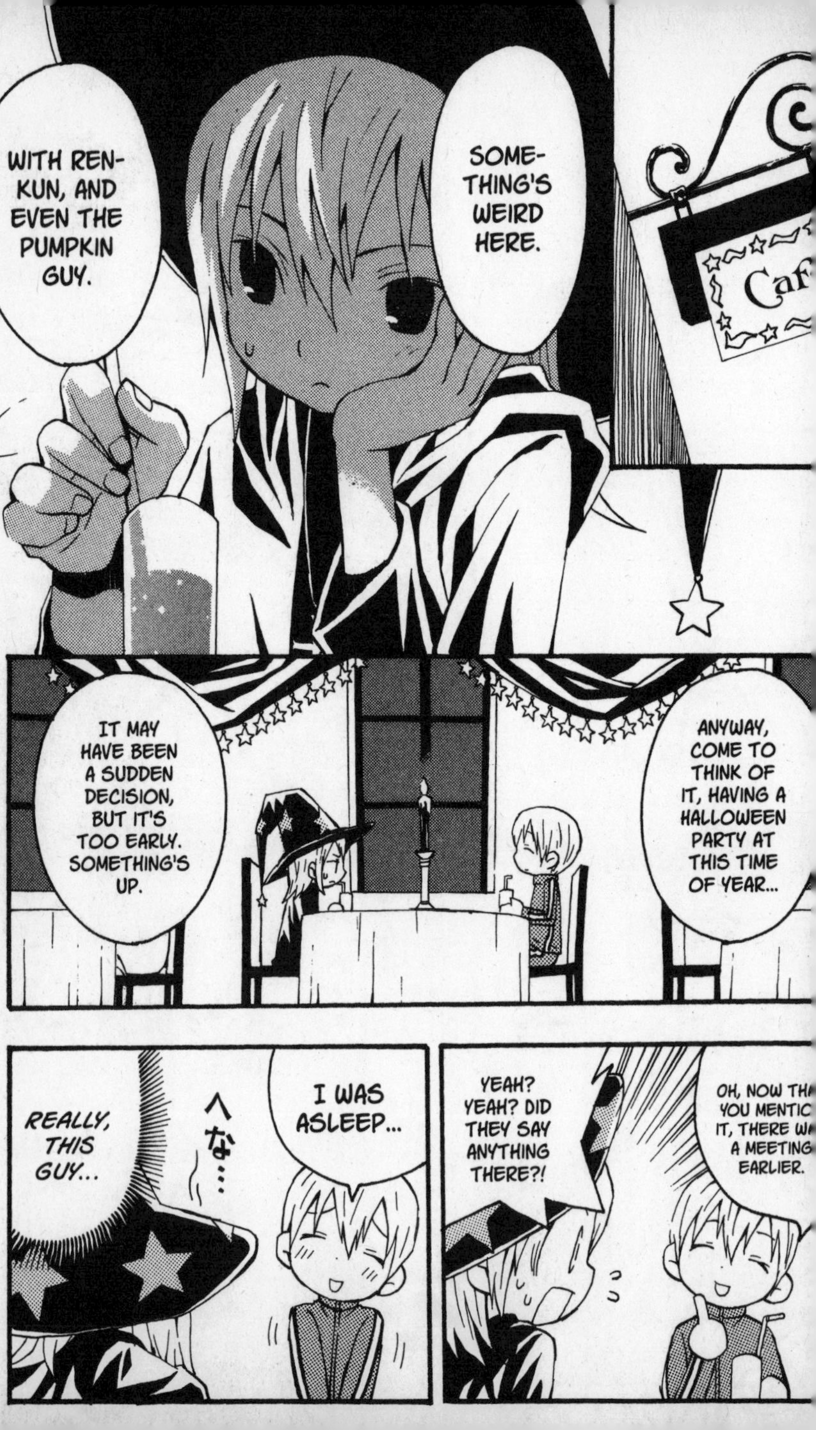
SOME-THING'S WEIRD HERE.
WITH REN-KUN, AND EVEN THE PUMPKIN GUY.
ANYWAY, COME TO THINK OF IT, HAVING A HALLOWEEN PARTY AT THIS TIME OF YEAR...
IT MAY HAVE BEEN A SUDDEN DECISION, BUT IT'S TOO EARLY. SOMETHING'S UP.
OH, NOW THA YOU MENTIC IT, THERE WA A MEETING EARLIER.
YEAH? YEAH? DID THEY SAY ANYTHING THERE?!
I WAS ASLEEP...
へな…
REALLY, THIS GUY...

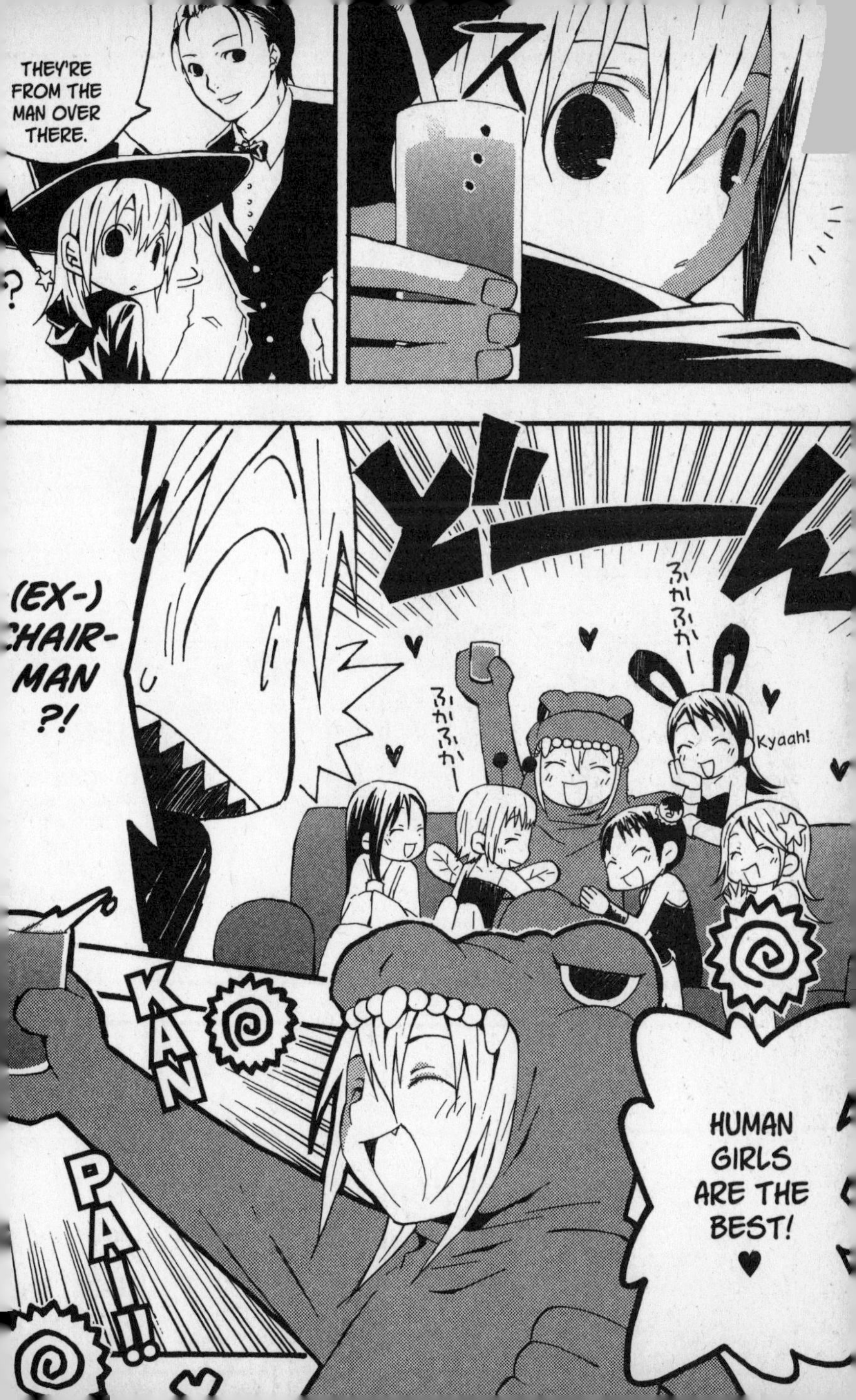

THEY'RE FROM THE MAN OVER THERE.
?
ふかふかー
Kyaah!
HUMAN GIRLS ARE THE BEST! ♥
ふかふかー
(EX-) CHAIRMAN ?!
KAN PAI!!

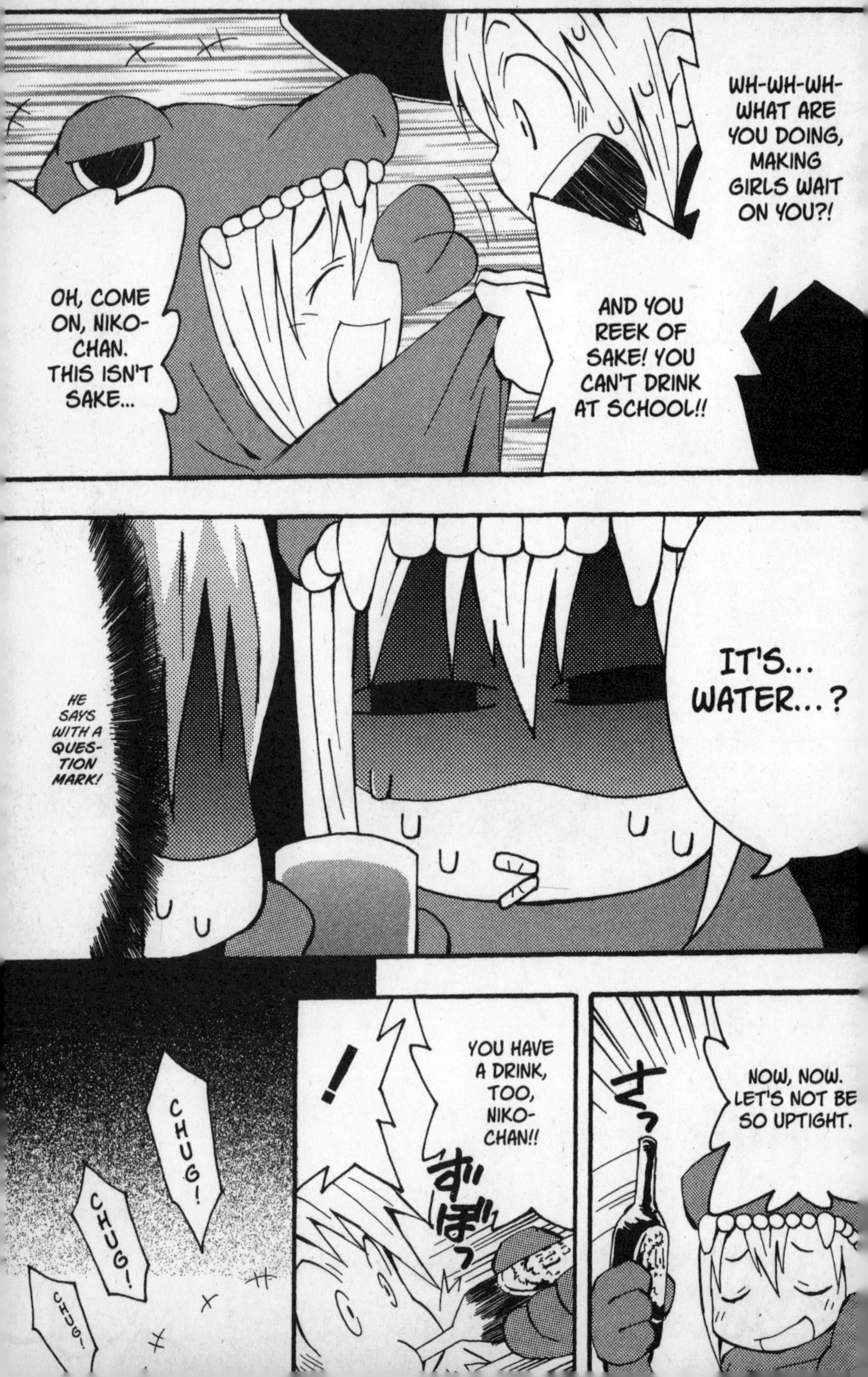

WH-WH-WH-WHAT ARE YOU DOING, MAKING GIRLS WAIT ON YOU?!
AND YOU REEK OF SAKE! YOU CAN'T DRINK AT SCHOOL!!
OH, COME ON, NIKO-CHAN. THIS ISN'T SAKE...
IT'S... WATER...?
HE SAYS WITH A QUESTION MARK!
NOW, NOW. LET'S NOT BE SO UPTIGHT.
さっ
YOU HAVE A DRINK, TOO, NIKO-CHAN!!
!
ずぼっ
CHUG!
CHUG!
CHUG!

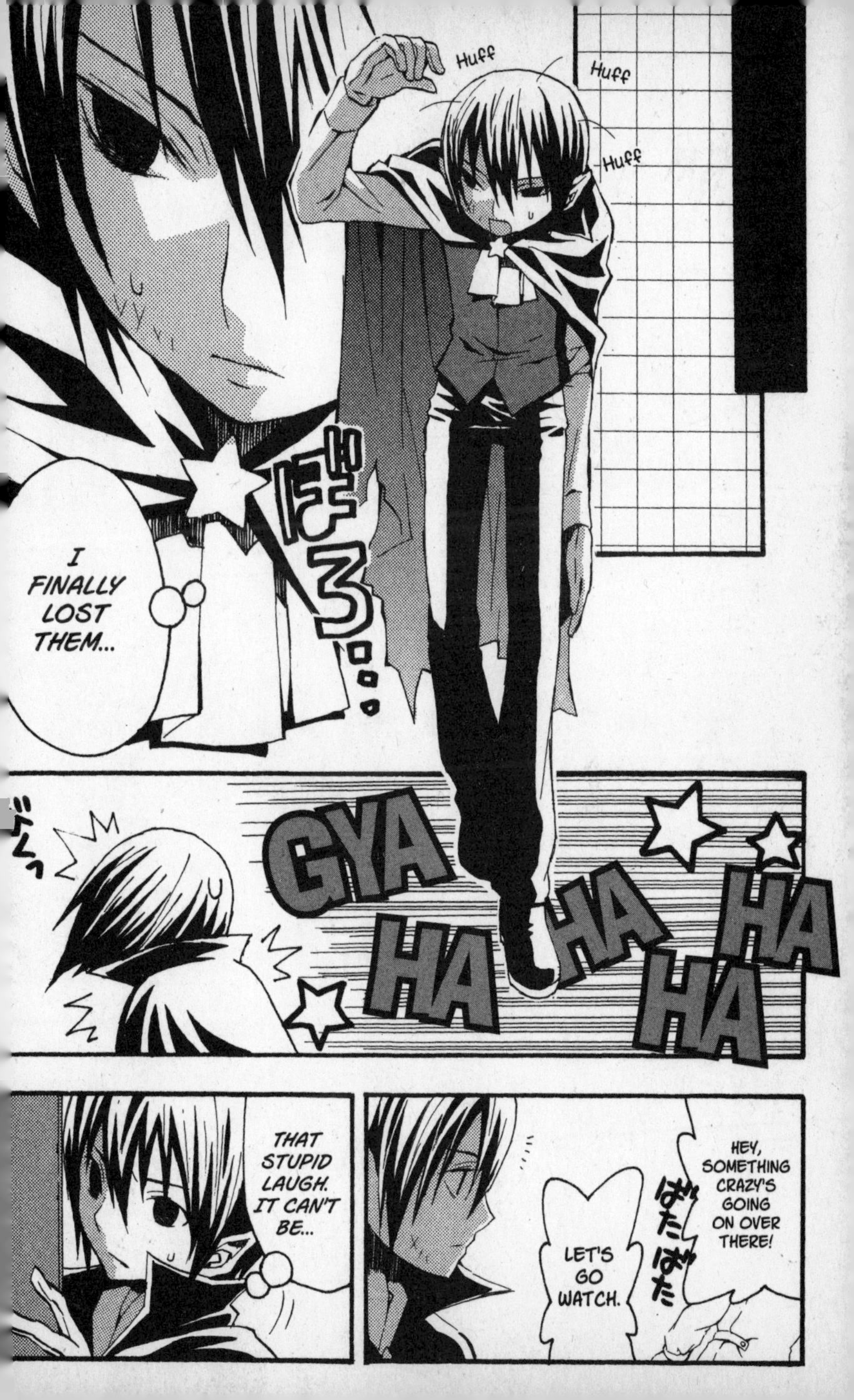

Huff
Huff
Huff
I FINALLY LOST THEM...
GYA HA HA HA HA
HEY, SOMETHING CRAZY'S GOING ON OVER THERE!
ばたばた
LET'S GO WATCH.
THAT STUPID LAUGH. IT CAN'T BE...

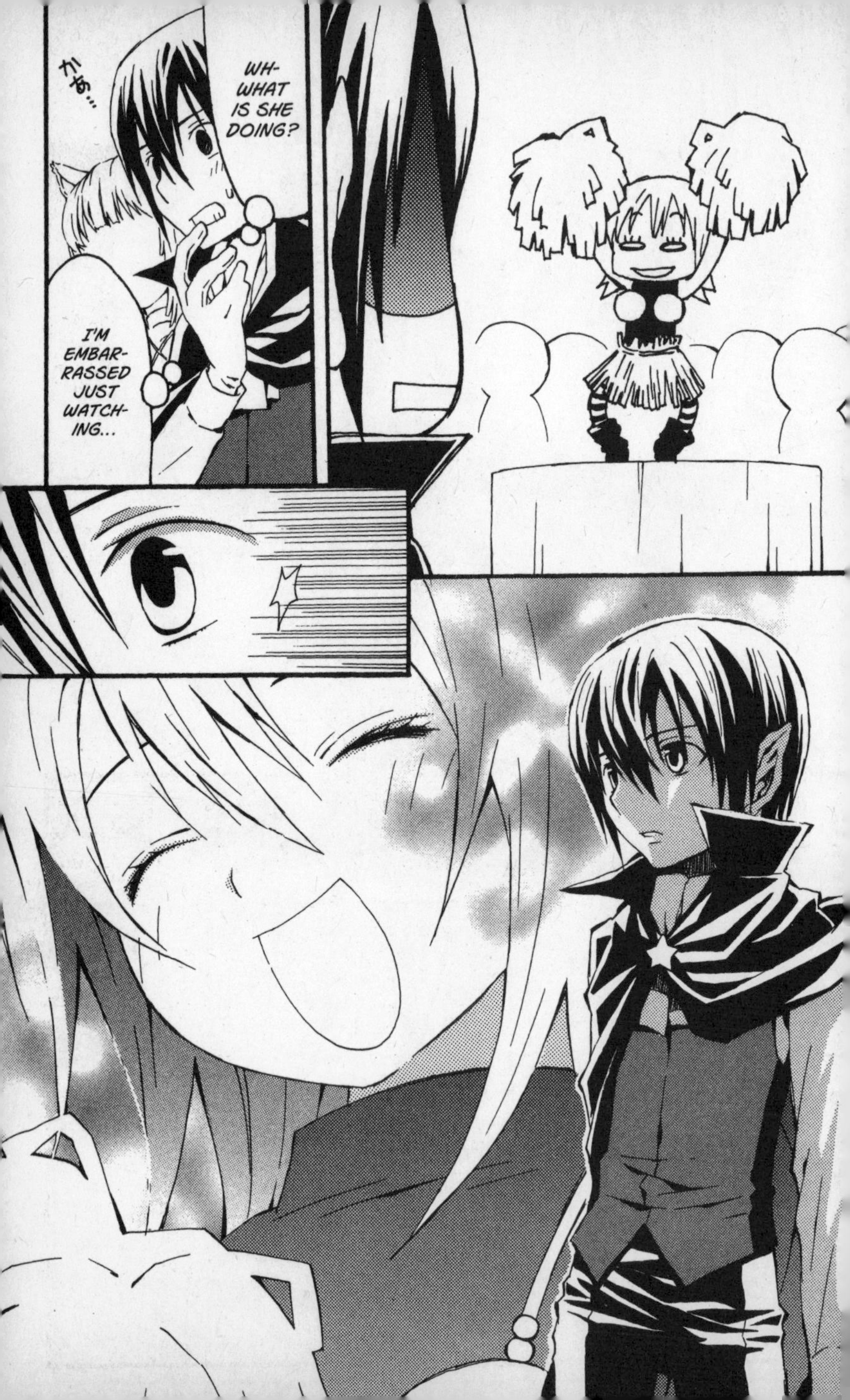
WH- WHAT IS SHE DOING?
かぁ…
I'M EMBARRASSED JUST WATCHING...

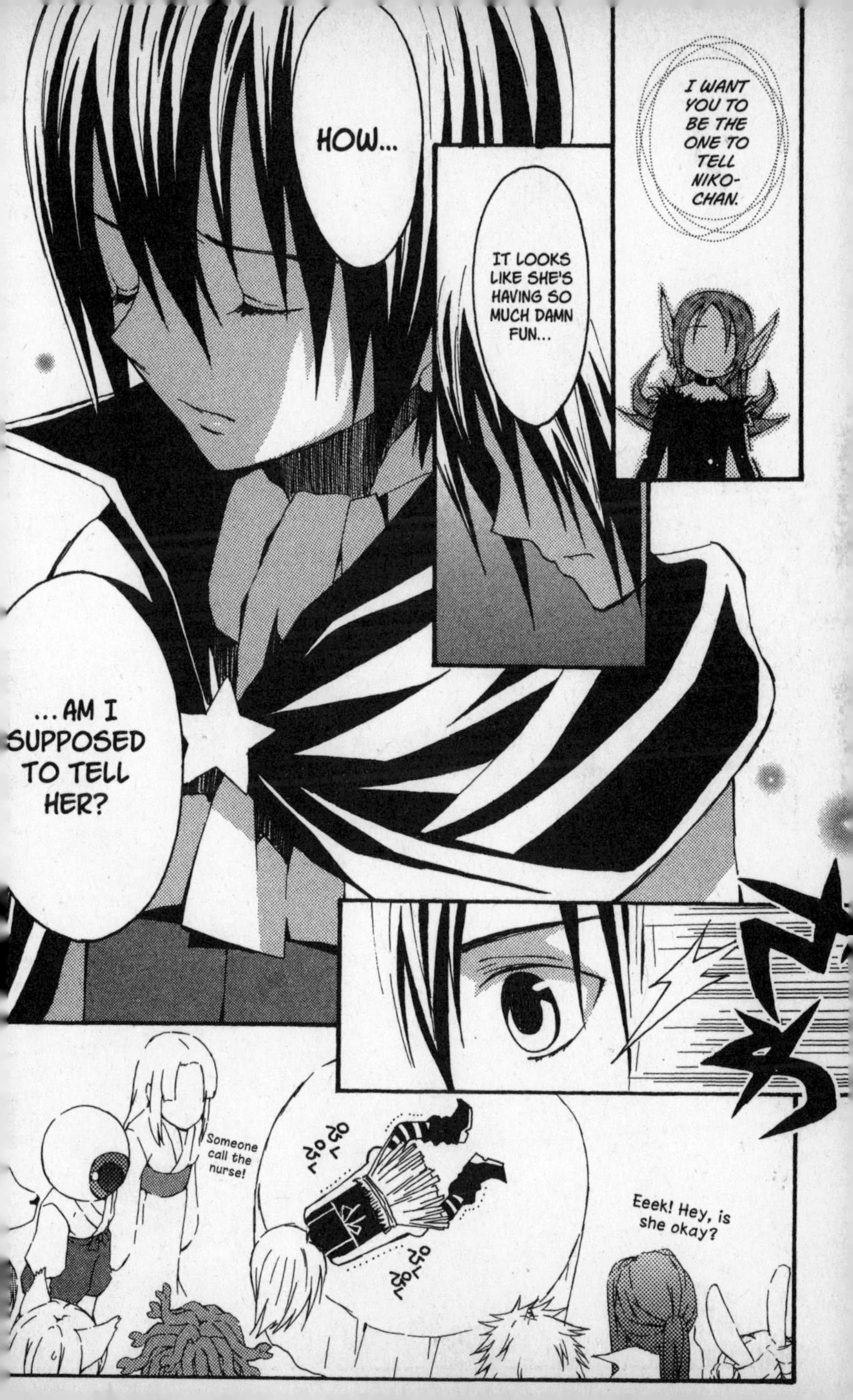
I WANT YOU TO BE THE ONE TO TELL NIKO-CHAN.
IT LOOKS LIKE SHE'S HAVING SO MUCH DAMN FUN...
HOW...
...AM I SUPPOSED TO TELL HER?
Eeek! Hey, is she okay?
Someone call the nurse!

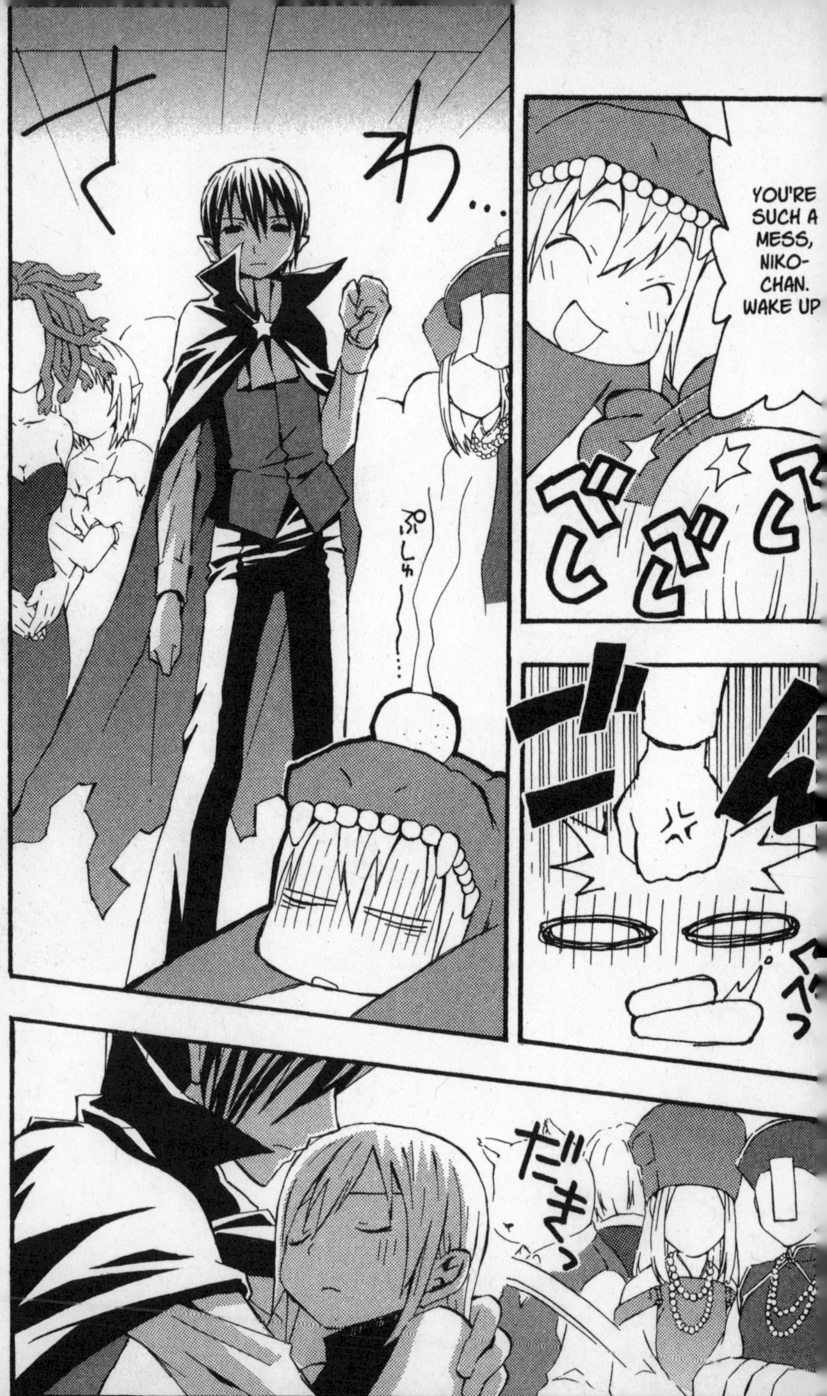

YOU'RE SUCH A MESS, NIKO-CHAN. WAKE UP
さわ…
ぷしゅ～～…
だきっ

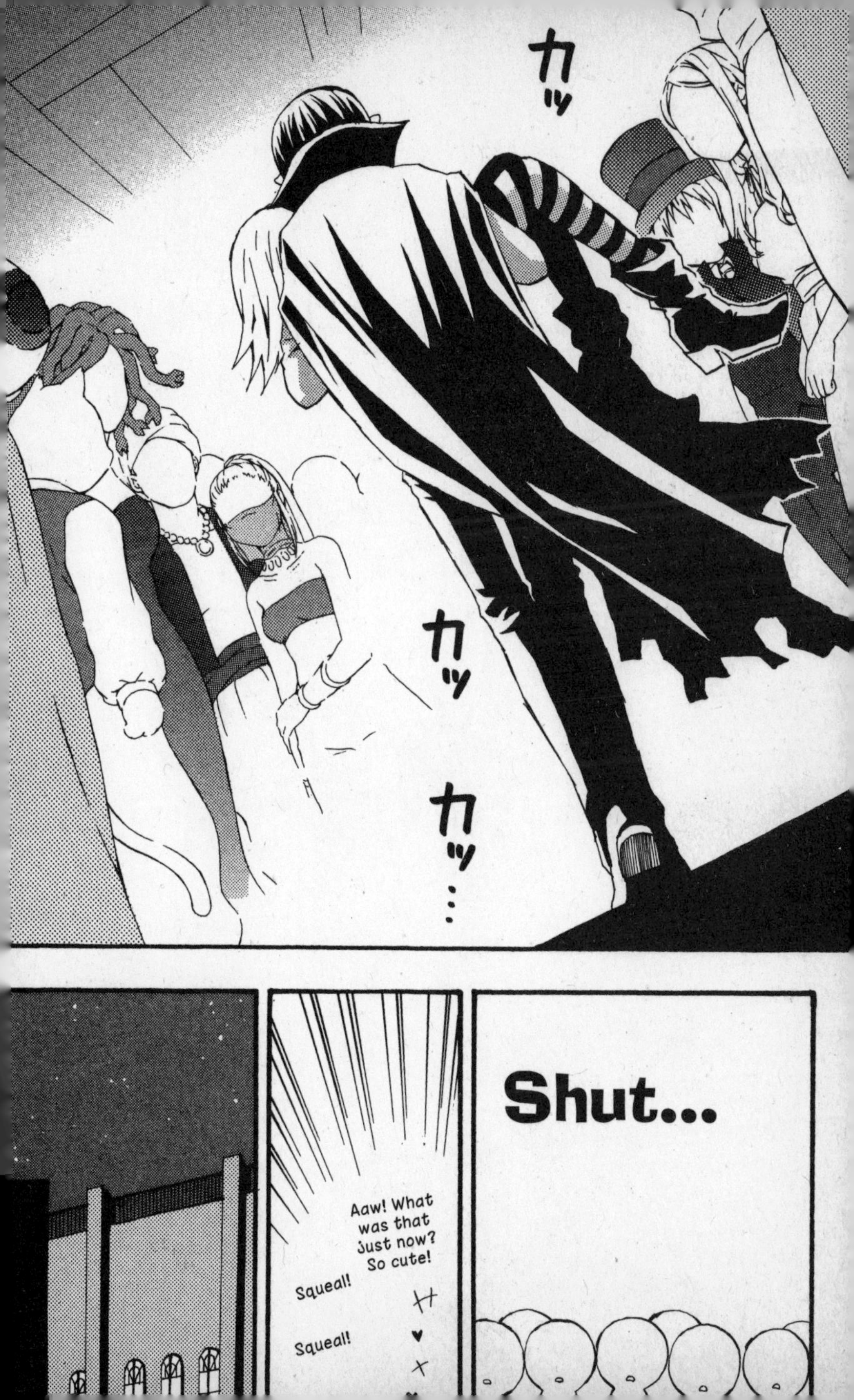
カッ
カッ
カッ…
Shut...
Aaw! What was that just now? So cute!
Squeal!
Squeal!

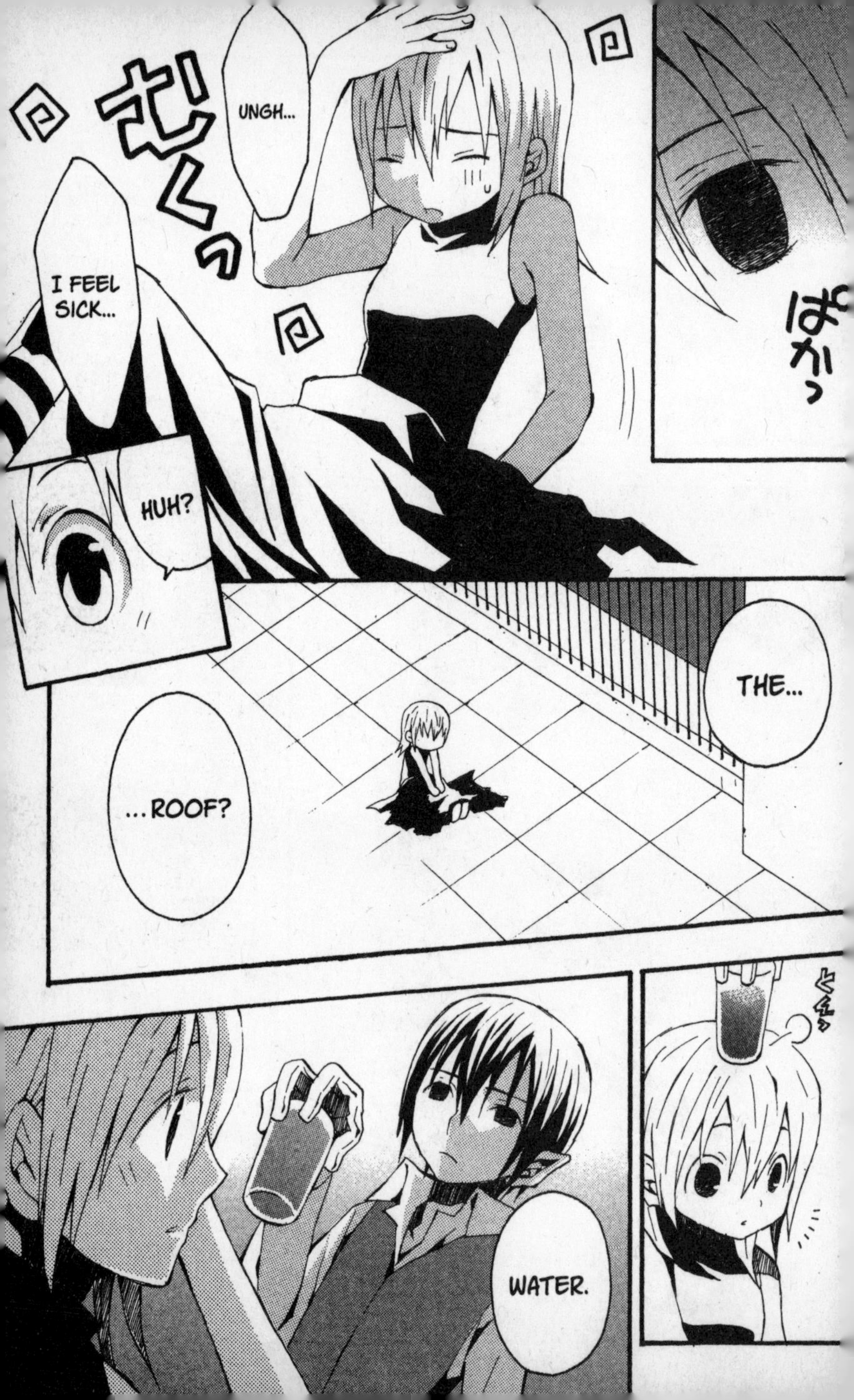
ぱかっ
むくっ
UNGH...
I FEEL SICK...
HUH?
THE...
...ROOF?
WATER.

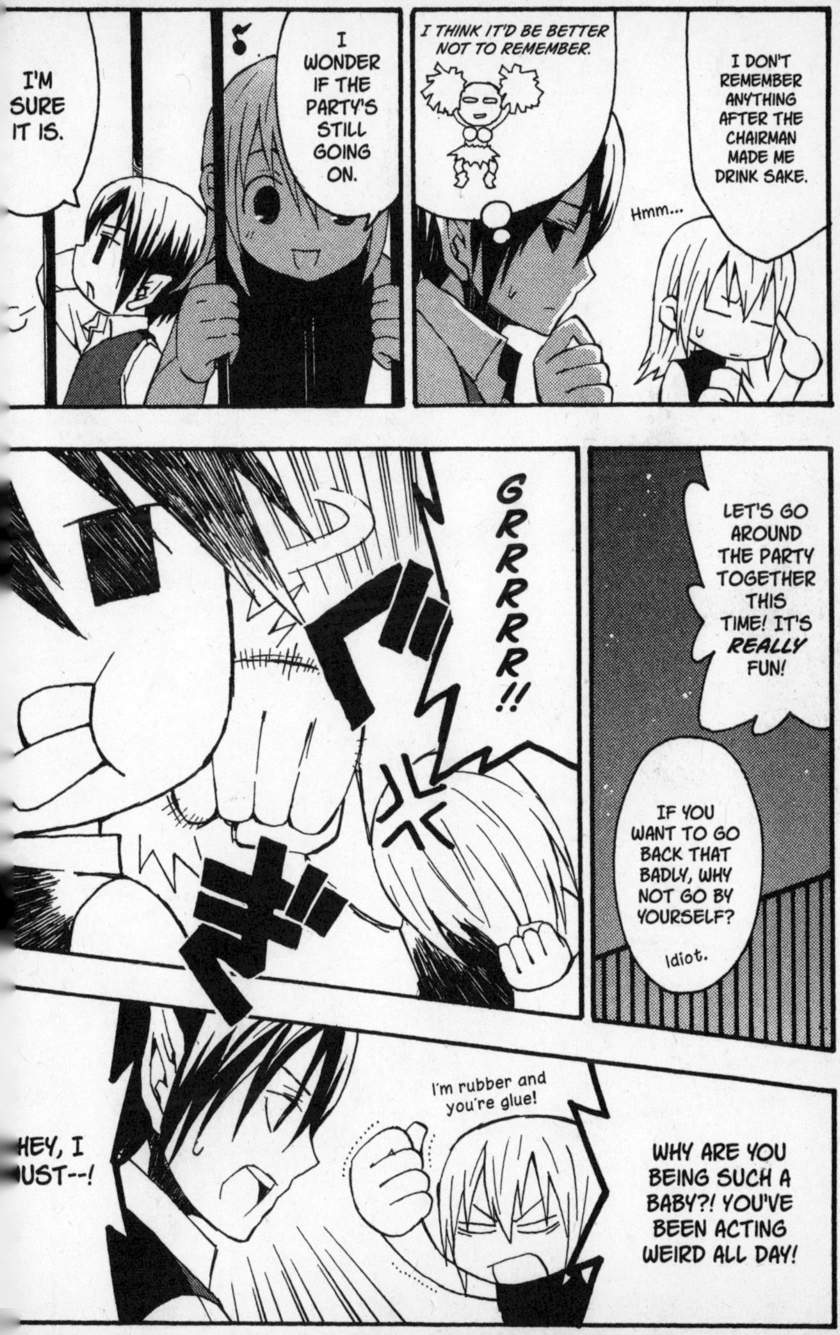
I DON'T REMEMBER ANYTHING AFTER THE CHAIRMAN MADE ME DRINK SAKE.
Hmm...
I THINK IT'D BE BETTER NOT TO REMEMBER.
I WONDER IF THE PARTY'S STILL GOING ON.
I'M SURE IT IS.
LET'S GO AROUND THE PARTY TOGETHER THIS TIME! IT'S REALLY FUN!
IF YOU WANT TO GO BACK THAT BADLY, WHY NOT GO BY YOURSELF?
Idiot.
GRRRRRR!!
WHY ARE YOU BEING SUCH A BABY?! YOU'VE BEEN ACTING WEIRD ALL DAY!
I'm rubber and you're glue!
HEY, I JUST--!

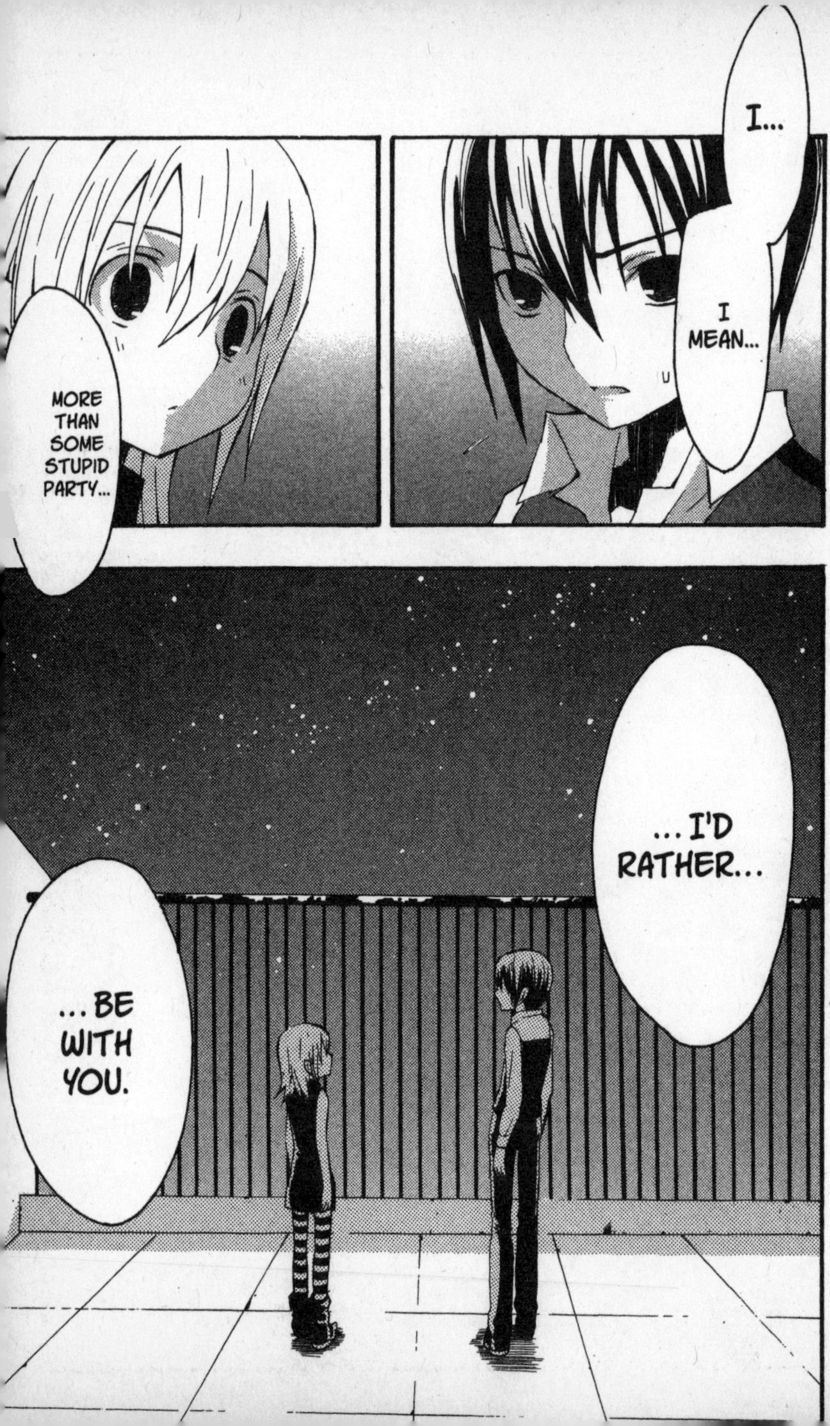
I...
I MEAN...
MORE THAN SOME STUPID PARTY...
... I'D RATHER...
... BE WITH YOU.

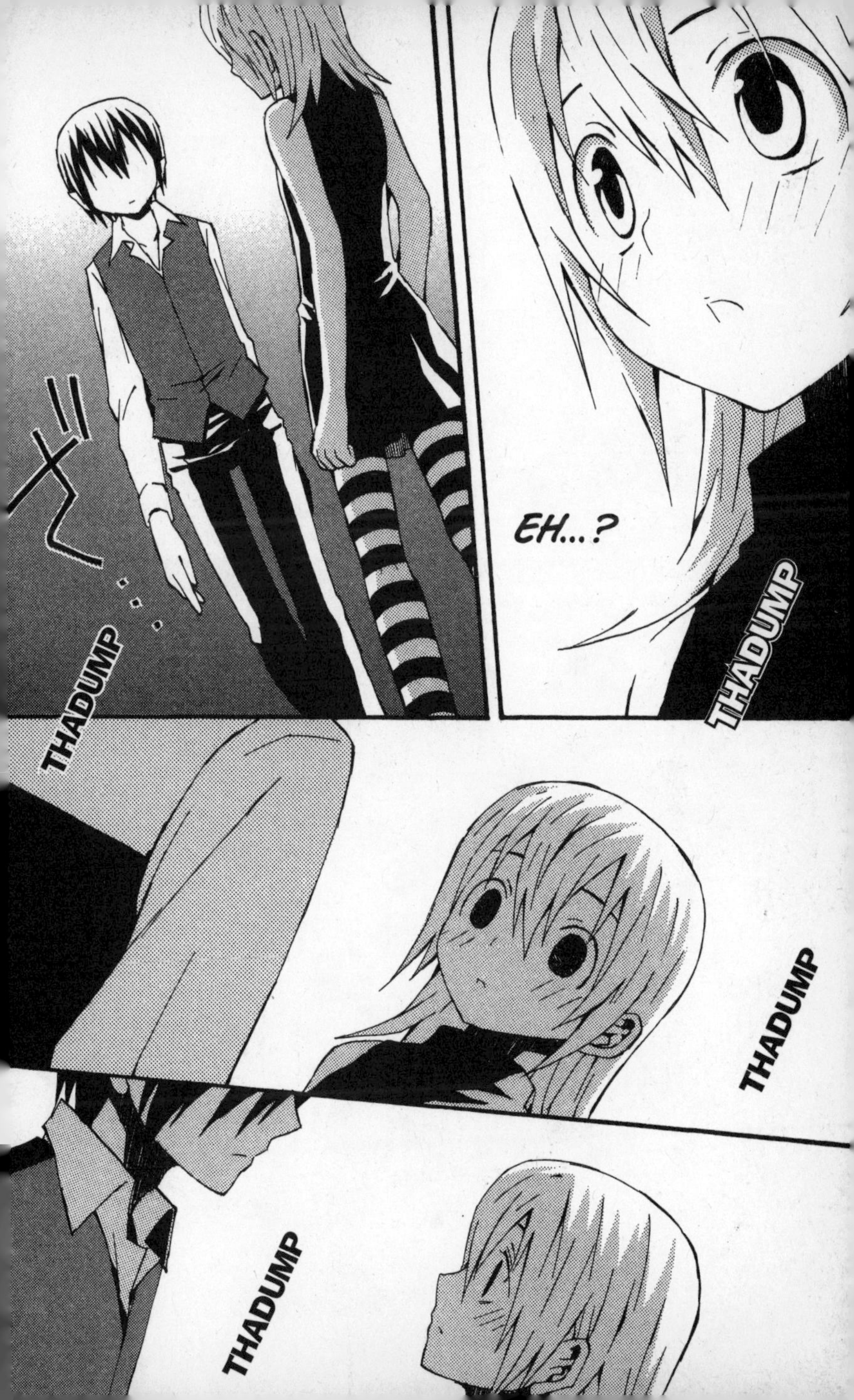
EH...?
THADUMP
THADUMP
THADUMP
THADUMP

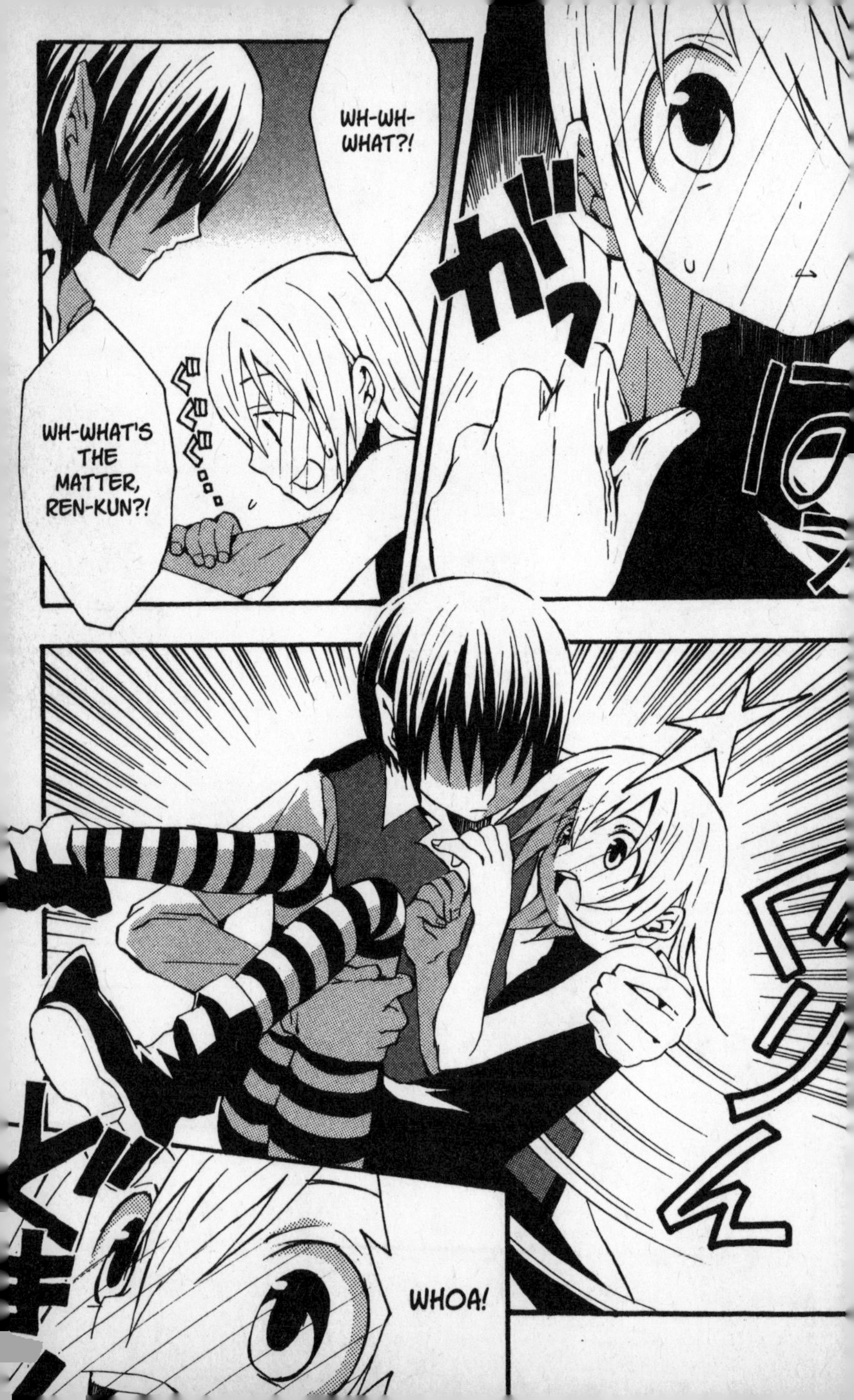
WH-WH-WHAT?!
WH-WHAT'S THE MATTER, REN-KUN?!
WHOA!

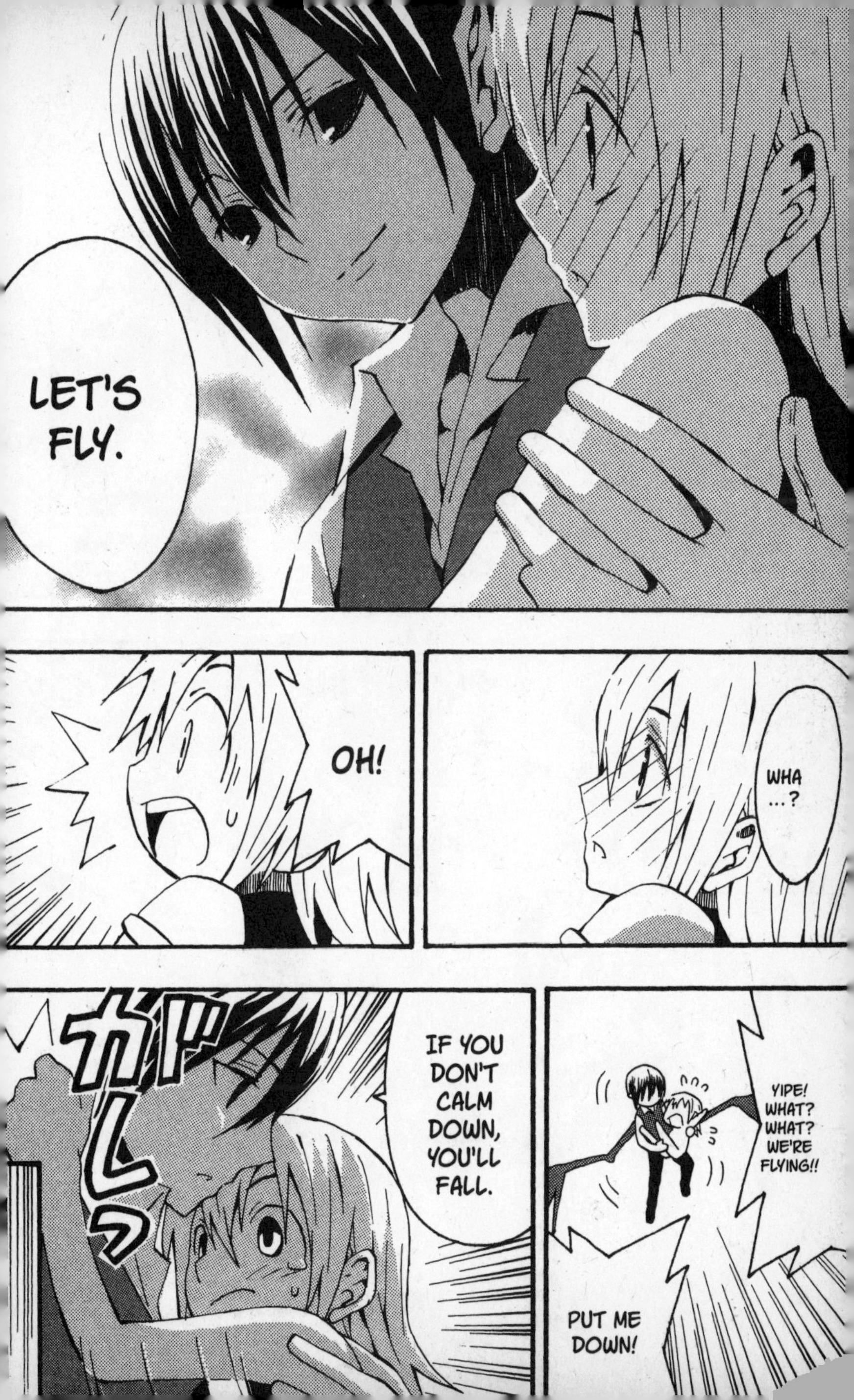
LET'S FLY.
WHA ...?
OH!
YIPE! WHAT? WHAT? WE'RE FLYING!!
PUT ME DOWN!
IF YOU DON'T CALM DOWN, YOU'LL FALL.
ガしっ

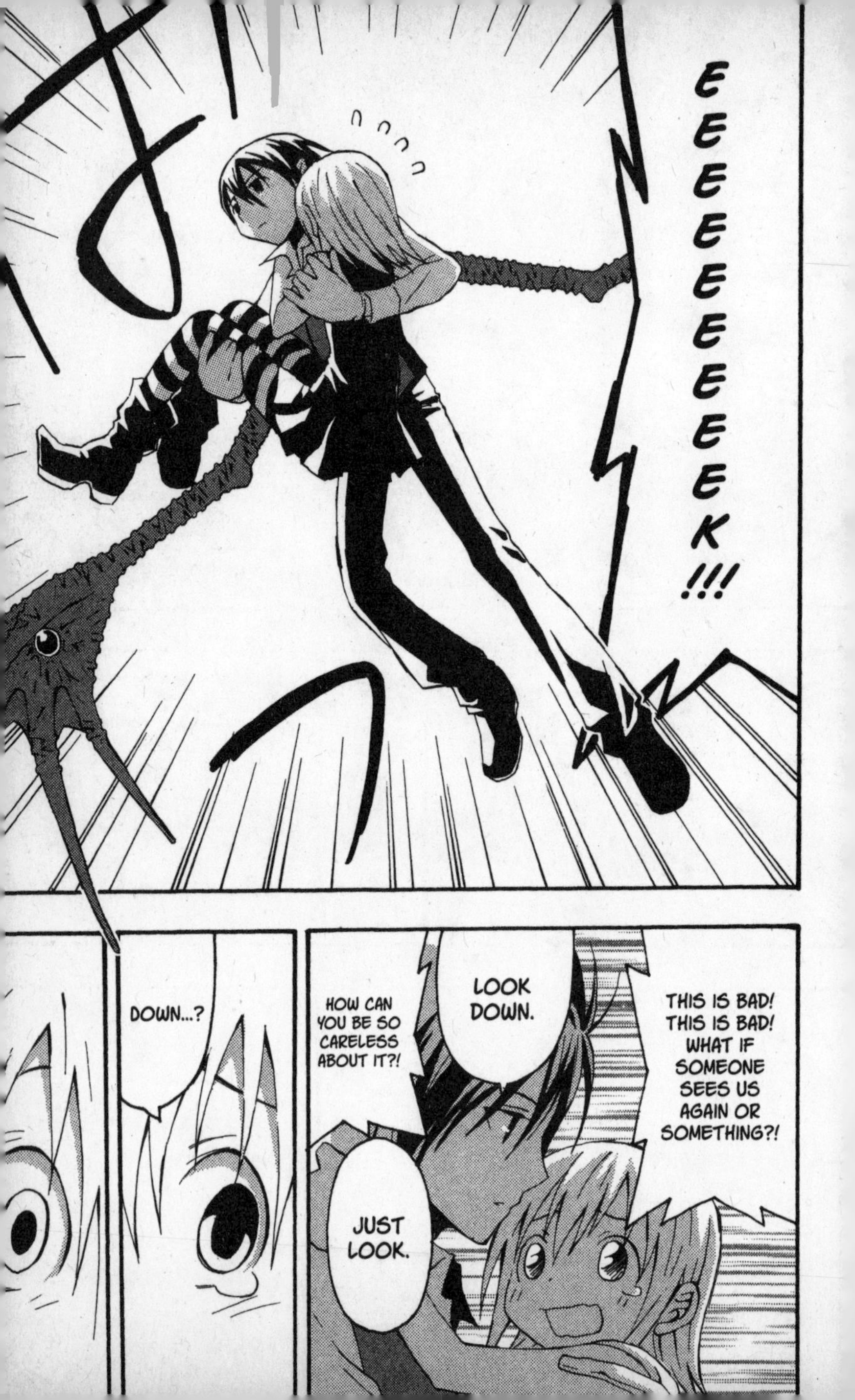
EEEEEEEEEK!!!
THIS IS BAD! THIS IS BAD! WHAT IF SOMEONE SEES US AGAIN OR SOMETHING?!
LOOK DOWN.
HOW CAN YOU BE SO CARELESS ABOUT IT?!
JUST LOOK.
DOWN...?

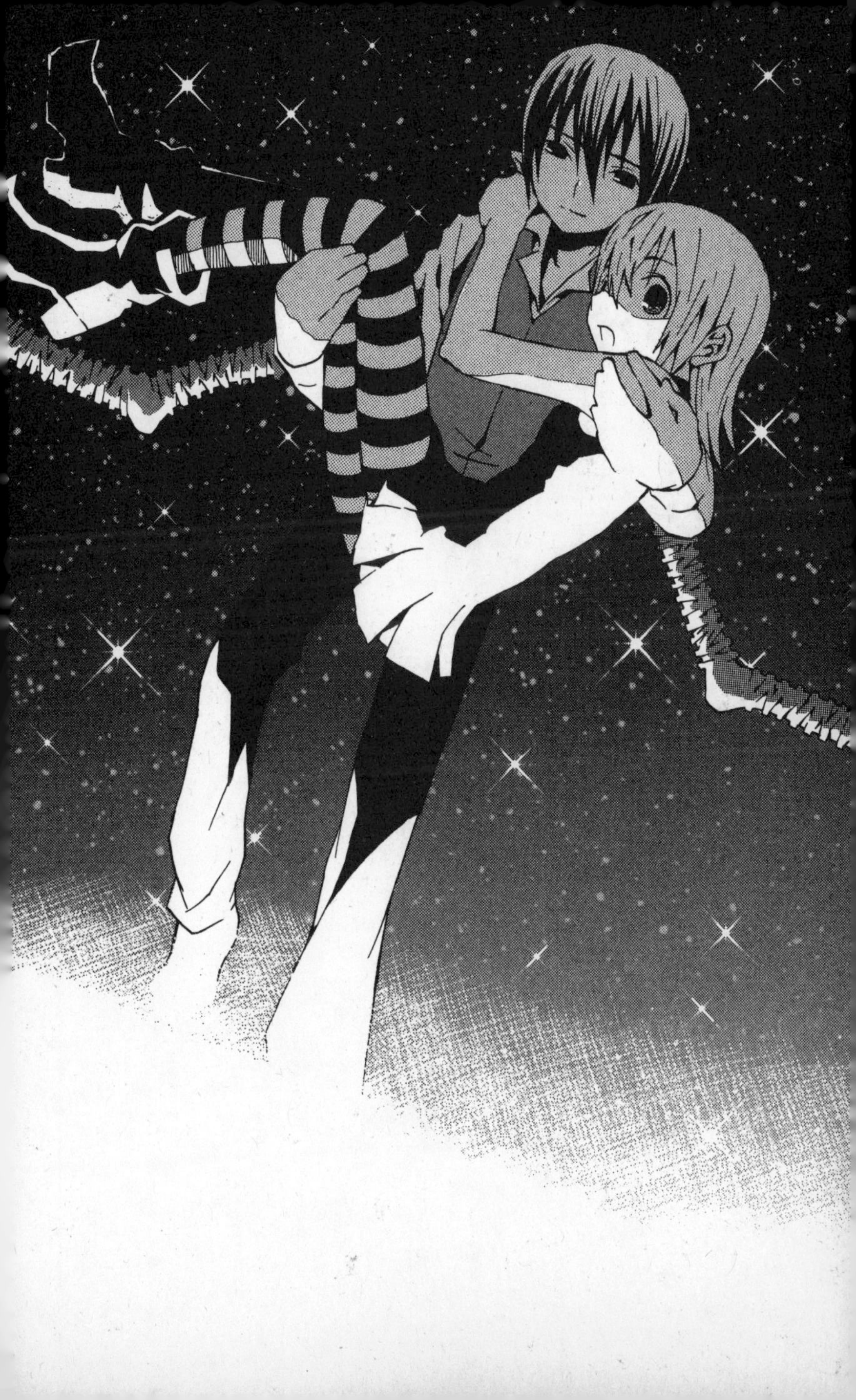

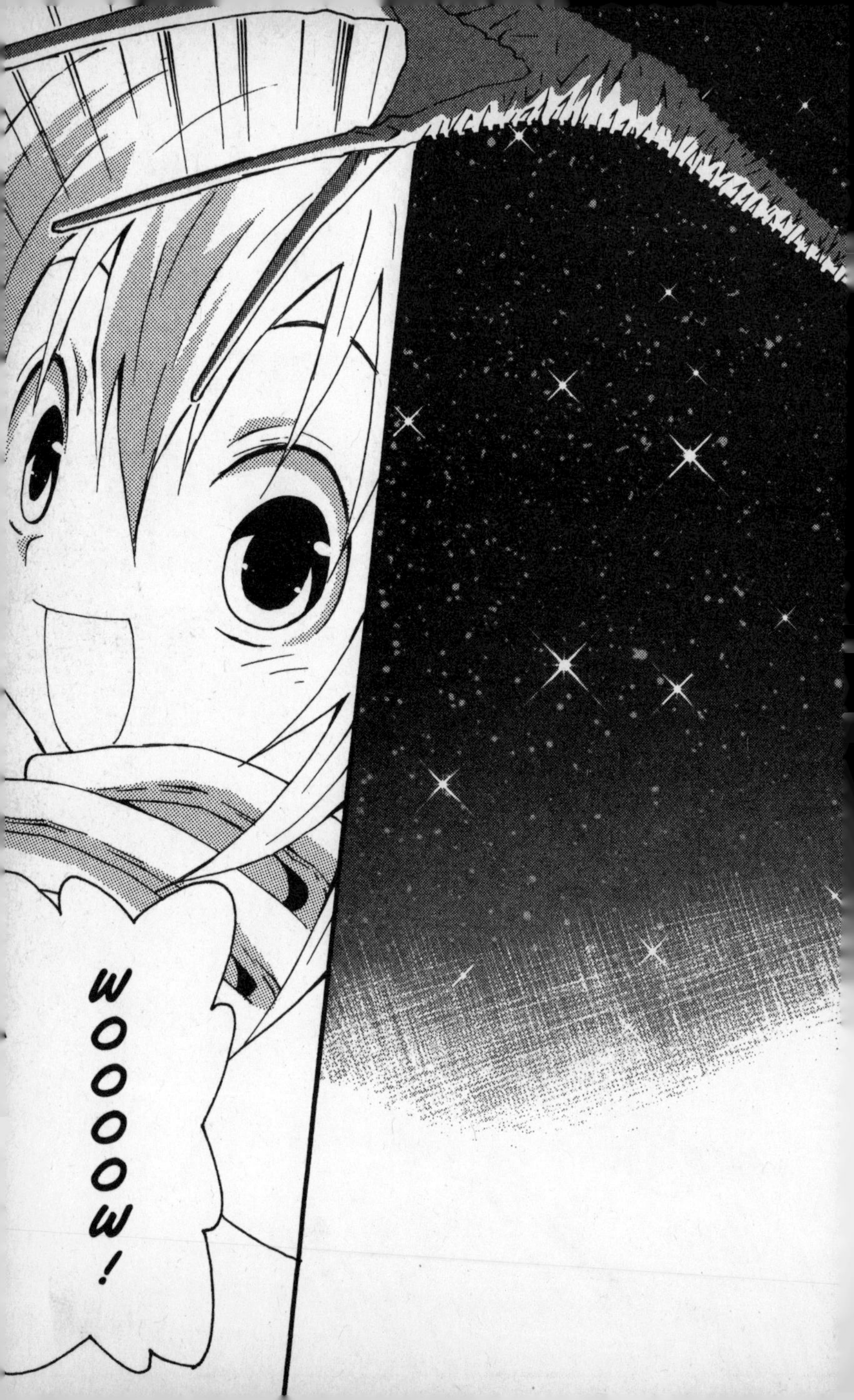
WOOOOOW!

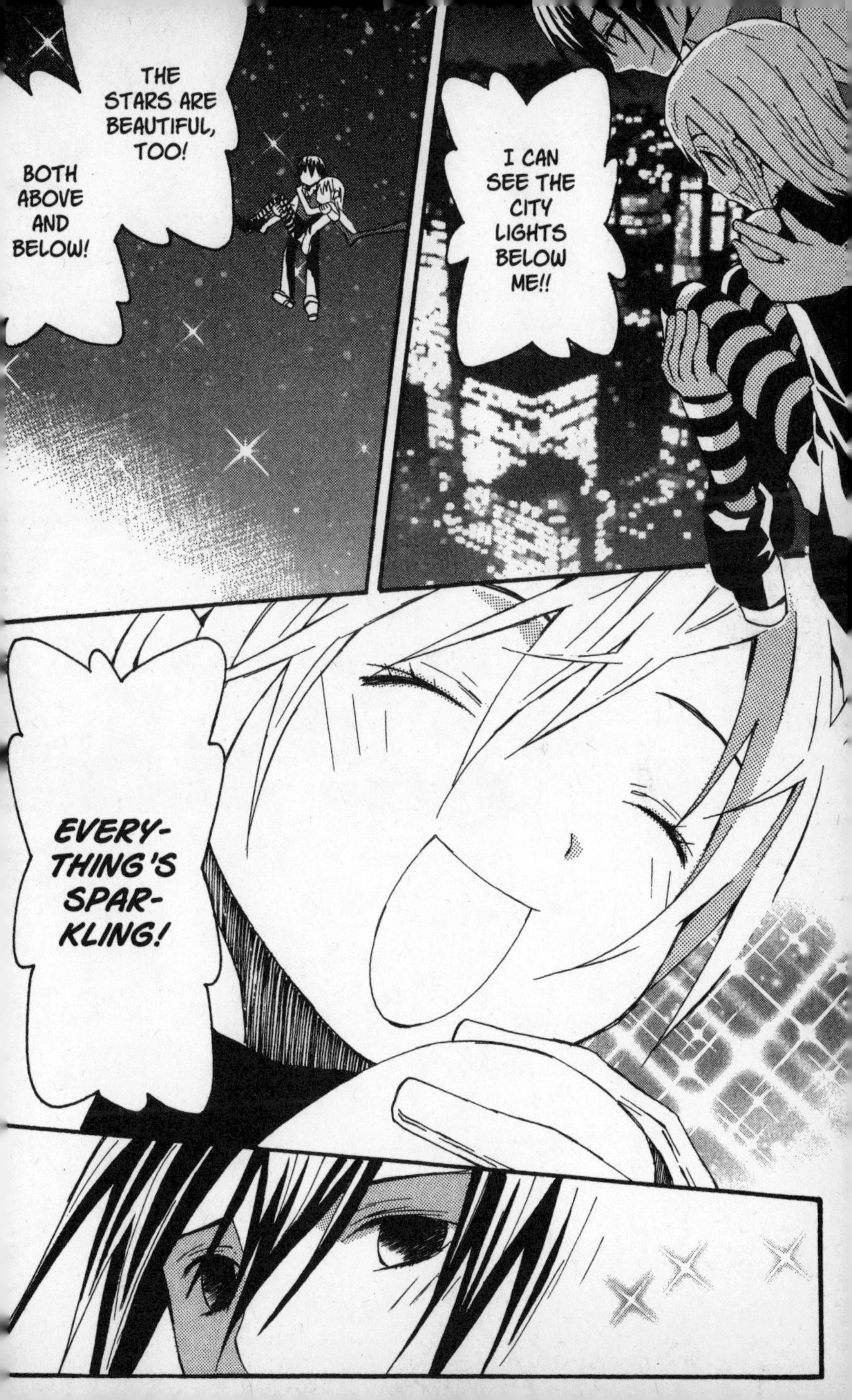
I CAN SEE THE CITY LIGHTS BELOW ME!!
THE STARS ARE BEAUTIFUL, TOO!
BOTH ABOVE AND BELOW!
EVERY-THING'S SPAR-KLING!

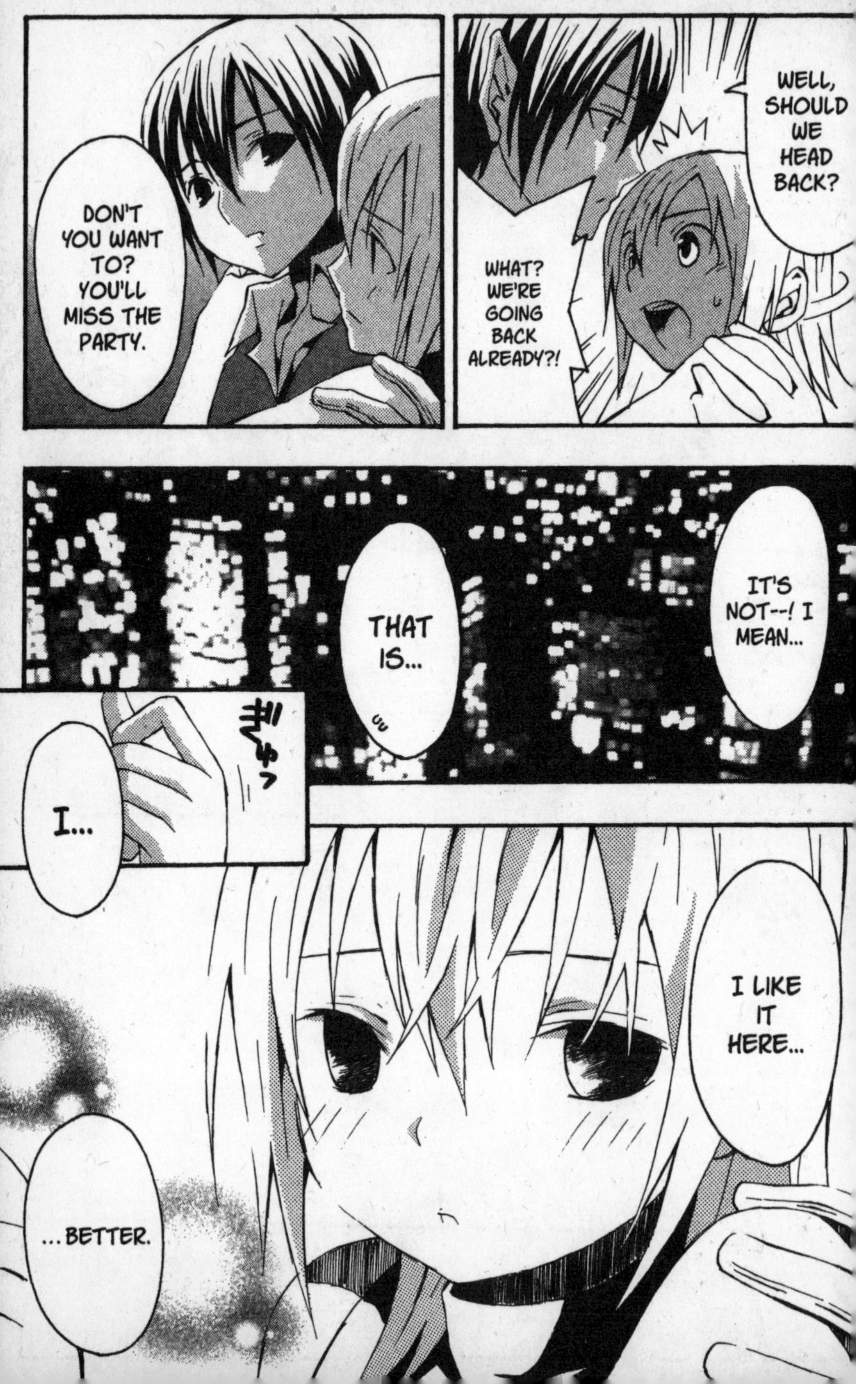
WELL, SHOULD WE HEAD BACK?
WHAT? WE'RE GOING BACK ALREADY?!
DON'T YOU WANT TO? YOU'LL MISS THE PARTY.
IT'S NOT--! I MEAN...
THAT IS...
ぎゅっ
I...
I LIKE IT HERE...
...BETTER.

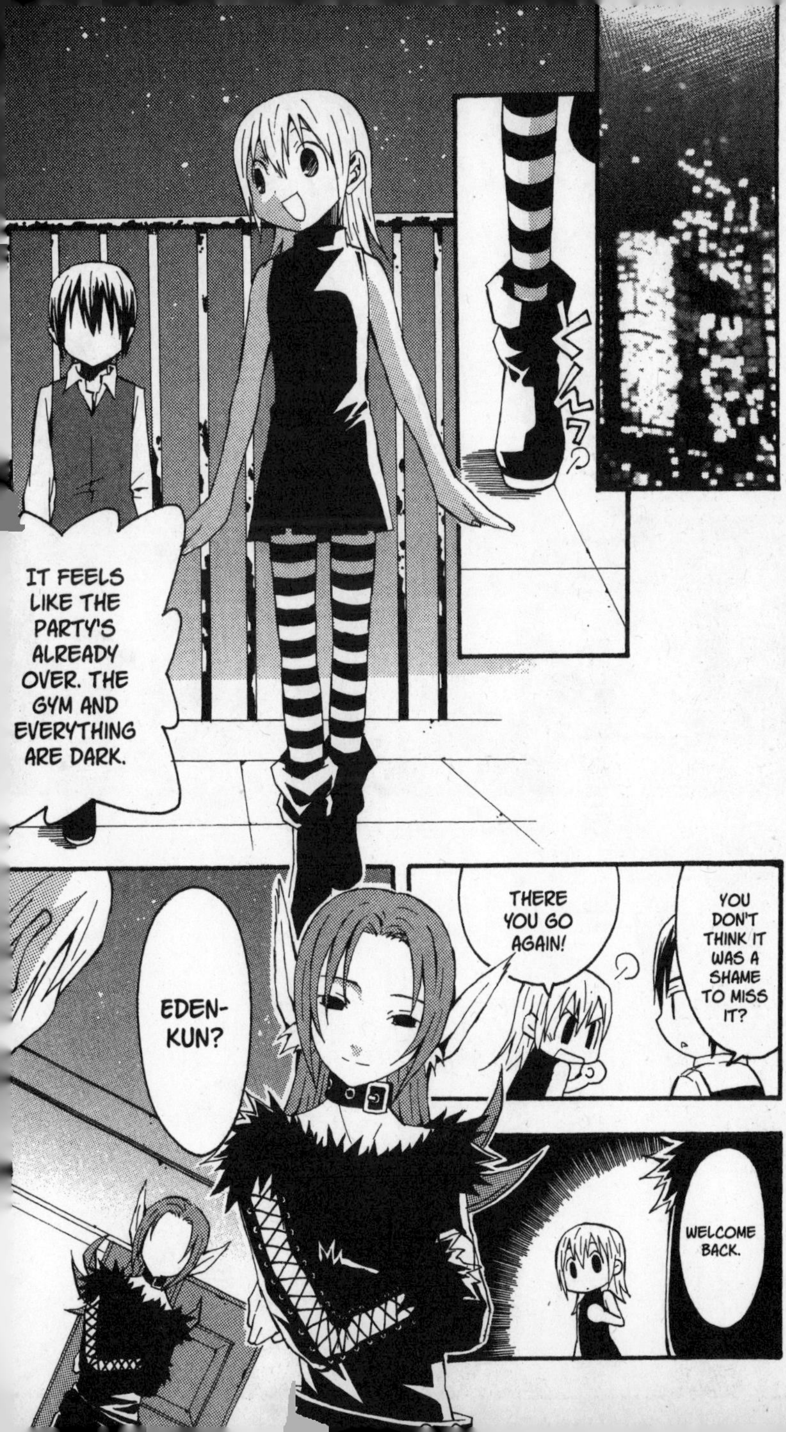
IT FEELS LIKE THE PARTY'S ALREADY OVER. THE GYM AND EVERYTHING ARE DARK.
YOU DON'T THINK IT WAS A SHAME TO MISS IT?
THERE YOU GO AGAIN!
WELCOME BACK.
EDEN-KUN?

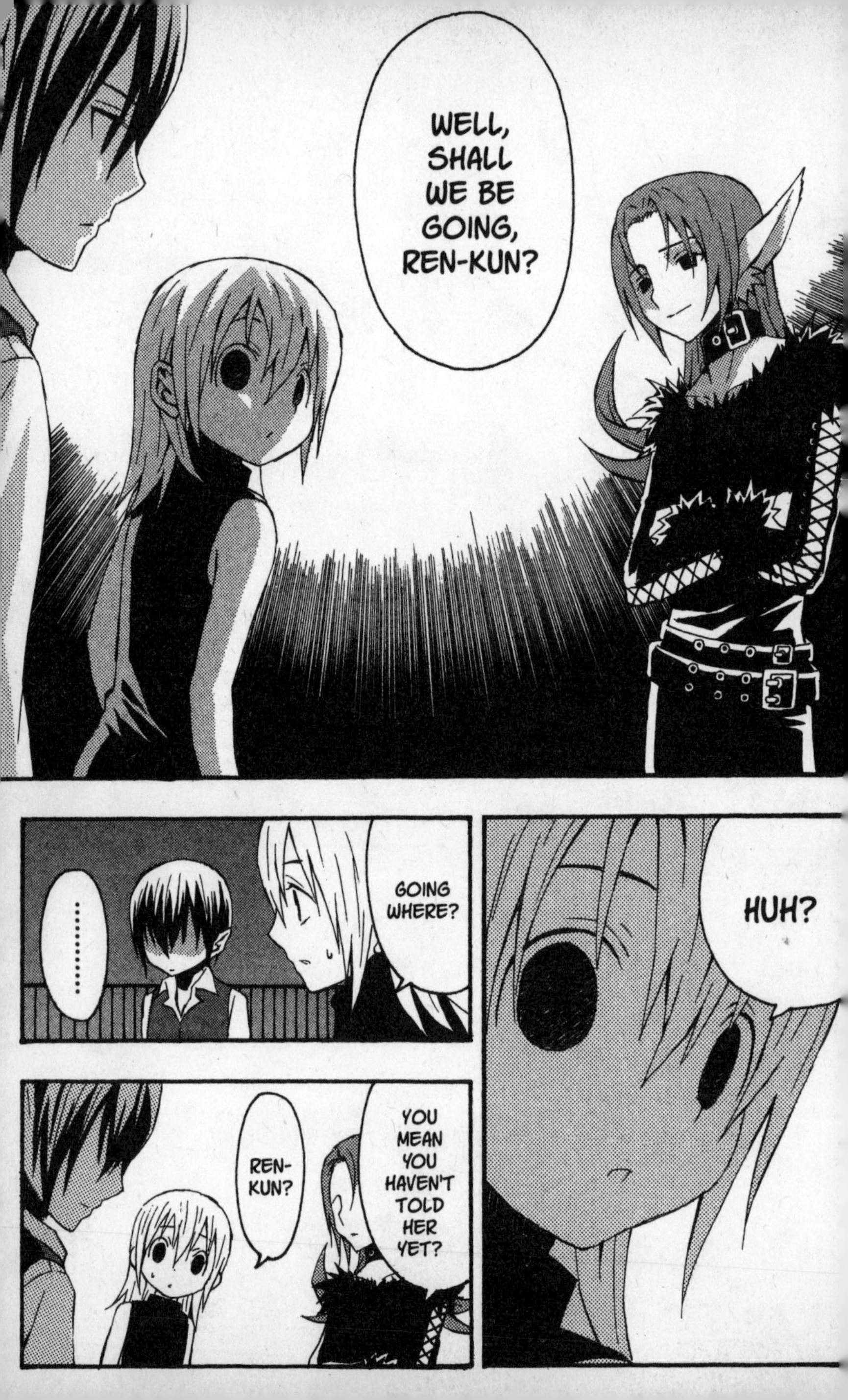
WELL, SHALL WE BE GOING, REN-KUN?
HUH?
GOING WHERE?
....
YOU MEAN YOU HAVEN'T TOLD HER YET?
REN-KUN?

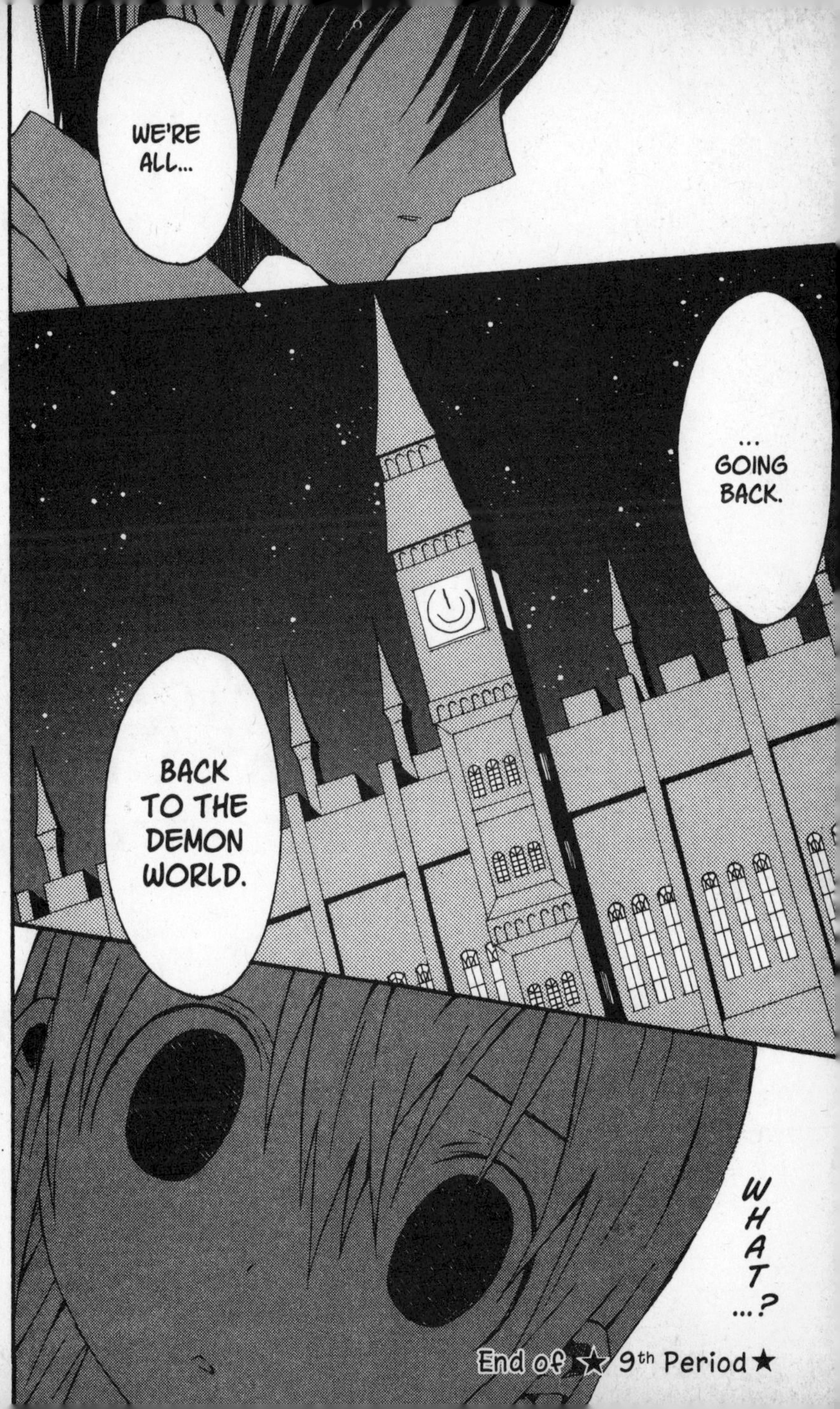
WE'RE ALL...
... GOING BACK.
BACK TO THE DEMON WORLD.
WHAT ...?
End of ★ 9th Period ★

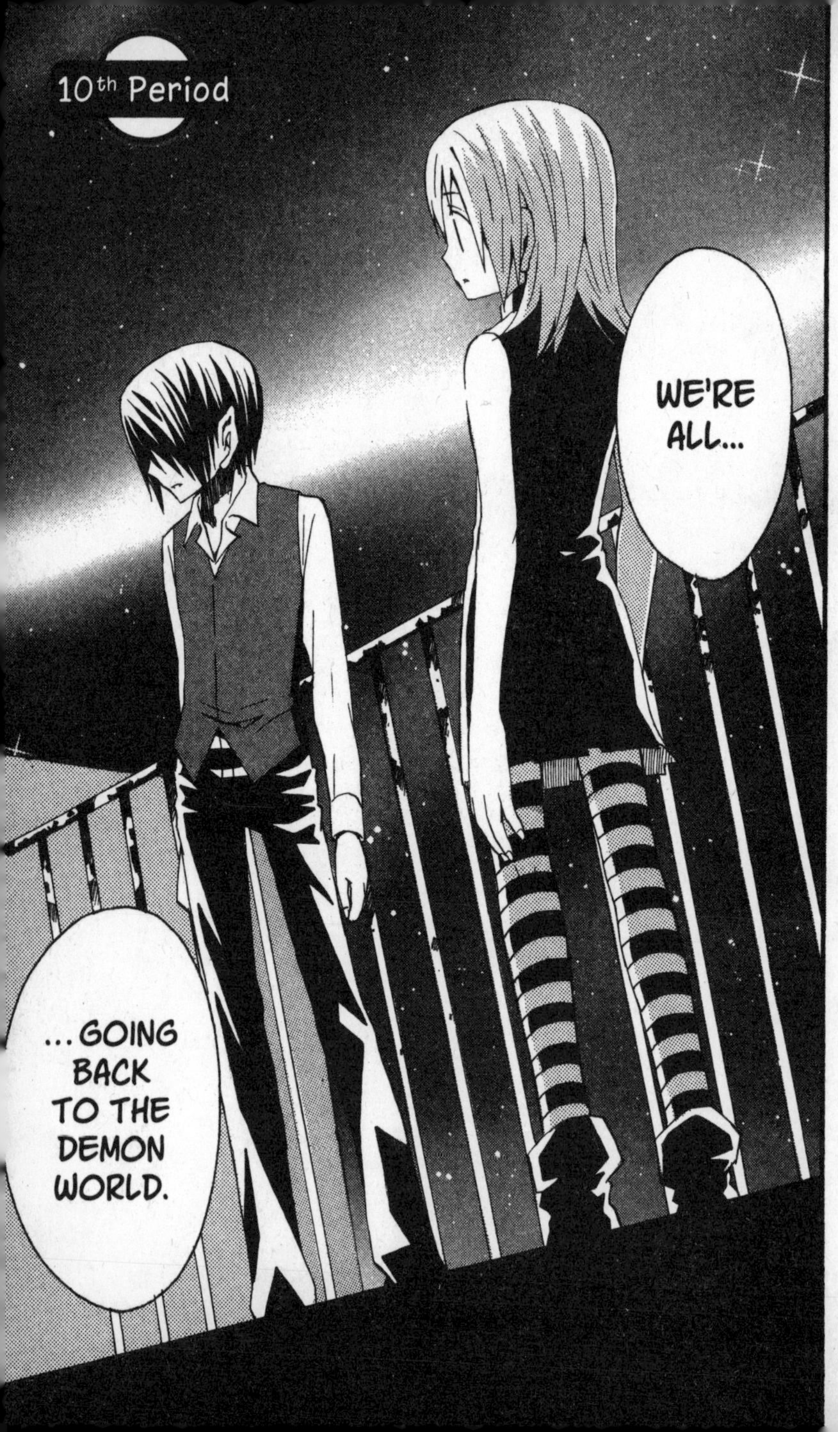
10th Period
WE'RE ALL...
...GOING BACK TO THE DEMON WORLD.

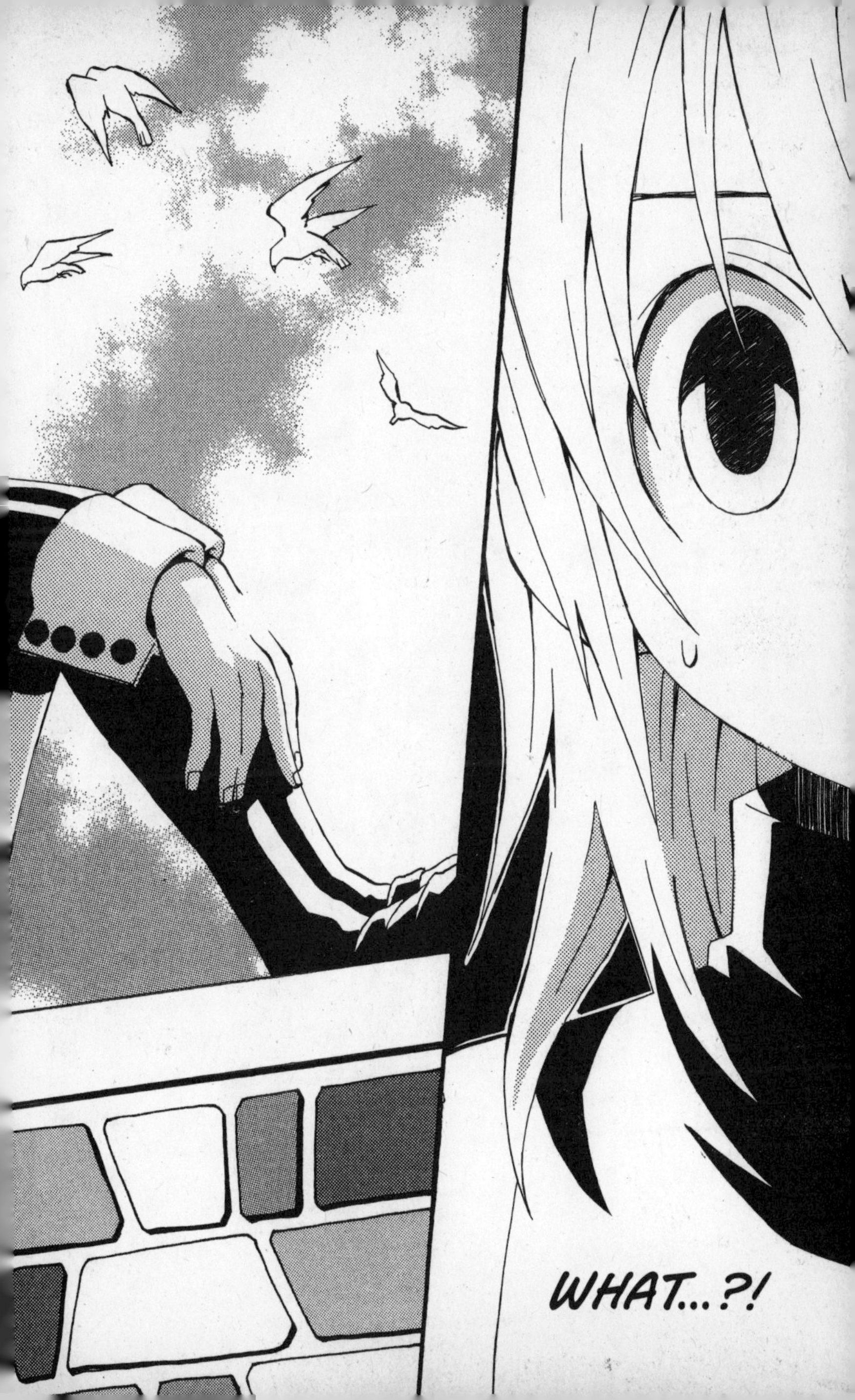
WHAT...?!

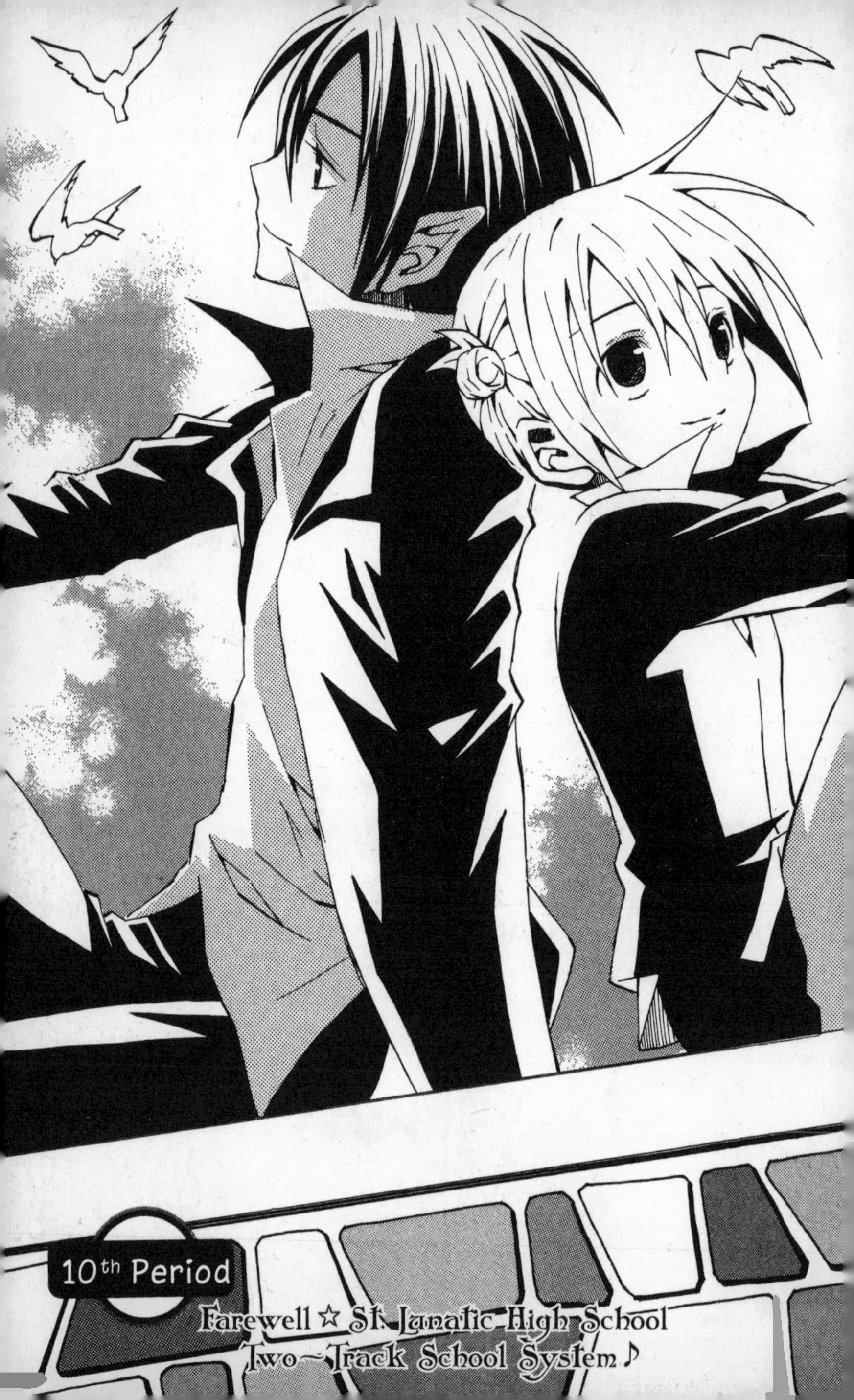
10th Period
Farewell ☆ St. Lunatic High School
Two~Track School System♪

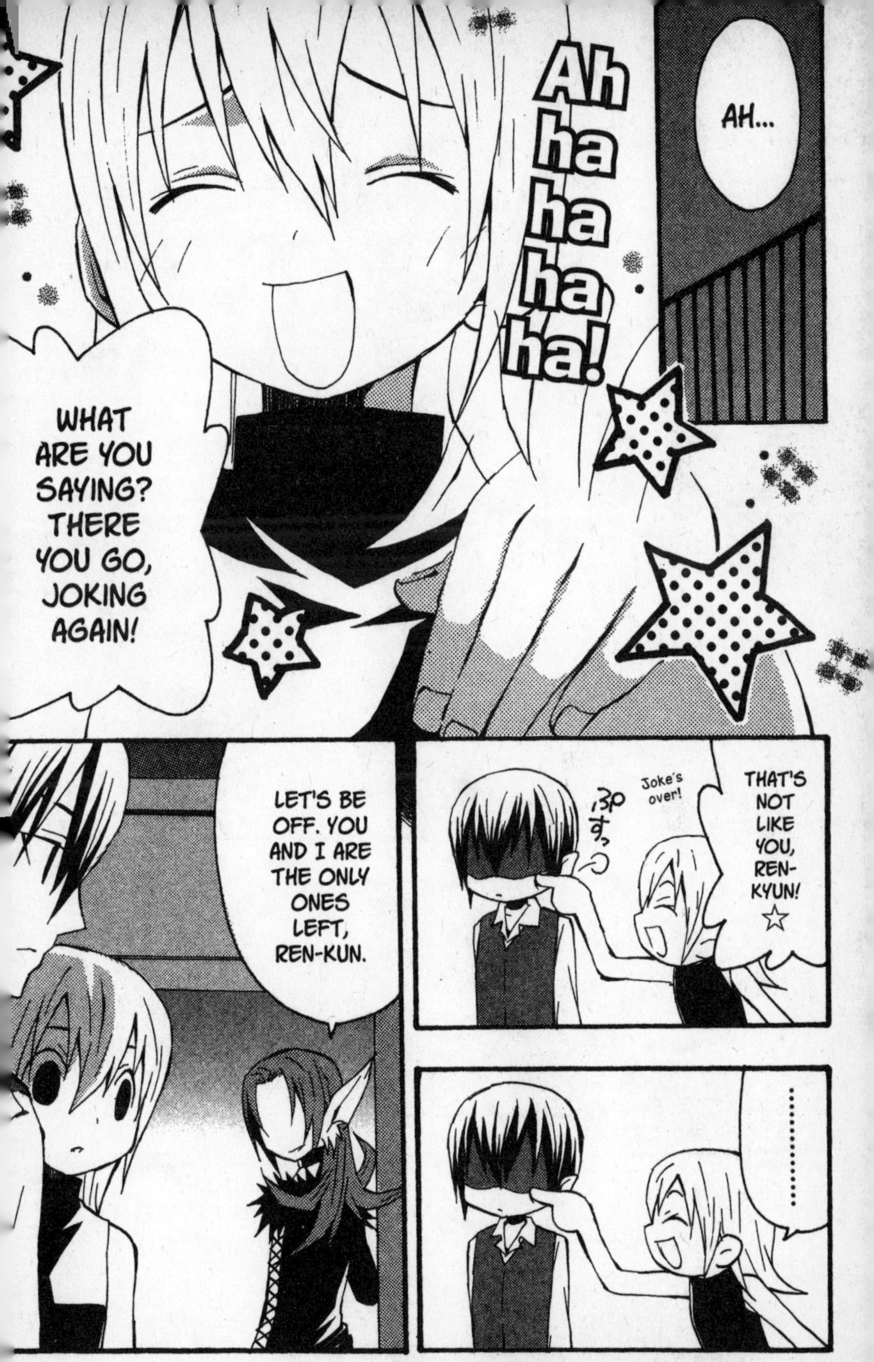
AH...
Ah ha ha ha ha ha!
WHAT ARE YOU SAYING? THERE YOU GO, JOKING AGAIN!
THAT'S NOT LIKE YOU, REN-KYUN! ☆
Joke's over!
ぷすっ
......
LET'S BE OFF. YOU AND I ARE THE ONLY ONES LEFT, REN-KUN.

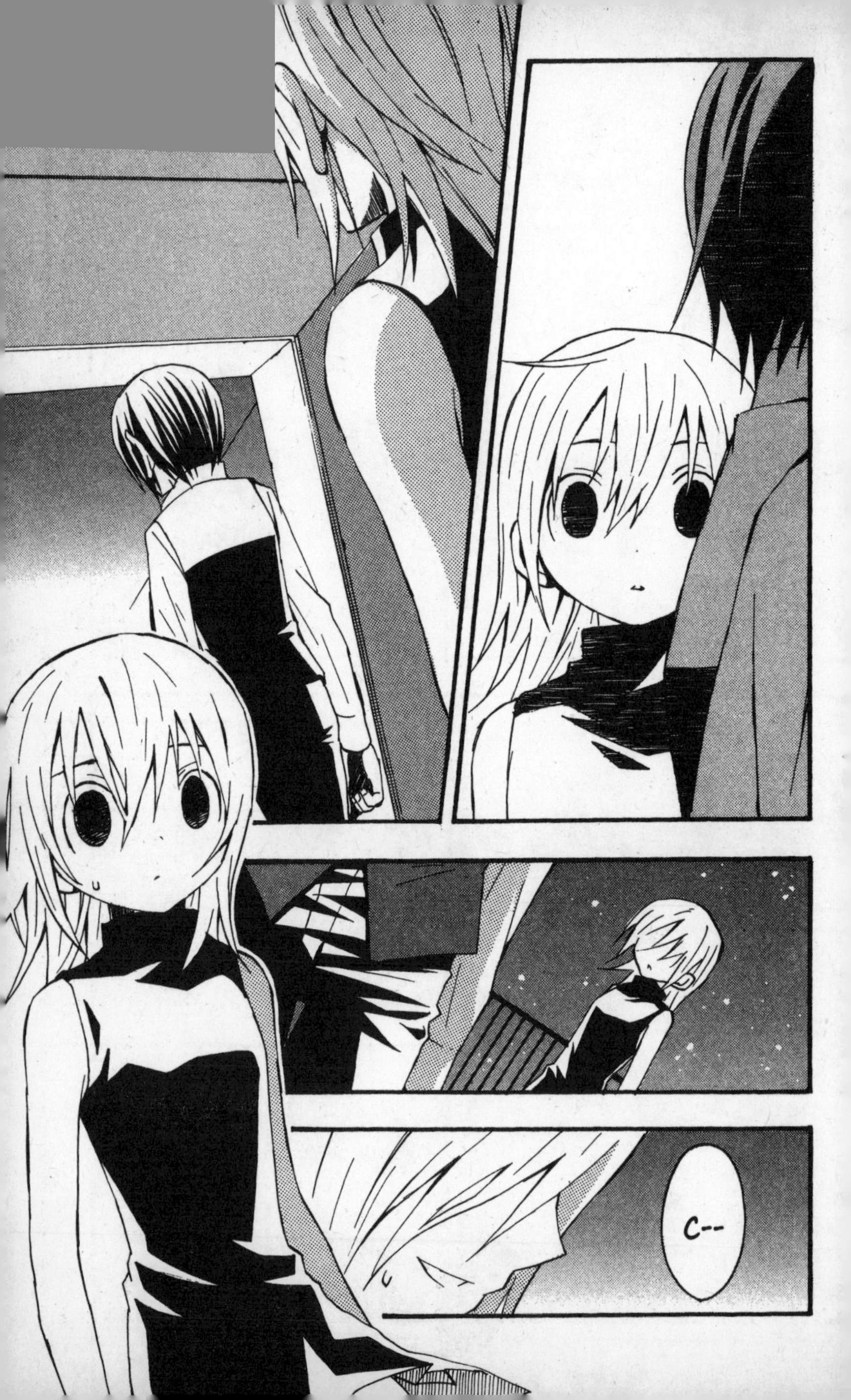
C--

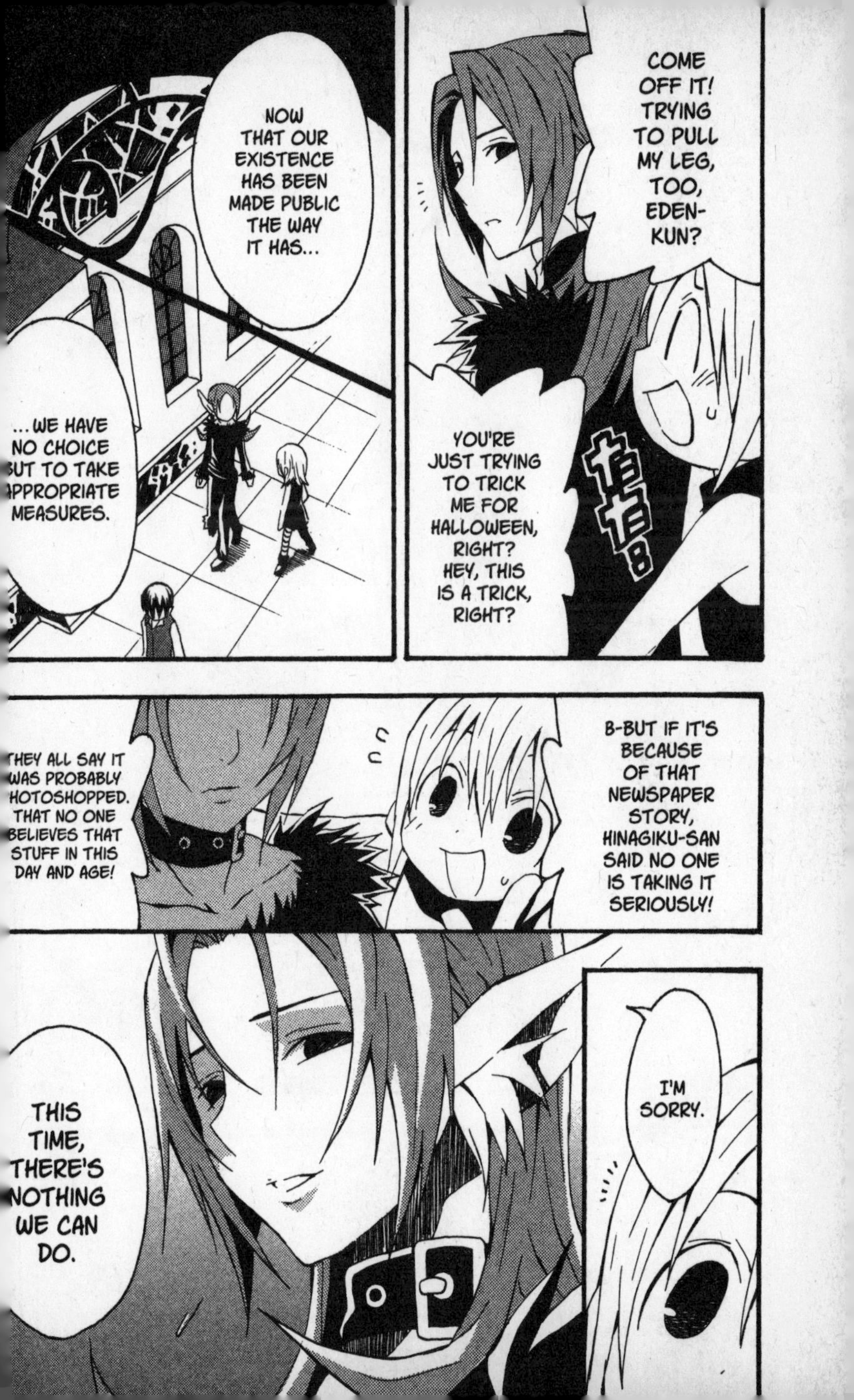
COME OFF IT! TRYING TO PULL MY LEG, TOO, EDEN-KUN?
YOU'RE JUST TRYING TO TRICK ME FOR HALLOWEEN, RIGHT? HEY, THIS IS A TRICK, RIGHT?
NOW THAT OUR EXISTENCE HAS BEEN MADE PUBLIC THE WAY IT HAS...
...WE HAVE NO CHOICE BUT TO TAKE APPROPRIATE MEASURES.
B-BUT IF IT'S BECAUSE OF THAT NEWSPAPER STORY, HINAGIKU-SAN SAID NO ONE IS TAKING IT SERIOUSLY!
THEY ALL SAY IT WAS PROBABLY PHOTOSHOPPED. THAT NO ONE BELIEVES THAT STUFF IN THIS DAY AND AGE!
I'M SORRY.
THIS TIME, THERE'S NOTHING WE CAN DO.

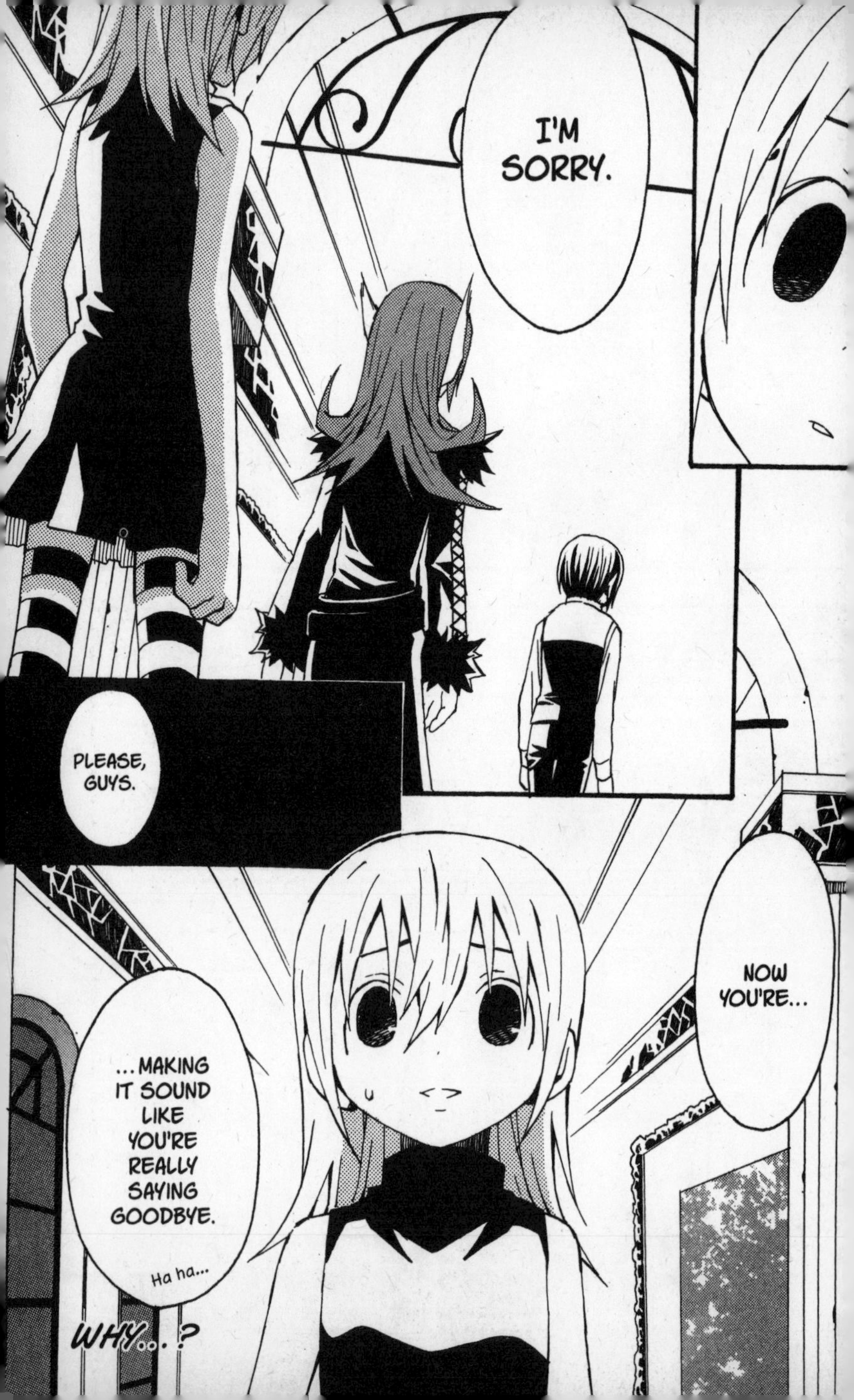
I'M SORRY.
PLEASE, GUYS.
NOW YOU'RE...
...MAKING IT SOUND LIKE YOU'RE REALLY SAYING GOODBYE.
Ha ha...
WHY...?

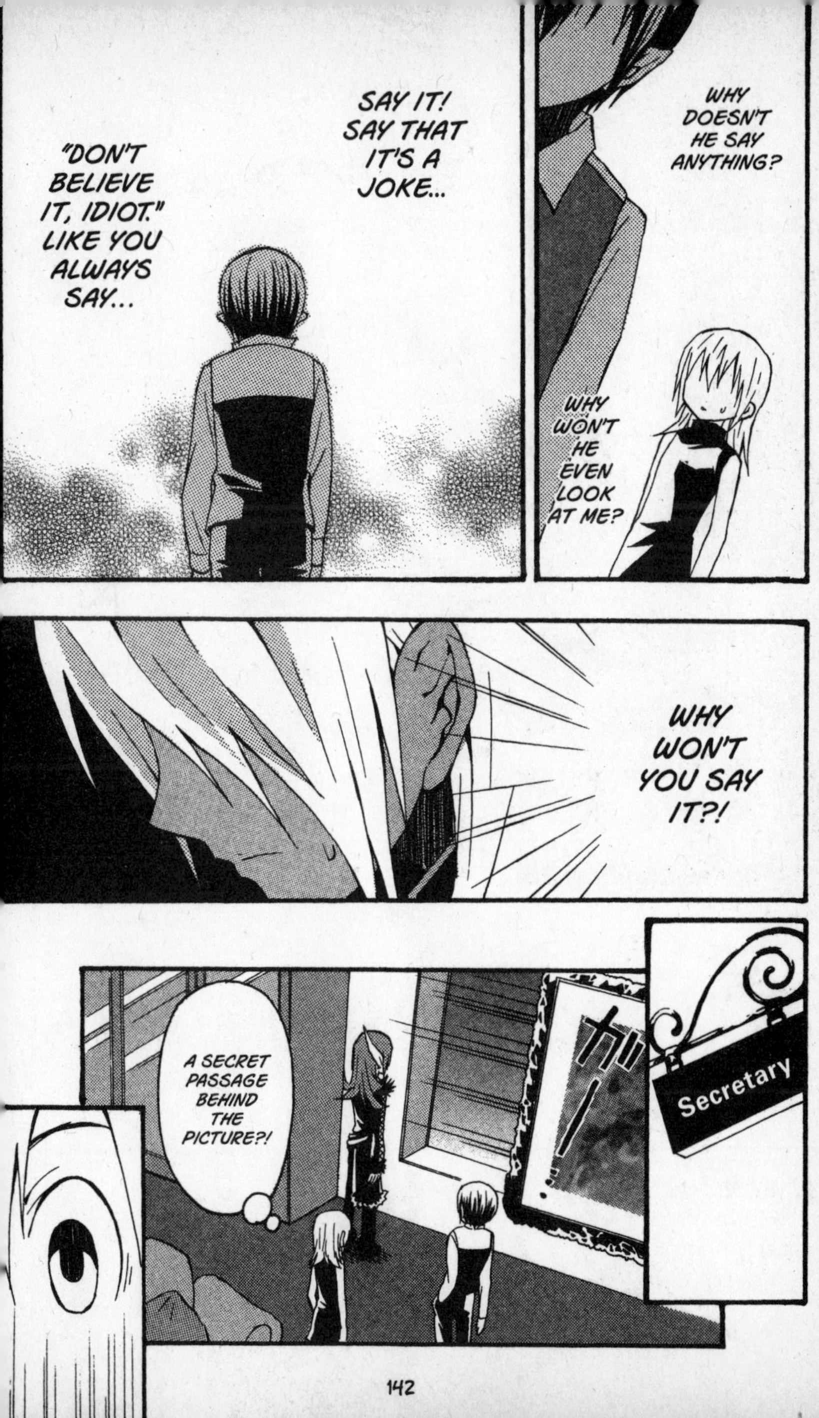
WHY DOESN'T HE SAY ANYTHING?
WHY WON'T HE EVEN LOOK AT ME?
SAY IT! SAY THAT IT'S A JOKE...
"DON'T BELIEVE IT, IDIOT." LIKE YOU ALWAYS SAY...
WHY WON'T YOU SAY IT?!
Secretary
A SECRET PASSAGE BEHIND THE PICTURE?!

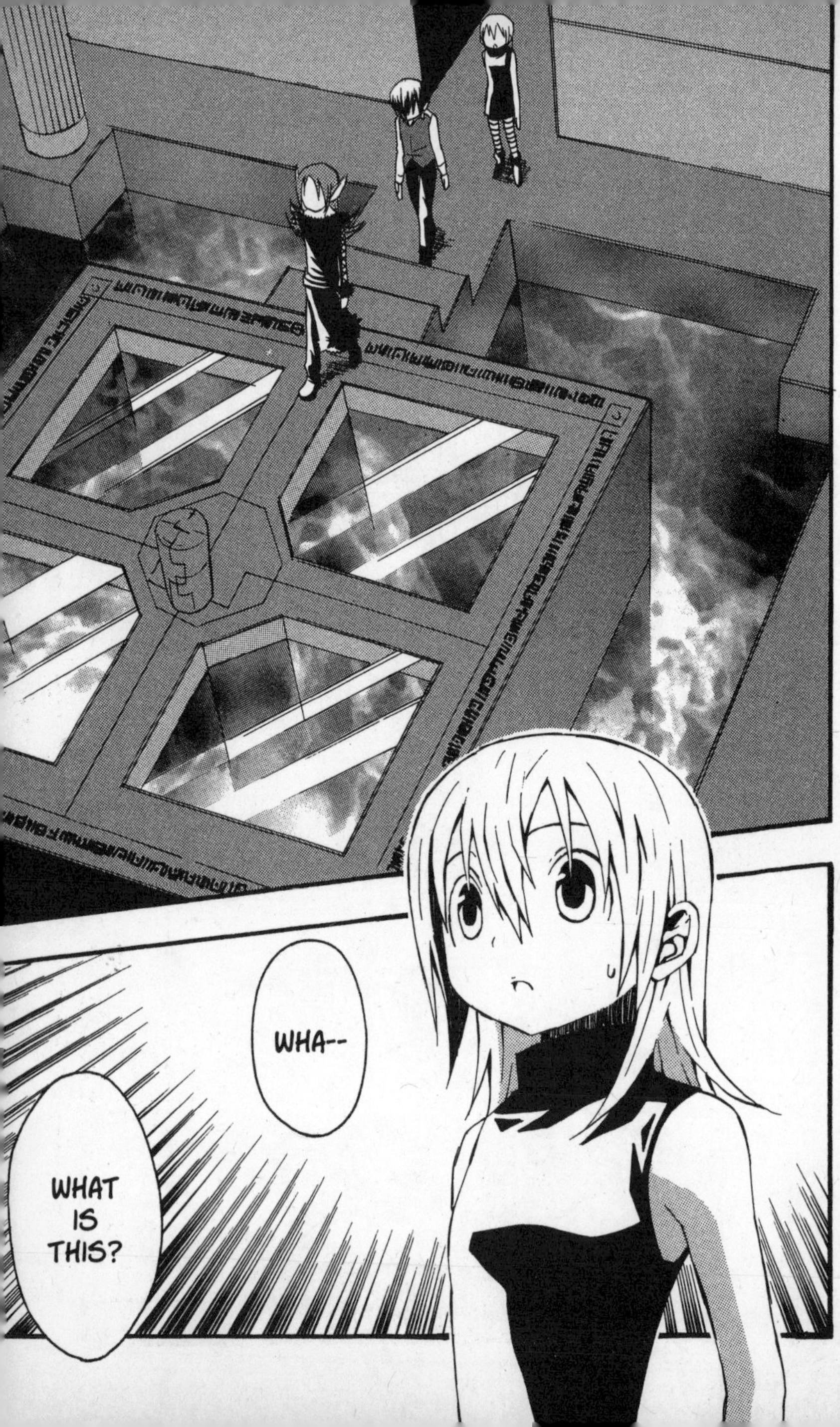
WHA--
WHAT IS THIS?

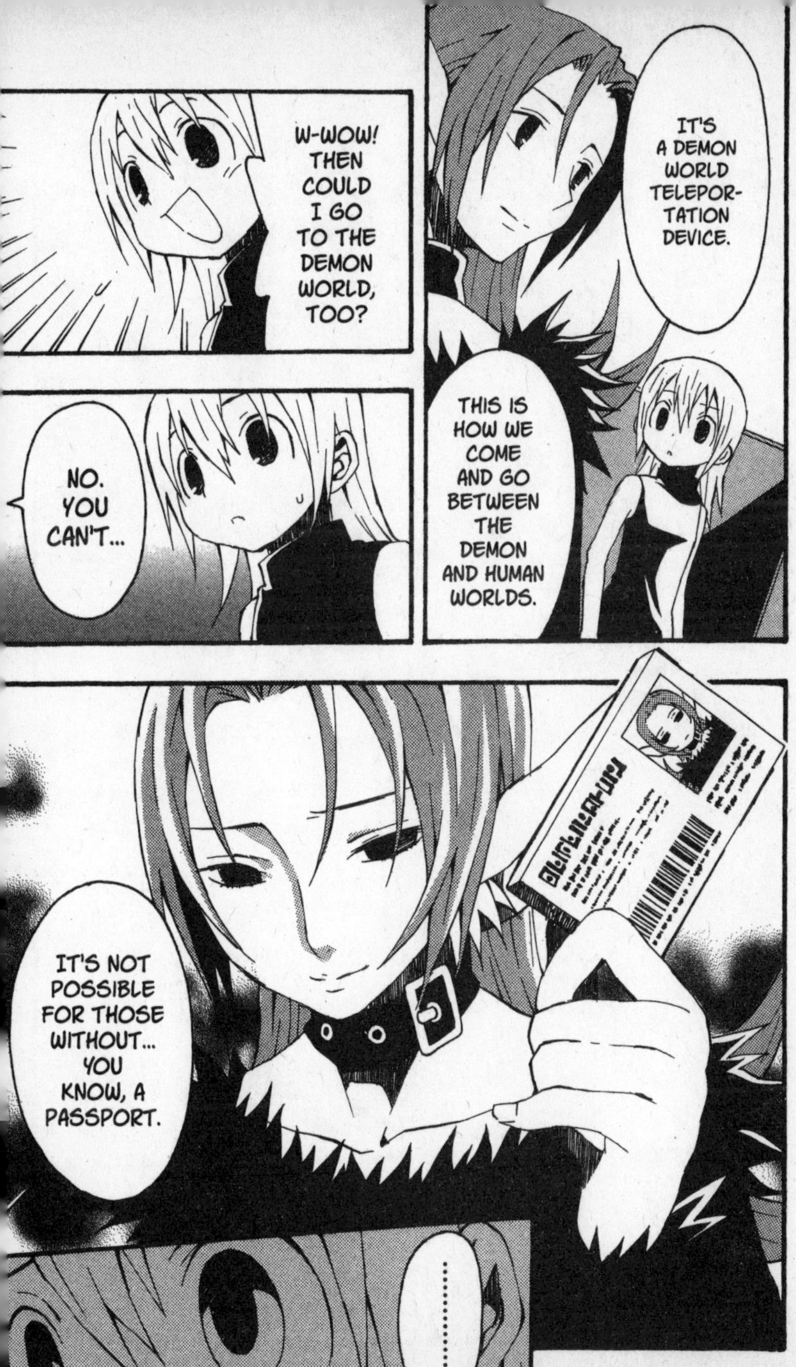
IT'S A DEMON WORLD TELEPOR-TATION DEVICE.
THIS IS HOW WE COME AND GO BETWEEN THE DEMON AND HUMAN WORLDS.
W-WOW! THEN COULD I GO TO THE DEMON WORLD, TOO?
NO. YOU CAN'T...
IT'S NOT POSSIBLE FOR THOSE WITHOUT... YOU KNOW, A PASSPORT.
....

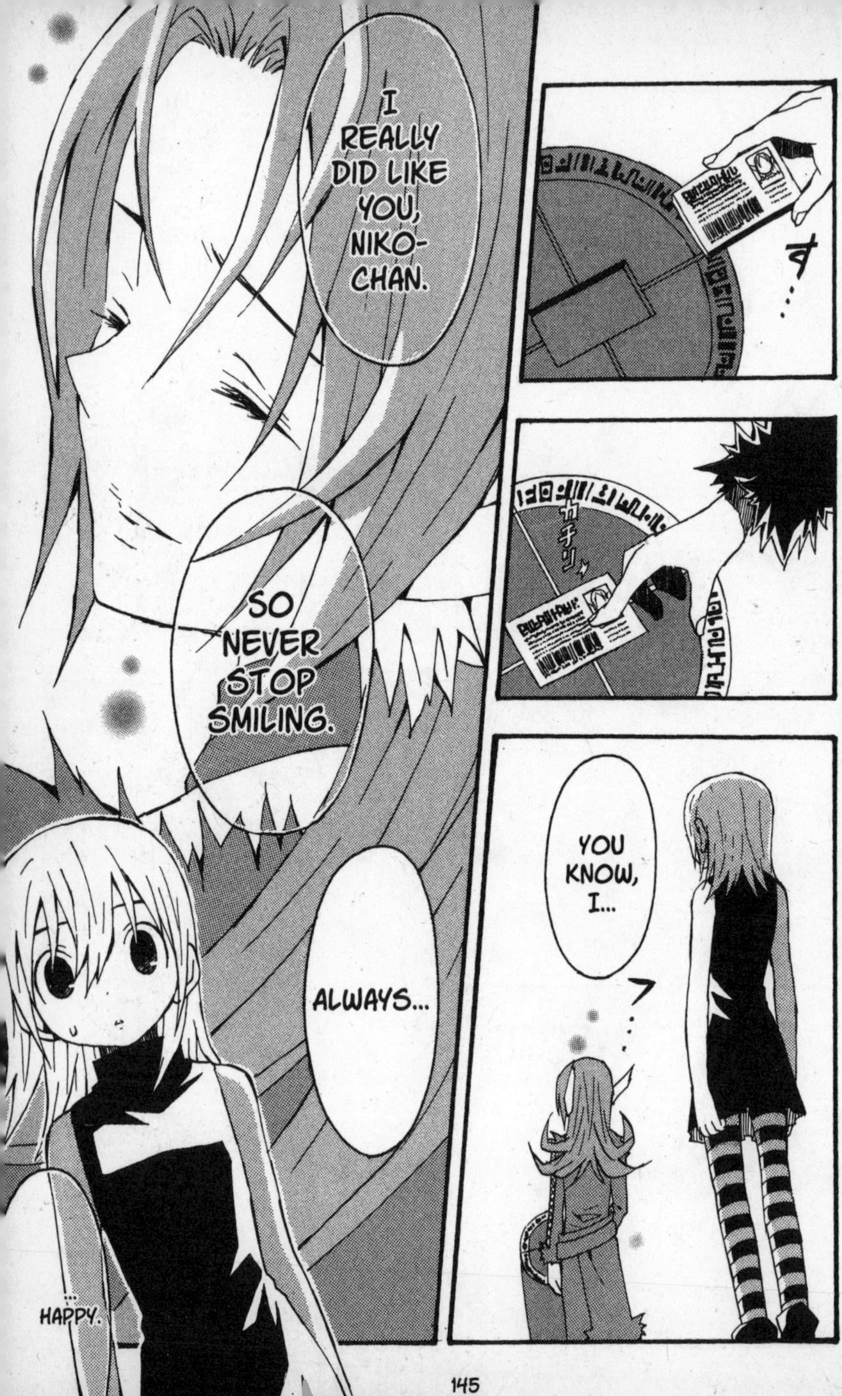
す…
カチリ
YOU KNOW, I...
?...
I REALLY DID LIKE YOU, NIKO-CHAN.
SO NEVER STOP SMILING.
ALWAYS...
...HAPPY.

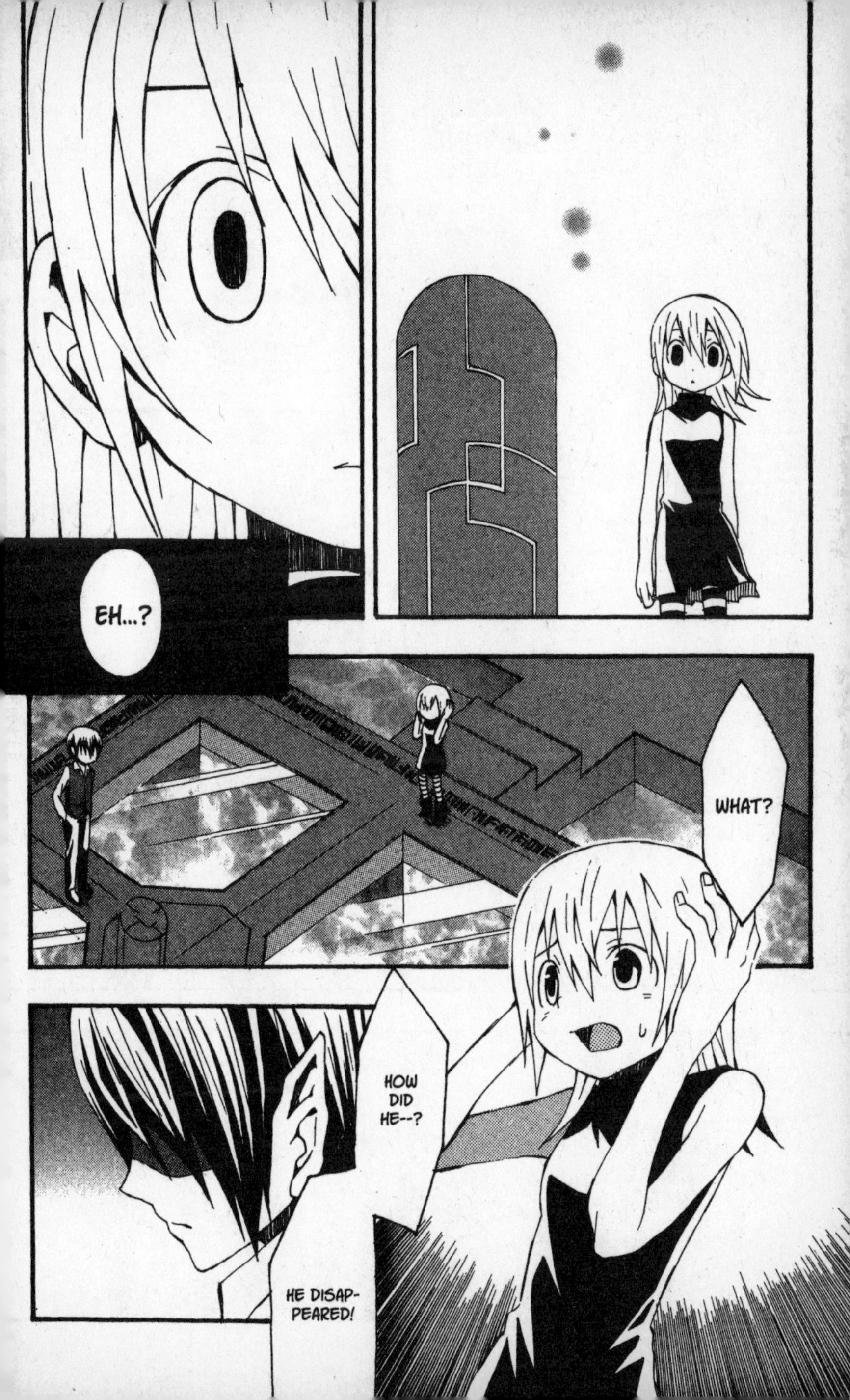
EH...?
WHAT?
HOW DID HE--?
HE DISAP-PEARED!

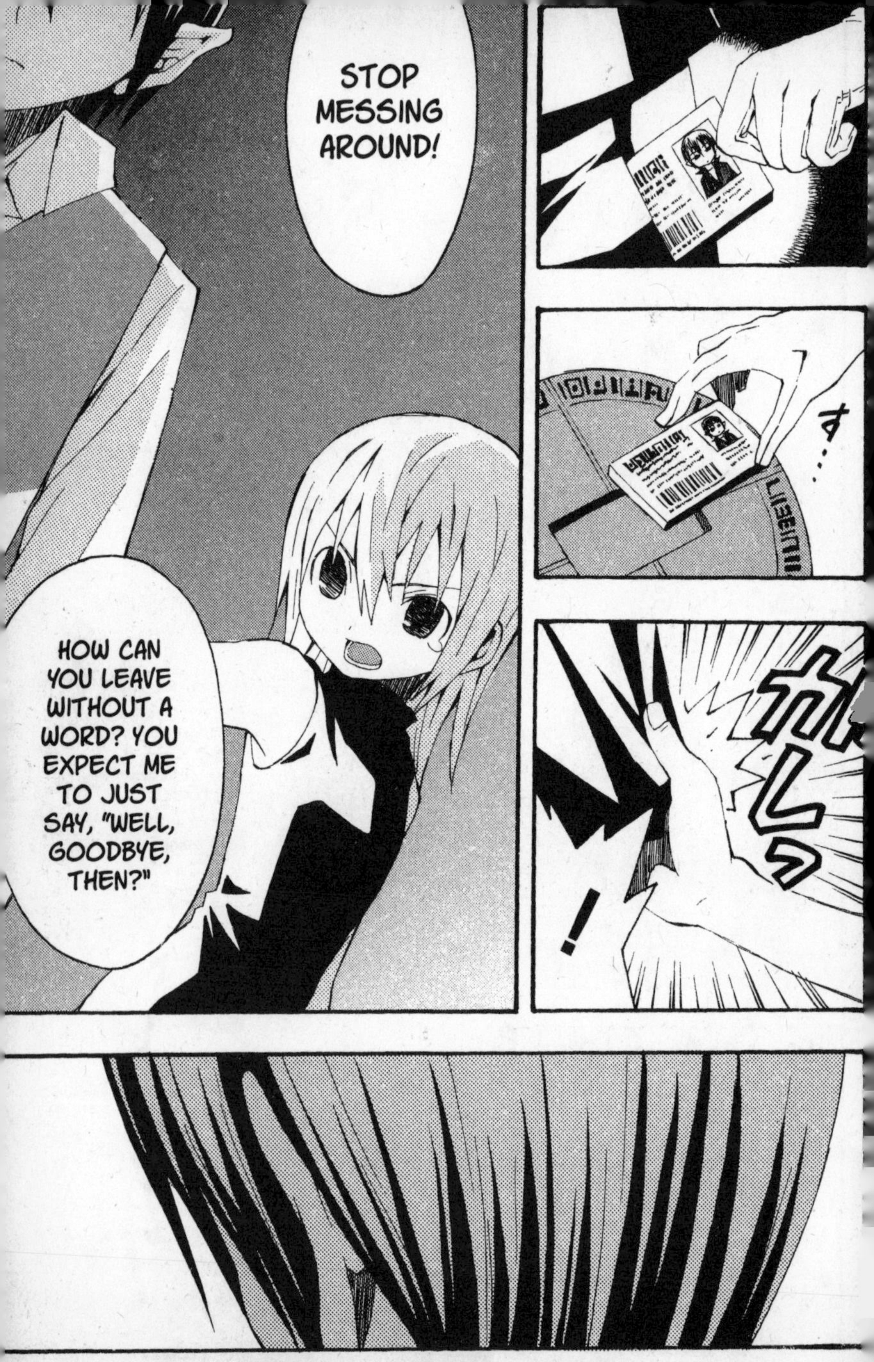
す…
!
STOP MESSING AROUND!
HOW CAN YOU LEAVE WITHOUT A WORD? YOU EXPECT ME TO JUST SAY, "WELL, GOODBYE, THEN?"

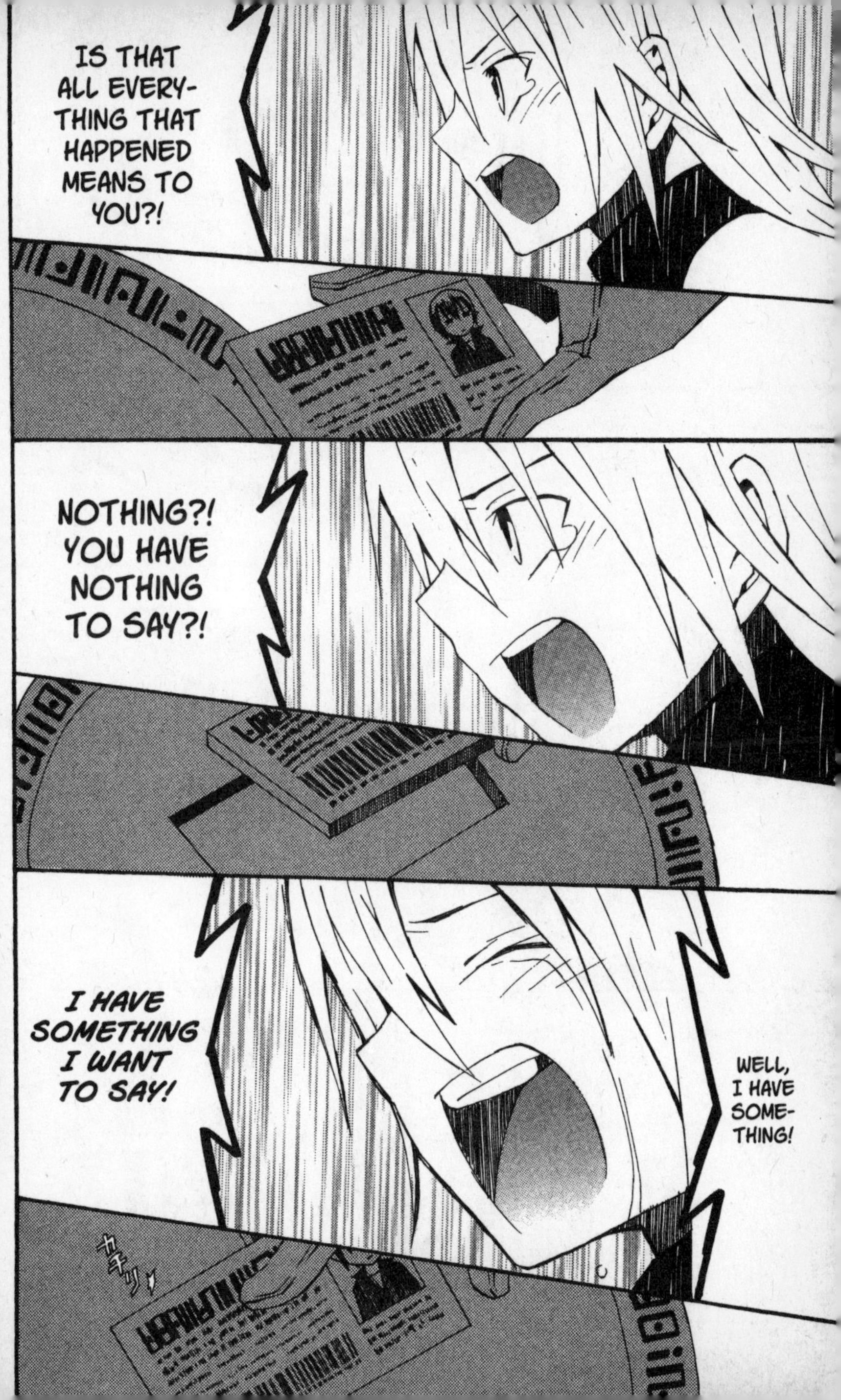
IS THAT ALL EVERY-THING THAT HAPPENED MEANS TO YOU?!
NOTHING?! YOU HAVE NOTHING TO SAY?!
WELL, I HAVE SOME-THING!
I HAVE SOMETHING I WANT TO SAY!

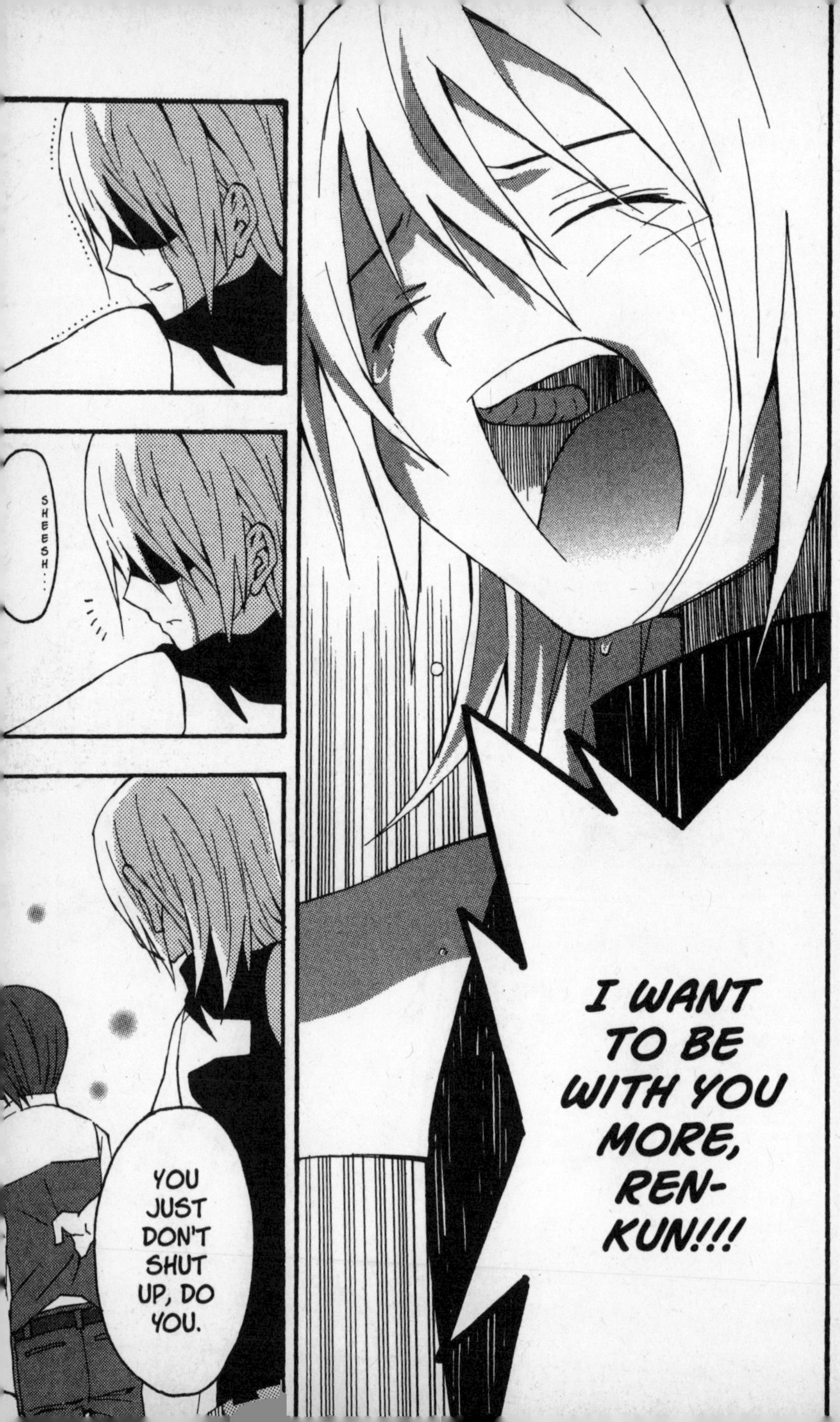
I WANT TO BE WITH YOU MORE, REN-KUN!!!
SHEESH...
YOU JUST DON'T SHUT UP, DO YOU.

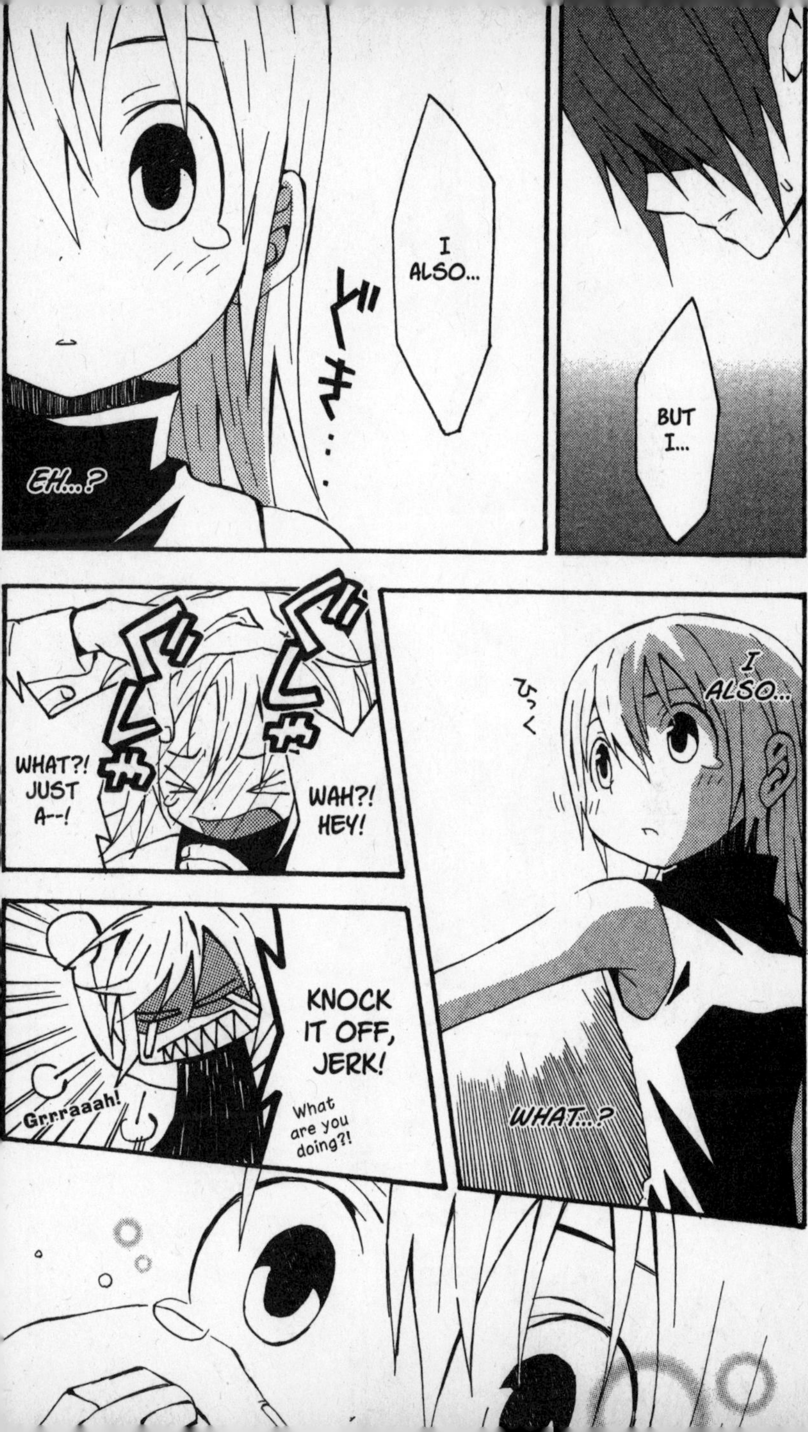
BUT I...
I ALSO...
どき…
EH...?
I ALSO...
WHAT...?
ぐしゃ
WAH?! HEY!
ぐしゃ
WHAT?! JUST A--!
KNOCK IT OFF, JERK!
What are you doing?!
Grrraaah!

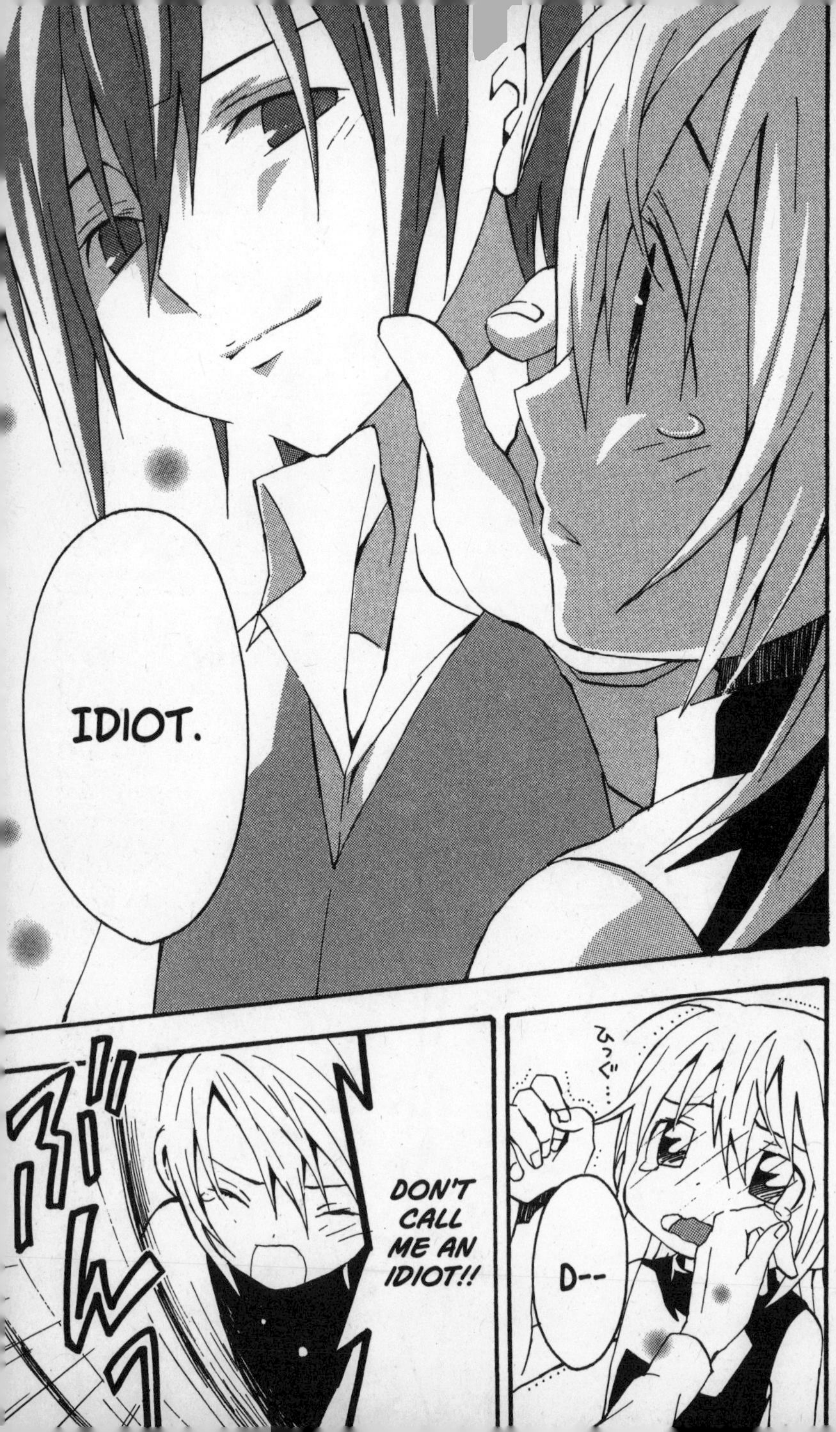
IDIOT.
ひっぐ…
D--
DON'T CALL ME AN IDIOT!!

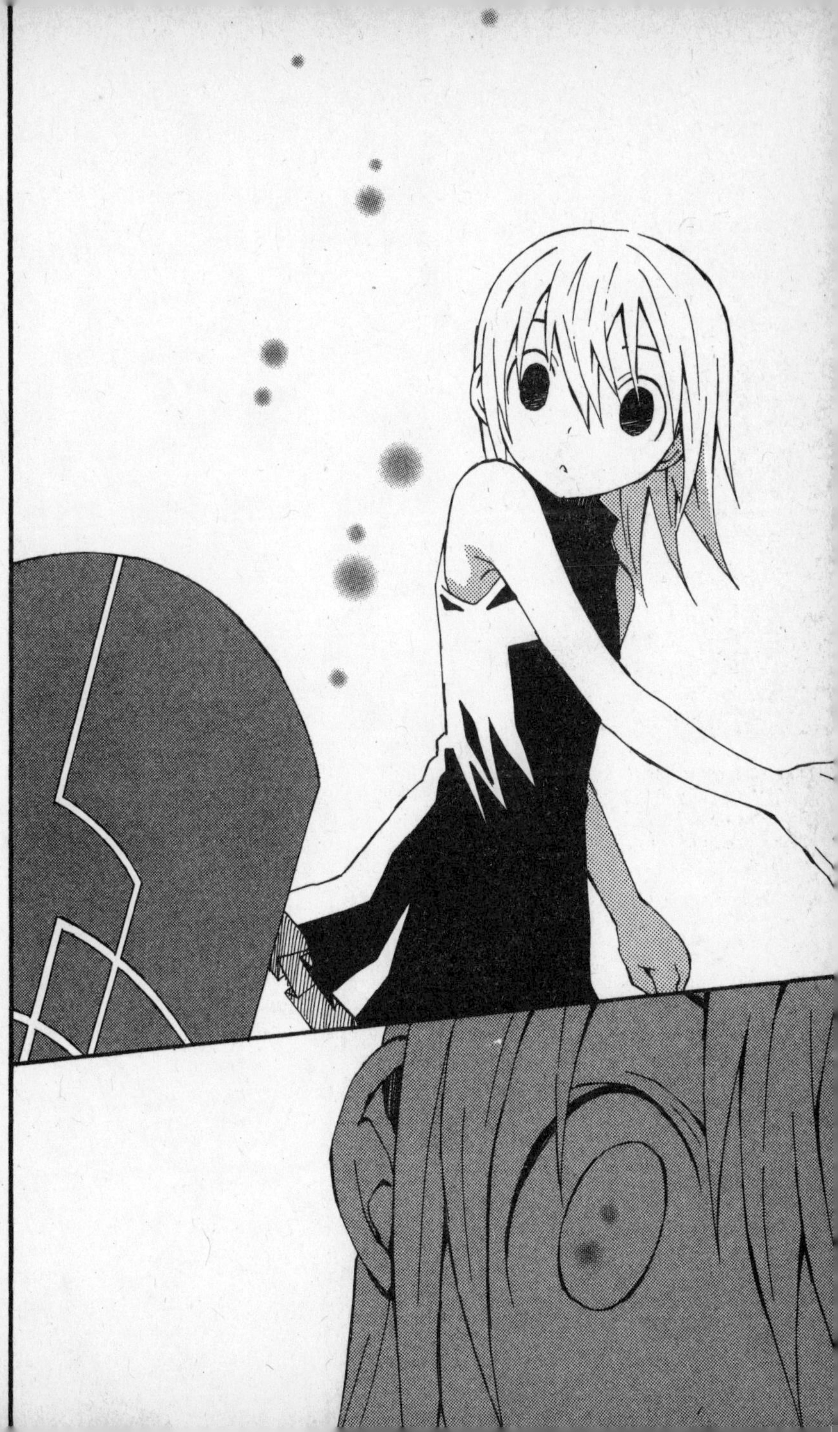

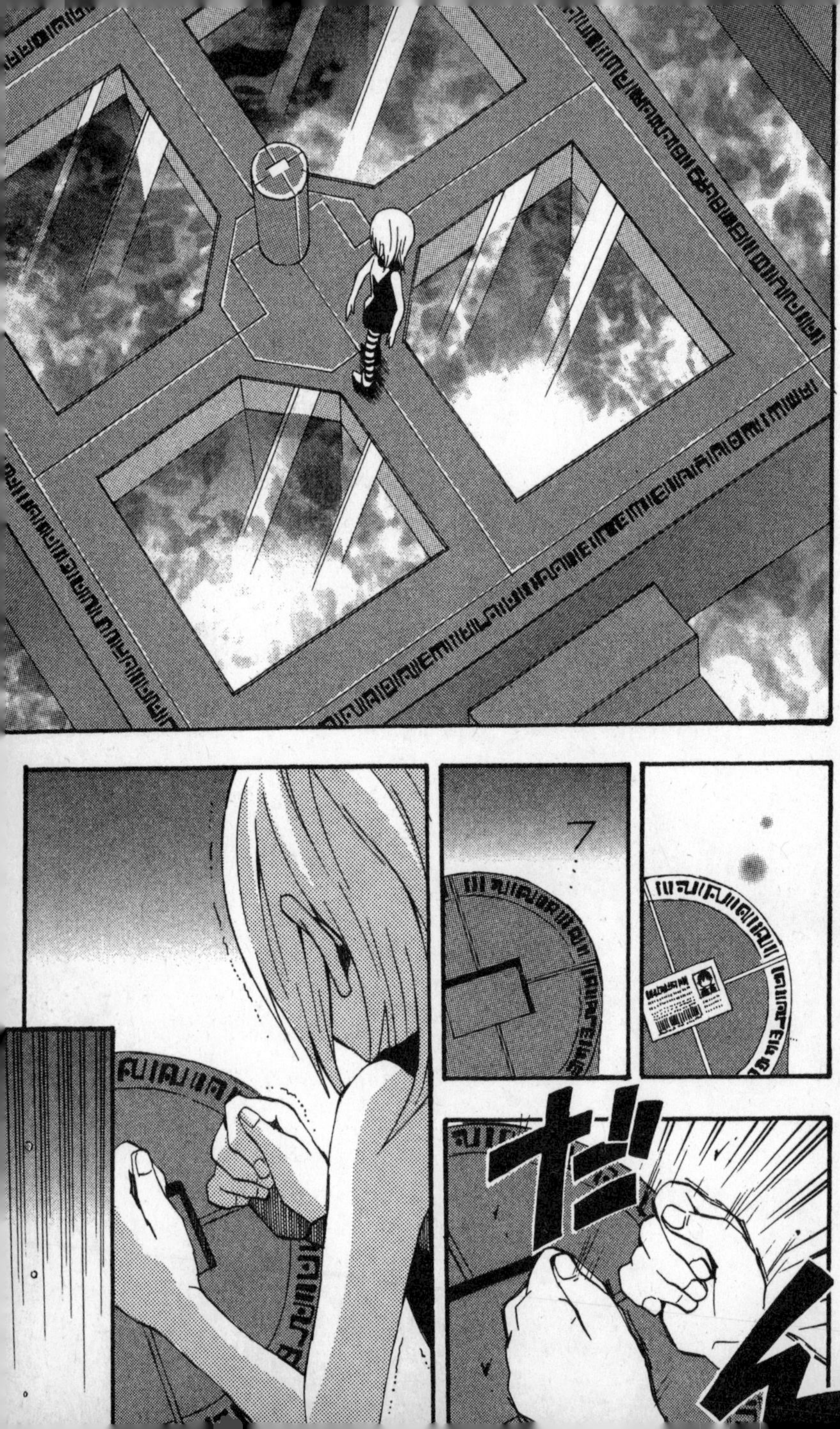

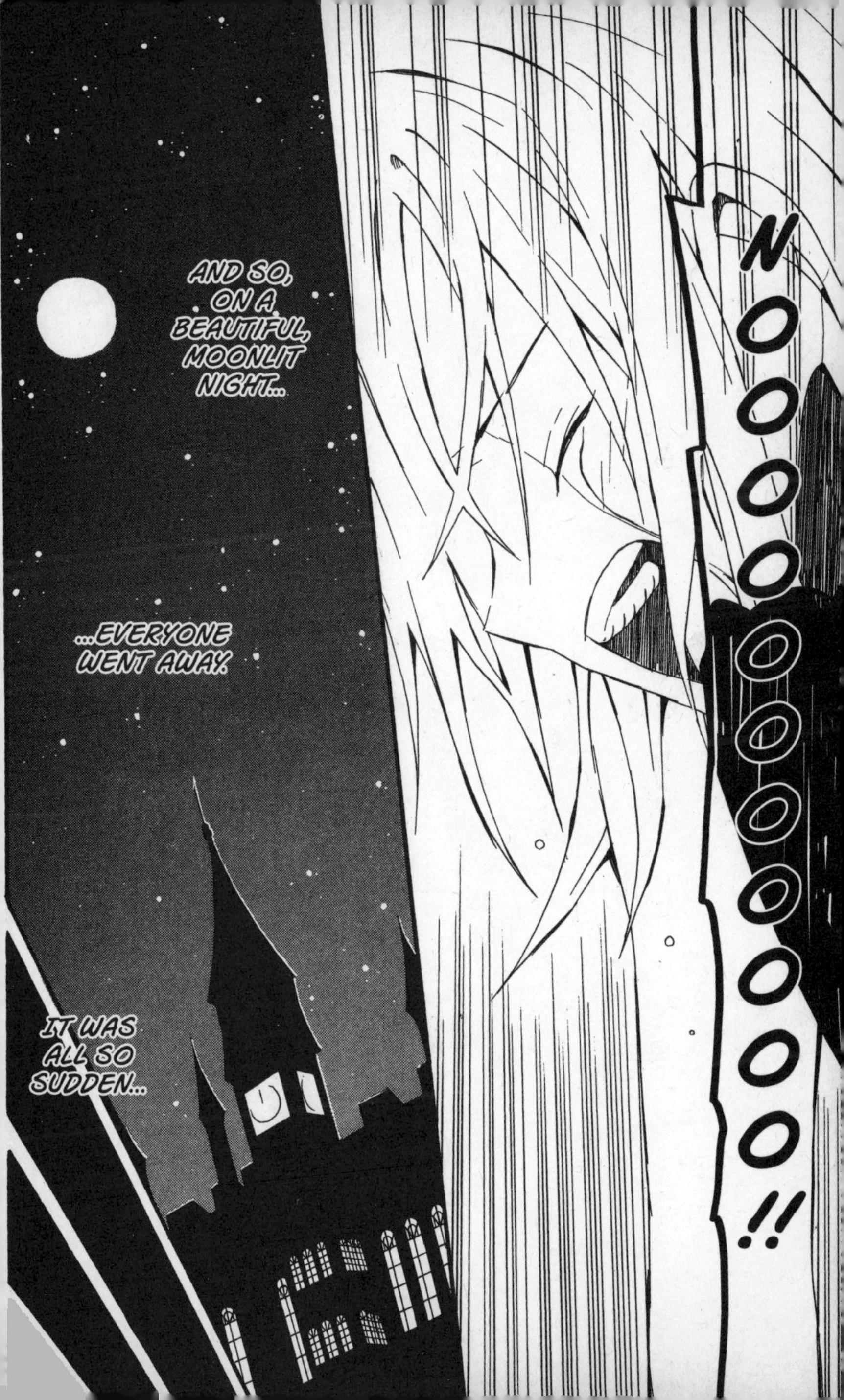
NOOOOOOOOOOOO!!
AND SO, ON A BEAUTIFUL, MOONLIT NIGHT...
...EVERYONE WENT AWAY.
IT WAS ALL SO SUDDEN...

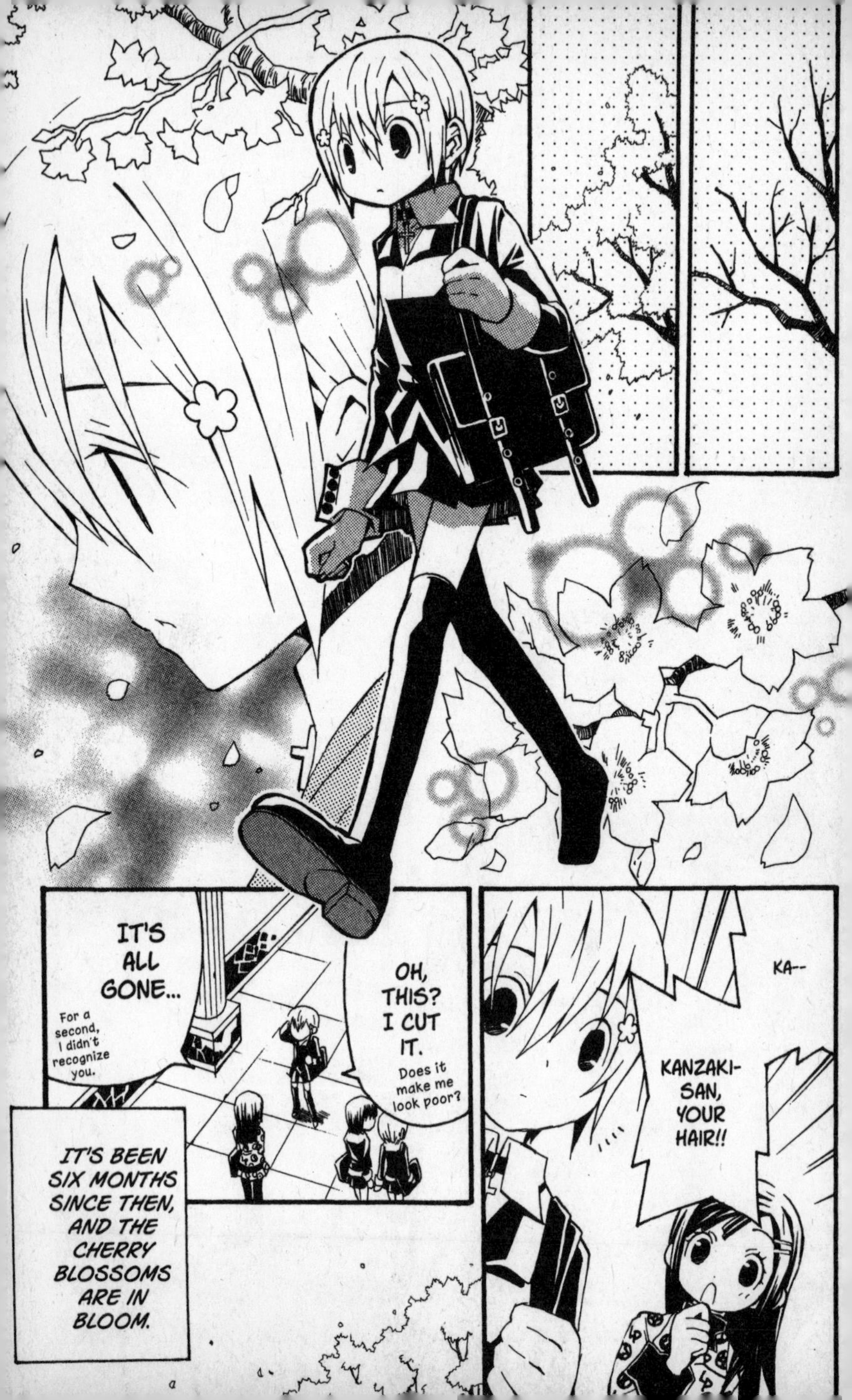
KA--
KANZAKI-SAN, YOUR HAIR!!
IT'S ALL GONE...
For a second, I didn't recognize you.
OH, THIS? I CUT IT.
Does it make me look poor?
IT'S BEEN SIX MONTHS SINCE THEN, AND THE CHERRY BLOSSOMS ARE IN BLOOM.

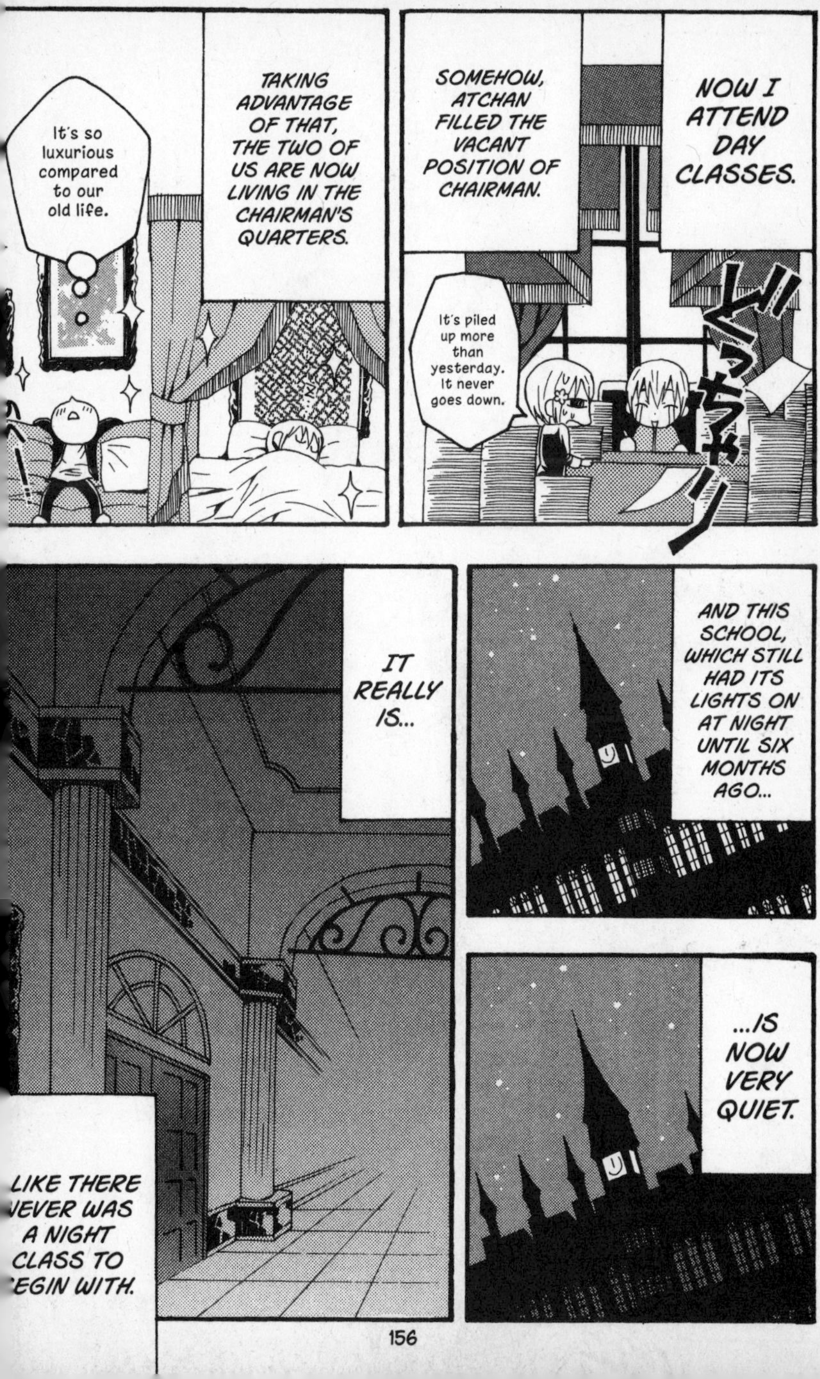
NOW I ATTEND DAY CLASSES.
SOMEHOW, ATCHAN FILLED THE VACANT POSITION OF CHAIRMAN.
It's piled up more than yesterday. It never goes down.
どっちゃり
TAKING ADVANTAGE OF THAT, THE TWO OF US ARE NOW LIVING IN THE CHAIRMAN'S QUARTERS.
It's so luxurious compared to our old life.
AND THIS SCHOOL, WHICH STILL HAD ITS LIGHTS ON AT NIGHT UNTIL SIX MONTHS AGO...
...IS NOW VERY QUIET.
IT REALLY IS...
LIKE THERE NEVER WAS A NIGHT CLASS TO BEGIN WITH.

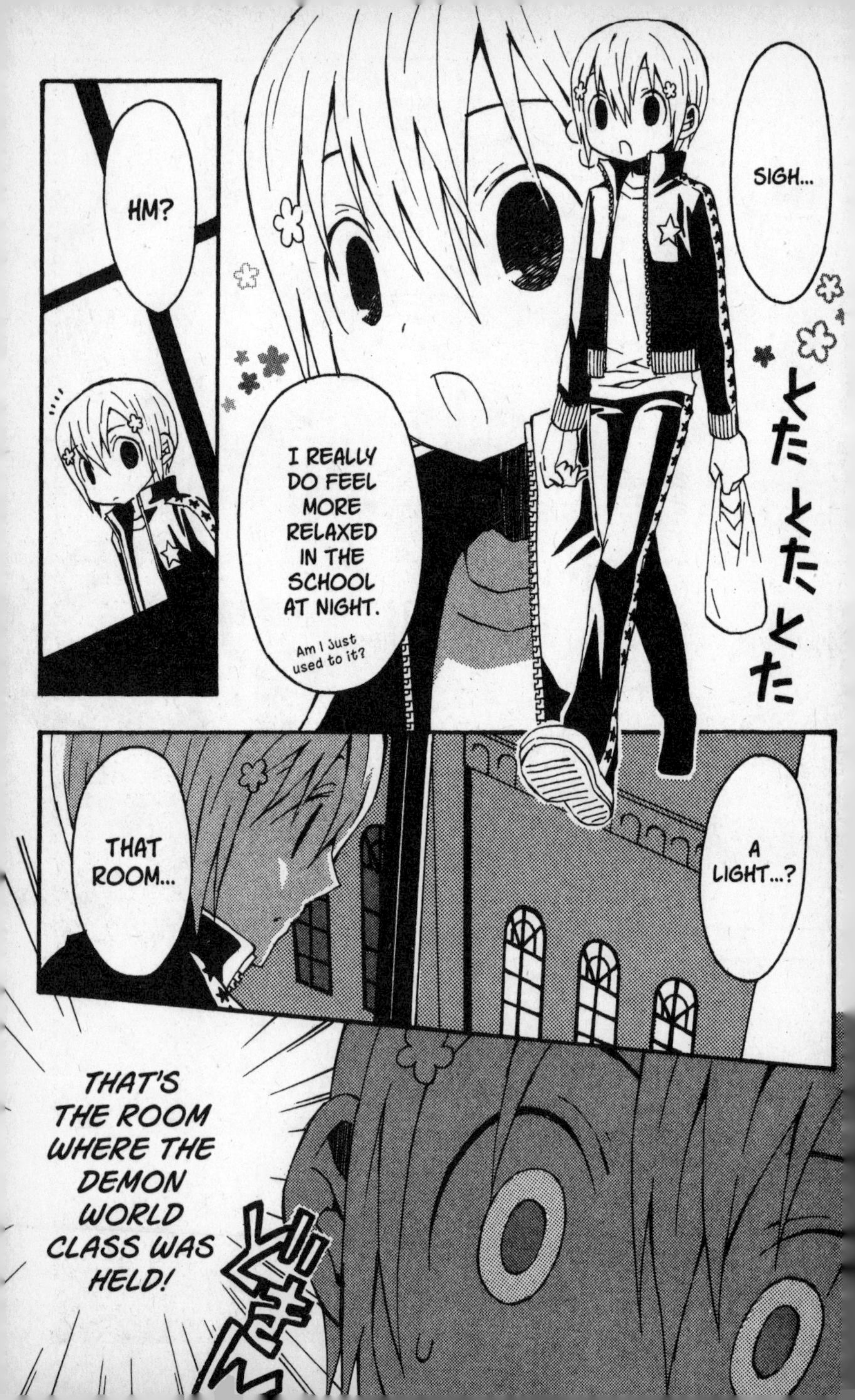
SIGH...
とたとたとた
I REALLY DO FEEL MORE RELAXED IN THE SCHOOL AT NIGHT.
Am I just used to it?
HM?
A LIGHT...?
THAT ROOM...
THAT'S THE ROOM WHERE THE DEMON WORLD CLASS WAS HELD!

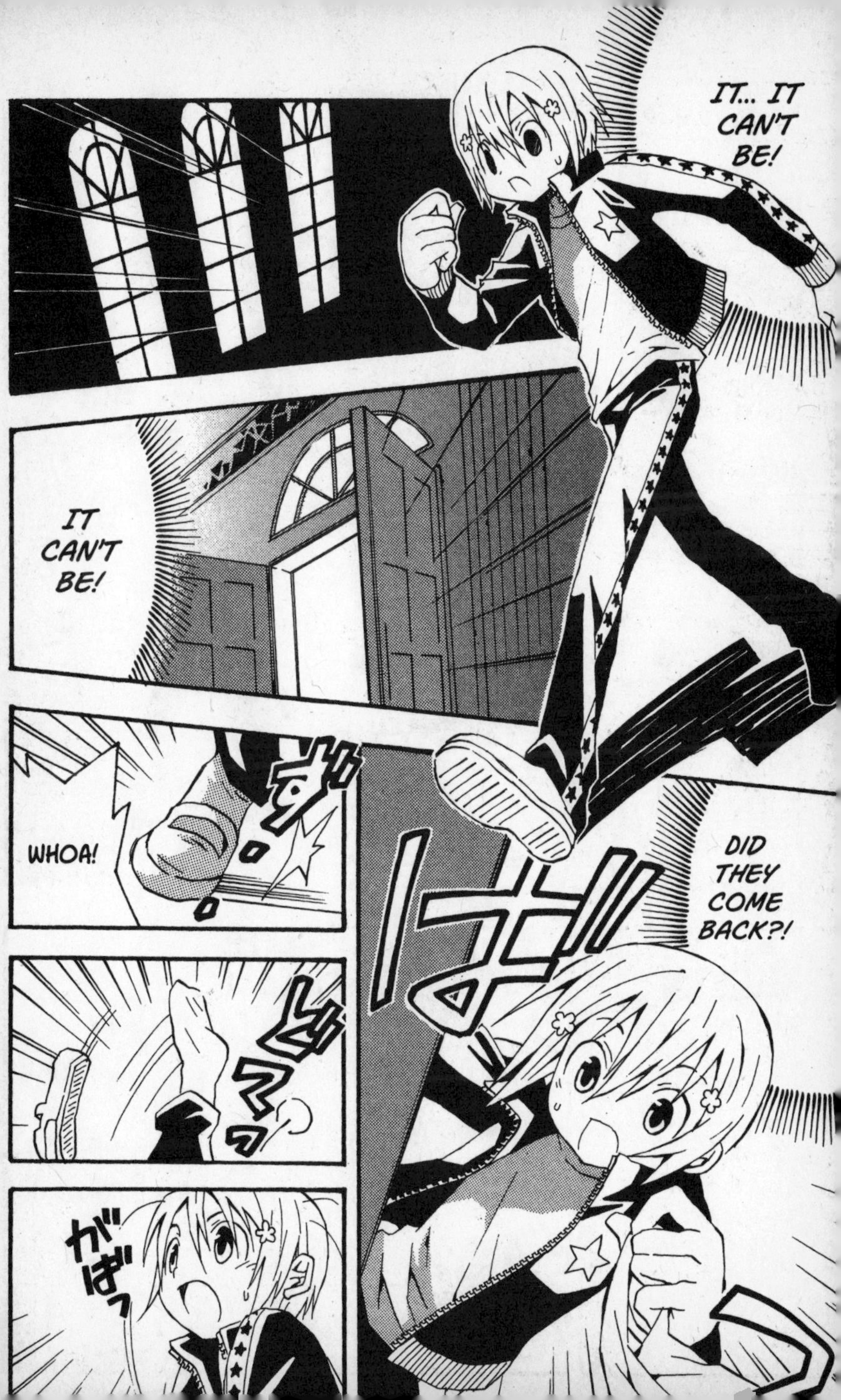

IT... IT CAN'T BE!
IT CAN'T BE!
DID THEY COME BACK?!
ばっ
WHOA!
ずっ
どてっ
がばっ

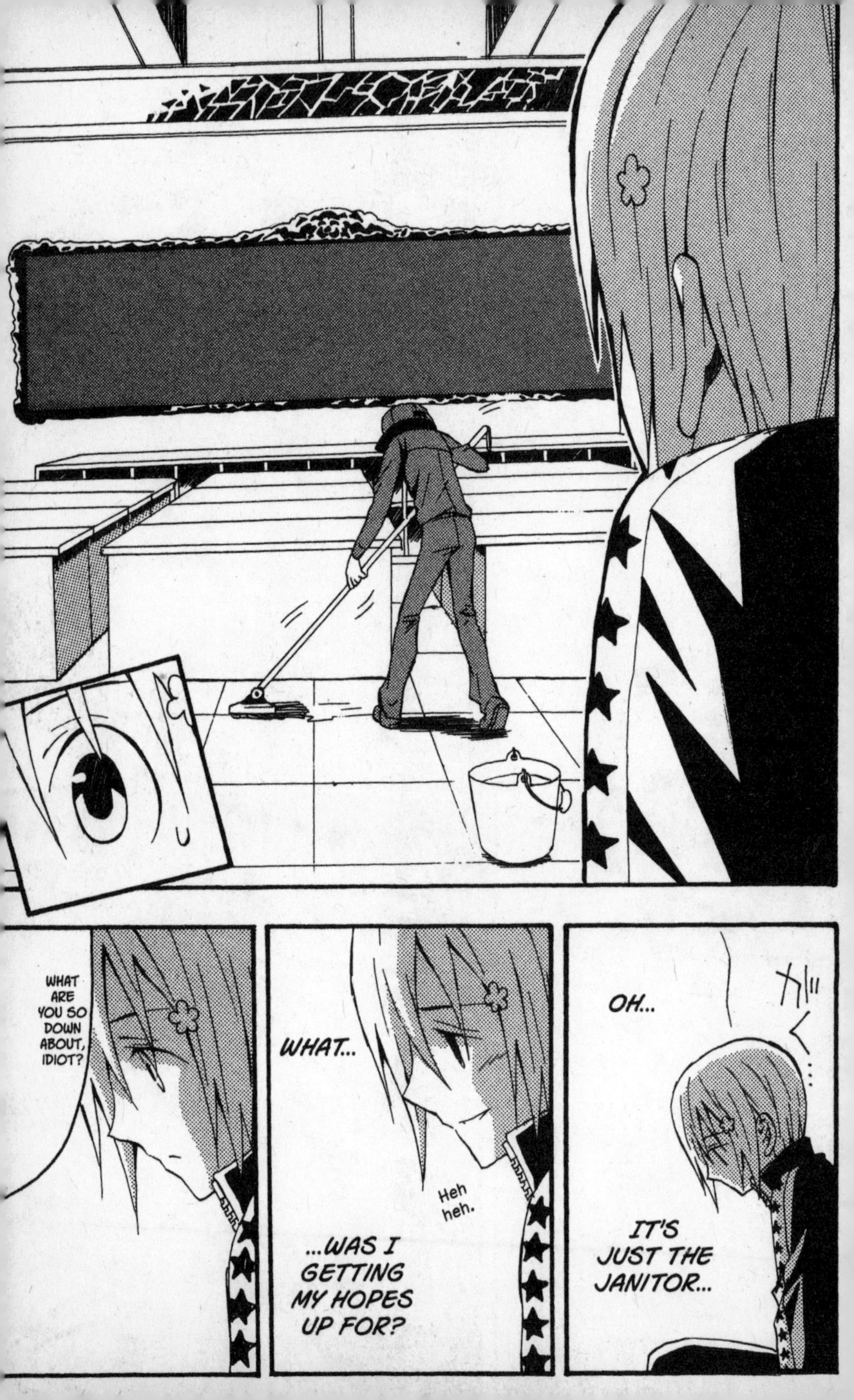
OH...
IT'S JUST THE JANITOR...
WHAT...
Heh heh.
...WAS I GETTING MY HOPES UP FOR?
WHAT ARE YOU SO DOWN ABOUT, IDIOT?

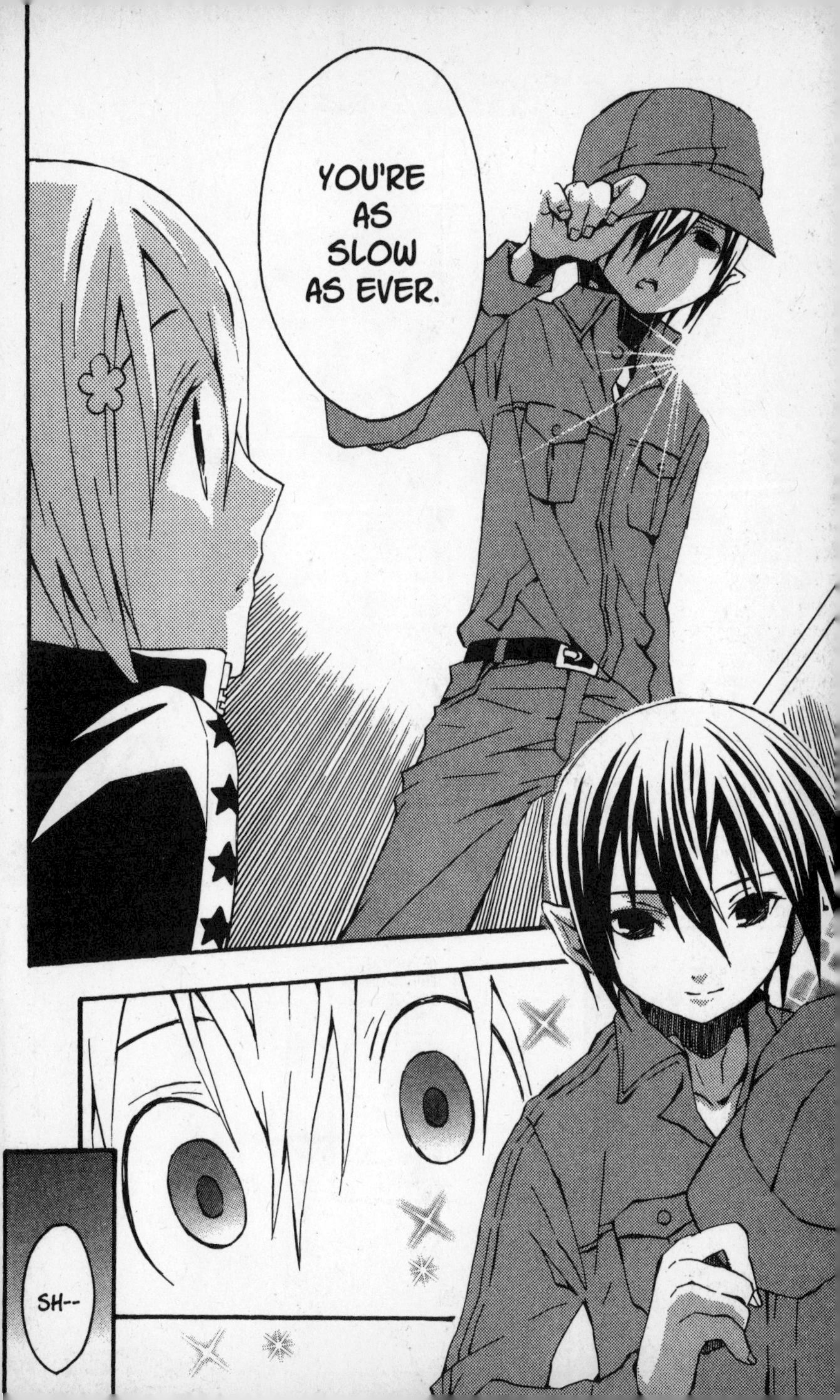
YOU'RE AS SLOW AS EVER.
SH--

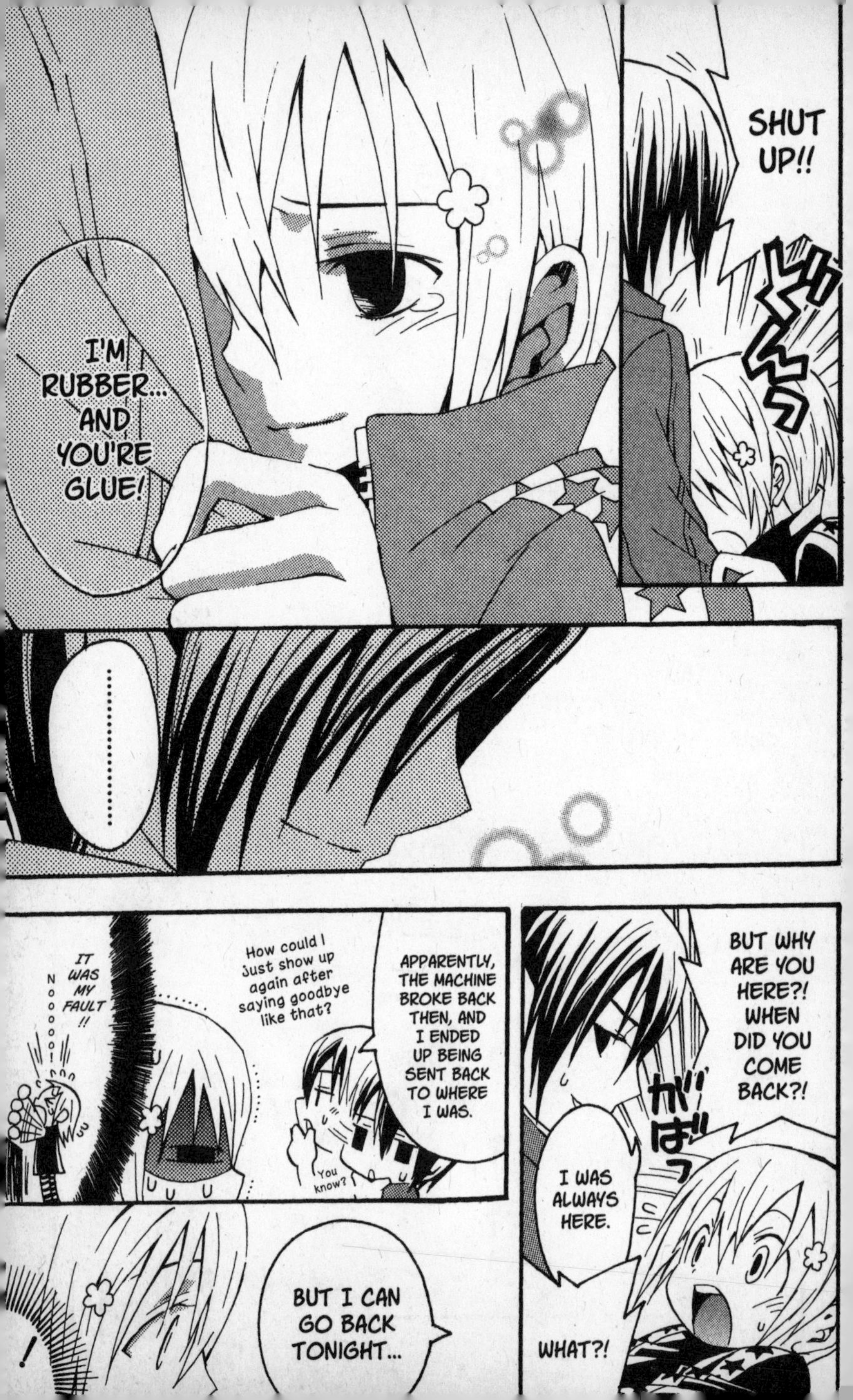
SHUT UP!!
I'M RUBBER... AND YOU'RE GLUE!
......
BUT WHY ARE YOU HERE?! WHEN DID YOU COME BACK?!
I WAS ALWAYS HERE.
WHAT?!
APPARENTLY, THE MACHINE BROKE BACK THEN, AND I ENDED UP BEING SENT BACK TO WHERE I WAS.
How could I just show up again after saying goodbye like that?
You know?
IT WAS MY FAULT!!
Noooooo!
BUT I CAN GO BACK TONIGHT...
!

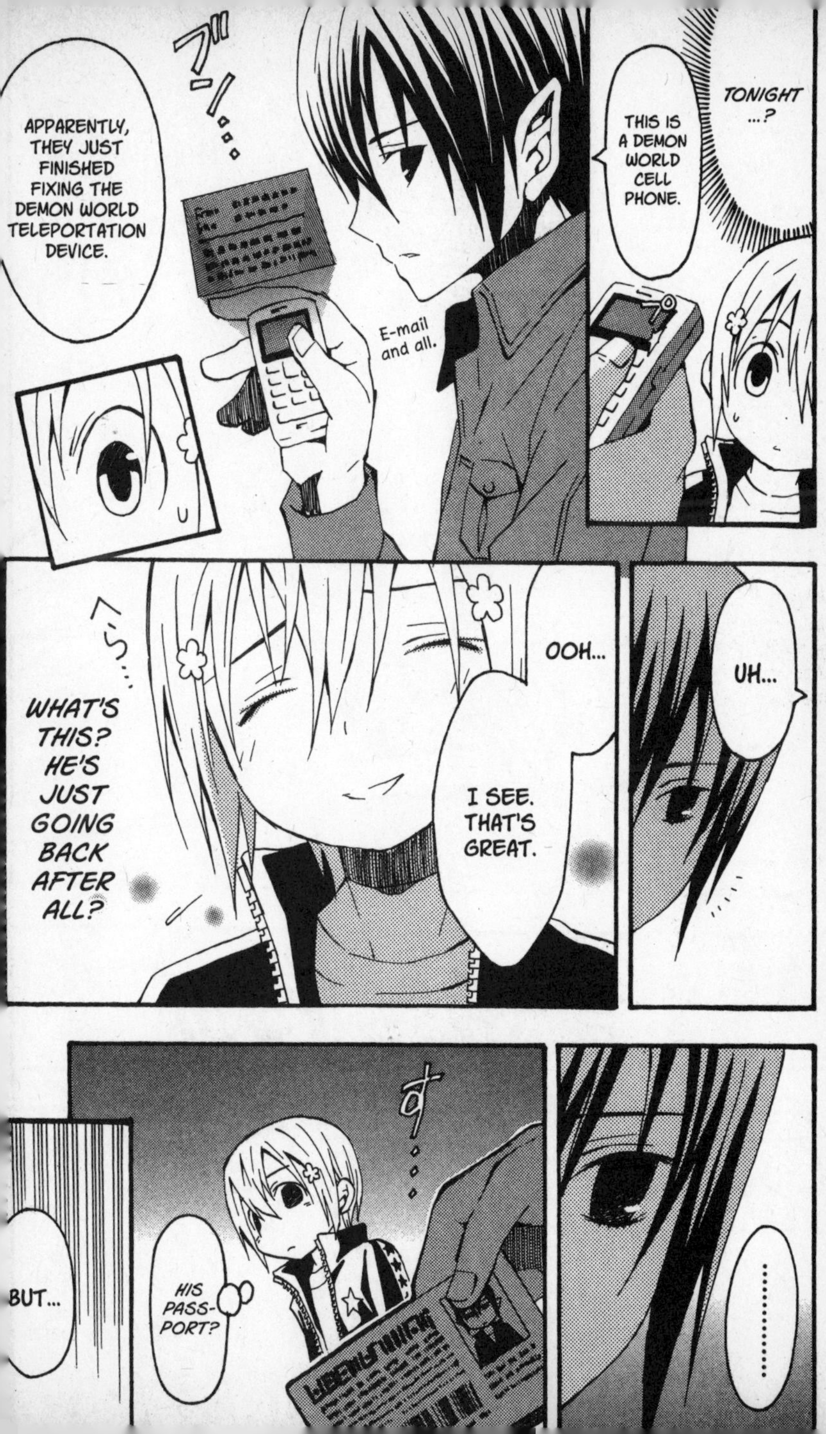

TONIGHT ...?
THIS IS A DEMON WORLD CELL PHONE.
ブー…
APPARENTLY, THEY JUST FINISHED FIXING THE DEMON WORLD TELEPORTATION DEVICE.
E-mail and all.
UH...
OOH...
I SEE. THAT'S GREAT.
WHAT'S THIS? HE'S JUST GOING BACK AFTER ALL?
....
HIS PASSPORT?
BUT...

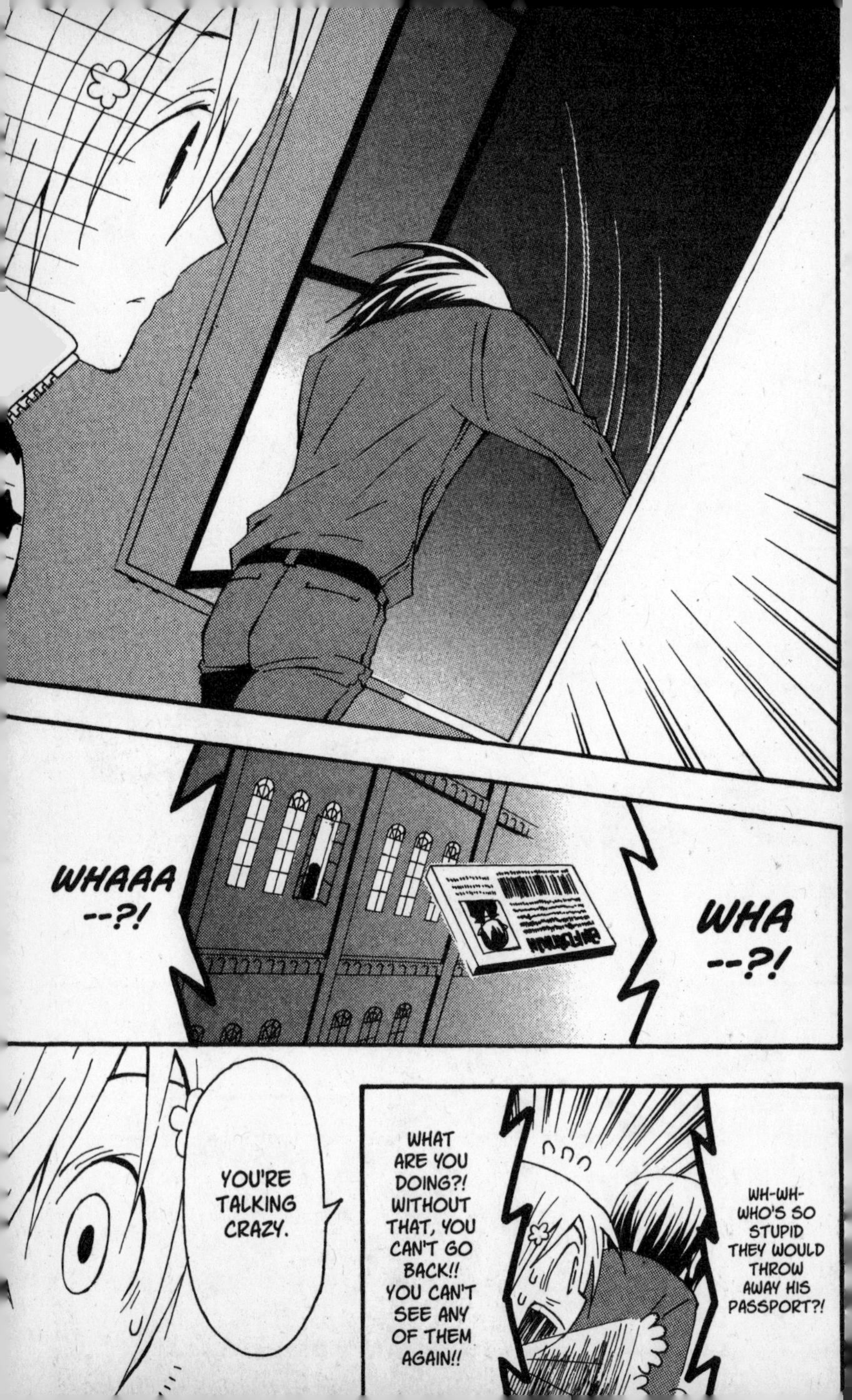
WHA --?!
WHAAA --?!
WH-WH-WHO'S SO STUPID THEY WOULD THROW AWAY HIS PASSPORT?!
WHAT ARE YOU DOING?! WITHOUT THAT, YOU CAN'T GO BACK!! YOU CAN'T SEE ANY OF THEM AGAIN!!
YOU'RE TALKING CRAZY.

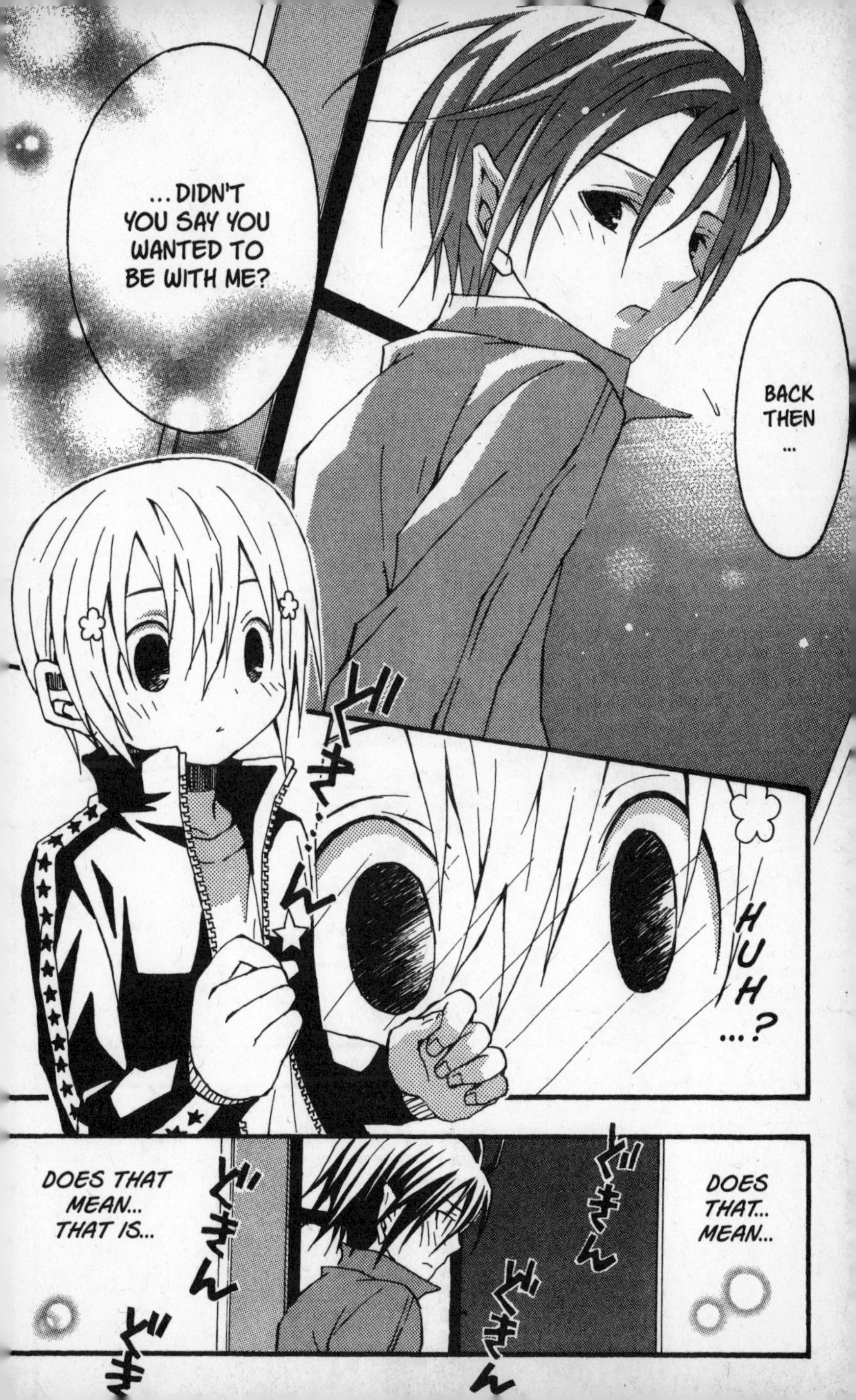
BACK THEN ...
... DIDN'T YOU SAY YOU WANTED TO BE WITH ME?
どきん
HUH ...?
DOES THAT... MEAN...
どきん
どきん
DOES THAT MEAN... THAT IS...
どきん
どきん

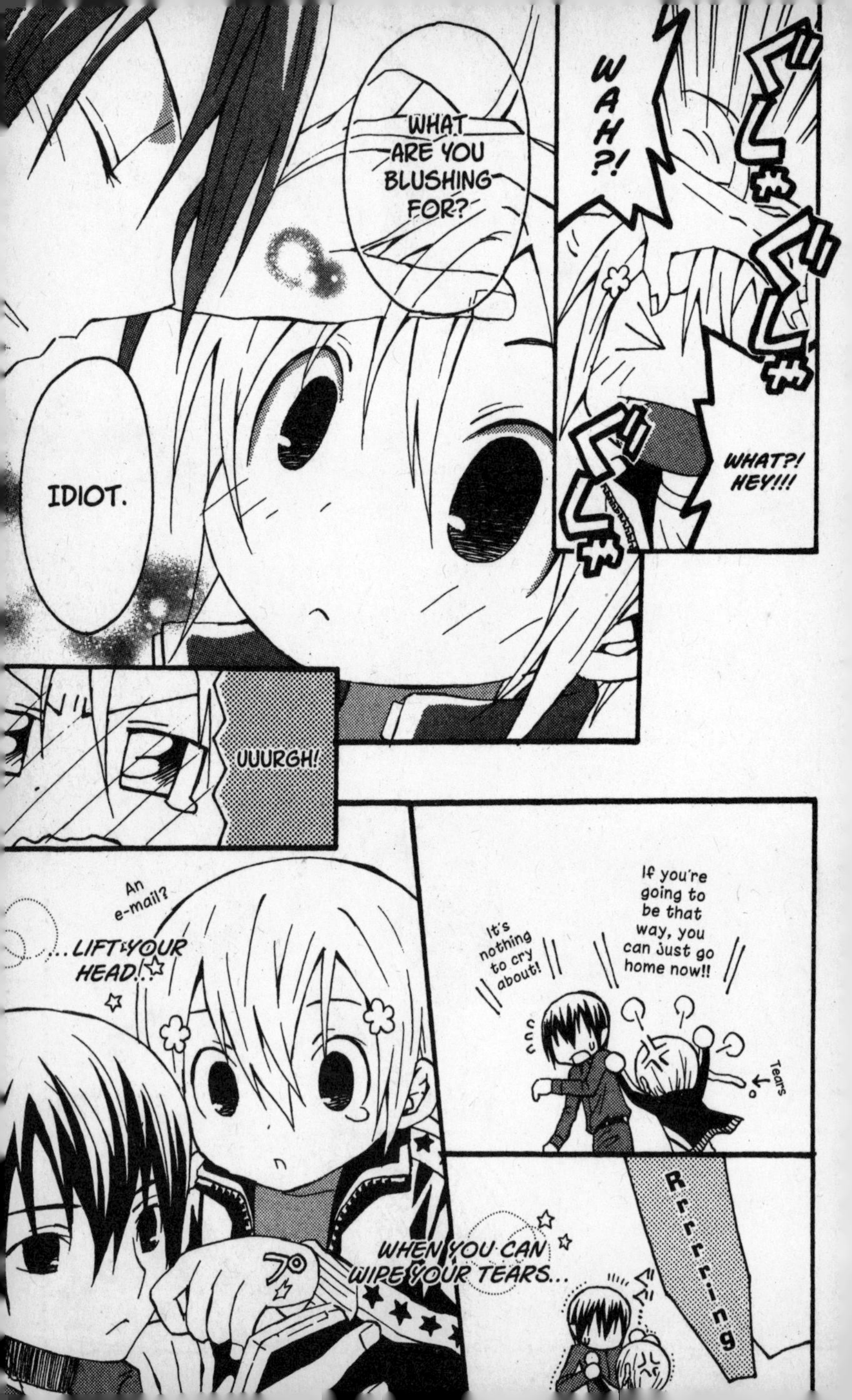
WAH?!
WHAT?! HEY!!!
WHAT ARE YOU BLUSHING FOR?
IDIOT.
UUURGH!
If you're going to be that way, you can just go home now!!
It's nothing to cry about!
Tears
Rrrring
An e-mail?
...LIFT YOUR HEAD!
WHEN YOU CAN WIPE YOUR TEARS...

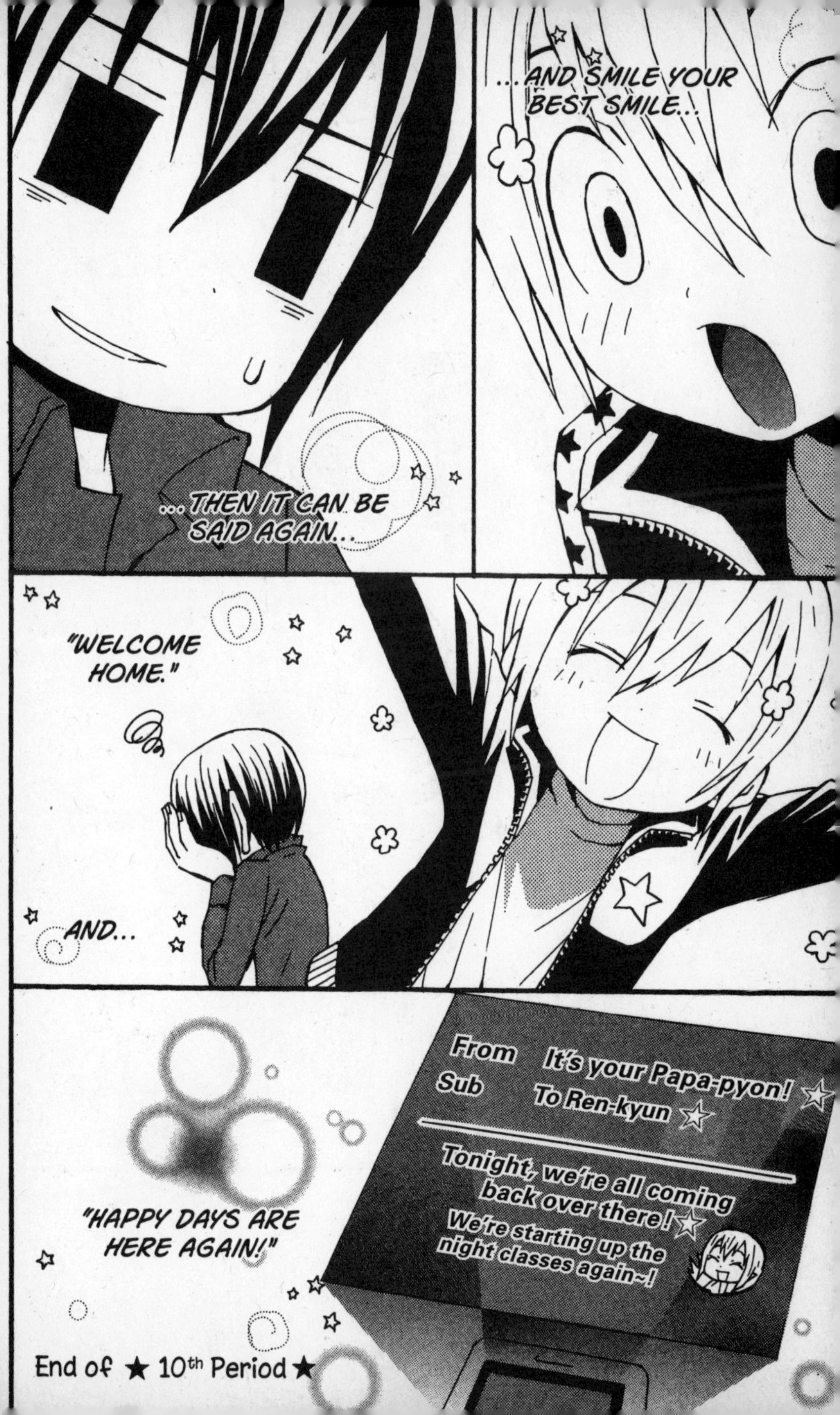
...AND SMILE YOUR BEST SMILE...
...THEN IT CAN BE SAID AGAIN...
"WELCOME HOME."
AND...
From It's your Papa-pyon! ☆
Sub To Ren-kyun ☆
Tonight, we're all coming back over there! ☆
We're starting up the night classes again~!
"HAPPY DAYS ARE HERE AGAIN!"
End of ★ 10th Period ★

The end!

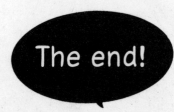

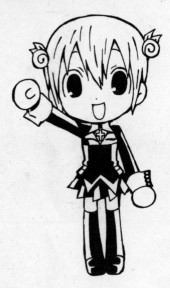

Here's an ← extra bonus chapter.

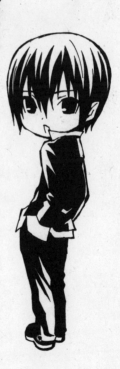

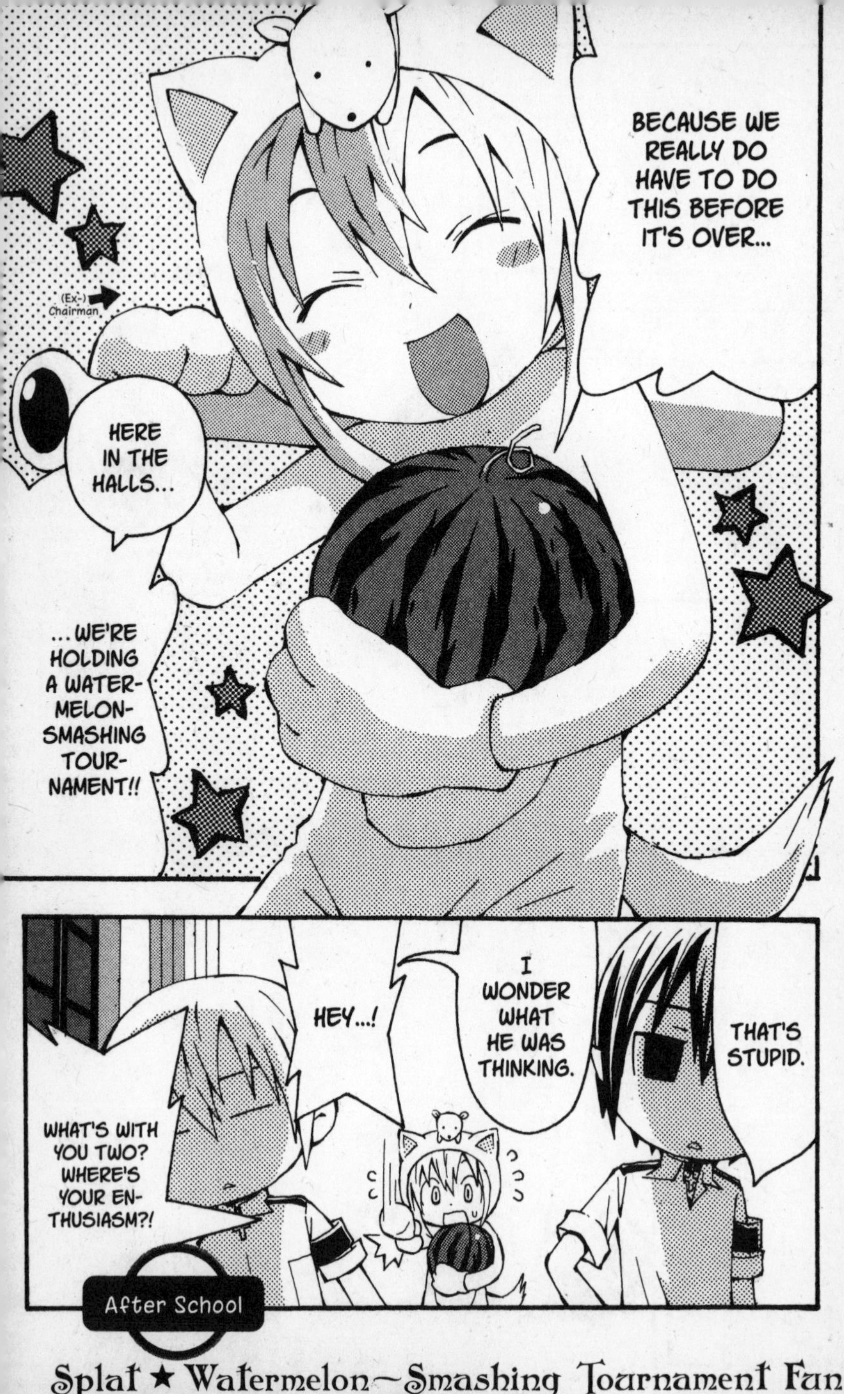
BECAUSE WE REALLY DO HAVE TO DO THIS BEFORE IT'S OVER...
(Ex-) Chairman
HERE IN THE HALLS...
...WE'RE HOLDING A WATER-MELON-SMASHING TOUR-NAMENT!!
THAT'S STUPID.
I WONDER WHAT HE WAS THINKING.
HEY...!
WHAT'S WITH YOU TWO? WHERE'S YOUR EN-THUSIASM?!
After School

Splat ★ Watermelon~Smashing Tournament Fun

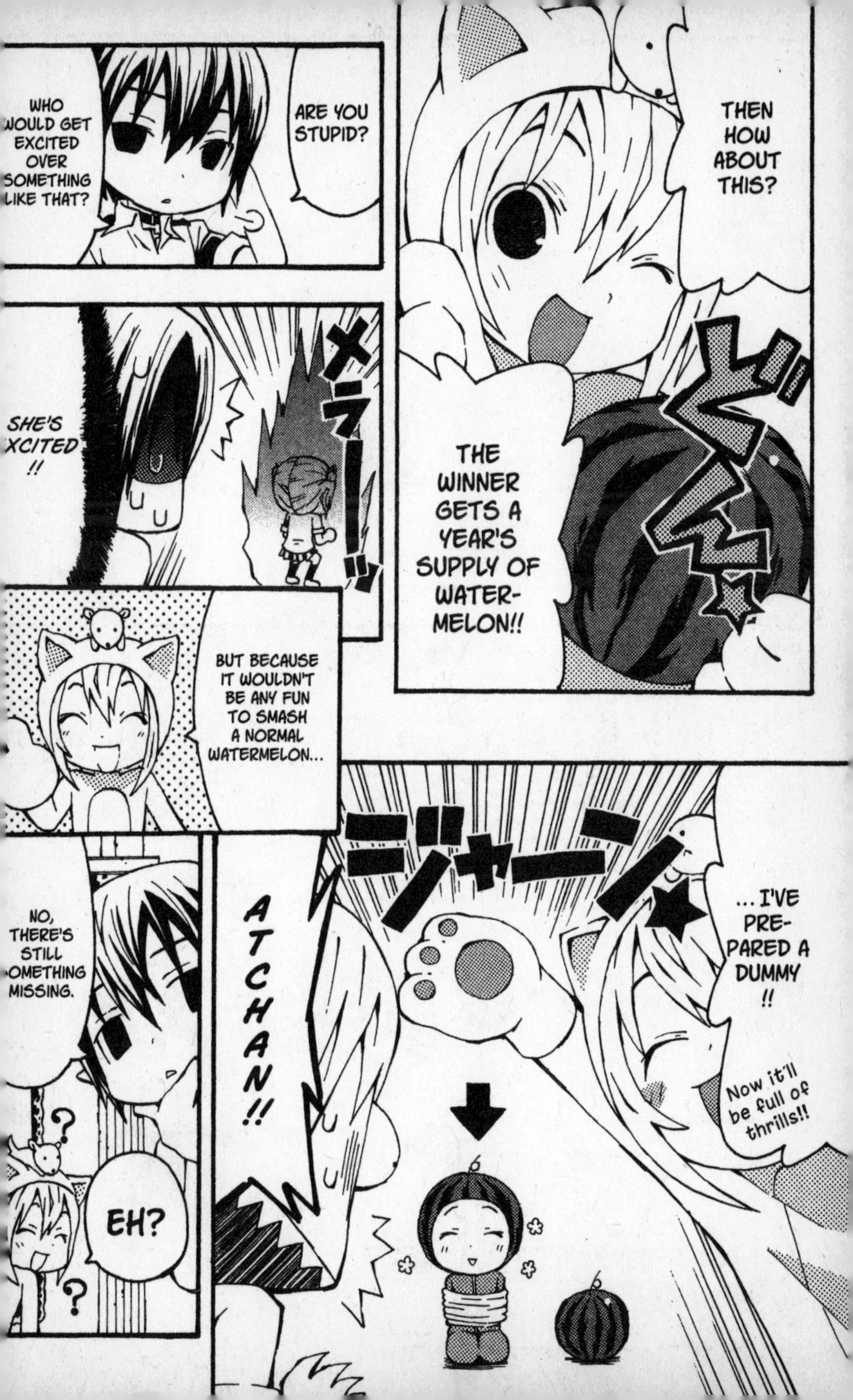
THEN HOW ABOUT THIS?
THE WINNER GETS A YEAR'S SUPPLY OF WATER-MELON!!
ARE YOU STUPID?
WHO WOULD GET EXCITED OVER SOMETHING LIKE THAT?
SHE'S EXCITED!!
BUT BECAUSE IT WOULDN'T BE ANY FUN TO SMASH A NORMAL WATERMELON...
...I'VE PRE-PARED A DUMMY!!
Now it'll be full of thrills!!
ATCHAN!!
NO, THERE'S STILL SOMETHING MISSING.
EH?

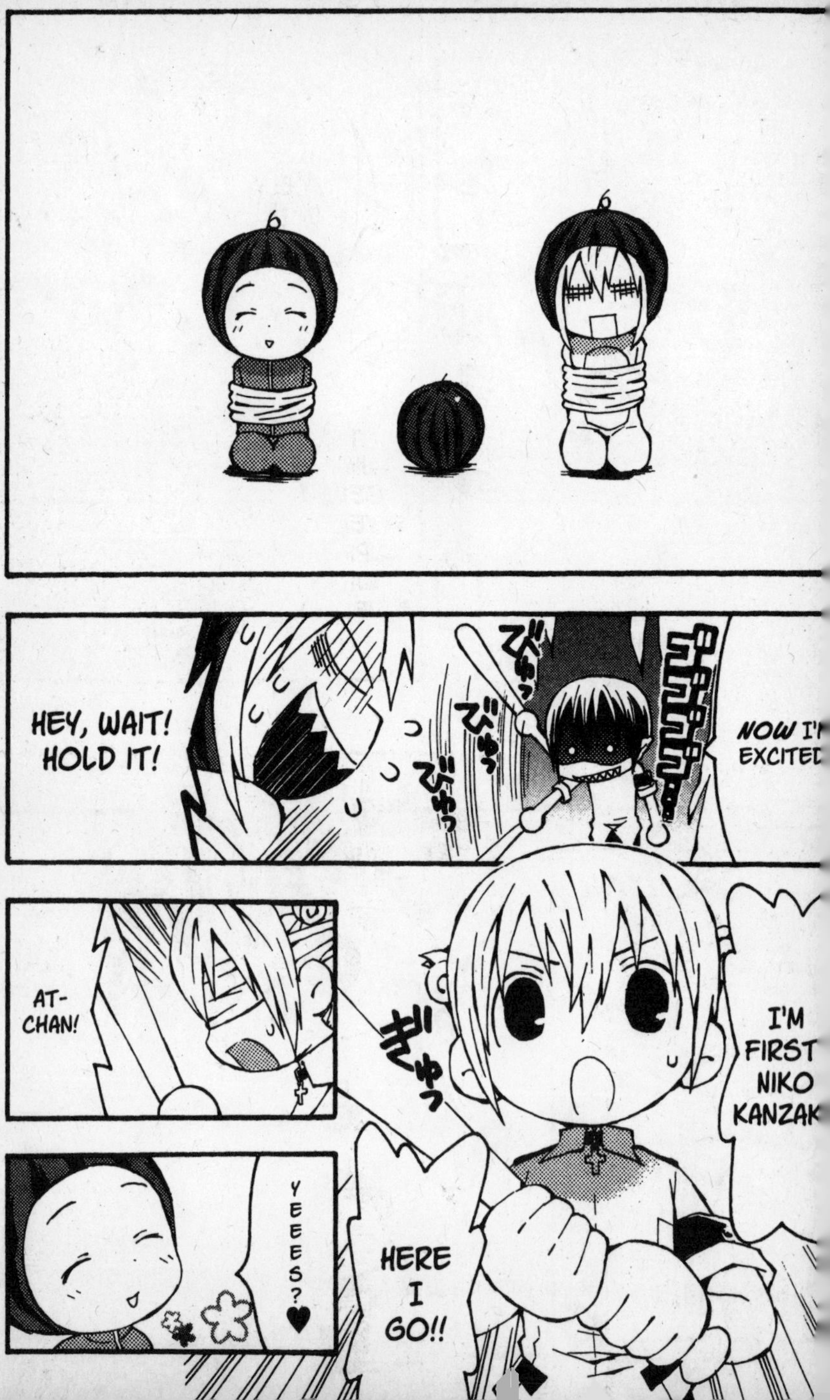
NOW I'
EXCITED
HEY, WAIT! HOLD IT!
I'M FIRST NIKO KANZAK
ぎゅっ
HERE I GO!!
AT-CHAN!
YEEEES?♥

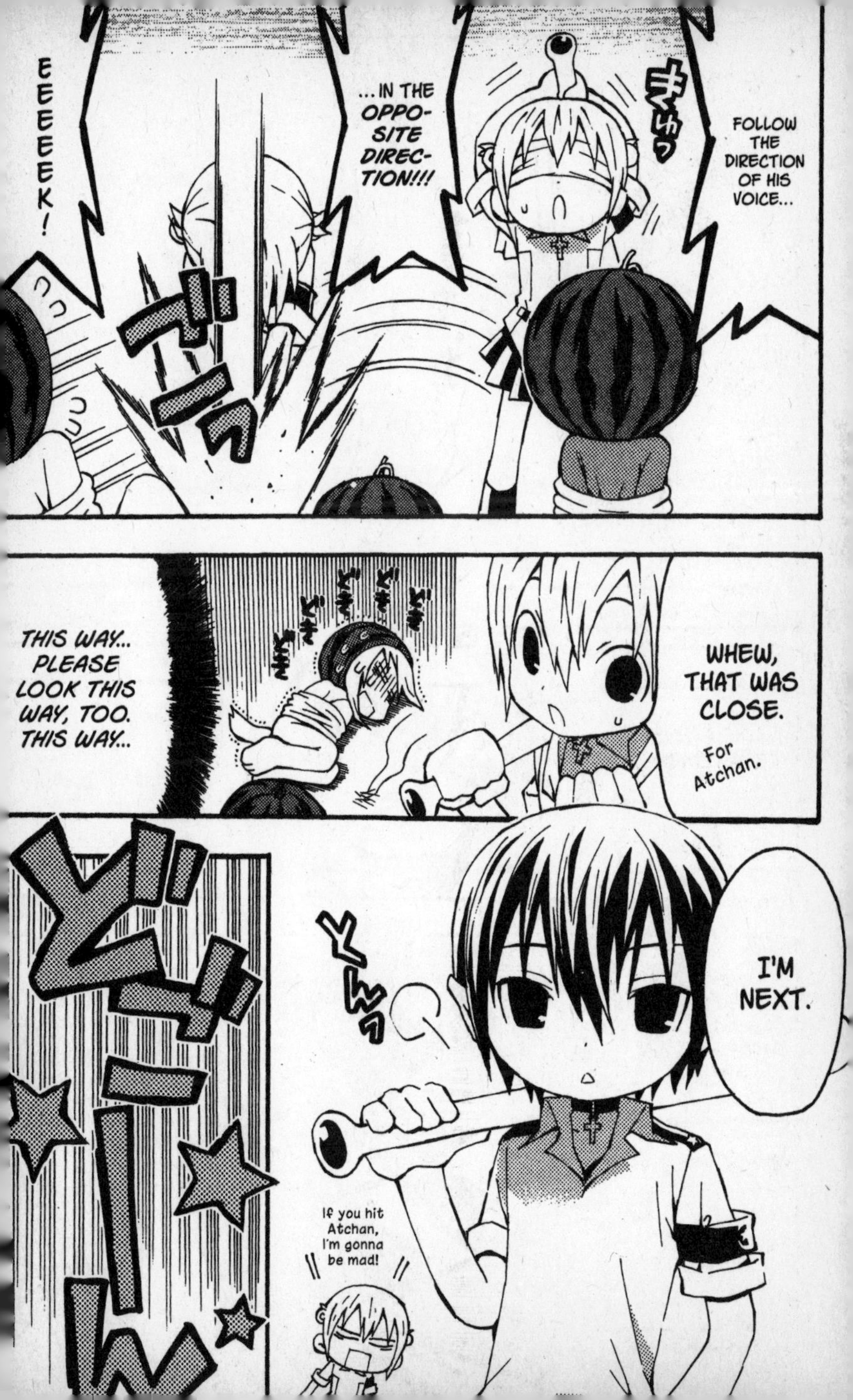
FOLLOW THE DIRECTION OF HIS VOICE...
...IN THE OPPOSITE DIRECTION!!!
EEEEEEK!
WHEW, THAT WAS CLOSE.
For Atchan.
THIS WAY... PLEASE LOOK THIS WAY, TOO. THIS WAY...
I'M NEXT.
If you hit Atchan, I'm gonna be mad!

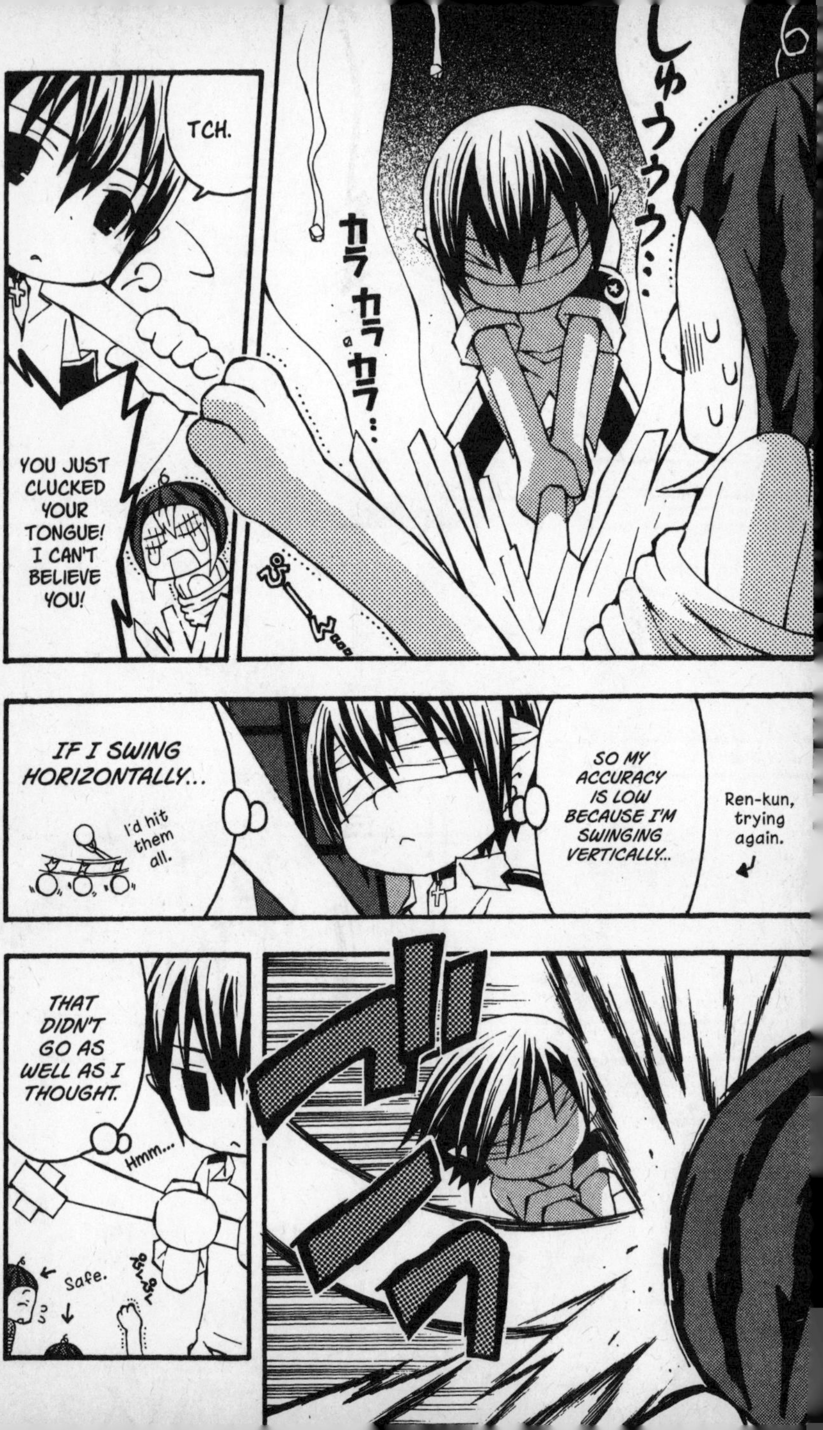
しゅううう…
カラ カラ カラ…
TCH.
YOU JUST CLUCKED YOUR TONGUE! I CAN'T BELIEVE YOU!
Ren-kun, trying again.
SO MY ACCURACY IS LOW BECAUSE I'M SWINGING VERTICALLY...
IF I SWING HORIZONTALLY...
I'd hit them all.
THAT DIDN'T GO AS WELL AS I THOUGHT.
Hmm...
Safe.

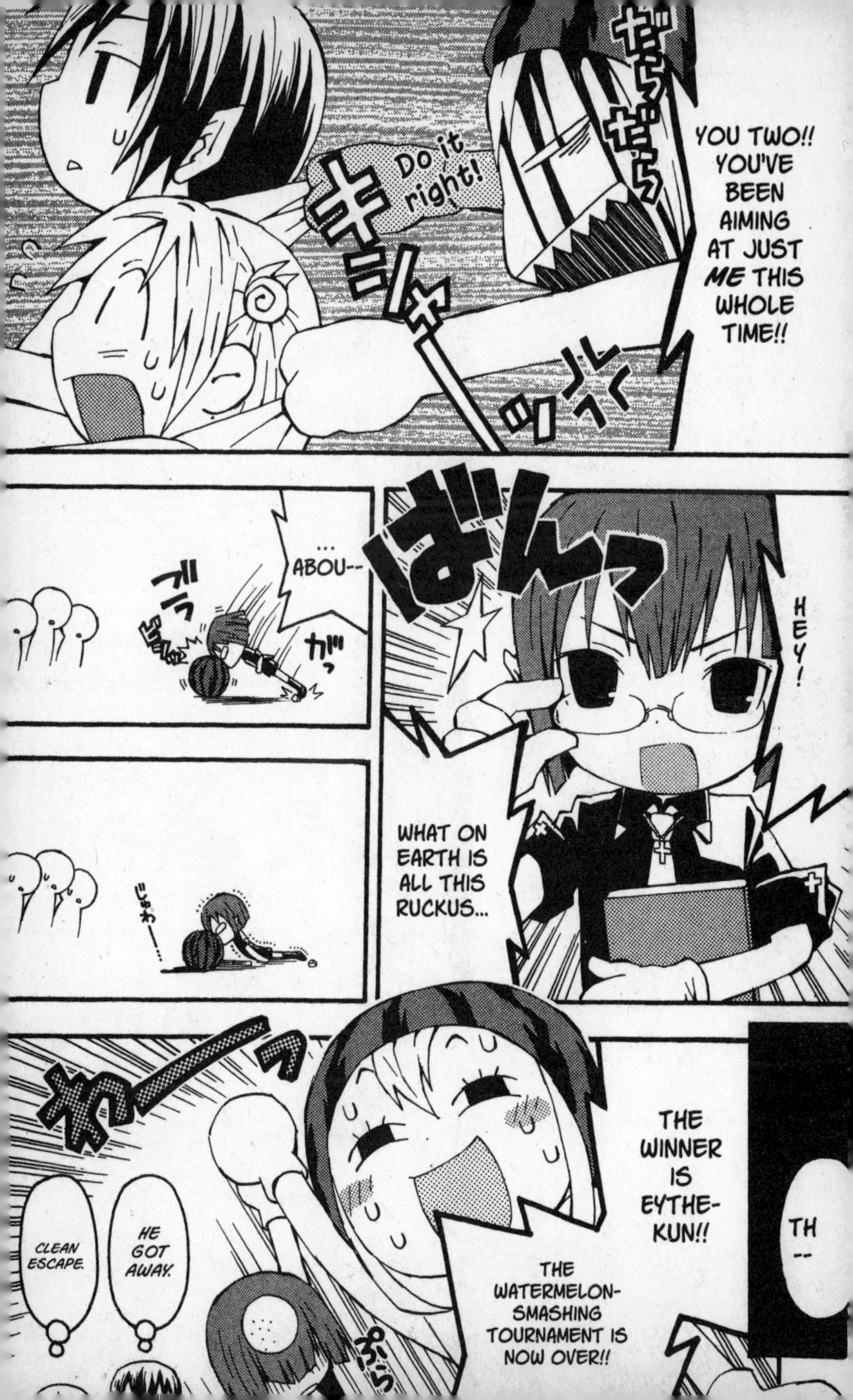
YOU TWO!! YOU'VE BEEN AIMING AT JUST *ME* THIS WHOLE TIME!!
Do it right!
HEY!
WHAT ON EARTH IS ALL THIS RUCKUS...
...ABOU--
TH--
THE WINNER IS EYTHE-KUN!!
THE WATERMELON-SMASHING TOURNAMENT IS NOW OVER!!
HE GOT AWAY.
CLEAN ESCAPE.

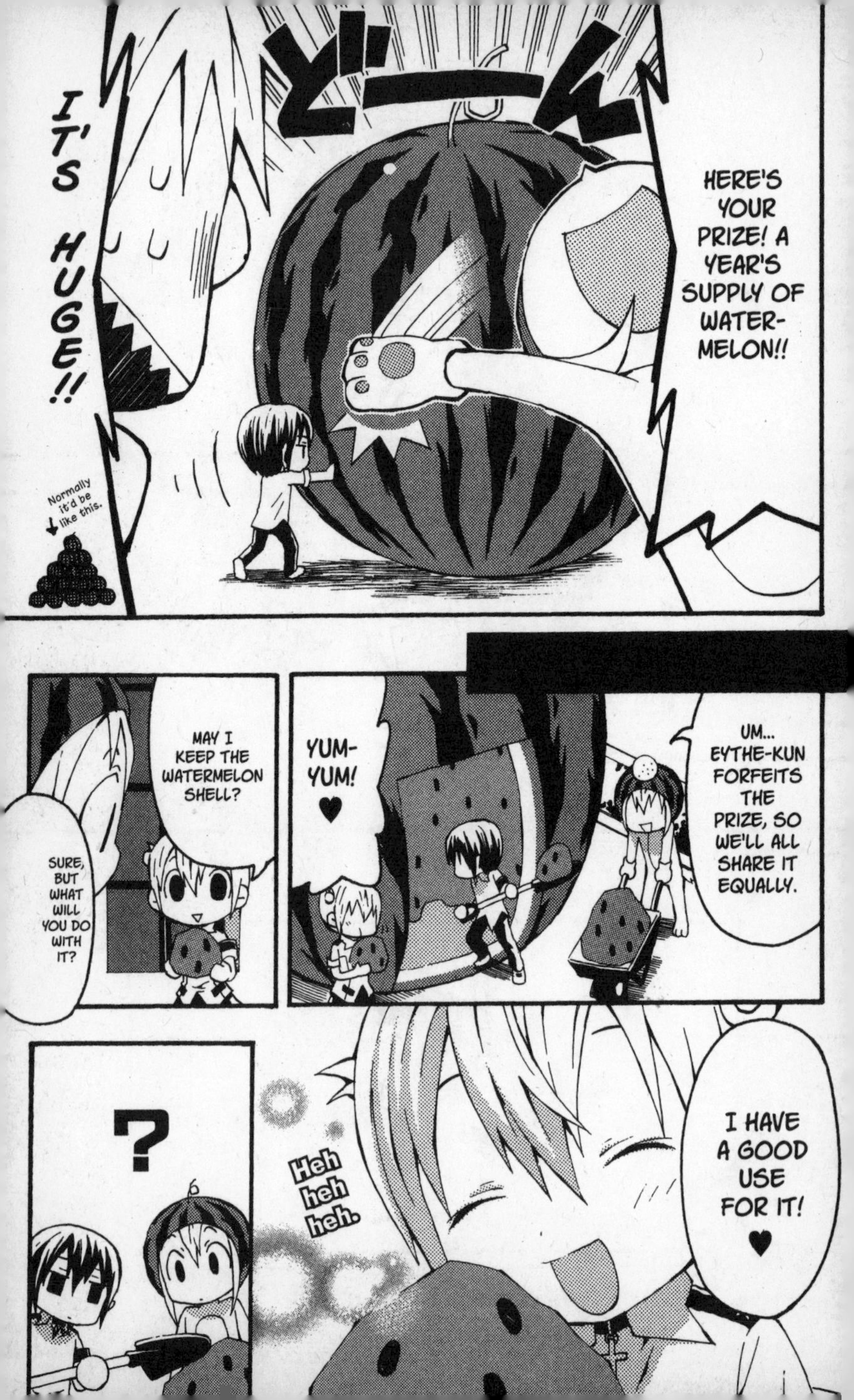

どーん
HERE'S YOUR PRIZE! A YEAR'S SUPPLY OF WATER-MELON!!
IT'S HUGE!!
Normally it'd be like this.
UM... EYTHE-KUN FORFEITS THE PRIZE, SO WE'LL ALL SHARE IT EQUALLY.
YUM-YUM! ♥
MAY I KEEP THE WATERMELON SHELL?
SURE, BUT WHAT WILL YOU DO WITH IT?
I HAVE A GOOD USE FOR IT! ♥
Heh heh heh.
?

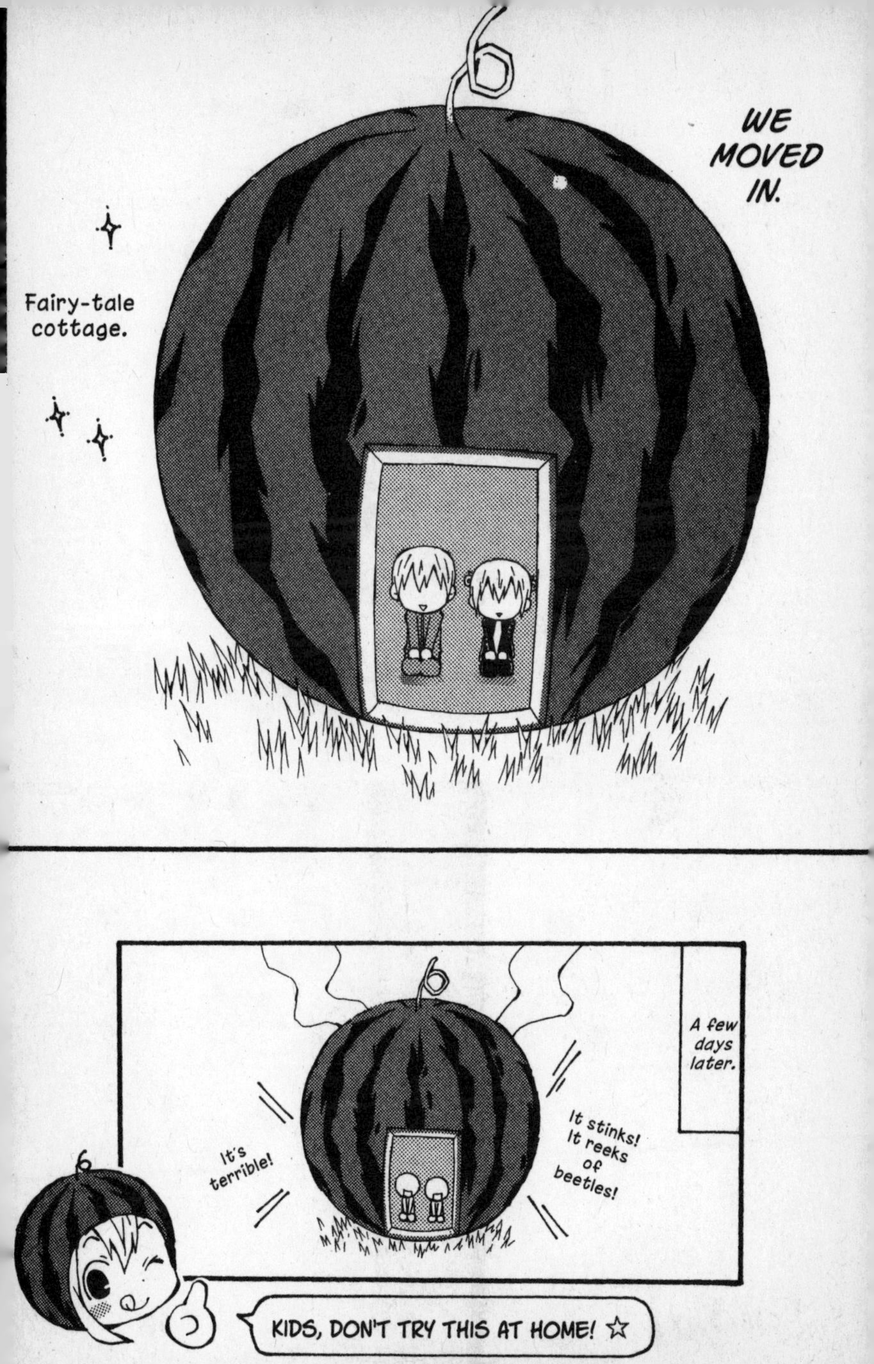
WE MOVED IN.
Fairy-tale cottage.
A few days later.
It stinks! It reeks of beetles!
It's terrible!
KIDS, DON'T TRY THIS AT HOME! ☆

End of ★ After School ★

Postscript

★ Hello. I'm Majiko!. This is the conclusion--volume 2. First, thank you for your support. And good work, me! (Ha ha!)

★ Actually, at first we talked about *St. Lunatic High School* as a one-chapter short. But it got longer bit-by-bit, and I was able to draw two volumes' worth. All of it is thanks to all you who supported me. Really. Thank you very much.

★ I would like to talk just a little about the characters...
The most popular character in *St. Lunatic* is Ren-kun, but while I intended to have him be a cool character that can do anything, I got more and more comments saying, "He's a natural!" I myself didn't intend for him to come across that way at all, so I was surprised. I've also been told, "All of your characters are naturals!" Is that so?! (Ha ha!) About Eden-kun's skirt thing...I think it might be hard to tell from the angles it's always drawn at, but it has a rose print on it. Incidentally, I also took the name "Eden" from the name of a rose. Finally, about Niko-chan...her brightness, her optimism, her strength, her indomitable spirit that doesn't sweat the small stuff... Actually, I may have put all my wishes of what I want to be like into her. (But for some strange reason, I'm told I'm a lot like her already.)
At any rate, they're all characters I put a lot of thought into. The story of *St. Lunatic High School* has ended, but I would really be happy if you would always hold this work dear.

★ I think I would like to keep on trying new works. I'll do my best.
And I sincerely thank you for reading.

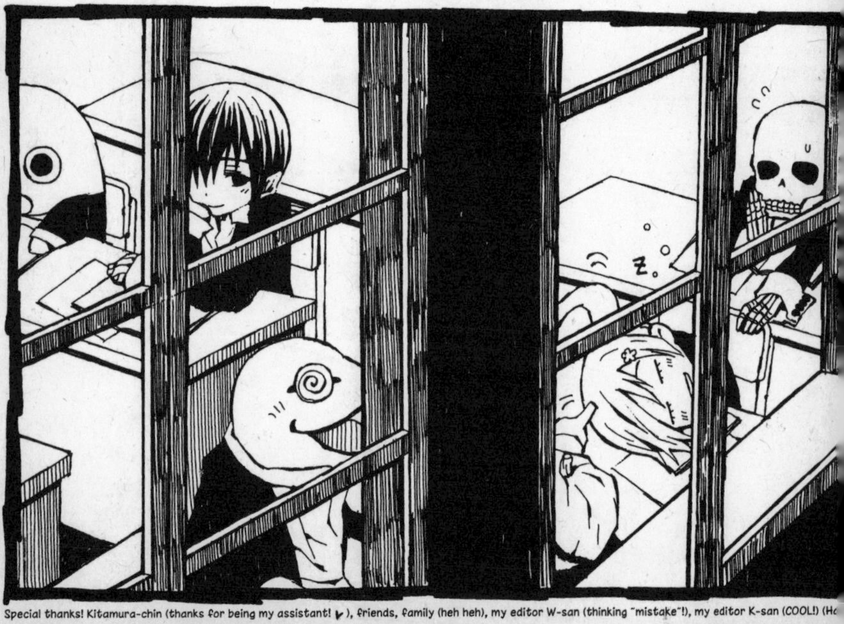

Z.

Special thanks! Kitamura-chin (thanks for being my assistant!), friends, family (heh heh), my editor W-san (thinking "mistake"!), my editor K-san (COOL!) (Ha

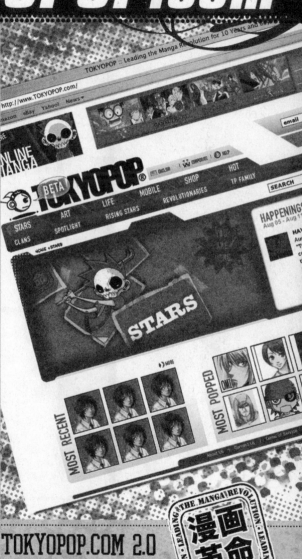
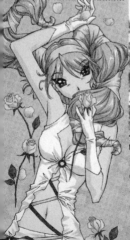
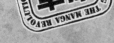

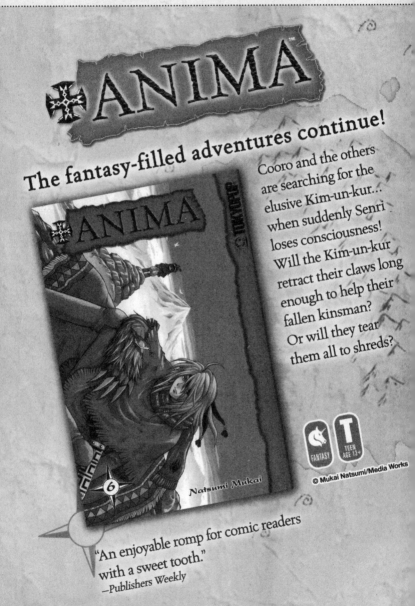

MISSING
KAMIKAKUSHI NO MONOGATARI

2

ANYONE WHO MEETS *HER* DISAPPEARS

When Kyoichi, a.k.a. "His Majesty, Lord of Darkness," disappears, his friends in the Literature Club suspect he's been spirited away by a girl posing as his girlfriend. Their desperate investigation quickly spirals into a paranormal nightmare, where a fate worse than death waits on the "other side"...

FOR MORE INFORMATION VISIT: WWW.TOKYOPOP.COM

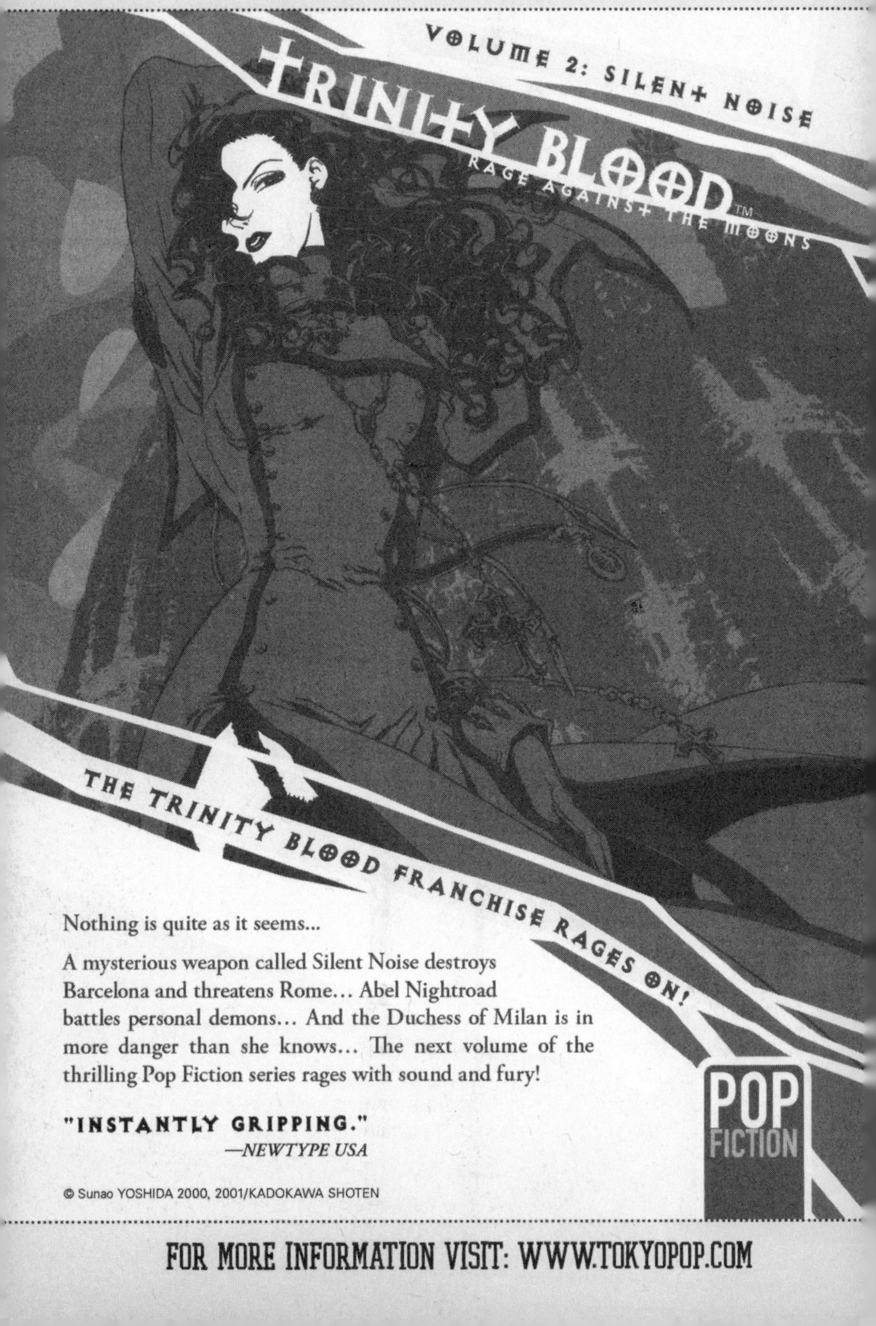
VOLUME 2: SILENT NOISE
TRINITY BLOOD™
RAGE AGAINST THE MOONS
THE TRINITY BLOOD FRANCHISE RAGES ON!

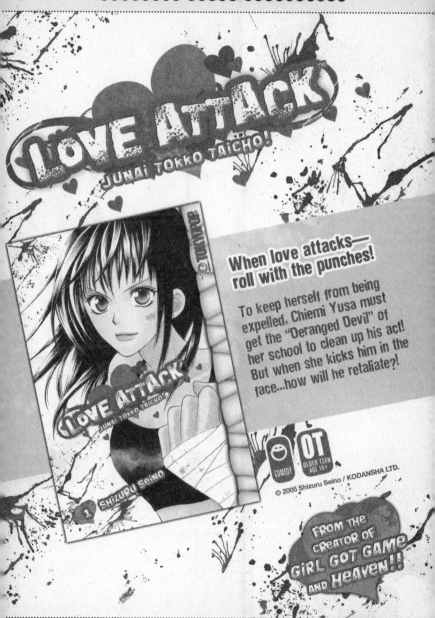

STOP!

This is the back of the book.
You wouldn't want to spoil a great ending!

This book is printed "manga-style," in the authentic Japanese right-to-left format. Since none of the artwork has been flipped or altered, readers get to experience the story just as the creator intended. You've been asking for it, so TOKYOPOP® delivered: authentic, hot-off-the-press, and far more fun!

DIRECTIONS

If this is your first time reading manga-style, here's a quick guide to help you understand how it works.

It's easy... just start in the top right panel and follow the numbers. Have fun, and look for more 100% authentic manga from TOKYOPOP®!